STORM GRAZER RISING

STORM GRAZER RISING
THE LAVONSHIA CHRONICLES: BOOK ONE
ERIC MUNGER

True Mark Publishing

Copyright © 2026 by Eric Munger

All rights reserved.

No portion of this book may be reproduced in any form without written permission from the publisher or author, except as permitted by U.S. copyright law.

This book is a work of fiction. The characters, places, cultures, and events within it arise from the author's imagination. Any resemblance to real people, places, or events is coincidental.

True Mark Publishing

First Edition, March 2026

ISBN: 978-1-971248-01-1

10 9 8 7 6 5 4 3 2 1

Printed in the United States of America

Music From The Lavonshia Chronicles

Experience the original music composed for *Storm Grazer Rising* by Elias Breidenbach.

Listen now by scanning the QR code, or search **Storm Grazer Rising** on Youtube or Spotify.

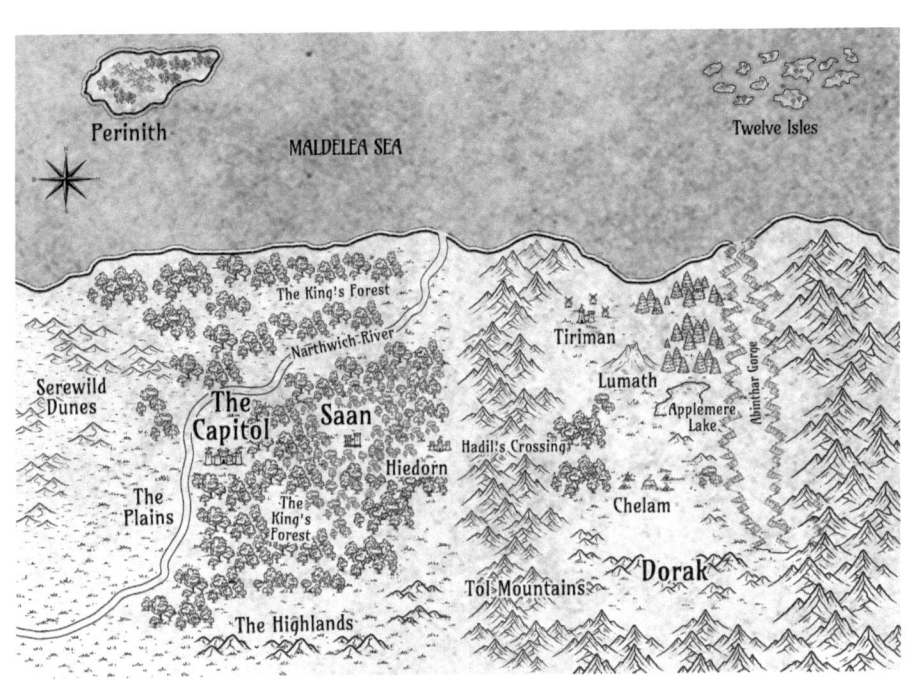

CONTENTS

The Storm Grazer Prophecy	1
Prologue	3
1. We Will	7
2. It Was Time	11
3. To Clean Our Blades	19
4. The Land's Whispers Grew Louder	25
5. They Always Come In Twos	27
6. They'll Pay For This	35
7. Say Your Goodbyes	39
8. Ghostly Figures	49
9. He Had Never Looked More Alone	55
10. What Hope Do We Have	61
11. Bravely Clutching Pots And Pans	67
12. Won't Go Unpunished	73
13. Before The Storm Could Break	79
14. Stole Past The Sleeping Ka	91
15. For Anyone Fond Of Mud	95
16. Welcome To Lumath	101

17.	Cutting Off Her Scream	113
18.	The Assault On Lumath	123
19.	Lumath Shares Its Pain	131
20.	Hack At The Roots	137
21.	It Was Magnus	147
22.	Fatal Choices Bury Men	151
23.	Close To Her Heart	155
24.	The Colorful Scarf	165
25.	Nothing	173
26.	The Spiral Staircase	185
27.	They'll Be Mine Again	191
28.	He Speaks Of Himself	203
29.	He Wept	213
30.	Again, Her Green Eyes Sparkled	221
31.	Clasped Hands	227
32.	They've Found Us	235
33.	Weak And Losing Blood	247
34.	The Face Staring Back	251
35.	Bound In Irons	255
36.	Stuck In Her Throat	267
37.	Never Such A Scene	271
38.	If I Must	275
39.	Headlong Into The Dark	283
40.	The King's Presence	293

41.	The Last Divesting	301
42.	Hacked Their Way Clear	305
43.	You've Earned It	311
44.	After Sunfall	317
45.	Quite An Impression	327
46.	Beyond A Visit With The King	337
47.	Horse And Rider	343
48.	Eating Away At His Heart	349
49.	Pitiful Mews	359
50.	A Rush Of Wind	367
51.	His Last Breath	375
52.	The Light Receded	383
53.	Not Since The Red War	391
54.	You Are	401
55.	Across The Narthwich Bridge	411
Acknowledgements		415
About the Author		416
Glossary		417
Cast of Characters		432

He who was Light awakens to Night,
exiled from the hearth that once held him.
Rise, Storm Grazer, leave all you hold dear;
Bloom, Flower of Lies, lest you perish in the fading sun;
Stand, Day-Son, your shadow brings ruin and gloom;
Seek, Bookkeeper, what memory dares not name;
For true to each other the Four must remain,
lest darkness consume all that is known.

PROLOGUE

An icy wind sliced across the eastern Tol mountains, pregnant with winter's first snow and a death long foretold. Nestled in the mountains' shadow, the foothills braced for the worst. Yet the one-room cottage radiated coziness, a fire crackling and popping in the open hearth, providing all the warmth needed. A child barely past infancy slept on, unaware of the gathering storm.

First hints of gray speckling his beard, a man paced, restless as a caged frit, while a woman sat motionless, only her eyes betraying movement as they tracked the man's pacing. Her outward appearance suggested she was near enough his age, though the white stone embedded in her forehead spoke of a path unlike his and a depth in her eyes hinted at a wisdom few achieved in a lifetime.

"How can she demand this, Aisling?" the man cried, slumping into a chair. "There has to be another way."

He spoke to the seated woman, though he did not speak *of* her, his gaze directed instead at a corner of the room resisting the fire's flickering light, to a figure cloaked in shadows.

Aisling frowned at his outburst and glanced toward the child, reassuring herself the little one still slept.

"There is no other way." Sensing the time appointed, the shadowed figure stepped into the light. "The child cannot survive the shadows or the storm without the stone."

The figure crossed the room with practiced grace, unhurried. In the light, her nature was plain: an Elder-Mother. Her cloak's hood concealed a flat brown stone embedded in her forehead, as it also hid the tears on her face. Kneeling at the bedside, she rested her hand on the child's forehead. Not gently, nor lovingly, for her hand trembled with fear.

"May the Great Binding speak to you. May it speak to all of us."

The Elder-Mother shuddered, knowing what was to come. Knowing the sacrifice to be made.

At the door's threshold, she glanced back, vowing never to forget that moment, before closing the door behind her. Outside, she wavered, one hand still on the latch, unsure she could walk away, the soft glow of an exterior lantern capturing her hesitation.

A long, slow exhale.

She vanished into the darkness, into the howling wind and approaching storm.

Inside, the man shot to his feet and made as if to follow her—into the storm, or to the Serewild Dunes, or even to the Twelve Isles if need be, but his pacing feet failed him. He swayed in place, trembling, hands clenched. In anger. Or perhaps fear. Was there room left to care?

He sank to the floor, rested his head in the seated woman's lap. "What can we do, Aisling?" The question tore as a sob from his throat.

Aisling rested a comforting hand on his arm but knew he wasn't expecting an answer.

There was none to give.

Determined, she stood and crossed to where the little one slept before bending to kiss the soft forehead.

Together we will change the world, my child, the whisper so quiet it was nearly unspoken. Aisling prayed it was true and prayed for the strength to do what must be done.

A knife secreted in her tunic slid effortlessly into her palm. She raised it high to accomplish the night's terror. The knife gouged into flesh, severing the stark white stone embedded in Aisling's own forehead. She collapsed with a sickening thud. The knife slipped from her hand and clattered across the plank floor, while the bloodied stone rolled and teetered on its rounded edge before coming to a stop.

The man wept.

Awakened by the noise, the child's wails pierced the room. Scooping the child into his arms, calloused hands brushed away tiny tears. He paced the room again, but like a boat on gentle waves, rocking the little one back to sleep while he crooned a lullaby. It didn't matter that it was off-key. The child knew his voice, and that was enough. When the cries subsided and the little one again slept, none the wiser to the night's horror, he tucked the child back into bed and kissed the tiny, tear-reddened nose.

He retrieved the knife and stone. Placed them almost reverently on the table, unsure for a moment, considering, gathering courage.

Kneeling beside the woman, he tucked a wild strand of hair behind her ear, the way he had so many times before.

But no answering smile lit the room. No soft laugh. No sweet kiss. She was gone, knowing instinctively where to cut at the stone, it being a part of her as not even he could have ever been.

May we meet again in a better tomorrow.

He choked on the familiar goodbye as he cradled her, like he'd cradled the child, sobbing against her skin. Her warmth was still there, but she wasn't. He kissed her cheek, her lips, her hair. Took one last breath of the lilac petal scent she so adored, and gathered her up in his arms.

At the door he paused, remembering the first time he'd crossed that threshold with her in his arms. Recalled the joy that night, bittersweet now, a fading memory, before disappearing into the gloom to bury his wife.

An icy breath of wind slipped in as the door closed. The wind shuddered at the loss haunting the one-room cottage. It recoiled at the bloodied stone and knife abandoned on the table, before hovering like a brewing storm over the sleeping

ERIC MUNGER

child, its breath tender for the first time. Its pulse quickened, answering the power dreaming below.

Chapter One
We Will

20 years later...

"Never seen it like this."

Tobias leaned against a merchant stall, a dagger in hand, picking bits of meat from between his teeth. The young woman manning the stall eyed him angrily. Admirably, she held her tongue, but then there were no customers to scare away today.

Kymn rolled his eyes, Magnus laughed, knowing Tobias didn't mean any harm. Not really. It was his nature. Nonchalant, relaxed, occasionally oblivious.

Magnus stretched, his eyes sweeping a nearby rooftop. Glanced down a row of stalls. Studied the man shuttering his shop across the street. A woman sweeping out her stall.

Quiet. Too quiet.

Their patrol took them through the markets—the Capitol's lifeblood—though today even that pulse felt weak. Magnus preferred the River Market when it was alive; it was rough, loud, and honest, the kind of place where people said what they meant and smelled like their work. The Grand Bazaar was nearly as intriguing, stalls replete with goods hailing from every corner of the kingdom; its chaos drew him in. Merchant's Row, by contrast, could rot for all he cared. *Silk and perfume masking greed and contempt.* Yet if he was honest, he still liked looking at the polished wares and imported fabrics. But today, even the river smelled wrong. Too still. The Capitol depended on the markets thriving, and so soon after the famine, the silence felt dangerous.

But it wasn't only the market that bled customers, drained like a man beneath a barber-surgeon's leech. No, it was how every Capitol street and alley felt empty, soulless, citizens scurrying along on errands with heads bowed, ignoring friends and neighbors, eyeing strangers warily.

Even the pickpockets were noticeably absent. Most days you spotted them easily enough, if you knew what to watch for. Shifty eyes, clothes too large for scrawny frames, and hands clawing for what belonged to others. It was said the Capitol's best could pick you clean. Blindfolded.

Magnus had learned the hard way to recognize the slight sensation, the brush of a hand pinching a last decri coin. During his first eight-day in the Capitol, they'd filched every decri he carried. Swearing it wouldn't happen again, he learned to identify every deliberate bump. To recognize the innocent from the ill-intentioned. A quick twist of the wrist and a threatening glare sent a pickpocket scampering. If the glare didn't work, a sweep of his cloak revealing the sword at his side did the trick. Or perhaps it was the uniform he now wore.

"How'd he take it?" asked Kymn, interrupting his thoughts.

"Ah ..." Magnus waved dismissively. "You know our commander ... he isn't happy with anyone leaving. Ever."

"You don't owe him anything." Tobias pushed off from the stall post, twirled the dagger in his hand. "Your contract's almost up. Go home."

Home.

The Plains.

Magnus closed his eyes and pictured fields stretching vast, innumerable, to the horizon. Heads of grain bending to the winds. The feel of the chaff, rough between his fingers. The intoxicating smell of warm, just-baked waybread, shared in every home and tavern of the Plains. And his home. Quiet conversations at night with his father. Just the two of them, while his sisters slept.

Didn't know the ache would bite so deep.

And then the pickpockets took worse than the decri—his knife gone too. A gift from home. From his father. The last thing he'd carried that still felt like the Plains.

"We all envy you, you know?" said Tobias. "Should have signed a shorter contract too. Fewer days like this."

He's right. What a waste.

Magnus quit scanning the alleys and rooftops. Who would have the heart for trouble after the morning's tremors? He couldn't recall hearing of earthquakes in the Capitol. Sure, they were common in the Highlands. Even on the Plains once when he was young. But in the Capitol? No. Never. But twice that morning, rumbling earth shattered stalls and upended carts laden with food, as if the land itself roiled in turmoil because of what happened at Saan.

Saan. The Capitol's closest neighbor, if not quite in distance then certainly in trade and social connection. There was hardly a citizen who hadn't lost friend or family in its desecration. The populace demanded blood. Revenge. Enlistment in the Ka, already up significantly during the famine, swelled to record numbers.

An urgent shout, sharp and piercing, snapped Magnus' attention, his patrol converging on the sound, discovering an effigy of a Gray Cloak hanging from a stone crosswalk. A sign around its lumpy straw-stuffed head bore four chilling words, dripping bright red in childish scrawling:

Death To Gray Cloaks!

The sight drew a crowd, until an onlooker picked up the phrase, joined by another, and another, as it swelled to a chant, the crowd swept along in the frenzy. Nearby merchants beat a hasty retreat, closing stalls and hastening away with their carts.

"Cut it down," ordered Magnus, "before this gets out of hand."

Kymn drew his sword, but a woman burst from the crowd, torch raised toward the dangling figure. Her face was wet with tears—grief had found something to burn. Onlookers cheered as flames leaped across the straw-padded clothing, engulfing the dummy, licking hungrily at the gray cloak it wore and the sign around its neck. Singed, the rope snapped. Flaming debris cascaded onto the street, scattering the crowd.

"Think we'll be sent east?" asked Kymn as he stamped out the fire.

Magnus scratched at the stubble on his cheeks, his hand resting on the hilt of his sword, considering the question and the sputtering flames.

Do I tell them? That east means war? That war means some of us may not return?

The orders would come soon enough, and it appeared the Ka wanted blood as badly as Capitol citizens did. He saw it in their eyes, heard it in the tone of Kymn's question, noticed it in the way his men stiffened when the effigy burst in flames and the crowd roared.

"We will."

Chapter Two
It Was Time

While earthquakes buckled Capitol streets and calls for Gray Cloak blood echoed across western Lavonshia, to the east the foothills of Dorak lay quiet and still. Few there worried about war. Centuries had passed since even a rumor of war so much as touched their province, and the old-timers swore many more would pass before it ever did.

Fortunate visitors to Dorak found lush meadows, rolling hills, and fields ripe with amaranth grain, where cobblestone pathways ambled between villages, interrupted only by groves of fruit trees laden with apples, chockberries, and mountain oranges.

Some claimed it to be the Kingdom of Lavonshia's best-kept secret—pleasant, hospitable—though difficult to reach.

Nestled in a bowl-shaped curve surrounded on three sides by the Tol Mountains and bordered by Gray Cloak territory to the north, Dorak's only connection to western Lavonshia was through a narrow gap: Hadil's Crossing. The gap was only passable this time of year, after late spring thaws melted winter snowdrifts and summer heat hardened the impossibly thick mud left behind. For a short moon's cycle, before another long winter descended on the mountains, one could travel to and from Dorak.

But for Dorakians, it was no occasion to travel, for it was harvest season, and a pleasant hum of conversation drifted over the fields as they labored side by side.

Aurelia Talbot glanced up from the harvest, brushing aside an unruly strand of her coal-black hair to check on her father. She worried about him more often these days; his once speckled gray beard now white as winter snow, his face sporting too many wrinkles to count, though the corners of his mouth still lifted in an amiable smile. A jest from a passing neighbor—*you gather less harvest than your daughter; you're getting old, Mahan!*—was as likely now as ever to spark a hearty laugh.

Aurelia scanned the contents of her grain cart and snorted. She'd managed, but only just barely, to keep up with him so far that morning. Even at his advanced age, she knew few who could match his harvesting speed.

But his eyes told a different story than the quick smile on his lips. They held a hint of fear she hadn't seen before.

After all, in Aurelia's nearly twenty-two years of life, trouble had never visited Dorak. When her father spoke of the past, of his life *before*, the stories reminded her how good life was in Chelam. She couldn't remember the last crime committed in their village. It was safe, and she was quite content with that, while the thought of *out there* unnerved her. Trouble belonged to the stories her father told, not to quiet fields and sun-warmed grain.

She sighed.

"What is it, little Aurie?"

Her lips twitched. She hadn't been little in many hunter's moons, but he still preferred the pet name even though she stood half a span taller than he—and taller still than the mother she'd never known. *You had tall uncles*, he'd joke if she asked. But no matter her height, to Mahan she'd always be his little Aurie.

"Chelam. Dorak," she said. "Don't you think it's perfect the way things are?"

"You know change is the season of the future."

The fear was gone now, replaced by the usual twinkle in his eyes. Mahan was fond of his many sayings.

"Seriously, Father?" Aurelia blew an exasperated breath. "What about Saan? Yesterday, Peddler Ibben said the Gray Cloaks were being blamed. Will what happened in Saan affect us?"

Mahan paused. Shrugged. "Hard to say. Unlikely though."

A flash of irritation at how quickly he dismissed the danger. As if saying they were safe would make it true. Despite his assurances, she had her doubts, and his eyes betrayed that he did too.

Though Gray Cloak clans kept mostly to themselves, Dorakians had long lived beside them in peace, and Aurelia was no fool. *Won't war to the north spill onto our land?*

"Did I ever tell you about my adventures in Perinith?"

Aurelia snorted at the change of subject. She knew what was coming. Her father's tales were so tall even the elders rolled their eyes. *Stories of a life he wished he had,* they whispered. As much as she wanted to believe him, her father's imagination was an active one. Still, she indulged him.

Leaning her scythe against the cart, Aurelia stretched from the backbreaking work, half-listening as her father lost himself in a meandering story.

"You should have seen it, little Aurie ... there I stood on the shores of Perinith -"

Eken's breathless arrival interrupted the tale, but then her best friend was easily excited and often breathless. As usual, the worn-out corner of a book peeked from his tunic pocket. A pair of reading spectacles perched haphazardly on his nose, an expensive rarity in Dorak, but he'd saved six years for them. Since then he'd read every book in the village four times over. Not that Dorakians despised learning. Any subject covering harvest or festivals was a bestseller and Peddler Ibben couldn't keep those books stocked. But Eken devoured anything and everything written on a page, bestseller or not.

"Aurelia! Aren't you coming?" he shouted, his lean frame catching its breath, with an aside, "Oh hello Mahan." Unwilling to await an answer, his legs had already carried him past the Talbots' field and towards the village square.

Aurelia glanced at her father for approval, not that she needed it; she was a grown woman after all, but she hated leaving with her cart half full and so much still to harvest.

He pretended not to notice, his scythe sweeping tirelessly across the heads of grain. He stretched, an exaggerated groan escaping his lips.

"Father?" she said, her hands on her hips.

He gave a start as if surprised to find her there.

"Yes, little Aurie?"

Is he going to make me ask? she wondered. She couldn't help but love him for the way he teased, even when he drove her mad.

"Yes, little Aurie." His eyes twinkled merrily.

With a giddy laugh, one she knew inappropriate for a woman her age, she planted a kiss on his bearded cheek, tossed her scythe to the ground, and vaulted the fence marking their field's boundary. She might act a school-aged child, but she couldn't help it. Tonight was a big night. Of all their festivals, the Harvest Festival was the highlight of the year.

A grin stretched from ear to ear as she chased Eken past fields lined with rows of grain waiting to be gleaned, where harvesters stopped to watch. They couldn't help their grins either, for hers was infectious, and they knew where she headed.

The Great Hall.

For the final night of festivities, and to see the Grand Unveiling.

A fast runner, she caught Eken well before they'd reached it.

"Come on, Mudboots!" she teased as she slipped past him.

As a young girl, she'd kept up with boys her own age, and that hardly changed as she became of age, not that as a grown woman she ran much. Festival games were the exception, and at those competitions she held her own against any challenger, male or female.

It explained her few female friends, this tomboyish side of hers. Gossip circles held no appeal, nor did chasing suitors. The suitors gave her the same wide berth, preferring the coy ones who batted their eyelashes. No, for Aurelia, she found pleasure in the sun's warmth as she worked the fields. Or in a cool sip of water at day's end, surveying the finished harvest. Evenings found her most often at the

Plow & Lantern, the village-square tavern, dancing to the fiddler's tune. And she never missed a festival, with Eken always at her side.

Then along came Col.

A couple years her junior, he had still played at juvenile games while she matured into a young woman. But then he came of age, and chose her for reasons she couldn't explain, though she had yet to choose him.

By far the most eligible bachelor in town, Col was outgoing, good-looking, son of a prominent family. A marriage to him would ensure wealth and status. In a small village like Chelam, word spread of Col's pursuit, and overnight she became the envy of every girl and woman in town.

Her father had placed few restrictions on Aurelia growing up. It wasn't intentional, though despite Mahan's best efforts to spoil her, she turned out remarkably well adjusted, even without a mother around. And now, as a grown woman with a serious suitor, Mahan insisted to friends that the choice and timing were hers. She was free to choose whom she wanted, when she wanted. But at home he gently suggested it was time. In his heart, at his most selfish moments, he wished she wouldn't marry. His daughter was the joy of his life, and he couldn't imagine being alone. But he was aging and she should wed—*build a life with a man who'll protect you when I'm gone* as he liked to say.

He broached the subject one day over dinner preparations, sprinkling spices into the boiling pot and dropping in chunks of meat while Aurelia prepped the vegetables.

Perhaps he wished he'd kept quiet.

"I don't need someone providing for me!" Her knife sliced savagely through a carrot's end. "Perfectly able to take care of myself, thank you very much."

"Yes, I agree." Mahan eyed the knife warily. "You're more capable than most—that's your mother you take after. She was feisty, like you."

Aurelia didn't take the bait. She'd grown tired a long time ago reminiscing about the mother she'd never known. If her father wanted to live in the past in his spare time, that was his choice.

Aurelia's legs blurred, heart pounding, breath catching in the chill air as she rounded the cobblestone village square, the setting sun casting long shadows from the timber-framed buildings. And there, looming before her, stood the Great Hall.

While homes in Chelam were small, often a single room, the Great Hall was a magnificent structure, towering above all others. It was the focal point of Dorakian life, holding official Elder Conclaves and many of Chelam's beloved festivals.

A crowd gathered, impatient, the hall doors still closed and locked. Anticipation hung thick in the air, as thick as Old Lady Cridge's soup. This was it. The last night of the Harvest Festival. The night of the courting dance.

For the unmarried, it was no ordinary dance. Accepting a dance on this night was tantamount to accepting an offer of marriage, their hand in yours a binding contract—declining to marry later risked being shunned from society. So those still single hovered nervously on the outskirts of the hall. The stakes were too high to venture onto the floor where married folk danced merrily, unfettered by such rules. Instead they watched with envy as the married or widowed—granted an exception singles didn't enjoy—danced with friends, family, neighbors, even their enemies should they have any, for Dorakians happily set aside long-standing feuds on such a night of celebration.

Outside the hall, the crowd jostled each other good-naturedly, neighbor greeting neighbor. There were no strangers in Chelam. Eken and Aurelia squeezed their way through, hoping to be first inside once the doors opened.

Nearby, a group of women prattled incessantly, one of the gossip circles Aurelia despised. To her horror, she was the subject.

"She's embarrassed to marry him," said Edme, the ringleader, not even attempting a whisper. "It's obvious his height bothers her."

Aurelia ignored the comment, especially coming from Edme, the worst offender. But by this point in her will-they-won't-they with Col, she was used to such talk, though it never ceased to amaze her how easily tongues wagged over foolish rumors.

"It's clear he'll return to his first love—the Ka," whispered another woman. "A shame to waste all those years of training."

"Mind your tongues," cut in a woman nearby, "that girl's worth ten of you."

But if the gossipers heard, they gave no sign beyond tightening their circle as the next chimed in.

"Or is he too honorable to withdraw his offer? Be proof pudding-thick that he's too good for the girl."

Where do they come up with such things? Aurelia wondered.

True, it was odd for a girl of marrying age to deny the advances of a well-meaning suitor, especially one as wealthy and well-connected as Col. He was a catch, and most thought her a fool to deny him.

"Jusel told me in confidence that he plans to forbid the marriage." Edme again, clearly with more on her mind needing to be voiced. "Even he thinks Aurelia isn't good enough for his son. What girl could be, raised without a mother? I tell you, Mahan's far too openhanded with her. That girl needed a good thrashing long ago."

Aurelia had heard enough. Blood boiling, she whirled to face the women. "How dare you, Edme! You have no right to speak such nonsense! You should be ashamed of yourselves."

Grabbing Eken's hand, she turned to leave and ran headlong into Col.

"Oh! Col ..." Her face turned a bright flaming red, as did his.

"Don't pay them any attention, they -"

"It's okay Col, I -"

She ducked away, plunged into the crowd, anxious to be anywhere but near him.

I ... what? she wondered. *What do I say to a man I've refused at the last two Harvest Festival dances?*

"I'll see you tonight?" shouted Col as she fled, the question lingering in the air.

Yes, I'll be there, she thought. *But will I dance with him?*

The list of reasons to continue refusing had all but disappeared. Wasn't his dogged pursuit enough proof he was the right man to choose? Tonight she must dance with him, or risk never being married at all.

Who else will want me after refusing him for a third time?

The tower bells struck.

An excited hush fell over the crowd.

It was time.

Chapter Three
To Clean Our Blades

Magnus wiped spittle from the corners of his mouth, the taste of vomit still fresh, stomach roiling. It wasn't the death that bothered him—he'd seen plenty during the famine—but how they died. What the magic bindings had done to the Ka ... and what the Ka had done in return.

He tried to stand, but legs shaking, he sank back to the ground.

Magnus thought little of magic as a boy. To speak of it in anything more than nursery rhymes had been forbidden in Lavonshia for the past four hundred years. Only the seediest of taverns dared whisper rumors of its reality.

He shuddered to think what powers Gray Cloaks forged in the dark while the kingdom pretended magic merely a fairytale. No, the truth was obvious now. They hadn't abandoned magic to myth and legend as all other good Lavonshians had. *How long have they secretly persisted in their bindings?* wondered Magnus. The Tol Mountains had certainly played their role in allowing it—dividing the two provinces as they did—with densely populated cities of the west, like the Capitol and Saan, busying themselves in the ho-hum of ordinary lives, leaving Gray Cloaks to the east with their anonymity. If one were to ask a typical Lavonshian who or what a Gray Cloak was, they would be as likely to get a blank stare as any sort of answer.

Until Saan.

Overnight a headline sensation, its inhabitants missing, the city ash and silence, and the Gray Cloaks blamed for it. Now even the children played games of Ka and Gray Cloak, though none wanted to play the Gray Cloak.

Royal advisors warned Saan was only the beginning, so the King ordered a Ka regiment east, as Magnus predicted. Their mission—rescue missing citizens of Saan and subdue or kill Gray Cloak resistors.

In four days of hard marching, the Ka reached Hadil's Crossing. Two days later found them in Gray Cloak territory, on the outskirts of a village. Their maps showed its name as Tiriman.

"Just like at the Capitol, only stronger."

Daylight had not yet pierced night's veil. A weak moon cast a dim pall on Kymn's face. Perspiration glistened his brow, despite the cool night air.

Magnus wiped his hand against his tunic, his palms sweaty, damp. To his right, Tobias appeared calm, though his hand fidgeted at his sword's pommel.

"Aye. It was."

Another tremor, the earth rumbling. A cry of alarm in Tiriman, followed by silence.

The Ka waited breathlessly for orders. Men prayed who believed in such things, a fleeing coward impaled on an officer's sword, first casualty of the impending battle. There would be no mercy for deserters.

A torch flared below, then another—Tiriman villagers awakening early, investigating the quake's aftermath.

A Ka trumpet blast. The order given.

Bellowing their battle cry, the Ka surged into Tiriman. The once-level ground, torn asunder by the earlier tremor, only added to the chaos as soldiers and fleeing Gray Cloaks stumbled over buckled rock and earth. Men, women and children streamed from their homes in panic.

A home erupted in flames, the efforts of an overzealous soldier. Screams pierced the veil of smoke as the fire spread and more homes blazed.

As a second wave of Ka rolled transport wagons into the village, Magnus herded a frightened family into the nearest one. His heart sickened at the sight of so many with tear-streaked ashen cheeks. In their eyes, in their faces, he saw his sisters. The youngest pressed a doll close to her chest, its cornsack-dress and horsetail-hair blackened from flame. *Like the one Ella carries.*

Desperate pleas for mercy fell on deaf ears as a company of soldiers slaughtered villagers.

"Tobias -" Magnus gestured towards a family huddled outside their home, desperate to save any he could as the wanton killing reached a frenzy.

"Take prisoners!" he shouted to his unit. "They are no threat!"

As the command repeated across the village, a fragile order settled over the ruin, while soldiers continued to search homes and herd prisoners towards the wagons.

A rising sun laid bare the truth—no songs, no victory, only the hush of death and smoke. The Ka had subdued a village of unarmed men, women and children. Soldiers refused to meet each other's eyes, shame writ clear across their faces.

Magnus approached a prisoner transport wagon, appraising the prisoners inside while he removed his helmet and wiped sweat from his brow.

An old man bound to the wagon's rail observed him thoughtfully. A large knot on the man's temple threatened to turn an ugly black and blue, while a cut at his jawline dripped blood. He waited calmly enough, though his white-knuckled grip on the wagon's bars betrayed him.

"Do you speak Lavon?" asked Magnus.

"Of course. Why have you done this?"

"I'll ask the questions. Where's your cloak? Your stone?"

The man seemed puzzled by the question. "I don't understand."

"This is a Gray Cloak settlement, yes?"

"It is. But why are you here? What have we done to deserve this?"

"Where is your stone?" asked Magnus again, refusing to be distracted.

"I bear no stone," said the prisoner, adding a shrug. "I never have."

Magnus scanned the occupants secured behind the wagon's bars. Children and elderly. A soot-streaked girl clutched her brother's sleeve the way his own sister used to clutch his when thunder pealed across the Plains.

"Can anyone here speak plainly? Where are your stones? Your cloaks?"

The prisoners stared blankly.

"Magnus," interrupted Tobias, directing his attention towards a commotion at the north end of Tiriman.

Thunder cracked, and rain erupted from a cloudless sky, a torrent so powerful that within moments it flooded a cross street and swept a soldier away. A geyser of flame shot from a crack in the ground, setting another on fire. He stumbled, burning, into the nearest building. It too caught fire, flame and smoke soon rising from its rooftop. Magnus strained to see through the smoke as the world turned unreal.

A melodic song floated on the breeze, jarring in the chaos. A rushing sound like thousands of beating wings heralded a flock of birds, and lifting a soldier bodily into the air, they carried him away screaming.

Cloaks billowed and swirled as a band of women entered Tiriman, deft hands tracing strange patterns, binding land and element to their will while the stones they bore in their foreheads pulsed with power.

These were the ones the Ka hunted.

Magnus rushed into the fray, his blade soon slick with blood. Beside him, his friends and fellow-soldiers fought. Tobias. Kymn. Morco and others. Earth and wind clogged their lungs; flame singed their skin. Ka soldiers and Gray Cloaks fell slain together, sightless eyes demanding an explanation for such sacrifice.

A second band of Gray Cloaks entered Tiriman from the south, moving among the wagons, breaking open the bars, setting prisoners free.

The resistance doomed Tiriman. In the chaos of battle, fire spread gleefully, whether set by soldiers or errant streaking flame no one afterward could say. Homes and transport wagons burned, some still with villagers trapped inside.

When the battle ended, no buildings remained standing, and Gray Cloak resisters who still lived, fled. The Ka victory came at a horrible cost.

Shell-shocked, Magnus wandered the ashes of Tiriman. His fellow soldiers had slaughtered women, children, fathers cradling babies in their arms, sparing few. Innocents lay scattered among resisters.

But in the battle's aftermath, the talk wasn't of the innocent, but of the bindings. The magic the Ka witnessed that day. Power that hurled earth and compelled flame. Forces that pulled the very air from your lungs. Grizzled veterans had laughed at such reports after Saan. *Nothing but fairytales*, they claimed.

No one laughed in Tiriman.

"You okay? Magnus?" It was Kymn and Tobias searching for their friend and captain after the battle.

"Did I ever tell you what I hated most as a child?" Magnus rubbed absent-mindedly at a spot of blood on his boots. "Slaughter days."

"Don't go there," said Tobias.

"I tried anything I could to get out of one," continued Magnus, ignoring the interruption, his thoughts returning to moments that built him. "Feigned sickness. Hid in the fields. Even ran away from home once to avoid it. But father always found me. Told me it was a necessary part of life. Animals died to put food on our plates, so we could live."

"Magnus, we should see to the survivors, to the -"

"Children." He continued to rub at the spot of blood. "Why doesn't anyone keep them from the death? And all the blood?"

"We had our orders." Kymn shrugged.

"The odor on a slaughter day ..." Magnus shuddered. "Rancid. Foul. Mother tried to help, before the yellow death took her. She'd make my favorite goat stew. I could eat it any other day, but not then."

"We did what we had to today."

"My father said the same." Magnus laughed, a humorless laugh, and grunted as he struggled to his feet. "Is that what we had to do?" His sword jabbed viciously at the smoking husk of a body lying nearby. A small frame.

"You know that's not what he meant," said Tobias.

"Who? Kymn or my father?" This time Magnus' laugh was bitter. "I've wanted to go home for so long, but I'd forgotten about the slaughter days. Is there no escaping the killing?"

"Easy, brother." Tobias embraced his friend in a fierce hug, holding him tight as Magnus wept. Soldiers nearby looked away.

"Come," said Tobias. "Let's find a stream to clean our blades."

Chapter Four
The Land's Whispers Grew Louder

The old man always waited in the same place by the dusty road from dusk until moonrise. Few ever noticed him. Dressed in garments that seemed stitched from moss and stone, he blended with the forest behind him. At least the day's worst heat had come and gone, though dust from passing travelers still brought on coughing fits from time to time.

It wasn't the waiting that was difficult. Four hundred years teaches one a good amount of patience. No, he was content to wait. It was the not knowing that frustrated.

Was this the right spot? The right time of day? Frustrated, he sighed. It was the listening that was tough, the magic in the land weak, lying dormant for too long. Although there wasn't much he missed from *before*, he missed the way it used to feel. The Sensing of it. He feared the magic would never recover if it wasn't awoken soon.

He brightened at the sight of a harpy eagle wheeling high above, its keen eyes searching the ground below for easy prey. The old man enjoyed birds, mesmerized by their freedom in flight as they cartwheeled through the sky.

This part of the country had its fair share of brilliantly colored ones: bluebirds, orange-breasted songbirds, the white lily jay, and the shimmering green spowe. But the giant harpy eagle reigned supreme. Other creatures—both those who winged currents of the sky and those who trod earthen paths—learned to fear it or face its talons and hooked beak. Some claimed the harpy was an omen, a harbinger of doom. But he had never bought into such things. The eagle had no magical properties; it was simply an animal.

Now, the creature sitting by his side was a different story altogether. The old man scratched the creature's head fondly.

They'd been friends for many years, for so long they rarely had to speak anymore. In fact, it was as if they read each other's minds. The old man knew, for example, that his friend was watching the eagle too, albeit with a decidedly more predatory eye. He could sense his friend tensing, muscles taut, ready to pounce should the harpy fly near. The largest of eagles sought easy targets, even a human if small and frail enough. Parents kept a watchful eye on their children when harpy eagles flew near. But of course his friend was no human child, though he wasn't especially imposing in stature.

The eagle wisely kept its distance.

"Do you think it'll be today?" asked his companion, tail swishing contentedly. Nothing much bothered him.

This was the routine, the same question every day, just before the waiting ended.

The old man sighed, sticking to the routine. "No, not today." He brightened, remembering the stew simmering over the fire. "Come, my friend, a hot meal awaits!"

Turning their backs on the dusty road, they made their way up the winding path towards home.

Another fruitless waiting. Today was not that day, though the old man Sensed it would be soon. The Storm Grazer was coming and the land's whispers grew louder.

Chapter Five
They Always Come in Twos

"Get out!" roared Drael, flinging his helmet at the nearest officer, who fled the tent in his desperation to escape the commander's temper. Soldiers feared few regiment commanders as much as Drael.

It had been near a moon's cycle since the ruin of Tiriman, and there'd been no Gray Cloak sightings since. Not even a whisper of one.

Ka maps showed where Gray Cloak villages should be, but when the Ka reached those villages, they were gone, as if they never existed. No buildings, homes or hastily discarded belongings, and not a scrap of evidence anyone had ever lived there. Surely the King's cartographers weren't fools.

When one of his officers had dared suggest, timidly, that they turn tail and head home, it had been the last straw. Drael made a mental note to demote the officer. He leaned over his desk, closing his eyes, and cradled his head in his hands.

"What is it?" he asked, sensing an officer remained behind. He opened an eye, recognized Magnus, one of his best and brightest. Drael sighed. *Everyone always wants to go home.*

"My contract," said Magnus, "it ends in a few days, as you know. I'd hoped to buy my horse off your hands."

"I can't afford to lose you, or any horse. Not now. We're in the middle of a campaign here. What can I do to convince you to stay? To see this through."

"My family, sir. They're expecting me. I ... I can't stay."

"We just need a good win." Drael slammed a hand on the desk. "You'll think differently then."

Orders came the following morning to strike camp. They were heading south. To Dorak. Perhaps a Dorakian could be convinced to reveal the whereabouts of their northern neighbors.

The bells' clamor pealed across Chelam's square.

The crowd waited, expectant, with a pent-up energy liable to snap should the doors fail to open. But then, the same as at every Harvest Festival for the last thousand years, the Great Hall doors swung inward and the crowd surged inside, eager to witness the hall's transformation.

Each year, the privilege of decorating the hall for Harvest Festival passed to a new family. This year, the Elders bestowed that honor on Eken's family, the Potterfelds. It explained his heightened excitement.

That he'd kept his family's preparations a secret surprised Aurelia. It was common knowledge that sharing a secret with Eken was akin to sharing it with all of Chelam, but try as she might, she'd failed to pry details from him, for even he appreciated the gravity of the time-honored tradition.

As tradition went, the Great Hall's doors remained locked and barred for a moon's cycle prior to the final night. Only the family decorating the hall could enter, forcing the Elder Conclaves to relocate each year during Harvest Festival, accompanied by much good-natured grumbling from the Elders.

To conceal the work inside, giant tapestries covered the floor-to-ceiling windows on the north and south sides of the building. Only as the bells tolled and the doors burst open were the tapestries tossed aside. As villagers streamed into the hall, so too did the light, freed at last to display the transformation within its walls.

Every year, Aurelia delighted in those first moments.

The Grand Unveiling.

Last year had been the best in recent memory, and she doubted the Potterfelds could outdo it.

The crowd pressed forward, sweeping her and Eken along with it.

Watching his friend absorb the hall's newly decorated splendor, Eken reached for the book wedged in his tunic pocket, wrapping his fingers around its spine—a nervous tic he'd developed. "See, I told you it would be amazing, didn't I?"

"I just can't ... oh, Eken! It's spectacular!"

The Potterfelds had outdone themselves, and her first impression of the hall's transformation was that it might rival last year's after all.

Rugs quilted for the occasion covered the floor, forming a vibrant patchwork of reds, yellows, blues, and greens. Each had been sewn with scenes from Dorakian life—festivals, plantings and harvests, feasting and dancing, Great Halls and village squares. Garlands of flowers hung overhead in bright gold and purple strands. The Potterfelds had wrapped the hall's giant pillars in leather panels etched with Dorakian legends and myths.

Despite the hall's size, food and spiced ale were never more than a few steps away. Rich aromas drifted from piled meats, cheeses, and fruits. Aurelia's stomach rumbled.

Each table featured an ornate centerpiece, hand-carved by local artisans, fashioned of lanthanum metal into woodland creatures. She spotted an elk at one, a bear at another, an otter at the next, and so on.

Eken tugged Aurelia by the hand from one marvel to the next, drawing her eyes to details she'd have missed in the grandeur of it all. Around them, gitterns rang, tabors thumped, and music swelled. The luckiest festival-goers shrieked as the dance claimed them while Aurelia watched from the sidelines with envy.

Her father, fashionably late as usual, arrived as the party reached its height. As he reached her, she rose on her toes to smooth his collar before he could protest. He looked splendid in the fine clothes she'd tailored over the summer, a rich blue with gold-colored accents. They had cost most of her savings for the right material at market, and many evenings since to fashion. She was glad she'd splurged.

He winked at her as he danced by, though sadness lingered behind him despite his arms around an attractive widow. They twirled, talking, laughing, admiring the decorations, before catching their collective breath, loading plates with food and downing mugs of spiced wine. Aurelia joined them to fill her own plate. Old Lady Cridge hovered dangerously close, a ladle in one hand, passing out bowls of her too-thick soup. They avoided her and the soup. For the moment at least.

The festival spilled outdoors as more Dorakians arrived than could fit inside. Friends and relatives from nearby villages often came for the final evening, especially when their own celebration fell on a different day. Everyone loved a lively dance, a bountiful feast, and the swirling rumors over which singles might dance.

Making their way outside, Mahan and Aurelia claimed a pair of empty seats, eating in companionable silence until her father asked, "Will you dance?"

She took her time considering an answer, picking at her food, no longer hungry. "I think I must. Can't go unmarried forever, and I've never had another suitor."

"But ...?"

"I ... I don't know. One moment I'm ready, the next ... is he right for me? Will he give me the space I need to be myself? I've seen how Jusel Blackwood treats his wife, and well, Col seems very much like his father."

"What do you mean?"

Aurelia sighed. Her father was a good man, but a little slow with advice on love and relationships. "I want to be happy. Col's mother doesn't seem happy. Jusel tells her exactly how to think, what to say, what to do, what to wear. That wouldn't work for me! You know that."

"Truer words were never spoken." Mahan's full-bellied laugh sloshed the spiced ale in his mug. "You're not one to be controlled. Even I couldn't do that!"

"Hey! I'm still a dutiful daughter," protested Aurelia.

"Yes, always. I couldn't have asked for better." He leaned over and planted a kiss on her forehead. "My little Aurie. I'm simply agreeing with you. You don't need someone controlling you, but someone you can build a life with. Together."

"Then how do I know Col is right for me?"

"You'll know."

"But -"

Cheering erupted from the hall. Aurelia lost sight of her father as they joined the throng pressing its way inside, her heart fluttering in time with the music upon witnessing the first accepted singles dance. She glimpsed Col studying her from across the hall. He smiled when he caught her eye. Heat rose in her face—not from shyness, but from knowing too many eyes in the hall were on her.

No, not yet! Why must I choose at all?

Her eyes swept the room; there he was again, matching her step for step across the hall. Their eyes met. She longed to be anywhere else—another festival, another day in the field. His eyes glittered like sunlight over the pebbles in Liller's Creek that flowed beyond the Great Hall, and within them shone too much pleasure in the chase.

Frantic, she ducked, submerging into the sea of festival-goers, until she surfaced for air, peering from behind one of the hall's giant columns.

No Col.

She peeked round the other side.

Still no sign of him.

"Aurelia."

She shrieked and jumped, whirled to face him. His dark eyes bored into her own, with a smile honed by years of being told he was important. Another man, with a gentler smile, might have won her heart. *Or am I being impractical?* Precious few choices existed in Dorak.

Suddenly the column's art beside her quite fascinating. She traced a scene on the canvas with her finger as she cleared her throat.

"Col. I wasn't expecting -"

"You look beautiful tonight," he said. Heat touched her cheeks, wondering *did everyone hear that?* "You know how much I care for you, right?"

"Look at this scene here," she said, hoping he'd become as interested as she was in the leather's intricate stitching.

But he stepped back, extended a hand. "Dance with me?"

Her heart pounded, drowning out the tabor and the gittern.

This was it.

Stay unmarried. Comfortable, familiar, safe. The life she knew, with her father.

Or seize the moment, a leap of faith that a life with Col could deliver on its promises?

Whether from hope or fear, she extended a hand.

Later, she couldn't recall if she'd placed her hand or he'd seized it, but when she looked down, hers rested firmly in his.

"Aurelia!"

Eken—breathless as usual. Wider-eyed than normal, if that was possible, his spectacles dangled precariously on his face as he elbowed his way through the crowd, ignoring the sight of their hands joined.

She let go of Col's hand faster than she meant to, allowing her best friend to drag her towards the hall's entrance, two words enough to explain the interruption: "Gray Cloaks!"

She glanced back with an apologetic shrug and couldn't help but notice Col's clenched jaw, his hard stare at Eken.

But even Col understood the weight of Eken's news. Gray Cloaks were such infrequent visitors they'd all been children the last time any had visited Chelam. Still, despite the infrequent visits, the Dorakians welcomed them. It helped that they usually came bearing gifts, though the visits, as the visitors, remained shrouded in mystery. They rarely gave a reason for appearing so suddenly, or an explanation for leaving without warning. Some claimed the Elders knew more than they shared, but then Aurelia found many such rumors to be just that.

"The timing's strange," said Col as he followed Aurelia, in tow behind Eken. "Now? During festival? Father says Gray Cloaks would never appear unannounced at one."

Though uncertain why they'd care about Dorakian festivals, she assumed Col was right—as son of a High Elder and member of a Hearth Family he'd be one to know.

Word of their guests spread quickly, and the crowd parted, allowing the Gray Cloaks entrance into the hall, accompanied by the Elders. Being one of the tallest in attendance, she didn't have to crane her neck much to get a look at the mysterious figures.

Again the crowd parted, in deference to Mahan. For reasons not completely understood by Aurelia—*it's simply my age, little Aurie,* her father would say—the people of Chelam revered her father as they would an Elder, though he wasn't one. True, during harvest season he met often with the Elders, since in his role as Harvest Master there was no end of crop reports to discuss.

A nervous buzz threaded the room. The musicians stilled their instruments, echoes of final notes fading until only silence remained. For many gathered in the Great Hall, it was their first glimpse of a Gray Cloak.

Then Aurelia realized there weren't just two Gray Cloaks in their midst, but five. She'd never heard of so many together.

A chill rippled down her spine, but something deep within her stirred toward the new arrivals, even as she thought:

They always come in twos.

Chapter Six
They'll Pay for This

Magnus caught himself grinning ear to ear but didn't care who noticed or how foolish he looked.

What a perfect day!

Blue skies stretched over the valley, puffy white clouds the only imperfection in the expanse of blue, the sun's warmth a perfect complement to the otherwise cool day.

The regiment had descended into a valley, one the maps referred to as Breckei Valley. It was green, vibrant, early fall wildflowers dotted the landscape, blues and yellows with the occasional fiery red. A thick forest of towering trees crowned the valley slopes to either side. Beyond the forest lay the stunning Tol Mountains, its highest peaks snow-capped year-round.

At last, a day untouched by war.

Memories of Tiriman had faded, and it was the first day he didn't taste the acrid odor of burnt flesh on his tongue. But better yet, in two sunfalls he'd be leaving for home.

He gave the mare he rode an affectionate pat. She hadn't been his for long, but so far she'd proved reliable. Her armor jangled as they trotted across the valley floor. Turning in the saddle, he stretched to get a good look. The regiment snaked its way behind him into the valley, proceeding southward towards Dorak, men and women of the Ka marching triple file, smartly dressed in their black tunics and red leather trousers, their light armor glinting in the afternoon sun while the drums' steady beat maintained their steps in tandem. The relentless thud of a thousand feet comforting in its regularity.

The officers rode at the regiment's front, forming a protective circle around Drael, his white short-cropped hair visible amid a sea of younger officers. Drael was unusual for his age, a commander rumored to be approaching his seventy-fifth hunter's moon. Few could stand the rigors of the Ka for so long and so late in life.

Flanking the officers rode the cavalry guard, the Ka's finest and best trained, tasked with the duty of protecting the regiment officers. Beyond the officers and their guard, on the fastest horses of Lavonshian stables, rode the scouts. Fanning out across the valley, they kept well-trained eyes on the surrounding forest.

Magnus faced forward again in the saddle, smiling as he studied the closest cloud—*ah, there it is, the shape of an old man. Bulging belly. Long white wispy hair pulled back in a ponytail.* He could just make out the old man's face, a mouth and nose.

How many times had he and sisters done the same? Lying hidden among the tall grasses, avoiding chores, stretched out with heads touching as they gazed up, identifying shapes in the clouds. It was usually father who found them, as he worked the fields. More often than not, he'd plop down beside them and join in the fun.

"It's good to see you smile again, Magnus."

Struggling to stay seated, Tobias tried to steer his horse towards his captain. Riding didn't come naturally, but as Magnus' aide, Tobias got a horse, a privilege he sorely regretted.

"Thoughts of home, good thoughts of home," said Magnus. "When we were young, my sisters and I would guess at shapes in the clouds. See that face there?"

Tobias craned his neck, studying the sky. He shook his head ruefully. "Must be you Plainsfolk and your imagination—we Highlanders didn't idle our days away with such fancies."

Magnus' laughter was cut short by an ominous gathering of clouds at the valley's end. Out of place, thick and gray, compared to the few puffy white clouds.

Frantic shouts carried the valley. A scout galloped toward them at breakneck speed, chased by clouds that stretched unnaturally fast, as if a giant hand meant to snatch him from the earth. The clouds nearly blotted out the sun itself, a thin, graying darkness settling across the valley floor.

"Gray Cloaks!" the horse carried the rider near as quickly as the wind carried his words. The scout yanked hard on the reins, pulled up breathlessly beside the officers. "At the valley's end."

"How many?" asked Drael.

"Twenty or thirty, if not more," a terrified look on the scout's face as he added, "and ... I believe they're singing."

"Then we must shut their mouths!" barked Drael in response. "Give the order to strike."

The horn master raised horn to lips, but no command ever sounded. Lightning tore the sky apart, striking the column with merciless force. Soldiers who earlier had marched in perfect ranks now lay broken across the valley floor, or staggered about in a hollow-eyed daze. The wounded lifted their voices in agony, while the dead kept their silence.

The impact of the blast threw Magnus and a searing pain tore through his shoulder as he struck the ground. The valley floor tilted and spun. He blinked furiously, struggling to clear his vision. The metallic taste of lightning coated his tongue.

A shrill note filled his ears, and he wondered about the strangeness of it. *An odd time for the regiment band to strike up a tune.* He touched his left ear. It was wet. He stared at the bright red staining his hand.

He staggered to his feet, stumbling like a drunken soldier, breathing a prayer of thanks to see Tobias, also horseless and stunned, but alive.

"Magnus, rally your men!"

In his confused state, the words made no sense.

"You pathetic excuse for an officer, rally your troops!" A fist seized his tunic collar, and he found himself hauled so close he could smell Drael's breath. "You'll be the last officer I promote so fast if you don't act now."

Clarity slammed back into Magnus—scent, sight, sound flooding his senses. Months of grueling training surged to the surface, reminded him what to do. The horn master lay still, clutching his horn. Magnus wrenched it from the dead man's grasp and sounded three piercing blasts, while shouting a rallying cry: "To me, Ka, to me!"

Scaling a knoll, Magnus assessed the damage. The regiment had sustained significant losses, a good third dead or wounded. But they were Ka, and though momentarily stunned, at the horn's signal they quickly regrouped.

"Another blast like that and there won't be an army left to hunt down these cursed Binders." Magnus relayed the update to his commander. He motioned to the treeline topping the valley slope. "We need shelter. We're too exposed here."

As if on cue, another bolt of lightning burst from the clouds and struck the regiment's rear guard, though inflicting less damage than the first.

"To the forest then," ordered Drael.

As the horn signaled retreat, the living fled to the forest. No further blasts barred their flight.

At the treeline, Magnus' eyes swept the valley where too many lay fallen, men and women he'd trained with and fought with. Smoke from charred earth drifted low, obscuring his view. Still, he whispered the familiar Lavonshian blessing to send the fallen on their way, "May we meet again in a better tomorrow."

It rang hollow until a vow escaped his lips: "Curses on the Binders. They'll pay for this."

Chapter Seven
Say Your Goodbyes

In the thousand-year history of Harvest Festivals, never had one ended so early. But the Gray Cloaks' arrival descended over the gathering like a shadow, and no one in Chelam had the heart to keep celebrating. They dispersed in a muted shuffle from the Great Hall, clinging to memories of the festivities, the unmarried carrying a mix of disappointment and relief.

Aurelia hugged her father good night.

"Don't wait up," he said. "I'll likely be home late."

She lost sight of Col in the crowd. Eken walked her home, though he was unusually subdued, offering only a quiet goodnight outside her door.

She flopped into bed, lacking even the motivation to kick off her shoes. But sleep didn't come as her mind raced.

Why are they here? she wondered. *And why so many?*

Her father always said, *set your busy mind on busying your hands,* so heeding his advice, Aurelia set to threshing a bundle of amaranth grain stalks, intending to add the separated straw to the growing pile in the corner. Both beds had long ago turned uncomfortably flat, and they'd agreed to lay aside a portion of this season's harvest to replace the worn bedding.

Despite the work, her mind remained unsettled, drifting between Col and the unexpected visitors. Her pulse quickened as she ran her fingertips across her palm, where Col's hand had rested; and her cheeks flamed red as she thought of what it signified.

Did I take his hand?

We nearly danced!

Her heart seesawed between disappointment and a welcome relief that the Gray Cloaks' arrival had forever altered the evening. Unease trembled at what she'd left undone. To accept a hand but not dance—an unprecedented breach in the history of Harvest Festival dances—though who else could claim a Gray Cloak interruption?

It didn't feel like her father's solution to a busy mind was working.

In the night, her father must have removed her shoes and pulled a blanket over her. She didn't remember his arrival, let alone drifting off and falling asleep.

But when she woke, he'd already risen for the morning and left behind the usual evidence—his festival attire tossed aside and lying crumpled in the corner, his good pair of shoes near the fireplace where the heat would dry out the leather instead of tucked neatly under his bed as they should be, and dirty dishes piled beside the washbasin from a breakfast he'd scrounged up. How she'd slept through all that racket she couldn't imagine.

The sun was halfway through its upward trek when she joined him in the fields, where his scythe swung hungrily back and forth. He was so absorbed in his work, or his thoughts, that he didn't hear her approach. But Mahan wasn't one to startle easily; he merely glanced over his shoulder when she cleared her throat.

"Morning, Father."

"Morning, little Aurie."

Her muscles ached at the start, but finding their rhythm, she kept pace with him. It wouldn't last; it never did, but for now they were content to work side-by-side.

The day was pleasant enough, with blue-gray skies punctuated by low-hanging clouds. Occasionally, the sun peeked through—a perfect day for harvesting, at least on the surface.

But her thoughts weren't on the weather's impact on harvesting. Into the silence she burst out, "Why are they here?"

Mahan butted his scythe into the ground and leaned against it, wiping sweat from his brow. "They talk of war to the north. The Ka attacking their villages."

War. The word felt harsh and foreign to her ears. "So I was right. It will come here."

"No one can say for certain." He resumed the methodical swish of his scythe. "But we spoke late into the night about plans and contingencies for those plans. They've called for a meeting with the Hearth-Families and Elders."

"But what can they do about it?"

Mahan shrugged. "Impossible to say what may stem the tide of war, but the meeting's at peak sun, at the Great Hall. And ... they asked for you too."

"Me? Why?" Aurelia pulled up short on her scythe's swing and it nearly flew from her hand.

"I ... I'm not at liberty to say," he said, but his voice wavered. She'd been so absorbed with her own worries she hadn't noticed the tremor in his normally sure hands as he worked.

"Not at liberty?" she asked when he didn't elaborate. "I don't understand."

"Please, Aurelia Talbot. Just do your work and let me think. You'll know more soon."

The use of her full name was a sure sign something was wrong. Stung by his tone, she moved to another row and concentrated on cutting more grain than he did. She nearly succeeded. But as the day crawled by, her energy waned, and she glanced too often at the sun which seemed content to move at a snail's pace toward its peak.

Neither her heart nor her mind were in the work as aching muscles bore the tedium of every swing. There was little joy in it today. She despised the work and the sun's pace for keeping her from the meeting, though she dreaded the meeting and what it might mean, wishing she could stay in the fields forever. There she knew the shape and feel of the scythe, the familiar rustling of the grain stalks as the wind whispered, and the smell of earth and sweat. The rhythmic hum of harvest calmed her, its process at once so familiar and so comforting.

Her mind wandered. She shut her eyes and wished she hadn't as unbidden images flooded her thoughts. *War.* Chelam in flames. The harvest flattened and ruined. Dorakians lying dead in their fields.

She opened her eyes, relieved to find herself still working the field with her father. She inhaled the scent of grain and earth, centering her mind on its familiar heartiness.

Another break, her fourth of the morning. Twice more than usual, but her father made no comment as she sat in the shade of the lone tree gracing their fields, sipping tepid water from a flask.

Her eyes tracked him as he worked, but he ignored her. His tremors had stopped. Instead, he attacked the grain with such ferocity she knew his mood had turned angry. Whatever was planned at peak sun, he knew more than he'd admit, and what he knew troubled him.

Mercifully, the sun at last reached its peak, or at least close enough that Aurelia could contain herself no longer. Throwing her scythe to the ground, she announced she was heading to the Great Hall.

Mahan was quick to follow.

Word had spread of the planned meeting, and a crowd gathered outside the hall. When Mahan arrived, they parted with their usual deference, but his daughter they eyed with surprise, whispers floating on the breeze.

"What is she doing here?"

"She took Col's hand at the dance last night."

"But did they dance?"

"I didn't see them. Did you?"

"Sounds like Aurelia. Flighty girl."

Koram, Aurelia's favorite Elder, met them at the door.

"Please, please come in. Come in. The others gather, awaiting only the Gray Cloaks."

Ever since she was a little girl, Koram had reserved his biggest smile for her—one that usually accompanied an invitation to sit and play a game of Ji, a favorite Dorakian pastime. She'd happily agree; they'd roll out the square carpet and place the hand-carved pieces on their starting spaces. But today the smile was fleeting, and no invitation came as he led them inside.

The Hearth-Families and Elders gathered at the hall's far end, where the Potterfelds had hastily cleared away festival decorations. The well-worn council table had resumed its rightful place, with extra chairs added for the unusual number of guests. Around it, stray garlands and abandoned decor provided a jarring reminder of the festivities' interruption.

Aurelia hadn't expected to see Col and Eken in attendance, even though Col's father was a High Elder and Eken's family made the cut as the lowest ranked Hearth-Family. But family members were not council members and never attended meetings.

Except this one.

Eken waved as she entered the hall. Aurelia avoided Col's stare. She would give anything not to discuss their almost-dance.

"What do you think last night means?" asked Eken.

"I ... it could be ... that um, I ..." stammered Aurelia.

She glanced up and wished she hadn't.

Col's eyes burned into her own.

A blush of red crept up her neck and colored her cheeks, pulse quickening as she remembered her hand in his. His touch had been like ice against the fire in her skin. His eyes last night, just as they were now, intense in their burning gaze.

"My father won't tell me anything." Col interrupted her thoughts. "The meeting's a mystery."

Aurelia collapsed into the nearest chair, a sigh of relief escaping her lips. *They aren't talking about the dance!*

"You okay?" asked Col as he knelt beside her, the back of his hand against her forehead.

"I'm fine. Could you get me some water?"

When he'd left, she hissed at Eken to get his attention. Intent on watching the hall's entrance, he reluctantly tore his gaze away.

"Has Col said anything about me?" she asked.

"No, why would he?"

Col returned with a cup of water and Eken picked up the earlier thread of conversation as if there'd been no interruption.

"I checked the records. There's never been five of them."

"When did you have time to check the records?" asked Aurelia.

Chelam's tedious book of meetings, more widely known as *the records*, was kept within a single, massive tome that spanned a dozen hunter's moons worth of meeting notes, recording the mundane workings of a small village.

"Last night. Stayed up all night to satisfy my curiosity."

Col groaned and Aurelia laughed; their friend's obsession to uncover even the most obscure knowledge was legendary.

"Do you know why it's always two?" he asked. She cocked her head and waited, confident he already knew the answer. He didn't disappoint. "Because they live two in a cave, rarely seeing others of their kind."

She snorted. *Mere speculation. And, their kind?* It was clear they were human. True, a Gray Cloak wore heavy robes, obscuring their figure, and it was true they bore those strange stones in their foreheads. Still, they were human.

"I don't know what to make of it," she said, "but I'm sure we'll find out soon."

"I still say seeing five together is a bad sign. Worse than Old Lady Cridge and her festival soup."

Her laugh echoed across the hushed pockets of conversation. The Elders glanced her way, a frown or two among them, though High Elder Koram merely smiled.

She clamped a hand across her mouth.

Still, Eken was right. Old Lady Cridge's soup *was* awful, but no one had the heart to tell the poor woman. She was one hundred and three, after all. Every festival she made the same thick sludge, and if she caught you skipping a bowl, she took offense. Festival-goers often slipped out the hall's back door when she wasn't looking to dump their bowls into Liller's Creek. Once, when Aurelia did the same, she found her father already there. He'd winked as they emptied their bowls out together.

A commotion outside announced the Gray Cloaks' arrival.

"Sari told me they didn't bring gifts." Eken squeezed the book in his tunic pocket. "That can't be a good sign."

His comments earned an eye-roll from Col, but Aurelia couldn't help wondering if he was right to worry.

"Welcome, friends, to our gathering," Jusel Blackwood's voice carried the hall in a formal greeting, extending a hand in welcome and an invitation for all to sit. "Please join us; we await your wisdom."

Mahan added, "Honored Ones, you grace us with your presence."

For a moment, the title he'd used distracted her, and she puzzled over it. *Honored Ones. That's a new one.* The delay cost her a seat next to anyone she knew. Only one seat remained open. At the table's end. Beside a Gray Cloak.

She sat, swallowed a stubborn knot forming in her throat, and tried not to stare. But unable to help herself, she studied the Gray Cloak beside her.

Up close, the hood of the stranger's cloak hid little—a woman, mouth pursed in a tight line, wrinkles and age spots betraying her age, the embedded stone in her forehead a rich brown color.

Though the stranger stared straight ahead, she unexpectedly addressed Aurelia. "Child. Do tell me. At what do you study so intently?"

The voice was firm, somewhat musical, the pattern of her speech odd, rather formal. Aurelia might have laughed if not for the weight of the moment.

"I, um ..." Should she mention the woman's odd choice of words? The stone on her forehead? The strangeness of this meeting?

"Nevermind, Child. It is a blessing to speak with you." The woman turned to face her and she gulped at the penetrating stare. "Your father has told us much about you over the years."

"My name's Aurelia. Wait ... what, he has?"

The Gray Cloak woman laughed. "Aurelia you are. Thus I shall call you, save when you deserve to be called Child. You may call me Ophel until you know my name."

Didn't she just tell me her name?

Perhaps she meant her last name too, though it seemed if the woman was concerned about such a thing she could have simply shared it. Not wishing to be rude, Aurelia responded with a common formal greeting, "Well met, Ophel."

The woman nodded as High Elder Jusel cleared his throat. "We have much to discuss. Before we dive into more private conversations, we should dispense with the business that brings our younger Dorakians here. High Elder Koram, you wish to address Aurelia?"

"Why me?" asked a startled Aurelia. She glanced to her father for reassurance, but his face was an unreadable mask.

"Aurelia," began Koram, his tone kind as always, "what I share with you now is not to be shared with any outside this room."

That's an ominous start.

"Our northern friends deliver grave news. And a request." He paused, his eyes scanning those gathered around the council table, before plowing ahead. "They tell us the Ka have come east, through Hadil's Crossing, over the Tol. The shadow of war looms."

It was the first that some had heard of the Ka's presence in the eastern province and anxious murmurs exploded across the table. Aurelia's heart pounded, once more picturing Chelam in flames, soldiers marching its cobblestone streets. She knew nothing of the Ka, but the very thought of an army at Chelam's doorstep made her stomach cinch tight. Koram raised a hand to silence the outcry.

"There's been a battle to the north, but I fear the Ka may come here, to Dorak. Our friends, the Gray Cloaks, came to warn us."

"They have a request too, you said?" asked Aurelia.

Koram smiled at her interruption. "They do, and it concerns you. They're quite insistent that you depart with them. At once, by sunfall."

Aurelia's eyes widened. *Me? Why me?* She looked again to her father, but he turned away, unable to meet her gaze.

"What could they want with me?"

"I wish I could say for sure. And your father," Koram glanced accusingly at Mahan, "has said little, other than consenting to your departure."

"Father?" He still refused to look her way. "You're going with me, right?"

When their eyes finally met, the anguish he held surprised her.

"I ..." His voice broke.

"Aurelia," the one who'd introduced herself as Ophel intervened, "there is much we cannot tell you, much we still do not know. Even were I to share all we know, you would not understand. But what I can say is this. Your father cannot go with you; he has his own path to follow."

Aurelia glanced first at her father, then at Koram, even at Jusel though she despised the man. Surely someone could offer more than Ophel's evasive answer, but no one did.

"You must leave. On that point there is no question," said Ophel. "Your life is in danger."

"We can protect her!" Col shot to his feet, drawing the sword he often carried at his side, sending his chair crashing to the floor. "With my skills -"

"Sit down, you foolish young man," ordered Ophel, rising to her feet.

He hesitated before the woman's harsh glare returned him to his seat. Her eyes swept the room, daring further interruption, but only silence met her. Satisfied, she settled her gaze on Aurelia and continued as if there'd been no interruption.

"Not only is your own life in peril, but the lives of countless Dorakians depend on you. Come with us and you will save your people from destruction. If you stay, many Dorakians will die. Sensing has shown this to be true. You would not understand our Sensing, but you must trust me."

As Ophel spoke, the stone in her forehead pulsed a deep, chocolate-colored hue, and Aurelia found herself drawn to her voice, certain of the truth in her words.

"But know this—when you leave, it is likely you will never return."

Her father's weeping shattered the silence that settled on the room. Panic squeezed Aurelia's chest, the room spinning as she struggled to breathe. She'd never lived outside Chelam, or ventured beyond the borders of Dorak. In that room sat her friends, her family, the only people she'd ever known.

But Ophel wasn't done.

"If by some chance the Great Binding allows your return, I can promise this—you will not be the same person you once were. Your people will not recognize you. You will not recognize yourself. It can never be as it once was."

The words settled over Aurelia like a shroud and again the stone glowed.

My people won't recognize me?

She didn't understand, but she couldn't shake the feeling that Ophel spoke the truth.

"Time is short," said Ophel. "Say your goodbyes, but you must come with us."

Chapter Eight
Ghostly Figures

Word swept through camp: there would be a search for survivors. Like all rumors, it spread quickly. Unlike most, this one was true.

Magnus moved through the ranks, offering words of encouragement and checking on the injured while awaiting orders. Satisfied he'd done all he could, he joined friends gathered at a fire, greeted Tobias and Kymn, nodded hello to others.

"Hian didn't make it." Tobias' blade picked at bits of food in his teeth, but his trembling hand betrayed an otherwise calm demeanor. "Neither did Theldt."

Silence descended as the men reflected on their losses, a mumbled *may we meet again in a better tomorrow* escaping broken lips and hearts. Tobias sang a mournful tune. One of loss, but also of hope and courage. Some joined in, others simply listened, each choosing their own way to remember the dead.

Magnus stared into the crackling fire, his thoughts on home as much as anything, the ache in his heart for family and for the simple life of the Plainsfolk. The glory of battle was not what some claimed.

Beyond firelight's edge, a pair of eyes stared back. Decidedly not human. Then another pair. And another. Blinking rapidly, they never wavered, though their gaze wasn't predatory. He could just make out small fuzzy heads, oversized ears, long thin tails and two parchment-thin wings that fluttered anxiously from time to time. Little variance in color separated the creatures, each a solid brown marred by white spots on their haunches. They squatted on their back two legs, constantly shuffling, two little hands each sporting three fingers twitching nervously.

"What are those?" Magnus nodded at the creatures. An elbow in Kymn's side got his attention.

"No idea," said Kymn after staring at the creatures for a moment. "Hey Morco, you grew up in the Tol, right? Ever seen anything like that?"

"Those are frits." Morco hardly glanced up, hands and knife busy whittling a chunk of beechwood.

"A what?"

"A frit. You know, curious little creature. Friendly enough, but nervous, jumpy. They'll never let you too close."

A camp aide approached their fire—Magnus had been summoned.

"Form a company of ten. Search the valley." Drael's commands were brisk, to the point. "Look for survivors who can still march and fight. Burn or bury the dead once you've assessed the risk. Any others ..."

He didn't finish the sentence, but Magnus knew army policy.

"I've tasked Tarn to join you with a second unit, but it's your command on this one."

Magnus' heart sank. Tarn was notorious for his ruthlessness and outranked him—he'd been Ka far longer. Magnus suspected Drael was testing him.

"We'll break camp soon," continued his commander, "and proceed south. Rejoin us roughly ... here." He pointed to a spot on the map, close by a Dorakian village named Chelam.

"To the valley."

Magnus' command was simple, the familiar sounds and scents of the Ka camp fading as the men trudged heavy-hearted towards the valley. Even for the most hardened, the task ahead was grim.

Securing men for the search hadn't been easy. There were ones he would have preferred, for they were kind-hearted, good men, but they couldn't stomach such a search and he wouldn't in good conscience force this burden on anyone. He asked, but didn't demand. Many declined. In the end, he chose his ten, unsure whether they'd all obey him if his orders violated Ka policy.

Surprisingly, Tarn deferred command without comment, a slight nod of his head the only acknowledgment Magnus received.

"Unfortunate that we can't trust more of them," said Tobias, studying the men at their heels. "What an awful duty. Tell me again why we joined the Ka?"

"You don't remember? The decri, adventure ... to be admired by all the ladies."

Tobias looked left, then right. Sighed dramatically. "I don't see any ladies."

"No, my friend," Magnus said wryly, "unfortunately not."

As they drew near Breckei Valley, no one spoke, for they approached hallowed ground. The final resting spot of Ka.

In the silence, every forest noise alarmed.

A twig snap.

The rustle of clothing as it brushed against a tree branch or bush.

Are the Gray Cloaks still out here?

Oddly, no birds sang, no creatures called to one another, as if the valley massacre had scarred the forest inhabitants too. Or perhaps they awaited further tragedy.

Through the trees, Magnus thought he glimpsed a figure clothed in shadows. His breath hitched and his hand drifted toward his sword. "Tobias, you see that?"

"See what?"

Magnus ducked right, skirting thick brush obstructing his view, but he no longer saw a figure, only leaf and shadow. "Shadows trick me," he muttered, though he wasn't certain.

An advanced scout returned. "We're close. Treeline's just ahead."

"We'll settle in, wait for dark," ordered Magnus. "No fires."

He posted two men, Saul and Bochim, as sentries.

"Think we'll have enough moonlight for the search?" asked Tobias.

Magnus shrugged. "You know that moon cycles were never my strength."

"So what exactly got you promoted?" The question was innocent enough but the grin said otherwise.

"My name." Magnus smiled ruefully. It was a common joke between them ever since his promotion. He still remembered the smattering of laughter at his expense...

"Do you vow to protect the people of Lavonshia, give your life in service of the Ka, obey all given orders, and so fulfill your duty to King and Kingdom? Do you, Magnus Phimethous Codum Alwyn, so swear?" The laughter only ended at a harsh glare from the master of ceremonies...

But truthfully, his name had no particular significance. He wasn't noteworthy. No, he was simply a commoner from the Plains west of the Capitol, his family falling on hard times, as most had during the ashrot that ruined crops and led to a two-year famine, crippling the economy and ensuring jobs were as scarce as food.

Desperate, his father sent him to the Capitol, where he discovered a city faring as poorly as the surrounding countryside, though the King in his mercy had opened the palace stockpiles. The nation flocked to the Capitol. The stockpiles dwindled but never ran out; anyone with decri could buy.

Until the decri ran out. That's when the army began actively recruiting with the promise of good pay, encouraging thousands to enlist, desperate for coin to purchase grain for starving families back home.

Magnus joined the long enlistment lines.

It wasn't a hard choice. Hunger gnawed at every household, and anyone with a little sense and the ability to carry a sword enlisted. The Ka's ranks swelled with boys and graybeards alike, men mostly, though no law kept women out.

Magnus' duties at home had been simple: run the farm, work the fields, deliver grain to market. He was capable, intelligent, in the prime of his life, willing to follow orders. While the Ka's training was challenging it wasn't anything he couldn't handle, and with so many raw recruits needing officers, he was quickly promoted.

What surprised him was Tobias' failure to earn a similar promotion. The man was every bit as tough and smart, with an unflinching moral code, one admittedly above Magnus' own. The commanders noted the same, including instances where Tobias refused to follow orders he felt broke that moral code. In the end, it cost him a promotion. Magnus had been fortunate, avoiding impossible choices, somehow keeping his own conscience clean.

Letters from home confirmed things were getting better. Crops were growing again. The ashrot had moved on and first fruits of the season's harvest looked promising. Magnus' pay had seen them through the worst of it. Now it was time to go home. He was needed again to work the fields.

"Magnus, you listening?"

"What? Oh, sorry ... thinking of family. How about yours? You hardly mention them since the letter."

Tobias patted his pocket. He carried the letter with him everywhere, the only correspondence he'd received since leaving home. "They're always on my mind. I worry if *sisa* got better. If *papi* got the decri I sent. If he finished the planting."

Tobias slipped into the odd Highlander dialect when he spoke of family. Not that he needed to speak, his dark complexion gave him away. His family had fared better than most with the Jilted Leaf their primary crop, a medicinal herb the ashrot didn't ravage. With so many suffering during the famine and yellow death on the rise, sales of Jilted Leaf soared. Magnus wasn't a fan of the leaf. Its taste was bitter, its occasional hallucinatory side effects debilitating, but for some it was the only medicine that brought relief. Still, despite their crop's success, Tobias' family eventually had to send their son away to find work.

"I'm sure your family's okay," he reassured him. "Besides, no letters will reach us out here."

Night swallowed up dusk, enveloping them in its embrace. A cool breeze drifted in from the north, a welcome relief from the day's heat. The once quiet forest coming alive at sunfall with the chirps, clicks, and whines of creatures stirring in the dark.

The sentries returned to report all quiet in the valley. Magnus issued his orders and a band of ghostly figures swept down into the valley.

Chapter Nine
He Had Never Looked More Alone

Never in its long history had the Great Hall witnessed such a stunned audience. Dorakian lives in danger? Ophel's warning hung grim and heavy, polluting the air. And then, all at once, the hall erupted—voices shouting competing judgments, arguments spilling over one another—yet on one point there was no dissent: Aurelia must go.

Col and Eken piped up that if she left, they would too. The Blackwood and Potterfeld families accused the Elders of conspiring to take their sons from them. The Elders protested, deflecting blame—it was the Gray Cloaks' idea after all—while the two young men insisted they were of age and would do what they well pleased, despite their families' objections.

Aurelia's fingernails dug crescent-shaped moons into the carved wood of the chair, her blood boiling with every new opinion or argument. Not one person had thought to ask what she wanted. She leaped to her feet, chair scraping noisily against the floor. A hush settled across the room.

She'd decided two things.

First, she cared little for council meetings. This would be her first and last.

Second, she wouldn't give the satisfaction of an answer, there in the Great Hall. She had someone she wished to speak with first, making her response to the whole matter rather simple:

"I'm tired. I'm going home!"

The Hearth-Families shouted at Mahan to control his daughter. How dare she entertain thoughts of staying put in Chelam if it jeopardized the lives of other Dorakians?

Aurelia left without a backward glance, body shaking as she stalked home, hands clenching white-knuckled with each step.

Do I have no say in this? Why must they force me to leave?

Angry thoughts simmered. At the Gray Cloaks. At the Elders and the Hearth-Families. But especially at her father.

Why didn't he say anything? Not a word, not even to insist he'd go with her. *Of all the times!* She'd never known him to be without an opinion.

But as her anger cooled, dread replaced it. To go ... out there. Beyond Dorak. With Gray Cloak strangers. But if she stayed? If the things Ophel said came true? Her father, Eken, Col, the Elders, her people ... she couldn't place her life above theirs.

By the time she arrived home, she'd reached a decision.

She started packing.

Aurelia stoked a fire; evenings were cool in harvest season. Tonight though, the fire failed to warm.

With her packing long since finished, she cooked a simple venison stew, ladled bowls for herself and her father, and waited. While she waited, she fidgeted, tapping her spoon against the bowl, the table, sometimes her knuckles—anything to distract from her noisy thoughts—all while evening shadows crept over Chelam.

The stew turned cold.

Still she waited, eyes boring the door to their little home. Late into the evening, it creaked open and her father stepped inside. He busied himself washing his hands, removing his boots, checking his notes on the harvest numbers, each a seemingly deliberate delay before taking a seat at the table. And still he avoided her eyes.

He'd better be ready to apologize.

"Aurelia ..."

There it was again. Not using her pet name. Twice in one day.

"I ... there's ..." He toyed with his spoon, stirring the stew as if buying time.

Aurelia's fingers tightened around her bowl, the urge to fling it across the room rising sharp and hot. Her jaw locked as she forced it down, shoving the untouched stew aside as she shot to her feet. *I can't stay here anymore!* Her father reached for her, but she brushed past, snatching up her travel pack.

At the door's threshold, she glanced back. Tears threatened.

"Is that all?"

"There's so much I want to say, need to say -" His voice cracked.

"Now's your chance." She folded her arms across her chest. "I'm leaving if you hadn't noticed."

"Little Aurie ... what can a father say? I remember your tiny fingers clasped around my thumb. How early you started talking ... the Elders remarked how smart you were. Only three hunter's moons old, and outsmarting the six-years for the grain counting prize!"

Mahan ran his fingers through his hair, eyes glazed over.

"And your first Moon Festival, eyes wide at the firebomb colors, squealing as they exploded high above. I remember every Harvest Festival. I remember ... now, my only child, ripped away from me? Like this?"

"Father, I ..."

He raised a hand to stop her.

"I thought you'd get married, raise a family. Here. In this village. I'd have a little rootling or two to bounce upon my knees, and -" he faltered, paused, collected himself, swallowed hard, "at least I could have seen you from time to time."

The clench in her jaw softened. She ran into his embrace and hugged him as fiercely as he hugged her. His beard itched, but it was comforting, familiar. He kissed her forehead, brushed away his and her tears with calloused hands, worn from heavy labor in the fields.

"I can't hold on to you, and I won't hold you back." He pressed an object into her hands, closing her fingers around it. "Never forget how much I love you. When all seems lost, use this."

She recognized her pendant necklace, the one he'd crafted when she was little. Her expression puzzled, she wondered what he meant.

A commotion at the door and Jusel Blackwood burst in, breathless and panicked. "Campfires! North of here. It's the Ka. You must go."

A shiver coursed through Aurelia. *It's all happening too fast.* She hugged her father again, drawing strength from him.

"Will you ...?" The pendant necklace dangled from her hand.

He cupped it, almost reverently, his hands shaking, before securing it around her neck.

In the village square, it seemed most in the village had turned out. A matter so grave, so unheard of, could never stay private in Chelam. Torchlight bathed the onlookers in an eerie yellow glow.

Gray Cloaks and Elders awaited her, as if they'd known what she'd choose. Nearby, a cluster of frits rested on haunches, wings fluttering, curious eyes blinking rapidly, absorbing every movement. They sat unusually close and unusually still for such nervous creatures.

Ophel nodded at Aurelia's pack. "Do you carry what you need?"

She tightened her grip on the pack strap, jaw clenched. "Considering I don't know where we're going or how long we'll be gone, I've done the best I can."

Col jogged into the square, his handsome face determined, with a pack secured around his shoulders and his ever-present sword strapped to his waist, his smile disarming as usual.

"I should not need to remind you, young man," said Ophel, "this is not a countryside jaunt. There is no plan to return."

"I don't care. Where Aurelia goes, I go."

The older woman's disapproving look sized him up before she muttered, "Very well."

A clamor echoed across the square upon Eken's arrival. "Wait for me!" Pots and pans clanged, dangling from a bulging pack he'd secured haphazardly across his shoulders.

Aurelia expected Ophel would roll her eyes, but she merely gave a slight shake of her head, as if exasperated, before uttering a strange and tuneless chant while the stone in her forehead pulsed:

"True to each other the four must remain lest darkness consume all that is known."

A chill threaded down Aurelia's spine while an awkward silence settled on the square, but Ophel seemed not to notice, or care, her gaze solemn, capturing the three Dorakians in its spell.

"Then it shall be the four of you." She beckoned a nearby Gray Cloak to join them. "This is Daphne. She will accompany you."

At her introduction, Daphne lowered her cloak's hood, allowing it to fall across her shoulders. She was young—not even Aurelia's age, perhaps closer to Col's—and where Aurelia stood tall, Daphne was smaller in frame. But what Aurelia noticed most was the warmth in her eyes, accompanied by a welcoming bow to each Dorakian. She sensed the girl wasn't nearly as reserved as other Gray Cloaks, though there was still something guarded in her stance. Large blue eyes overwhelmed a petite face, set against a shaved-bald head with a gray stone in its prominent place. Ophel frowned at the familiarity Daphne displayed by lowering her hood. Not annoyance—something sharper, almost wary.

"We only get one of you?" asked Eken.

"There are other matters to which we must attend," said Ophel. "Now, no more questions. Go. You must set a brisk pace. May the Great Binding speak to you. May it speak to all of you."

Daphne smiled shyly, though her voice oozed confidence with a, "Come, follow me," before heading west across the square. Briskly, as commanded.

"Wait, Aurelia!" Koram shoved a well-worn Ji set in her hands. "Something to pass the time. And to remember fondly your old friend."

"Thank you, oh thank you!" Aurelia knew how much she'd miss her favorite Elder and their matches of Ji. "May we meet again in a better tomorrow," she blurted, praying it would be true.

At the western end of the square, she turned back for one last look. Chelam had always felt right to her, big enough for a girl with simple dreams. But tonight it seemed impossibly small. Torchlight flickered over the cluster of frits, rooted still to the same spot; over Ophel, her lips moving silently as if in prayer or recitation; and over her father, shoulders bowed beneath a grief she could not soothe, surrounded by Chelam villagers who'd come to see her away.

He had never looked more alone.

Chapter Ten
What Hope Do We Have

To comb through the fallen meant exhausting, heart-breaking, foul work, for the stench of death lingered, a sickly pall over the valley. Magnus listened for cries of help, however faint, and watched for signs of movement, however slight. But there was no stirring among the dead. Only the rustling movements of the living.

He had set lookouts, two at each end of the valley. Though he wouldn't admit it aloud, the mysterious figure from earlier weighed on his mind.

"One still lives."

He sighed, relieved at Kymn's report; but the relief proved fleeting at the sight of Tarn kneeling by the survivor, though Tobias stood guard, cupping a lantern in hand, allowing a little light to spill across the body.

"She's breathing," said Tobias, "but it's ragged."

The light revealed a pale face, a female, one of the regiment's few. Magnus recognized her, *Veyra*, though he didn't know her well as she'd joined their company only days before orders sent them east. Blood crusted at a gash across her jawline, a bow and satchel of arrows slung across her back, the familiar sword all Ka carried hung at her waist. She'd absorbed the fire of a lightning blast to her right side, leg charred, arm blackened and crusted a dull dried-blood red, bits of her lite-armor melded to her skin.

"She's not long for this world." Tarn drew a knife from the folds of his tunic. "Let's end it quickly. Mercifully."

Though he spoke of mercy, his tone carried no trace of it. He clutched a pair of scavenged boots while eyeing a ring on Veyra's finger. Magnus seized his wrist before he made good his threat.

"Not while I command." Magnus' hand strayed to the sword at his side.

"She'll slow us down," growled Tarn.

"It's Ka policy," said another, eyeing the bow and satchel of arrows strapped to Veyra's back.

"As long as she lives," repeated Magnus, "she goes with us."

Tarn spat at Magnus' feet, "She's all yours ... hero," and with a dismissive grunt, stalked away.

A howl pierced the night air. Magnus shivered, though he wasn't cold. An answering howl, closer in to the valley.

He stood guard over the unconscious woman, berating himself for not bringing a healer. If blood loss didn't take her, the infection setting in and the fever that was sure to follow would.

"There's a stream," said Kymn, "at the valley's opening. We should clean her wounds, bandage the worst of them."

She moaned when they laid her by the water, her eyes fluttering open for a moment before her head sagged limp.

"Veyra," began Magnus, "we're going to cut away the armor melded to your skin and clean your wounds with fresh water."

She moaned again as if to acknowledge him.

Another howl. Closer still.

Tobias severed the cords binding her forearm plate to the shoulder guard. As he tore the armor free, it dragged strips of skin fused to the metal by the blast. Veyra screamed, her eyes flashing open, before she went limp again. Magnus sawed at the thigh-plate, metal rasping beneath his blade as the girl drifted in and out of consciousness, a faint whimper each time he cut too deep. The work was crude, desperate, but a chorus of howls drove them faster.

Tarn approached. "We're leaving."

"As the commanding officer -"

"Wolves close around us, or worse perhaps, demons summoned by Gray Cloaks, and you command us to fool with this one? She lies at death's veil, but your actions would condemn us all there."

With a grunt of disapproval, he stalked off into the pitch-black forest. Men followed, a few hesitantly, most eagerly.

Seven remain, and the wounded girl, thought Magnus after a quick count. *Too few if wolves attack.*

Bending feverishly to the work, quickening his pace at a howl nearby, he cupped water from the stream and cleaned Veyra's wounds while Tobias cut a clean, spare tunic into strips and bound her arm and leg.

The howling even closer now, insistent. As one ended another began. Magnus' heart broke at the prospect of leaving the dead unburied, but they couldn't stay—the wolves would leave nothing to bury.

They hastened from the valley, the wounded girl borne between them, pressing south in hopes of rejoining the regiment. Magnus waited for the howls to fade, but they rose instead, echoing closer still in the dark. The wolves hunted.

"It makes no sense," said Tobias, fear scouring his mouth dry as if lined with sandpaper. "The valley offered an easy feast."

The forest thickened the deeper into the woods they went. An impossible thickness, with scant moonlight piercing the tree canopy, unseen vines grasping at ankles and feet, thorns and branches slicing at hands and face, while gnarled roots and wobbling stones threatened a broken ankle or worse. It seemed the forest itself was against them.

Wolves now surrounded them. Howls in every direction save forward, though Magnus had lost all concept of where forward might lead. *Is it still southward?* It mattered little. Forward remained their only chance to escape the tightening net.

Tension melted strength from limbs. Fear sapping energy. Dry mouths, sweaty palms, the bedlam of pounding hearts drowned by the ever-present howling. His legs screamed for rest, his arms drained of strength from bearing Veyra's weight. Ghostly shapes joined the howls, on the edge of visible sight, the terror of it fraying the soldiers' nerves.

A man's cry. Distant.

One of their own stumbled, caught in a thicket. Magnus turned, hesitated, but it was too late, wolves upon the man before he could break free.

"Go!" He ordered his men forward. "There's no helping him."

Kymn and Bochim hacked at tangled vines, clearing a path through which to carry Veyra.

Morco, a giant of a man, took point in their dwindling group, his warhammer at the ready. Another, Saul, removed his lantern's cover-plates. The wolves whimpered and fell back as light spilled out, enough to reveal they were no ordinary creatures, but feral beasts wrapped in shadows and far larger than any wolf had a right to be.

"Who can fight such as these!" cried Saul.

"Stay together," urged Magnus.

They slogged on, spent, exhausted, banding close, six men now, carrying a burden of one.

The howling ceased, and in its place a silence infinitely more terrifying, as if the wolves, knowing the end was near, listened now for a man's ragged and faltering breath. To pick off the weakest, the one to fall next. The men clung to a single truth—breathe. Again. Breathe. Once more. Breathe. Another breath, for as long as they breathed, they lived.

A figure ahead. Magnus certain it was the same he'd seen earlier. In the chaos of being hunted, he didn't know how he knew, but he did. As quickly as it appeared, the figure vanished, and in its place he glimpsed a break in the trees. An open glade lay before them.

"With me!" he shouted, "better to stand and fight."

Strength all but gone, they tumbled into the glade, forming a defensive ring around Veyra, joining a cluster of frits already occupying the glade. The creatures' wings beat frantically, fingers fidgeting, seemingly terrified by the soldiers, but more terrified of what howled from the dark. The men readied their stance and set lanterns to cast their brightest light. *Is this to be our end?*

Shadow-Wolves encircled the glade. Snarling, slobbering creatures, their eyes flashed hatred, suffocating the glade with their guttural growls, though none yet dared cross beyond the tree line.

"Does the glade protect us?" whispered Tobias, awed by the sight.

"It may," said Morco in a booming voice; he was not a man who whispered. "I remember nursery stories as a child, glades of magic providing solace and protection to weary travelers, though the stories say it matters not if the creature hunting you is born of a darker magic."

A moon cycle earlier and he'd have known a sharp rebuke and a reporting to their commander. Grown men did not speak of magic in Lavonshia. But their encounters with Gray Cloaks had forever changed that.

Magnus peered into the gloom. *What are they waiting for?*

The figure re-appeared in the wolves' midst, just inside the trees' shadows, at the glade's border. There was something oddly familiar …

A wolf stepped beyond the tree line, lantern light unable to pierce the shadows encircling it.

The alpha. A giant creature, thick-chested, long-legged and massive-pawed. Standing taller than any human, with fangs the length of a man's forearm.

Into the glade it strode, its fanged smile dripping death, followed by its pack; the glade's spell, if it had ever truly existed, broken.

In the chaos of shadows and wolves, Magnus lost sight of the figure.

The cluster of frits fled, screeching and jittering at the presence of the Shadow-Wolves.

The smell of sweat and fear, of wild wolf and rotting fangs, hung as a cloud over the glade. With shouts of courage to mask their fear, the soldiers lunged and stabbed with steel blades, but the wolves leapt aside with barks of laughter.

They're wearing us down, realized Magnus. *What hope do we have?*

Chapter Eleven
Bravely Clutching Pots and Pans

There was little conversation as Aurelia and her companions left Chelam behind. It was a cool evening, not entirely unpleasant. Moonlight lit their way past field and orchard, pleasant reminders of home that gradually surrendered to a thick wood, though a path wound through it.

Peak moon came and went, its light struggling to pierce the tree canopy. Despite it being harvest season, leaves clung desperately to their branches. It was late in the year to see them hold so fast, as if this season they feared earth's embrace.

Aurelia sensed her companions' excitement, here at their journey's start, but didn't share in it. Ophel's warning echoed in her ears—*when you leave, it is likely you will never return.*

But nature had long been a source of comfort for her and the night's calm worked its wonders, quieting her heart. The chirping of midnight bugs replaced words of warning, while chilled air breathed deep into her lungs worked its soothing magic.

Deep into the woods, they arrived at a polished marble pillar. Dorak's boundary marker. One she had never crossed. Beyond the marker, the world felt different—it lay dark, expectant, waiting.

Daphne walked by without a glance, before realizing she walked alone, for the three Dorakians halted at the marker.

"There's no going back, is there?" asked Aurelia.

Col shook his head.

Eken shuffled, the soft clink of pots and pans betraying his nervousness.

Daphne returned to stand by their side.

Aurelia placed a hand on the pillar. It was warm to the touch. The warmth seemed to infiltrate the pendant necklace at her throat. She traced the ancient runes, faded with age, carved into the pillar's surface.

"May the Great Binding lead us back here one day," said Daphne at last, when no one else spoke, raising her cloak's hood as if drawing courage from the anonymity it offered. The Gray Cloak nodded at each in turn and continued down the forest path.

Quickening her pace, Aurelia matched Daphne's stride, leaving the two men behind to talk about whatever men talk about. As she'd done earlier, Daphne pulled back her cloak's hood. Moonlight revealed a friendly, but curious smile.

"Why do you do that? Remove your hood. None of the other Gray Cloaks do."

"Honestly? It's itchy." She scratched her head vigorously as if to prove the point.

"New cloak?"

"To me it is. Ascended a moon's cycle ago. I'm still getting used to the role—haven't had years to hone my *acting mysterious* skills." She grinned a little wickedly.

Aurelia decided she liked this girl. She wouldn't mind some female company, or keeping a little distance from Col. *Have no wish to discuss last night!*

She glanced back to see how the men were getting along, caught Col frowning as Eken carried a one-sided conversation, caring little if Col took part.

She hooked her arm through Daphne's. "Here's to you and me getting along just fine."

The Gray Cloak studied her face. "You're not what I expected."

"What do you mean?"

"Ophel said to expect a girl who, having lived alone with her father, would be terrified to leave home. That I would need to *take charge* of the situation as Ophel put it. I don't think you need anyone taking charge of you."

"I ... I'm not sure what it is," said Aurelia after a moment's hesitation. "The outside world terrifies me, and I'm afraid of change, or, at least that's what I thought. Father always said don't fight it, embrace what comes. Now that I find myself in the moment, it's easier than I thought it would be."

"I wish I'd had someone like you to talk with sooner," Daphne confided. "Everything changed when I Ascended, but trying to talk to other Honored Ones about it is like talking to a rock."

"What did you call them?"

"A rock?"

Aurelia giggled. "No, not that—you said *Honored Ones*. First time I heard that used was earlier, by my father."

"Oh, sorry, right ... most people have it all wrong. Outsiders were the first to call us Gray Cloaks, but the name stuck. We know our true name. We are Fiadha. While those that Ascend become Honored Ones. Only an Honored One wears the cloak and bears the stone."

"Now I'm really confused. Why Gray Cloaks then?"

"Cause the color of the cloak of course."

"But you said not all Fiadha wear the gray cloak!"

Daphne shrugged and the two dissolved into laughter.

Following close behind, Col muttered, "Unbelievable. Laughing away like there's not a care in the world."

Ever the optimist, Eken gave him a hearty slap on the back. "Cheer up—we're on a grand adventure!"

"I'll be glad to reach a town," sulked Col. "The longer we're out here the more alone I feel. Two giggling girls and a bookworm. What a lot I've fallen in with."

"But it's the perfect setup to be the hero and steal the spotlight."

"For once you're right!" Col beamed cheerfully, missing the sarcasm. "A silly minded girl like Aurelia, who I admit is smarter than most, could fall for any old fool back home. But out here," he sucked in a lungful of the cool night air, "she'll see what I'm made of. I'll likely save her life at some point, and all my training to be Ka will have been worth it. I think I've already won." With a triumphant smile he clapped Eken on the back with such force it sent him sprawling, pots and pans clanging alarmingly.

Startled, the girls looked back, only to see Col's beaming smile as Eken struggled to his feet.

Daphne raised a hand to hush her companions. "Did you hear that?"

A final clanging echo of the pans. Then—wolves. Howling, snarling. Frantic shouts, men's voices raised in alarm. Eken hastened to tie his pots and pans tighter.

"No wait, don't do that," said Daphne. "Untie those. Give us each a pan and something to bang against it. Are these made of lanthanum?"

"Of course," he answered, delving deep into his bag until he'd equipped them each with kitchen utensils. "Only the finest metal will do for Dorakian smithing."

Aurelia laughed, a hesitant nervous laugh, eyeing the pan and spoon in her hands. "You can't be serious."

Col glared, refusing the tools offered. "I only need this." He pulled his sword free of its scabbard where it gleamed bright, reflecting moonlight.

Does he wax that thing every night? wondered Aurelia.

Daphne yanked a pan from Eken's hand and thrust it at Col. "Wolves won't fear your sword. They've killed plenty of men who believe a sword will save them. But the noise we make," and here she raised the pan and spoon in her hands to make a point, "will catch them off guard. More than that, lanthanum wards off all manner of evil."

"Ha," scoffed Col, though he swallowed, a first hint of nerves flickering across his face, "that's an old wives tale. Why should we care anyway? We don't know whoever's out there."

"Col!" exclaimed Aurelia.

"I was only jesting. Right, buddy?" He thumped Eken across the shoulder as if he'd been in on the joke. "Fine, we'll die together or save the day with our pots and pans." And laughing at his own wit, he snatched up a pan, while clanging his sword against it. "Oooh. Scary."

Daphne raised an eyebrow as Aurelia shrugged, apologetic.

Bravely clutching their pots and pans, they hastened towards the howling.

Chapter Twelve
Won't Go Unpunished

Saul lunged, his sword slashing empty air where a wolf once crouched. He slipped, fell to one knee. The creature bared its fangs in a hideous smile and he cried out as tooth and claw gouged deep, his sword clattering useless to the ground.

The Ka's circle threatened to collapse.

With a fierce bellow, Morco swung the full weight of his warhammer. It connected with a sickening crunch, hurtling a wolf across the clearing.

Backpedaling furiously, Tobias parried an attack.

Sensing movement, Magnus jabbed right, spearing a wolf. He yanked the sword free, and as the creature collapsed to the ground, its encircling shadows dissolved.

"Beneath the shadows—they die like wolves!" His voice rang across the glade, and the men drew fresh courage, renewing their desperate struggle. Sensing the tide turning, the wolves retreated, snarling and pacing out of reach, waiting for an opening.

In the brief lull, Magnus assessed the situation. They'd closed rank, a tight, worried knot of men, and dragged a pale-faced Saul into their midst. He lay beside Veyra, clutching his side, his fingers slick with the coppery tint of blood.

Five of us fit to stand and too many of them, Magnus thought as he counted several dozen wolves circling.

"What do they wait for?" Tobias leaned on the hilt of his sword, catching his breath.

"They're toying with us," answered Magnus.

Even as he spoke, the alpha sat its haunches, a wicked grin splayed across its face. Soulless eyes regarded the soldiers, and lifting its head, it howled, as if in cruel laughter. The pack responded, echoing their leader's cry.

Magnus forced a deep breath, closed his eyes as he allowed his thoughts to wander, picturing fields back home. He could almost smell the scent of hay gathered into bundles, see his father loading the wagons for delivery to Capitol markets.

He opened his eyes and offered a grim smile to his companions.

"I don't intend we die here today." He radiated confidence, staring each man square in the face. "But if we do, let's resolve to meet death bravely."

The wolves noted his tone, snarls quieting as they looked to their alpha for reassurance, while shadows recoiled and moonlight shone a little more brightly, the glade awash in its glow.

"We stand with you, Magnus!"

As one, the men raised sword to the sky. As one, they spoke a time-worn oath, the Red Oath, seared on the lips of every Lavonshian child from the time they could speak, even if none understood its meaning. "Though red is the night, we stand as one! Though mountains rise against us, we stand as one!"

For a moment, Magnus believed the glade itself would win the evening, for the moonlight burned so bright it shone like the sun, and he dared hope it would send the wolves and their shadows fleeing, but the glow faded and darkness returned to cloak the glade in gloom. Gleaming fangs reflected off what dim light remained, and the alpha stirred, its pack following, fur bristling as they charged.

Magnus prepared for the end.

A racket shattered the glade, a horrific din echoing from every corner of the forest, off every rock and tree, as if the world itself might end in one ear-splitting finale. Bewildered, the wolves halted mid-stride. They cowered, whimpering, tails tucked, senses buffeted by a distinct resonance, before fleeing the glade in a complete rout, howling as they went.

A ragged cheer erupted.

Magnus jabbed his sword into the ground, breathing hard as he propped his weight against it, astounded at the sudden turn of events and the sight of four individuals appearing at glade's edge. He could just make out the two standing closest: a man of average height with long blond hair and a woman who stood a little taller than the man, black hair falling loose down her back.

He observed no weapons other than a sword strapped to the young man's side. On their backs hung bulging travel packs and in their hands the noise's culprit. Magnus laughed until he clutched his side. Never would he have imagined salvation to arrive wielding pots and ladles.

"That's an odd way of expressing thanks."

"Col, don't fuss at them; they're exhausted. He laughs from sheer relief."

The woman stepped close enough for her features to come into focus. She was pretty, her frank, open face warmed by an engaging smile. She stuck out a hand in greeting.

"I'm Aurelia. Sounded like you needed help. We thought these might come in handy."

She grinned sheepishly, brandishing a pan and spoon.

"My apologies." Magnus steadied himself and clasped the hand she offered. It was soft but not delicate, and there was strength in it—the kind earned through labor. She stood close, too close for someone who had just saved his life, and he became suddenly aware of the warmth radiating from her. Her eyes held his in an appraising stare. "My uh, my name is Magnus. I meant no harm. You've done us a favor and we owe you a great debt."

He dropped her hand, though he couldn't pull away from her stare, adding on impulse, "My life is in your hands, and should any raise a sword against you or your companions I will defend your health and honor with my own."

Though he meant every word, the reckless swearing of another Lavonshian oath surprised even himself. His men responded with a hearty "Aye! Aye!"

The young woman inclined her head in thanks as he added, "We should go. The wolves will return when they come to their senses."

"I agree." Another woman's voice, but from the shadows at glade's edge. "Mountain wolves startle easily enough at strange noises, but they'll not scare so easy next time."

"These were no common mountain wolves," he replied. "And you are ...?"

His eyes strained to pierce the dark as a figure strode forward.

"You may call me Daphne until you know my name."

His eyes hardened, hand flinching toward his sword.

A Binder!

The embedded stone revealed her identity, and she seemed not to care to hide it, allowing her cloak's hood to rest carelessly against her shoulders. In an instant, the glade's merry mood changed; swords rasped against sheaths as the Ka pressed forward with angry mutterings of *Witch!* and *Binder!*

Magnus' eyes narrowed, anger's heat flooding his heart with images of dead Ka in Breckei Valley.

"What do we do?" whispered Tobias at his side. "You just vowed to defend their lives."

He would have thanked Tobias for the obvious, but was too busy balancing his sword in hand, picturing the Binder impaled at the end of it.

"We're exhausted," said Kymn, eyeing the girl with a sideways glance, "and we don't know what power she holds."

The Gray Cloak studied them as they whispered. "If you need privacy, happy to leave you here in this clearing." She smiled amicably enough, though to Magnus it reminded him of the alpha's smile.

Need time to think, to sort my thoughts. Besides, Kymn is right; we're in no condition to take on another fight.

"Daphne, well met," he said, his mind resolved for the moment. "We're indebted to you. Do you know of shelter close by? We are spent, thirsty, hungry ... and have two injured."

"Yes, I know of this glade. Belanor's Cave lies near. It's given refuge to many travelers. More importantly, the wolves fear it."

Her assurance that wolves would fear a cave made little sense, but he nodded his agreement. *What other choice do we have?*

The Gray Cloak who'd introduced herself as Daphne stiffened at the sight of their wounded. He tensed as she brushed by, so close he could have plunged a dagger in her heart. But she ignored him, kneeling at Saul's side, laying a hand on his forehead.

"He's lost a good bit of blood." She peeled back his blood-soaked tunic. "But he's fortunate; the wounds aren't especially deep. On our way to the cave, we should forage for bresha plants."

"Oh, I know those!" interjected the girl named Aurelia excitedly. "We use bresha back home." She followed the Gray Cloak into the circle of soldiers and knelt by Veyra's side. "Your friend here is far more grievously hurt, and her forehead's hot. She's fevered and may not last 'til tomorrow."

"Are you healers?" asked Magnus, taken aback by their unexpected kindness.

As if on cue, the women exclaimed, "We're not healers!" They looked at each other and laughed. Aurelia added, "I wish I was. Your friend here ..."

"Veyra," offered Magnus.

"... needs a true healer, but I've assisted our village healer many times, so I'll do what I can."

"Do you have food? Water? We separated from our company; we have no supplies."

"Belanor's Cave has water," said Daphne, "though our food supplies won't stretch far between us."

A wolf howled in the distance.

"None of that matters if the wolves find us again!" warned Kymn.

"Come, follow me." The Binder raised her cloak's hood, shadowing her face, and hastened from the glade.

Magnus marveled at the thought that Ka soldiers would follow one they once hunted. A lopsided grin and a friendly tone interrupted his thoughts.

"Hi! I'm Eken. So nice to meet you. Can't wait to talk more on the way."

Magnus couldn't help but smile, but his thoughts were elsewhere, eyeing his men, each in turn, conveying unspoken thoughts: *For now, we follow. Be patient. The Binder won't go unpunished.*

Chapter Thirteen
Before the Storm Could Break

The morning sun rose full-bodied above the horizon, retreated quickly, only to peek once more, as if debating whether it was safe to come out. It studied the odd gathering of humans making their way to Belanor's Cave—Ka, Gray Cloak, Dorakian—and wondered what strange portent the sight foretold. But at last it gathered its courage, its light, its warmth, and lifted itself purposefully above the horizon.

Aurelia shivered, chill bumps speckling her arms at the sudden change in temperature. Thankful for the new day's warmth, she rubbed her hands vigorously as she joined Daphne at the head of their procession.

"What was that about?" she asked, glancing back at the soldiers. A blush warmed her cheeks as she noticed Magnus watching—*me, or Daphne?* she wondered—his keen eyes absorbing every detail.

But Daphne didn't answer, choosing to wrap herself in silence. Aurelia turned instead to study their path and when she caught sight of wild-growing fruit, an edible plant, or the red-tipped bresha fern, she'd forage for a moment.

A chorus of morning birds chirped lustily in the trees. Ground moles peeked from their den, chittering at the heavy-footed intruders stomping by. Reveling in the world's stirring, she sucked in a lungful of air, surprised that she could feel so happy in the moment, despite earlier events.

I must have been possessed to charge toward howling wolves!

It would have been impossible to do such a thing alone, and she marveled at the courage she gained from her friends. But courage or no, she had doubted they'd see the morning sun. Now that it was here, she delighted in its warmth.

So engrossed was she in her surroundings that Daphne's sudden voice startled her, and she choked off a scream.

"I haven't known you long, Aurelia of Dorak, but you've shown me enough to believe I can trust you."

"So I have you fooled, then?"

Ignoring the tease, the Gray Cloak plunged ahead. "I covenant to be your faithful friend, to be true as the night star. To give counsel when counsel is needed, to offer silence when silence is needed. To utter only truth. This I covenant." She released a deep breath, adding as an afterthought, "Binding knows I need a friend out here."

"I, uh, I appreciate you too, Daphne, and um -"

"I'm such an idiot! I forget how strange our customs can be to outsiders, but the covenant of a faithful friend is not one we give lightly. Or often." She peeked at the Dorakian, while holding her breath.

Aurelia's answering smile was enough, wrapping her arm through Daphne's as they walked side by side. "Then I'm grateful for the honor, and promise to be your faithful friend too."

"Oh, what a beautiful day!" exclaimed Daphne.

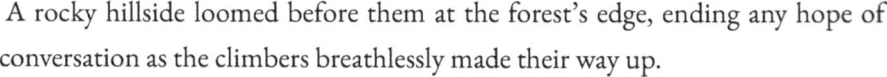

A rocky hillside loomed before them at the forest's edge, ending any hope of conversation as the climbers breathlessly made their way up.

Struggling to scale a large boulder, Aurelia's foot slipped, but a hand on her back steadied her as she wobbled. A soldier stepped beside her. An easy grin displayed yellow-stained, time-worn teeth. He was a brute of a man, pushing seven span tall, with burly shoulders and arms, and broad-chested. Past any hope of youthful prime, his face was weathered and scarred, graying hair pulled back in a ponytail. Across his back he'd slung a long-handled warhammer.

"Morco." He nodded a greeting, his eyes reflecting a kindness that surprised her. "Looked like you could use some help." His deep voice echoed across the hillside.

Touched by the kindness, she returned his smile, though her stomach flip-flopped at the sight of his teeth. "Thank you, Morco. I wouldn't have expected ... because of last night -"

"My apologies; it's just, well, it's not you ... it's her."

"If you can surprise me with your kindness, perhaps she can surprise you with her goodness."

Morco appeared to consider the advice as he steadied her on the next boulder, releasing her hand when she regained her footing. He laughed then, a full-bellied guffaw of a laugh.

"Hah! A woman's wisdom. You remind me of my mother. She always said never judge a book by its leather, but by the words scrawled across its pages. Later I understood she spoke of far more than books." He winked and bowed low, an awkward movement for a man his size. "I'll take your words to heart and hold judgment until I know your friend better."

Her heart warmed to the gentle giant as he helped her over the next boulder, curiosity piqued when he dug into the pack he carried.

"For you," he said, pressing an object into her hands, "as a thank you for saving our lives."

It was hand carved, the wood grain similar to basswood trees common in Dorak, the design delicate, intricate, the exact likeness of a frit.

"You made this yourself?"

"Aye."

"It's incredible! I shall treasure it and remember you fondly if our paths part." Impulsively, she stretched on her tiptoes and planted a kiss on his cheek. His face flamed a bright pink blush though his smile widened.

Eken's excited voice floated up from below, where he'd stayed behind, pretending to assist the soldiers with their wounded. At the moment he was engaged in a lively one-sided conversation, telling the Ka all about life in a Dorakian village.

"That fool never stops talking," muttered Col.

Aurelia would have scolded him, but he'd already pivoted to speak to Daphne. "The Ka came to hunt Gray Cloaks, didn't they? The way they reacted -"

"They mistook me for someone else." Daphne shrugged, though she glanced sideways at Morco who stood within earshot.

Seemingly content with the explanation, Col sprawled on the ground to rest. Aurelia met Daphne's gaze, caught the subtle shake of her head.

I can wait, thought Aurelia.

Unexpected words echoed in her mind, words she felt rather than heard: *You'll have your answers.*

Her eyes widened and she froze, confused. That hadn't been spoken aloud. Had it? She stared hard at her new Gray Cloak friend, but her face was an emotionless mask.

Daphne, was that you? There was no answer. *So tired my mind's playing tricks on me!*

With a shake of her head, she settled in beside Col. She couldn't resist sneaking glances at Magnus, his hands full hoisting Veyra onto a nearby ledge. The gentleness with which he handled the unconscious woman impressed her. He glanced up and caught Aurelia staring. A slight smile played on his lips, and she looked away.

"How much farther?" Magnus called up to Daphne, who pointed wordlessly up the slope. He sighed and struggled gamely to his feet.

A short time later, with the sun nearing its midday height, the small band arrived at a nondescript pile of gray and white boulders.

"We made it," said Daphne, "and none too soon."

A wolf stepped from the forest's shadowy embrace, lifting its snout to the sky in a blood-curdling howl. In daylight, the lone wolf seemed a far less scary sight, until another joined it, then another and another, and a pack some forty strong stood clear of the trees. They bounded up the hillside, surprisingly agile for their size.

"Quick!" cried Daphne. "Into the cave!"

Had she not vanished before their eyes, her companions would never have found the entrance to Belanor's Cave. It was a thin opening, tucked between two of the largest boulders. Morco only just squeezed his giant frame through. But once inside, the flames of hastily lit lanterns cast light deep into Belanor's Cave, revealing its size. The ceiling soared some height above, while paths wound through stalagmites poking up through the cave floor; and farther off in the distance, where shadows hid the cave's true size, could be heard a stream's gentle murmur.

"The wolves won't follow?" asked Bochim, his voice trembling, for even as he spoke one could hear the harsh baying of the wolves outside.

"No, they won't," said Daphne.

"Why are they so afraid of this cave?" asked Eken, his hand gripping the book in his pocket.

"A story for another time. We should rest."

Magnus gave instructions for first watch, unwilling to trust in the cave's goodwill for protection. Desperate for rest, others wandered off, searching for a flat space and a little peace and quiet.

Aurelia set up camp by a stream, where Eken and Daphne joined her. Eken soon slept, his snores echoing loudly. Whether it was the noise or that she was too excited from recent events, Aurelia remained wide awake.

"Can't sleep?" asked Daphne, striking her lantern. In the dim light, Aurelia could just make out her new friend's eyes, bright and inquisitive.

"No. You?"

Daphne nudged Eken and his snoring quieted for a moment. "That might help," she said with a mischievous grin. "You asked me a question earlier. Same as

Col, but ... I wasn't truthful with him. You, though, are now my covenant friend. What would you like to know?"

"Everything!"

"That could take a while ..." Daphne chuckled.

Aurelia loved that about her—the effortless laughter. "So then what was that last night? The tension between you and the soldiers. Is it true? About Gray Cloaks ... Saan ...?"

"A moon cycle ago we received an urgent message from clan Fi-Jal," Daphne's visage darkened, noticeable even in the dim light. "The Ka ransacked one of our villages: Tiriman. Few survived. Those who did journeyed east and south to warn the other clans."

"Were your people responsible for Saan?" asked Aurelia, as blunt as she could manage.

"No! Absolutely not. It's against our very nature."

She studied her friend's face but sensed she spoke the truth.

"The news about Tiriman outraged us, though some didn't believe it. We're a peaceful people. Why would they attack us?" Daphne pushed off an elbow and scooted close. "We debated for days—my people are good at that. We could never reach a consensus—we're good at that too. While we wasted precious time, a company of Honored Ones arrived, confirming the reports of Tiriman and sharing news of a battle in Breckei Valley. I think these soldiers came from that valley. The injured man—a wolf did that. But the girl? That's charred flesh. No wolf causes that, but a Binder with storm powers can."

"Storm powers? You mean like lightning?"

"Some control lightning. Others wind. Or earth. Metals. We each have our strengths, though we only use them in defense. But when provoked, our bindings can be devastating." Her eyes clouded, dark and stormy, setting Aurelia's heart to pounding.

I hope I never find myself at odds with her.

She hadn't said it aloud, but a response echoed in her mind: *you have nothing to fear from me.*

"Did you -"

Approaching footsteps interrupted her. It was Magnus, accompanied by one of his men. He'd noticed them there by the stream, but only his eyes conveyed any misgiving as he knelt to fill a flask.

"Ah, if it isn't the pot drummer," he said with a wry smile, his attention on Aurelia.

"Says the man we saved," she retorted.

"Apologies. I spoke in poor taste, and I'm sorry for the intrusion. We came to refill our flasks. This is Tobias."

He nodded at the soldier beside him, who waved a friendly greeting. Aurelia returned it with a smile, taking him in with a quick, curious glance. She'd heard of Highlanders with their dark complexion, but had never met one in person.

"The water is better upstream," said Daphne. "I can show you where it flows fresh from the rock."

Her lantern lit the way, light and shadow etching strange yet playful designs across cavern walls. The stream they followed gurgled merrily in a deep rutted trench, splashing over stalagmites worn by eons of waterflow to little more than nubs.

"That story then?" asked Magnus. "Belanor's Cave ..."

"It's an ancient tale, before humans walked this world." Daphne rubbed at the back of her neck, recalling the familiar myth. "A noble stag led his herd in search of fresh pasture. Those were days of want and vast desert wastelands, when even the most hale of creatures were found dead and dying. But this was no ordinary herd. *The Eldihi*. Creatures as much of another world as they were of this one. And he was their king, Belanor, a mighty beast with a many-pointed crown, thick golden fur, and the stamina of a dozen Eldihi stags. He led them through this very wood, where a pack of hungry beasts set upon them. Wolves. Not unlike what pursued you, wrapped in shadows and possessed of unnatural strength and cunning."

She paused in the telling, peering right and left, her lantern bobbing this way and that, considering the stream as it split before them.

"I thought you knew the way," said Magnus with a sigh.

"I do. Or did, rather. But it's been many hunter's moons since I was here." And then, her tone confident, "It's this way."

She followed a branch of the stream deeper into the cave, resuming her story as they went.

"The forest that night witnessed a sight it would never forget. To those who ask, elm and ash and beech will whisper the tale, and generations of my people have asked. As the story goes, the Eldihi grew weary, trembling at the wolves' pursuit, an endless pack of howling shadow, tooth and claw. Their kingly stag led the flight, and defended them when the howling pack closed in. The night was long, the battle's ebb and flow seemingly endless. When the Eldihi reached the forest edge and the rocky hill outside this cave, their courage faltered, for none had strength to brave its slope. They were legend, but they were still mortal. Their king Belanor would have none of it. He urged them up the hill. They fed on his energy and he gave them all he had, driving them forward even as he repelled the horde of Shadow-Wolves. As the last of his Eldihi fled safe into the cave, he fell mortally wounded at its entrance. But still he fought, though shadows pierced his eyes, his mouth, his lungs, as fang and claw sank deep into his flesh. The bodies of those wolves whose lives he claimed piled high until they blocked the very entrance to the cave. Only then did he close his eyes and breathe his last. His life given for his Eldihi. The King Stag. Belanor."

Aurelia hung on every word as Daphne told the tale, a story every bit as enchanting as any a Traveler ever shared. At its finish, she wiped away a tear.

Magnus cleared his throat. "That's uh ... quite a story." He grunted as Tobias elbowed him in his side.

"And here we are," said Daphne cheerfully, ignoring his comment. "Told you I could find it."

They had reached the stream's source, where it flowed clean from an opening in the rock face.

"But what of the Eldihi?" asked Aurelia, stepping aside, allowing the soldiers access to the stream.

"Time flowed never ending, until my people walked the land," said Daphne. "We discovered this cave and the bones of a thousand wolves blocking its entrance. Once cleared, we explored inside but found no trace of Eldihi, not even a single stag bone. Some believe that because of Belanor's sacrifice, the land spirited them all away. The forest can't, or won't, say."

"What were you and your companions doing in the forest, anyway?" asked Magnus.

"We travel to the Capitol," replied Daphne, "for an audience with the King."

Aurelia's heart flopped and she thought she might be sick. She couldn't have been more shocked if it were suggested they scale the Tol's highest peak.

"Oh?" asked Magnus, a touch of strain affecting his voice. "To what end?"

"To ask why the King's Army kills my people when we've done nothing to deserve it."

Aurelia winced. She hadn't expected such bluntness from her friend.

The Ka soldier whirled, took a forceful step toward them before his friend laid a restraining hand on his shoulder.

"Kill *your* people? What of Saan's?" He spoke in a clipped tone, his hand straying to the sword at his side. "I vowed no harm would come to you. Don't try my patience, Binder! My men would like nothing more than to avenge the loss of our brothers and sisters."

"Your loss? What about my people! A village wiped out. Men, women ... children, slaughtered."

The man flinched, his face draining of color. "I ... it wasn't our intention -" He inhaled a shuddering breath. "It's beyond regrettable. The killing of innocents was," he seemed to struggle for the right word, wincing even as he spoke it, "evil."

Aurelia found it hard to reconcile Ka soldiers killing innocent children with the man standing before her. But her friend seemed to have no such qualms.

"The innocent lie in their graves," her tone as icy and cold as any Aurelia ever heard, "yet still their cries drown out your hollow speech."

As she turned away, Tobias caught her wrist. "Don't judge him too harshly. Magnus is a good man. To our shame, we were there, but he'd never condone it. Never take part."

Daphne frowned at his restraining hand, though her face softened. She opened her mouth as if to speak again, but thinking better of it, she jerked her arm free and stalked off. Aurelia hurried to catch up.

"What do you think?" asked Magnus as they watched the womens' bobbing lantern shrink until darkness enveloped it. "Does it justify what the Binders did in that valley?"

"Perhaps."

"At least we have an answer to your question," he said, a quiet laugh at the apparent confusion. "The one where you asked why we joined the Ka ..."

"Ah," said Tobias, a grin spreading across his face, "Yes, there go two of them. Although I'd advise against getting mixed up with those two."

They finished filling their flasks and headed downstream.

"Do you believe her?" asked Tobias.

Magnus hesitated. His thoughts drifted toward the taller black-haired woman, though his friend had obviously referred to the Binder.

"She believes her people are innocent. But as an officer of the Ka, I have little choice. I must present them to Drael."

"He'll not deal kindly with them."

"To fulfill my vow, I'll request the right to accompany them to the King, where the Binder can plead her people's cause."

"Will they go with us though? To Drael?" asked Tobias.

"They must. I'll convince them it's their safest and best option to reach the Capitol."

"Ha!" Tobias laughed. "Good luck with that. You'll have your chance sooner than you might wish."

With a nod, he inclined his head towards a bobbing lantern returning their way.

"Earlier, I failed to defend my friend." Aurelia's eyes blazed as she drew near. "While I haven't known her long, I know a genuine person when I meet one. If she represents Gray Cloaks, then they aren't responsible for Saan."

Despite the angry tone, this fiery version intrigued Magnus. A vein on her temple pulsed as she spoke, and she brushed an unruly strand of hair from her eyes that refused to stay, a gesture that he found both distracting and fascinating. When she finished, he lifted his hands in a helpless gesture.

"It's noble to defend your friend, but the King himself knows of Gray Cloak plots against -"

"Plots?" Daphne's turn to bristle with outrage. "Hah! We can't even agree on dinner plans. We don't plot."

He waved dismissively. "We're not here to argue the point. The evidence against your people is more than sufficient." He looked to Tobias for backup, but his friend hesitated.

"I don't know what I have to do or say to prove our intentions," Daphne continued hotly, "but when I speak with the King, I'll clear my people's name."

"If anyone can convince him, I imagine you can, but I must present you to my commander first. It's his to decide what to do with you. I'll speak on your behalf, it's the least I can do after you rescued us, but this matter's above my head."

The Gray Cloak looked ready to explode, but it was Aurelia who spoke first. "Thank you for your help. Truly." And seizing her friend's arm, she dragged her away before the storm could break.

Chapter Fourteen
Stole Past the Sleeping Ka

"Thank goodness." Magnus sighed as they left. "I refuse to spar with those women."

Tobias laughed. "Because you'd lose!"

"At least everything's out in the open." He ignored the jab. "We know what they want, and they know who we are."

"It's obvious where Aurelia stands on the Gray Cloak matter."

Something softened in Magnus' expression. "She's quite a woman, I mean ... she's uh ..."

"Say no more. I understand."

"As if I need that out here, in the thick of a campaign, let alone I should be heading home tomorrow. And she's friends with a Binder!" Magnus growled, frustrated, shaking his head to clear his mind and focus his thoughts. "We can't forget what Binders are capable of—powers of persuasion. Maybe she's already turned Aurelia."

"You don't believe that."

"That's what troubles me." He kicked a loose rock, sending it skittering across the cave floor. "It's difficult to square what we were told of Binders with Daphne. She's been nothing but helpful."

"Maybe we were told half a story."

"Which would undermine everything we're doing ... and have done. Though even if Daphne is peaceful, Tiriman and Breckei Valley prove how vicious Gray

Cloaks can be." He'd known Tobias long enough to sense he held back. "Speak your mind."

"To lay the iron bare ... it's just, well, we were first to attack. Can you blame them? Defending their land, their villages, their homes." Tobias took a deep breath and plowed ahead. "Could it be we bear innocent blood on our hands?"

"If Saan was their doing, perhaps we were justified at Tiriman."

"Then it all hinges on Saan, doesn't it?"

While Tobias shared freshly drawn water among the men, Magnus checked on Veyra, who still slept. Bresha fronds wrapped her burns, and her forehead wasn't as hot. The bresha reminded him of Aurelia, her excitement at the first sign of the plant lining the forest path. How deftly her hands harvested the red-tipped fern. How a stray bit of early-morning light illuminated her face, while her hands wrapped the bresha around the soldiers' wounds, her mouth parting slightly as she concentrated, that same unruly strand of hair falling across her face. Her competence unsettled him more than her beauty—he felt himself drawn to her in ways he hadn't sought or welcomed.

At the cave's entrance, he found Kymn and Col engaged in a lively conversation.

"Been warning our Dorakian friend here about life in the Ka."

"I've always wanted to serve, and I'd do anything for Lavonshia," said Col. "A standing army protects her from foes within and without."

"And who are the foes within?" asked Magnus.

"I've had my eye on Daphne and her ilk." The Dorakian peered into the cave but, spying no eavesdroppers, leaned in as if they were conspirators to a plot. "I know the rumors about Saan. What they did there. And I tell you—there's something off about them. Secretive. Shifty, if you ask me. Always shrouded, always watching. Nothing honest hides its face in daylight. And that girl Daphne—appoints herself as the supposed leader of our group. Throws that hood back like she's better than the rest of us. And that smile? Too easy. I don't trust her one bit."

Magnus wanted to believe him, anything to confirm the treacherous nature of the Binders, but he had to admit the girl didn't seem at all as described. "Did she speak of their plans?"

"Not to me," Col shook his head, "but like I said, I don't trust her. Happy to keep an eye on her for you."

"Thank you, yes, we need more information, details of their plots."

"You can count on me."

The men shook firm hands before Magnus took his leave, slipping outside through the narrow opening, careful to scan his surroundings before going far. He took advantage of the moment alone to stretch sore muscles, walking a ridgeline that jutted out from the cave's opening. Though the sun shone bright, the air was crisp and cool, refreshing after the cave's damp interior.

Fear raked his gut when the figure that had shadowed him the past two days stepped into the light, out from beyond the treeline at the base of the hill. It stood wrapped in shadows, as the wolves had been.

"What do you want from me?" Magnus shouted, snatching up a stone and flinging it downslope. It fell short, but drew the figure's attention. It came on, scuttling up the hill with unnatural speed. Magnus dismissed any thought of fleeing to the cave, loathe to turn his back on the foul apparition. Steel hissed free and he dropped into a Ka battle stance—if this were to be his end, he would meet it fighting. The figure drew up short. Close enough to hear the rustle of its clothing, but outside the reach of his blade. It seemed to hover above the stones, though the shadows clinging to it made the truth impossible to see.

"Day-son," its whisper was harsh, tongue grating against teeth, as if speaking for the first time.

"Who are you?" There was something unpleasantly familiar about it.

"I am you. You are me."

The shadows dissipated, revealing a man's face, a face Magnus knew well. His own.

What evil is this? he wondered, staggering backwards. The world spun, ears ringing as his breath caught tight in his chest.

"Day-son, our time is near." The shadow-man's voice was like a snake's hissing and Magnus could almost imagine a double-forked tongue protruding from its mouth.

"I want no part of you!"

He lunged, only for his blade to slice through shadows as the shadow-man stepped nimbly aside.

"Day-son, do not fear your destiny."

The phrase rang mockingly and Magnus fell to his knees, fingers digging into rocky soil, seeking a hold on reality.

"Magnus. Magnus!"

Hands clawed at his shoulders, and he swung wildly with a fist, connecting with solid flesh that resulted in a grunted *oomph*.

"Hold friend, it's me! It's Kymn."

Magnus struggled to breathe. "I ..."

"It's okay. You're okay."

"It was so real." Shaking, he clung to his friend.

"I heard shouting -"

"That man ... the shadows. He was right here ... he wore my face."

"There was no one else here; come back inside."

At their campsite, the fire did its best to warm him, as did the company of men he trusted, but the cold of that whispered name, *Day-Son*, clung to his bones. Eventually he drifted asleep, wondering if the shadow-man had been real or whether exhaustion and fear played tricks on his mind.

Cloaked in the cave's shadows, three figures stole past the sleeping Ka.

Chapter Fifteen
For Anyone Fond of Mud

Earlier, arms flailing and lantern swinging violently, Daphne had stormed ahead of Aurelia, fuming at the gall of that pompous Ka soldier, and fuming at her new friend for dragging her away before she could unload a piece of her mind.

"I won't be taken prisoner and paraded before his commander. Regardless of whatever charm you think he carries." She waved off Aurelia's protests. "Oh, I see the way you look at him, and how he looks at you. But his army butchered my people. I won't -"

Aurelia embraced her in a fierce hug. "I can't imagine how you feel, but I only said those things so he'd think we'll play along. There's no way his commander gets anywhere near you." Aurelia peered into the shadows beyond the lantern's light, but they were alone. "We'll leave tonight, the four of us. Or just the two of us if the boys won't come."

"You are a covenant friend!"

At their campsite, Eken snored on, oblivious. A nudge from Daphne and he rolled onto his side, rewarding her efforts with even louder snoring.

"On this hard ground," Aurelia patted the cave's rock floor ruefully, "and with his snoring, I'll sleep fitfully at best. But you should rest, and I'll wake you both later. We'll find Col and make our escape."

Daphne soon slept, but as Aurelia feared, her own remained elusive.

Her mind strayed from planning their escape to thinking of Magnus—his steady strength caring for his men and for their wounded, the hard line of his jaw when he'd answered Daphne. Although guarded, his eyes held a measure of kindness. She had to admit he was charming, even handsome, as Daphne accused her of thinking. Though he wasn't handsome the way Travelers were.

Parents kept a close eye on children of marrying age when Travelers came to town, though Dorakians were too hospitable to turn their visitors away. Besides, they loved the theater and the death-defying acts as much as anyone. But more than a few Dorakians had succumbed to the enchanting beauty or handsome figures of the Travelers—one secret nighttime betrothal, and another villager gone, taking up the mantle of Traveler.

Aurelia understood their appeal, but she'd observed how their smiles faded too soon after the applause. For all their exuberance on stage, a quiet sadness clung to them.

She had once snuck to the edge of their camp, just beyond Chelam's boundary, expecting laughter, music, and dancing—the same spectacle they offered on stage. Instead, firelight illuminated a ring of wagons and weary, though still stunningly beautiful, faces gathered close around the flames. Their voices were low, their laughter stilled, while one strummed a gittern and sang a song so sorrowful it ached in her chest.

Transfixed, she lingered long into the night, returning every evening to the darkness outside their campfire, but it was always the same: a deep melancholy hovering like a gray mist. She longed to step into their circle, to ask why such sadness shadowed their joy and to learn the answers to their riddle, but some instinct warned her she trespassed on a truth not meant for her.

No, with Magnus, his features were more rugged than that of a Traveler. But though she barely knew him, she sensed that he, like a Traveler, carried a depth inside truer to who he was than the soldier's mantle he wore. If she could only study him from the darkness beyond a campfire's light, she might learn what that truth was.

She couldn't say how long she lay there, but at last, unwilling to wait any longer, she prodded her covenant friend awake.

"It's time?"

She nodded wordlessly.

It took a great deal more effort to wake Eken. But once they explained the urgency, he proved eager to go and hastened to secure his belongings.

Tip-toeing past sleeping soldiers, they hugged the cave's far wall, and found Col standing guard at the entrance.

"Keep quiet," whispered Aurelia, "we can't risk waking anyone."

"What are you doing here?" he asked, rubbing at red-rimmed eyes.

"We need to go—just the four of us. Daphne's not safe here."

He was silent for a moment, before glancing deeper into the cave where the soldiers slept.

"Please," she said, taking his hand.

He looked down, seemed surprised at her touch. "Like I said in Chelam, where you go, I go. I'll always protect you." He squeezed her hand, and she breathed a grateful sigh for his friendship. "Let me gather my things. I'll be right back."

He'd been gone far too long, it seemed; worry gnawed at the edge of Aurelia's mind, but then he was back, his pack in hand. A quick nod, hurried whispers, and they slipped through the narrow opening of Belanor's Cave.

———◆○◆———

"It's still my intention to address the King, but I expect the soldiers will turn west to intercept us once they discover we've gone." Daphne stared in turn at each companion, while they hung on every word. "So we'll go east, to Lumath; a Gray Cloak village and a guarded secret, so well hidden that if you didn't know the way, you'd never find it. We can shelter there until it's safe to venture west."

"That's a marvelous plan!" Aurelia clapped her hands in delight.

"Lumath," breathed Eken, enraptured by the idea. "A hidden village. What can be more exciting than that?"

"Besides rescuing a band of soldiers from Shadow-Wolves and then making a daring escape from said soldiers?" asked Aurelia, sharing a smile with her friend.

So it was that the three Dorakians followed their Gray Cloak guide on a circuitous route east, around the base of the hill. On the far side, the slope ended abruptly at a jutting rock wall, a narrow ledge hugging the cliff face the only way forward.

"We're crossing that?" asked Eken, a tremor in his voice.

"It's safe," their guide assured him, "unless it rains, then the ledge is slick. One of my clan fell to their death here. May the Great Binding speak to him still." She paused, considered recent weather patterns for a moment before adding cheerfully, "Thankfully, it's been a few days since it rained!"

Aurelia eyed the ledge. It was perilously thin, barely wide enough for a footstep. By her reckoning, it ran the length of a Great Hall—considerably farther than she wished to walk such a narrow path. At least the cliff wall offered a surface to hug, so she turned sideways and edged along, slow and careful, breath tight. But one glance below was a mistake and a wave of dizziness threatened to send her tumbling. It was a long way down, the forest floor impossibly distant. The world tilted. She froze, clinging to the stone, breathing slow until the moment passed.

Daphne, meanwhile, strode confidently ahead, nearly halfway across.

Seeing their progress, Eken placed a first foot, then another, onto the ledge. His grip on the book in his pocket threatened to snap it in two. Aurelia could hear the fear in his steps as he slid his feet forward.

"Take your time, Eken, don't rush it."

He'd faced the wall, palms flat against it, his back to the edge, face pale, his body like a listless boat at sea, teetering side to side, his bulging pack throwing him off balance. He glanced over his shoulder, couldn't help himself. A pan slid in his pack and he lurched backwards. Slipped. Swallowed a scream as he pitched toward an empty expanse.

Aurelia lunged, missing his hand. A strap from his pack flapped loose; her fingers closed around it, yanking him back against the cliff face. His feet scrambled, searching for solid footing, sending rock and debris flying off the ledge.

Her breath caught in her throat, heart hammering. *Too close.*

"Thank you," he panted, his face white.

"Don't look down!" called out Daphne over her shoulder.

"A warning sooner would've been a mercy!" Eken forced a cheerful tone.

The three were nearly across now, but Col had yet to set foot on the ledge. He leaned against a scraggly tree at the cliff's edge. When Aurelia glanced back, he caught her eye and returned her smile. Pushing off the trunk, he stepped onto the ledge.

"That was the worst of it, until Leaping Death …" Daphne shrugged at the anxious stares. "There's a reason the village is so well hidden."

"Leaping Death?" Col had finally crossed the narrow ledge and flopped, spent, to the ground. "You're sane as a frit or as doomed as one. I haven't decided which."

For once, Aurelia agreed with him, though the comparison was a little odd. Frits weren't known for their wise choices. As a little girl, she'd watched a frit leap too far between branches and tumble from the sky; her father saved the creature's life, catching it as it fell. Its wings broke in the fall, and Mahan spent the next few months nursing it back to health. He'd even named it. *Uiguo.* Wild One. The little creature latched onto him, becoming his shadow everywhere he went, until early one evening Uiguo stretched its nearly healed wings and flapped into a boiling stew pot. She never forgot the sound of the little creature hitting the pot, or the hollow ache in her stomach afterward—both for losing Uiguo and their dinner.

"Will we reach Lumath tonight?" asked Eken, as their Gray Cloak guide set a grueling pace.

"I doubt it. Besides, we'll need rest before tackling Lumath's summit."

They descended from the hills just as a steady drizzle of rain fell, finding themselves once again in a forest, this one sparse. Little underbrush hindered their way, though Col slowed their progress.

"Something's soured my stomach," he'd groan, clutching his middle and stepping off the path.

Still, reasoned Aurelia, *endurance finishes what haste abandons* as her father often said, and at last Daphne announced, "We're here."

She led them into a series of gullies and to a shallow cave. The shelter was welcome; drizzle had turned downpour.

"What's this cave called?" asked Eken, ever curious, his mood rarely dampened by a little rain.

"Don't think it has a name." Daphne shrugged. "Or any significance. Simply a welcome relief I discovered recently."

Though its opening was larger than Belanor's Cave, the space inside was small, proving to be more of a hollowed-out cleft in the rock than an actual cave. They huddled close, hugging its back wall, as water poured over the rock's lip, mud splattering. Before long, a giant puddle had formed and its muddy water lapped at their feet. Aurelia pulled her legs in close, tucking them under.

"Fine shelter," grumbled Col, "for anyone fond of mud."

Chapter Sixteen
Welcome to Lumath

The rain tapered off during the night. By the scant moonlight peeking into the cave, Aurelia could make out Eken and Daphne's forms, leaning back-to-back, fast asleep, Eken's heavy snores deafening in the tight space.

Col was gone.

She slipped on her cloak and stepped outside, tiptoeing around the mud puddle.

Moonlight illuminated the gully, but no Col.

Night sounds assaulted her senses. A screech, a hoot, clicking, growling, nocturnal animals awake and active. *Is it safe?* she wondered. *What predators roam the gullies?* She waited. Patient. Listening. Adjusting to the world around her. A light fog permeated the night and a gentle breeze rustled her hair, lifting the edges of her cloak.

Where are you Col?

Footfall ahead.

Her own steps light as she chased the noise through the gully and into the next. Here, six connected gullies fanned out in every direction. She caught a flash of movement, a wave of blond hair.

Col.

She crept forward, staying low behind rocks and trees, wanting to see but not be seen.

What's he doing sneaking around?

She lost sight of him. Peeked around a boulder. Brushed aside a snaggle of vines thick with berries.

Nothing.

Where is he?

"Hey."

She shrieked and jumped, a desperate thought of how foolish to be out here, utterly defenseless. But it was only Col, grimacing, his stomach cradled in his arms.

"What are you creeping around for?" he grunted.

"I ... uh, couldn't sleep." She realized she'd misjudged the situation, thinking fast, "And then you weren't in the cave, so I came out to find you."

"Yeah, well, you found me. And no, still not doing the best. Couldn't sleep with these cramps. Didn't know that was a crime," he finished sulkily.

"I'm sorry, I misread things."

She could have crawled under a rock. He'd accompanied her from Chelam, had been nothing but loyal, and she returned his affection with suspicion. She was glad of the cloud passing over the moon; her face burned red.

"I know!" She brightened. "There's got to be something out here for a tea, to help you feel better." She peered up and down the gully for inspiration.

"How about those?" he asked, pointing to a clump of bresha ferns.

"Good thinking," she said, surprised to see them growing in the rocky gully, "but no, you'd be even worse off if you ingested that."

"My mother was horribly sick when I was young." His eyes wandered, recalling an old memory. "Stomach cramps, couldn't keep anything down for days. She'd grown so weak, father feared for her. I can still remember the smell of that awful drink the healer forced down her throat and the tears my mother cried. I screamed at him to stop, but Koram led me away and told me to hush. Said to let the healer work, he knew what he was doing. He called the tea something then, what was that ..." He snapped his fingers. "Pepper tea."

"Why didn't I think of that?!" Aurelia smacked her forehead. "Of course, pepper tea."

"Like the spice?"

"Actually, no, but a funny name for a tea. I doubt the plant grows in these gullies. The forest should though. Let me go look, stay here!"

She dashed off, eager to redeem her attitude toward him. If she could help ease his pain, she'd feel better.

The forest proved a prolific source. She easily spotted the plant's telltale yellow-tipped leaves and white flower, plucking enough leaves to make tea for Col and a dozen more like him.

A sound startled her—a rustling in the trees, perhaps a whispered voice. Or so she imagined.

She froze, scanned the trees. A deer bounded past. She let out a thin, shaky laugh at being spooked so easily, and realizing she'd gathered more than enough pepper tea leaves, made her way back to Col.

It wasn't a chilly night, but the fire was comforting and necessary to boil the flowers and steep the tea. Stoking the fire woke the others, who sleepily crawled near, huddling around the flames. Aurelia studied her friends as they stared mesmerized into the fire.

Was it really just two days ago Father and I worked the harvest?

"I think you've stirred that tea to death," remarked Daphne dryly.

A small smile from Aurelia as she blinked back a tear—the homesickness bit deep. She added a touch of honey from a bottle in her pack as pepper tea was awfully bitter without a little help.

Eken wrinkled his nose. "What's that smell?"

"Pepper tea." She poured a cup. "For Col."

On cue, he groaned, bent nearly double.

"Drink this," she said, his smile grateful in response and more gentle than usual.

As he took the cup, his fingers curled over hers, his touch less possessive, stripped of any claim. Her heart skipped a beat.

Can two days change a man?

When his eyes lifted and met hers, it was the same look she'd seen many times: in the fields, at the festival dance, in the village square, over a game of Ji at the Plow & Lantern. His touch might feel different, but it was clear his intentions hadn't changed.

Why don't I feel the same?

When she looked away, it wasn't his face she saw, but Magnus. She sighed. *I don't even know the man. And I ran from him!* Yet Col was here, beside her, his feelings clear. She peeked at him as he slurped the hot tea with a grimace. Slurped again, then a large gulp. Too much. An *ouch* as it burned going down.

He noticed her watching, and in that moment, in his pain, he was more vulnerable. *Less cocky*, she thought. She could like this Col.

Eken cleared his throat. "What's the plan? More sleep tonight?" as he stifled a yawn.

"The sooner we make it to Lumath, the sooner we'll be safe. And a healer there could help Col."

"I like the sound of that," said Col.

"It's settled then. Col, finish your delightful tea," said Daphne. The Dorakian grimaced as he took another swallow of the bitter brew. "Let's put out the fire and get on with it."

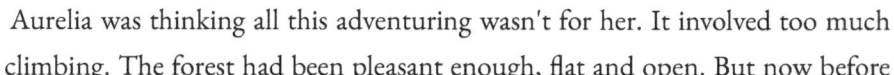

Aurelia was thinking all this adventuring wasn't for her. It involved too much climbing. The forest had been pleasant enough, flat and open. But now before them lay another steep hill, hemmed in by even steeper, towering hills and a volcanic cone. It wasn't the Tol, but it was close enough.

"We're almost there," said Daphne. "At the top is Leaping Death, and once we're through that—Lumath!"

She bounded ahead, Aurelia marveling at her energy. There was no choice but to keep up. At least there were no rocks or boulders to climb on this hill. Huffing and puffing, the three Dorakians reached the summit, only for Daphne to push on, into a thicket crowning the hill's summit.

"Watch for thorns," she warned.

"Ouch!" Eken stuck a thumb in his mouth as a spot of blood welled up. "These aren't thorns, they're daggers!"

"What'd I say, Eken!" laughed Daphne, with practiced ease pushing aside a vine prickling with thorns.

Beyond the thicket, a thundering waterfall cascaded over a sheer cliff face, before plummeting into a chasm below. Impregnable walls of rock rose steeply to either side of the waterfall. Aurelia couldn't see any way past. *A dead end?* She stepped carefully to the chasm edge, peered into its depths. A refreshing mist wet her skin, but there was no way down.

With a playful smile and a finger to her lips, Daphne took a leaping run into the waterfall. Aurelia shrieked, lunged to snatch her friend from certain death, but she was too late.

Daphne was gone.

A knot formed in her stomach. *Daphne?* she cried out in her mind.

It's okay, covenant friend. I'm here.

She sagged to the ground, relieved, but more than a little angry.

Next time, warn me. And you owe me an explanation about ... this ... this mind thing.

She sensed her friend's smile.

Staring into the curtain of water, Eken could just make out a form on the other side. "She's okay!"

"Come on!" Daphne called, "But don't leap short!"

Her outline disappeared. Wherever she was going, she wouldn't wait long.

Eken took a few steps back, shrugged, grinned, and with a running head start and a whoop that was part delight, part fear, leapt into the waterfall.

He appeared safe on the other side, a hazy outline, before he too was gone.

Aurelia took a deep breath. *This is crazy!* She ran, jumped, the breath knocked from her as a sheet of ice-cold water pummeled her. A jarring landing on the other side, but she was safely through as Col followed moments later. She stood, brushing off her knees, *that'll leave a bruise*, and shaking off clinging droplets.

Daphne welcomed them with a lopsided grin.

"And that, my friends, was Leaping Death! Well done. We're almost there now."

The Dorakians found themselves disappointed on the other side of Leaping Death, greeted by a small grassy knoll with another sheer cliff rising at its back. They'd expected more. But Daphne led them over the knoll to an opening tucked in the cliff face, and what lay beyond proved more enchanting than anything they'd ever seen.

A garden oasis.

No one cultivated it; rather, it grew wild, or so Aurelia thought until recognizing signs of human hands discreetly guiding the wildness.

Wildflowers grew thick along the path that wound its way through the garden. A babbling stream meandered by its side, water droplets dancing on pebbles, notes of wild laughter in their wake, drifting lazily to her ears.

And oh, the fruit that dangled from every branch, bush and vine! An astounding variety of apples, damsons, blackberries, chockberries, sloes, grapes of every imaginable color and size, pears, melons and oranges, and other varieties unfamiliar to her. An abundance of butterflies and birds fluttered among the flora.

There were other creatures too: mountain squirrels dashing, whisper-hares loping, toads hopping and hedgehogs plodding. But most of all there were frits.

Dozens upon dozens of them. Though these frits were unusually calm, resting quietly beneath the branches, their twitching fingers at peace and their typical nervous tittering replaced by slow whuffling snorts.

The explosion of life and color in every direction took Aurelia's breath away, while Daphne laughed in delight at the wonder on her friend's face.

"Isn't it magical?" She whispered in Aurelia's ear, with a quick hug before bounding off to pluck a pear from the closest tree. She bit happily into it, juice leaking down her chin.

"Oh!" she cried, throwing her hands up in ecstasy. "How I've missed you, pears of Lumath!" With a contented sigh, she plopped down on a rough-hewn bench beside the stream.

For once, Eken was stunned to silence, but only for a moment, before bouncing between the trees and bushes, exclaiming with every new sight, "Oh my! Oh my!" while plucking oranges and apples and strawberries, stuffing his pack full.

"No need to hoard Eken! There's plenty," shouted Daphne with a laugh.

Col's response was far more subdued, though he was no less awed by the garden than his friends. He meandered through the garden, touching this tree or that plant, examining the fruits, smiling at the antics of the animals, soaking up the sun and reveling in all the garden offered.

Aurelia sucked in such a deep lungful of air she thought she might burst. Even the air felt fresher, the sunlight a little more comforting, and the clouds overhead seemed carved into soft, perfect shapes.

Contented, she basked in the happiness of her friends and the garden's beauty. Strolled the path for a moment, surprised but delighted by the tightly furled blooms that opened and bent towards her as she passed. She knelt at the stream, allowing its flow to pass refreshingly between her fingers; she danced from tree to tree, studying each fruit she passed.

It was all perfect.

Then she saw it.

A cluster of chockberries. Gleaming dark blue.

Everyone knew a perfect cluster of chockberries was an elusive thing, ripening so fast they usually skipped that phase altogether, turning from sour to rotten overnight. Despite this, Dorakians still planted chockberry vines—pursuing perfection—though at best, its fruit was tolerable. But there was something about the taste that always left her wanting more. A yearning for what they could be.

She plucked a cluster, considering for a moment whether eating one would ruin Lumath's spell. Surely its perfection couldn't reach as far as chockberries ... could it?

She broke off a single berry and popped it in her mouth.

Exquisite.

It was summertime and festivals, warm hugs, campfires at night and dances with friends, the comfort of home and family all at once.

She sighed and took a seat beside her friend, staring wistfully at the berry cluster.

"Why didn't you tell me about this place?"

"I didn't want to spoil it. And it's ... a tough place to explain."

"It's paradise!" gushed Aurelia.

Paradise it was, even setting the two Dorakian men at ease as they laughed over a shared moment, picking fruit side by side, loading their packs.

"Lumath," Daphne's voice breathless with excitement, "I've known nothing like it. The joy it brings. Just wait till you see our homes, every bit as enchanting."

"Excited to see your people?"

"Yes! And introduce them to my new covenant friend."

They linked arms and sat in contented silence for a time. Until Aurelia, pensive, "Do we ever have to leave?"

"This place ... it will change you." Daphne spoke slowly, weighing her words, explaining Lumath never easy. "There's an old magic here. Deep in the land. More powerful than any of our bindings. Some say Lumath was here long before we were. This garden. Perhaps the world started here."

She paused in the telling, but Aurelia felt no need to rush her. There couldn't be any sense of urgency, not here. So she waited, losing track of how long, but the passing of time only pleasant, removing her shoes and digging her toes into the grass. It was green, thick, slightly warm and perfectly damp, like a fine morning dew. A sweet scent floated along on the breeze. She puzzled at it before realizing it was simply the abundance of fruit in the garden, a scent so perfectly sweet, you got a little taste every time you breathed in. Not too thick. Not too overwhelming. Just right.

Daphne picked up her telling as if she'd never paused. "And for a time, what you're feeling, it's all you'll feel. And with it, that desire to never leave." Another pause, so long this time Aurelia suspected she was done, but it was only another pause as there was something about Lumath that made one take their time. "You'll feel whole, content to stay forever. It happens every time I'm here. I always imagine I'll never leave. But then ... I do. And it's okay. I realize I'm not meant to stay. Not yet. I have too much to give ... out there." Finishing the telling, her voice took on a wistful quality, as if she must convince herself again that leaving would be the right choice.

"Your people, do they live here permanently?"

"Only those who've finished their journey. Most stay a short time before moving on."

Aurelia doubted she would ever feel like moving on. Not the way she felt right then. She could think of no better way to pass the time than to sit right there in that garden for moon cycles to come.

She sensed too the land's magic Daphne spoke of. Though she'd never felt such a thing before, she was certain she felt it now.

"The magic. I can feel it. Coursing through the land."

Daphne's eyes widened, appraising her friend. "I've never heard of an outsider who can feel it, not that many come here. We call it Sensing. What does it feel like to you?"

"I don't know. Like a presence here with us? Warmth, light. Coming from the land. It's odd, feels a little ... fuzzy." She grinned sheepishly at the description. "The magic here is stunning. And those flowers too—the way they leaned towards me and bloomed at just the moment I passed by. Spectacular."

Daphne's eyes jerked toward her. "They what?"

"The flowers," she answered, a little alarmed, *did I do something wrong?* "they uh, bloomed. When I walked by."

"I've never heard of that happening. To anyone here." Daphne's eyes widened, wondering. "The council didn't tell me to expect that."

"What exactly did they tell you?"

"That you weren't all you appeared to be. Whatever that means. They love their mysterious phrases as much as they love anything. I'm determined not to be like that, no matter how long I've been an Honored One."

She wondered at that—*not all she appeared to be?*—and said, "What else?"

"Let's see, they uh ... there's always the prophecy they repeat when they talk about you. Seems you're connected to it."

"My life is changing so quickly." Aurelia laid her head on her friend's shoulder. "I think if it weren't for you and the calm here, I'd feel lost. And now there's a prophecy?"

Daphne's face drained to a strange pale hue. "Let me see if I can get this right ..."

Her eyes rolled behind her eyelids as she intoned:

"He who was Light awakens to Night, exiled from the hearth that once held him.
Rise, Storm Grazer, leave all you hold dear;
Bloom, Flower of Lies, lest you perish in the fading sun;
Stand, Day-Son, your shadow brings ruin and gloom;
Seek, Bookkeeper, what memory dares not name;
For true to each other the Four must remain, lest darkness consume all that is known."

She slumped forward, sweat glistening her brow. Her eyes refocused and she searched Aurelia's face, a question on her lips, "Did I ...?"

Aurelia gulped, nodded. "What was that?"

"A trance. It happens when my people speak the Storm Grazer Prophecy. Don't know why."

"Storm Grazer?"

"It's said the Storm Grazer will be one who rides the storm clouds and holds lightning in hand. My people pass the prophecy down from generation to generation, though I don't think they understand its truths, shrouded in mystery and lost to time as it is."

"The last phrase, about the four remaining true, Ophel said that very thing back home, before we left." Aurelia's voice rose an octave, her eyes widening. "Was she talking about us?"

Daphne shrugged, her eyes uncertain. "Maybe. Maybe not. Hard to know when it comes to Ophel and anything she says."

"But if it is us, what can it mean? True to each other the four must remain?" Her voice trembled. "To avoid darkness consuming ..."

"Lumath is no place for fear, so enough about prophecies!"

And seizing her hand, Daphne dragged her through the garden to marvel at one sight or another, until soon Lumath's wonder had dimmed her fear, though the prophecy lingered like a thorn beneath the skin.

Eken and Col rejoined them, their packs overflowing.

"I'm feeling much better," Col announced, his ruddy complexion regained.

"Even the fruit works wonders," marveled Aurelia. "What else are you keeping secret from us, covenant friend?" she teased.

"Let me show you!"

Daphne led them deeper down the garden path, stopping occasionally to point out a tasty fruit, a flowering tree, or a pair of waterfalls marvelously constructed by human hands though not out of place in Lumath's wild beauty.

They weren't alone now, Lumath residents wandering the garden too. Gray Cloaks, or Fiadha, as Daphne called her people, wearing simple tunics and trousers and bearing no stones. But here and there an Honored One, with the heavy gray cloak and the embedded stone. These greeted Daphne and her guests with a solemn bow.

"Don't worry, they're not all like this," she assured her friends after the latest dour greeting. Moments later, shouts of *Daphne!* proved her right as a trio of children bowled into her, knocking her to the ground with squeals of laughter. Accompanying the children were a pair of gray-haired adults, whose joy at reuniting with Daphne was no less enthusiastic and real.

When they reached the garden's end, Aurelia was sorry to see it go. A meadow stretched far beyond the garden, thick with a swaying sea of grass. The wind carried the sound of blade rasping against blade. Color abounded here too. Blue and yellow wildflowers strewn across the meadow, their scent tickling the nose. Massive oak trees, eons old, their height dizzying to the eye, dotted the landscape, giving sporadic shade in the meadow; while towering cliffs of gray and brown and black hemmed it all in; and the sky above bluer and brighter than any sky she ever saw.

Daphne spread wide her arms and spun in giddy circles, tossing her head back to the sky with a resounding "Welcome to Lumath!"

Chapter Seventeen
Cutting Off Her Scream

This is Lumath? wondered Aurelia. *Grass and trees?*

Nearby Gray Cloaks laughed; winked knowingly at their children.

A little girl took her by the hand.

"Look closer!"

The girl giggled as she towed a puzzled Aurelia into the meadow. They plunged through grass neck high, the *whisp whisp* rustle of blades rushing past, though they never cut, the grass too fine, too delicate. The girl released her hand and disappeared from view. Aurelia came to a jarring stop, off-balance, dizzyingly short of breath, peering through the meadow grass, puzzled by the vanishing act. Then she saw the sunken path, and a wooden door at its end. The girl, her hand at the door, winked, with a mischievous giggle, and vanished inside.

And it wasn't just one path, realized Aurelia, but dozens and dozens of them. She saw them now, the furrows in the grass where paths tangled, criss-crossing and intersecting, this way and that.

Eken watched Aurelia's head dip from view. "They live underground?"

"But not just underground—look!" Daphne pointed to a nearby tree.

It was a giant, dwarfing the tallest Chelam boasted, though nothing more than that at first glance, until closer inspection revealed surprising details. The tree held dozens of tiny houses, square, round, octagonal, tucked in and among the enormous branches, camouflaged by leaves.

"It's amazing!" exclaimed Eken.

The days following their introduction to Lumath provided both rest and excitement for the Dorakians. While the Fiadha, especially the Honored Ones, proved rather reserved as a whole, they welcomed their new guests. Each night, a new host welcomed them to their table. The food was plentiful, fresh and delicious; the garden's bounty a feast for eye and stomach.

They learned the Fiadha called the underground dwellings *Lowers* and the tree-houses *Uppers*, each a marvel in their own right, built to take advantage of the natural surroundings.

The Lowers used protruding roots as hooks for a cloak, or for hanging cups and pans in the dining area. Large rocks became tables for mealtime. Smaller ones jutting from clay walls served as shelving. Underground streams were a source of water and a place to rest and reflect.

The Uppers used leaves for bedding, smaller branches for hooks and shelves, and the widest of branches as natural hammocks for rest; while vines served as a pulley system to lift humans, food or other resources to their homes.

Aurelia couldn't quite decide whether she preferred Lowers or Uppers. She relished her time in both.

The Lowers were cool, quiet. Though worried at first she'd feel claustrophobic, the rooms instead felt cozy, their diminutive size reminding her of home. One wall always faced up and out, with windows allowing for natural light and ventilation. Somehow it was never dusty in a Lower, a result of the soil's composition she was told.

The Uppers were breathtaking. From the first exhilarating rush as a pulley hoisted her at break-neck speed towards the top, to the expansive views across the meadow, the Uppers never ceased to delight.

As sunfall approached, she set her foot nervously into the cupped seat of a vine swing for the first time.

"Grab tight here, like this, and give it a sharp tug when you're ready," a young Gray Cloak boy advised her. "I'll be with you all the way up."

To prove his point, he stepped into a swing beside her and grabbed hold of the vine with one hand, though his grip looked loose for Aurelia's taste and he hung halfway out with practiced ease.

She wrapped her arms around the vine, a full-bodied cling, squeezed her eyes shut and gave the vine a gentle tug.

Nothing happened.

She opened one eye, and the boy laughed, though it was good-natured. "A little harder."

Her body tensed as she gave the vine a sharp tug. This time it worked. Too well. An unseen force jerked her up, and she shrieked, clinging desperately to the vine, a rush of wind buffeting her as she soared up, up and up.

She remembered a childhood dare, scaling the Great Hall, believing then its height something to marvel at, sitting on its rooftop, gazing over Chelam's rooftops and across orchard and field.

But when she willed her eyes open, she realized how laughable that thought was now. This was a height like nothing she'd experienced before. Easily three times that of the Great Hall. When the ride ended, she stepped onto a platform crafted from branches, the panoramic view both dizzying and exhilarating all at once. She clung to a branch, willing herself not to look down, soaking in the sunfall casting shadowed orange hues across the meadow, the crisscrossing paths, and the garden wild.

She didn't miss another sunfall while in Lumath.

A sunfall in an Upper was unlike any other, for even the sun fell below the horizon in brighter colors there. From the treetops, one could nearly see over Lumath's outer cliff walls, though why anyone would care to view the dull world outside Lumath was beyond her.

Aurelia saw little of Daphne in those first days, who was too busy re-acquainting herself with old friends. When they did cross paths, she'd breath a heart-felt apology, all the while hopping anxiously from one foot to another and glancing frequently across the meadow. Aurelia assured her all was fine, though the lack of attention stung. Thanking her for understanding, Daphne would give a quick hug, a kiss on the cheek and bound across the meadow, leaving Aurelia to stare wistfully after, wondering what she'd done to lose her friend.

She would have sought out Eken, but he'd abandoned her as well. At first, he'd only slept, woke to eat, and slept some more, reminding her that he needed a solid night's rest to be at his best and that their adventures had deprived him of said rest since leaving Chelam.

His story changed when he discovered Lumath had a library. Sleep no longer mattered, and from that moment on he spent his days nose-buried in a book.

That left Col.

He wouldn't have been her first choice, but curiosity about all things Lumath filled Aurelia's waking and dreaming, and he proved a willing companion. Together they explored the wonders of Lumath—garden and meadow paths, dug-out nooks of the Lowers, and the many-branched splendors of the Uppers.

He joined her at every sunfall, their conversation often of Dorak, reminiscing of childhood memories and dreaming of the future. Following their second sunfall together, they agreed to meet the next morning for a sunrise; from that moment onward, her days began and ended with Col.

"What's the plan today, Aurelia?"

There was a distinct gleam in his eyes, bright, cheerful, and she liked it. He smiled more often, laughed more frequently—all without his usual sarcasm—and in conversation he was more vulnerable than she'd thought possible.

He wasn't perfect. More than once she caught a snide remark about Eken, or mocking an uptight Gray Cloak, but he was quicker to apologize and admit it was mean-spirited. Perhaps it was Lumath's air, but she couldn't quite remember why in Chelam she'd hesitated.

You should wed, build a life with a man who'll protect you. Her father's words pierced her muddled thoughts.

She pictured them back in Chelam, after all this excitement over Gray Cloaks and Ka and prophecies blew over. Her and Col. Together. It made sense somehow, two Dorakians from the same village.

Could he become the man I hope exists beneath the swagger?

Early one morning she caught herself stealing glances, his profile back-lit by morning rays, the beginnings of a sunrise peaking over the treetops.

On the eighth day of their stay, Aurelia decided she needed a few moments alone. It had been another day of exploration with Col, but begging for some time off, he reluctantly agreed. Her hand lingered briefly on his before she slipped away.

As she strolled through the garden wilds in the evening's cool, his voice and face filled her thoughts. She marveled at the strength of her affection for him. *Maybe I need a few days away.* But no, she wanted more of him and knew he felt the same.

Most of all, she cherished the way he looked at her now. Different from before, when he'd seen her as an object, a thing to possess and control. The way that Jusel looked at Col's mother.

But now?

Now his eyes bore a genuine sense of caring for how she felt and what she thought. She wasn't oblivious to his faults. He still had a sharp tongue, but lately he would catch himself.

Although he hadn't asked since leaving Chelam, she knew his opinion on the matter of *them* hadn't changed. He'd asked a hundred times before, every eight-day in Chelam and at every Harvest Festival dance, patient, waiting for her to be ready. And now, for the first time, *yes* felt possible.

A twinge of doubt flickered, but she pushed it down. Buried it deep. It was time, she knew it was. *Right?* After all, she'd taken his hand at the Harvest Festival dance.

She's embarrassed to marry him, it's obvious his height bothers her. The gossiper Edme's words rang in her ears. *It's clear he'll return to his first love—the Ka.*

Aurelia's jaw tightened, fist clenched. Outside Lumath, a peal of thunder rolled. *I could show them! One word quiets all their whispers. All of Chelam would see me differently then.*

Lost in thought, she bumped into a door, looked up, surprised to find herself outside the library. She smiled, delighted. *What good timing!* She'd talk with Eken and unburden her soul, certain he'd be excited for her.

The largest of all the Lowers housed the library, divided into multiple rooms, books filling every nook and cranny, jammed and piled high everywhere one looked, an uncountable horde. A scholar's dream. Personally, Aurelia found it a little overwhelming and more than a little stuffy.

Don't mind a good read, but not like this.

Nearly walking right by him, she discovered Eken tucked in the back, hidden behind books stacked as tall as summer amaranth. Piles of ancient manuscripts and other books cluttered the floor, his face buried deep in an impressively large tome, spectacles wedged snug to his face and his mouth hung open as he read.

When she pulled a chair close, its legs scraped across the floor, jarring in the silence, but he remained oblivious to her presence. She peeked at the title written on the book's spine: *History of the Kingdom, Volume II.*

Booorrrring, she thought to herself and snorted.

The noise snapped Eken's focus, and he glanced up, his eyes blank, a glassy stare unreadable behind the spectacles. He didn't seem to recognize her, didn't even flinch, and though she waved her hand in his face he returned trance-like to his reading.

"Eken."

No answer.

"EKEN."

Louder this time, demanding. Still no answer. *This is ridiculous!* She ripped the book from his hands and tossed it on a nearby pile.

"Hey wait! I was ..." he blinked repeatedly. Bits of whiskery hair dotted his chin and cheeks, a troublesome sign as he made a point to shave daily what he referred to as *my shame*—a patchy, wispy man-child beard.

Aurelia grabbed him by the shoulders and shook him. Hard.

"No need for that!" he cried out as the fog lifted from his face. "Oh hey, Aurelia, I've been reading the most fascinating things. Did you know -"

She pressed a finger to his lips.

"Eken, whoa buddy. Have you spent all your time here? When did you last eat?" Now that she thought about it, she hadn't seen him since their third day in Lumath. "And why haven't you shaved?" she asked, then teasingly, "You look awful, you know."

"I um, uh ..." He blinked again, rapid, quick-fire succession, scrunched his nose and rubbed at his temple, before offering her a shrug. "Time seems a little blurry. What day is it?"

"It's uh ..." Aurelia thought for a moment, realized she wasn't sure. *Has it been an eight-day since we arrived in Lumath?* Time felt slippery, like it slid between her fingers when she tried to grasp it. She counted all the sunfalls and sunrises but lost track. "Let's get some fresh air."

Eken hesitated, stared longingly at the books piled high. "But I ... I didn't quite finish. Let me finish these, all I had left ..." He waved vaguely at the books.

Didn't quite finish? There were countless thousands of books in the library, he couldn't mean the piles beside him were all he had left? She laughed at the thought. "Eken Paul Kestermin Potterfeld, you are leaving this library right now even if I have to drag you out myself!"

Reluctantly, he allowed himself to be dragged away. Daylight was fast fading; the air cool compared to the library's stuffiness.

"That helps," said Eken. "I ... I, it's uh ... strange. All I wanna do is read, consume the knowledge in that library. It feels like I just got started this morning, but I'm guessing by the look on your face it's been longer?"

She shrugged. "Don't know, but I haven't seen you in four or five days, maybe more. Got a little distracted myself."

He whistled, long and low. "I can't remember the last time I've eaten or even stepped foot outside. I'm starving."

It didn't take long to find a feast in progress, deep in a Lower's bowels, where a family happily welcomed them. Three young children, wiggling and wide-eyed, made room on the stone bench they occupied, while their parents, gray haired and wrinkled—*seen their share of hunter's moons*, thought Aurelia—distributed place settings to the new arrivals.

Eken scarfed down three heaping bowlfuls of a spicy vegetable stew, four slices of melon, a cluster of chockberries, a mixed vegetable platter of cabbage, carrots and tomatoes, and a thick slice of apple pie to top it off. Two mugs of spiced wine washed it all down. Aurelia was far more moderate, enjoying a single bowl of stew and a small piece of apple pie, but then she and Col had joined regularly in meals the past several days.

With a full belly, Eken looked more like himself. They wandered companionably outside.

"What did I miss?" asked Eken.

"Let's see, Daphne's preoccupied with old friends, though that's fine with me." Her strained tone suggested otherwise. "I've had a lovely time with Col. We've grown close these past few days, and -"

"Close? With Col?" He belched. Her comment didn't sit well with the food he'd eaten. "That's the worst news I've heard this past eight-day. Not someone I'd recommend getting close to."

"Can't you be happy for me?" Her blood boiled. Thunder cracked outside Lumath. "That a man loves me and that perhaps I could say yes? You think you know what's best for me, but you didn't even hear me out. This after I saved your life dragging you away from those stupid dusty books, watched as you stuffed your fat mouth ..." She regretted the words as soon as she spoke them.

"My what!" Another belch, louder this time, with a nauseating odor. "For your information, I was quite content spending time in those books. They don't disappoint like people do."

Perhaps he hadn't intended to look so pointedly at her, but he had.

"Well, I ...!" Aurelia snorted. "I'm going to Col! At least he prefers my company over that of books!"

Holding back tears, she stormed off.

What is going on? This place was meant to be magical, different. And it was. But she didn't feel quite right. *Where's Col when I need him?* Maybe he could help sort things out.

Her feet once again carried her where she hadn't asked them. To the garden wilds, near the bench where she'd first sat and talked with Daphne about magic. A blur of blond-haired motion caught her attention.

Col. Slipping through the opening in the rock that led back out to the waterfall.

What's he doing here?

She heard his voice raised—*desperate? angry?*—and rushing through the rock-face opening, stumbled headlong into him.

"Oh Col! I -"

The words stuck in her throat as she looked over his shoulder and straight into a face she remembered too well. A face she'd seen often in her dreams.

Magnus.

And behind him, soldiers, crowding the grassy knoll that bordered the waterfall. Even as she watched, another leaped through.

Col's hand closed over her mouth, cutting off her scream.

Chapter Eighteen
The Assault on Lumath

Days earlier, in Belanor's Cave, Magnus had wondered if he'd made the right decision.

It began when a shadowy figure startled him awake. Magnus' sword was at the intruder's throat in an instant, the blade nicking the neck, a spot of blood pooling.

"Wait! It's me! It's Col." A panicked voice, a face materialized into view, matching it. "I came to warn you—they're making a run for it. What should I do?"

Magnus' instincts said to rouse the men and secure ... the prisoners? He wasn't sure what to call them. Or, instead, he could let them go and consider his debt repaid.

Perhaps there's a better play.

With his decision made, he explained his plan to Col, starting with the brightbeetles. A moment's rummaging in Bochim's pack produced a jar of glowing insects, which he stowed away in Col's pack. A word of encouragement—the man seemed hesitant at the plan—then a clasp of hands, a farewell nod, before Col stole back into the shadows.

Magnus allowed his men to sleep, knowing such luxury wouldn't come to him. He thought of Aurelia, picturing her face, her smile, the way she brushed that loose strand of hair behind her ears. Her bravery to run towards howling wolves and the cries of desperate men. The tenderness she'd shown in caring for the wounded.

He sensed her genuineness, that she was someone you could trust. He'd met few women like that in his lifetime. And there it was. The truth. *I'm smitten with her.* He knew it, couldn't deny it. That she was involved in their campaign against the Gray Cloaks was regrettable, but then war never cared which side you chose. He could only hope she'd understand the choices he made now. He was still an officer after all, with a duty to perform.

He dozed off only to be awakened by an anxious Kymn, until Magnus assured him all was well and gathered his friends round. Tobias, Kymn, Bochim, Morco, Saul. His heart stirred with affection for these men who stood with him.

"I let them go." Magnus held up a hand for silence as murmurs flooded the cave. "But only to lull them to thinking they're free of us, to track their movements, learn their plans. Col is on our side, a spy in their camp, and with the help of these," he held up a brightbeetle, "we'll follow from a safe distance." The murmurs turned to appreciation of his plan.

He was certain the brightbeetles would prove the perfect tracking tool and briefly instructed Col on their use—how Ka trackers crushed them against bark, stone, or the leaves of a low-hanging branch, leaving a bright yellow residue that marked an easy trail to follow.

He instructed Col to eat one a day. They'd cause a mild stomach ache, unpleasant, but a believable excuse for lagging behind, giving ample opportunity to smear a glowing trail the Ka could follow.

In the end, the first mark proved hardest to find. Assuming the Binder had spoken truthfully of her plans, they hunted west into the forest, in the general direction of the Capitol. After a lengthy and fruitless search, Magnus widened the perimeter, sending some north and south to skirt the hillside, while the rest continued to scour the forest.

It was an excited Morco who reported he'd found the first mark on a scraggly tree by a narrow ledge, a yellow stain smeared so thick Col must have used a handful of brightbeetles.

Once they'd found the first, following the trail was relatively easy; and when Col placed markings too far apart, signs of recent human passage aided in the search. Bochim proved his worth as a tracker, spotting a footprint in a dry creek bed, a snapped twig beside a trail, or a piece of cloth snagged by a thorn.

Entering a series of gullies late one evening, they discovered Col sitting bent-double, near the trailhead, an arm cradling his stomach.

"You didn't tell me I'd get this sick," Col's tone accusing, his face ashen, sweat beading his brow.

"How many'd you eat? I said one a day."

"Oh." Col grabbed the jar from his pack, appeared to count, before shoving the jar back inside wordlessly.

"The others near?"

"Asleep in a cave the next gully over." Col pointed south. "Daphne's taking us to a place called Lumath."

"You've done well, Col, keep marking the trail. Now go. There's no need to risk discovery."

The plan was working as well as he'd hoped. *Then what?* he wondered. A twinge of doubt nibbled at his mind, but he ignored it, remembering his Ka oath.

The soldiers retreated from the gully. Magnus posted first watch and scarcely settled in when Aurelia burst into the forest, her eyes scanning the forest floor.

His breath caught, enchanting as she was in the moonlight. If he'd not known her, he might have believed her a magical creature, leaping nimbly as she did from plant to plant, her feet light as dew upon the ground. He sensed her delight, shared secretly in her joy when she found what she sought, felt her pleasure in the simple discovery as she plucked the leaves from a white flowering plant.

The moonlight bathed her in an ethereal glow, yet she was real, right there in front of him. He fought the urge to step out from behind the concealing shrubbery, if only for the chance to see her face up close, to hear her speak and watch her lips move. Even if only for a moment.

Her gathering finished, she turned back towards the gully. Stopped, stiffened. He heard it too. One of his men, unaware of Aurelia's presence, moved through the trees.

Aurelia stared unblinking into the forest's shadows. Her stare pierced him, thrilling him. His breath caught again in his throat, and he almost wished to be discovered.

A deer crashed through the undergrowth, bounding past Aurelia. She laughed and disappeared into the gully. Magnus sighed and settled in for a long sleepless night.

The following day proved rather puzzling.

Morco had been on watch as their prey left the gully. The soldiers tracked them through the forest, halting at the wood's edge, where a steep incline rose to meet a ridge, towering cliffs and a volcanic cone forming a stunning backdrop. They waited. The slope's exposure too great a risk in broad daylight.

Time stood still for the waiting, the sun impossibly slow as it dipped towards the horizon. At dusk, they ascended the hill. A glowing mark stained a vine in the thorny thicket, but then, nothing. Only a chasm, sheer-cliff walls and a cascading waterfall.

The markings had clearly led them here. *Is it a trick?* Had the others discovered Col's ploy? Or how do four people pass this way and simply disappear?

Magnus studied the waterfall, intuition telling him the answer lay within it.

Securing Kymn by a length of rope, they lowered him deep into the chasm.

"Nothing," he said upon his return to the surface, "only deeper into darkness and mist."

"Magnus, over here." Bochim knelt at the chasm edge, tracing a footprint in the moss growing there. "This isn't ours."

Magnus studied the print. Glanced at the waterfall. Back down to the footprint. A thought formed, planted and took hold.

"Oh, no you don't." Tobias shook his head, recognizing the gleam in his friend's eye. "Absolutely not. Through? You don't know if that's safe."

"Then secure me to a rope with enough play in it," said Magnus. "If there's no through, I'll count on you to keep me from falling. I don't see any other way. It has to be through. They didn't just disappear."

Though his men volunteered to take the leap, Magnus insisted it was his idea, his risk to take.

"Is this for the Ka? For Saan?" asked Tobias, tugging a knotted rope tight around Magnus' waist. "Or for her?"

Wondering at his own stupidity, Magnus took a running start and leapt towards the waterfall. For a breathless moment, the chasm grasped at his flailing feet, and Magnus pictured his men failing to hold his free-falling weight, rope searing through their fingers as he plunged to his death.

Then he was through—a chilling burst of water—but he was through.

The days following their discovery were as monotonous as winter field plantings back home.

They'd returned to the forest, while Magnus sent Bochim to report to Drael.

Only a slew of arriving or departing Gray Cloak interrupted their boredom. It began as a trickle, a lone Gray Cloak here or there, ascending the hill and entering the ridgeline thicket. But then larger companies began arriving daily. Despite the fact that only a few wore the actual gray cloak, it was enough to convince the waiting men that the hidden village was a hotbed of seditious activity.

While waiting for reinforcements, both Veyra and Saul continued to heal, rest and bresha working wonders. It was the sixth day of their watch as Magnus took his shift on sentry duty when Veyra approached him.

"Mind if I join you?" she asked.

He nodded, studying her as she sat gingerly, favoring her scarred leg. Her right arm hung limp. *Will she lift a sword in battle again?* he wondered. White and pink scar tissue—vivid, thick, crusted—lined her leg and arm.

"I wanted to thank you," she said. "I haven't done so properly, and I understand I owe you my life."

"It was nothing." Magnus waved a dismissive hand. "Anyone would have done the same."

"I know Ka policy, and Tobias tells me others that day wished to end my life." She stared frankly. "You chose otherwise."

"I, um ..." He cleared his throat. "Tobias talks too much."

"He also tells me there were others, not Ka, who aided me. The four we've tracked here? A Gray Cloak, who helped heal me?"

Magnus nodded absentmindedly, his thoughts on Daphne ... and Aurelia.

"The story gets stranger, I'm told. That you vowed an oath of protection before realizing her identity. Do you plan to keep your vow?"

He wondered at her impudence in asking such a thing. "Are you always this bold?"

"I'm sorry," Veyra responded, her face flaming red. "My parents, they uh ... often tell me I speak when I shouldn't and ask questions when I shouldn't."

"Should I regret saving your life?" asked Magnus teasingly. Her smile reached her eyes, pale green eyes Magnus noticed for the first time. Eyes that reminded him of home. She bore the look of his people, the Plainsfolk. "Where's home?"

"Perinith."

"Really? I thought the women there were, uh ..." He stopped, embarrassed, his turn for his cheeks to flame red. *How do I say this nicely?* He plunged ahead. "Hairy."

"How do you know I'm not?" She asked with a laugh. "I wasn't born Perinithian. My parents moved to the island when I was a child, but they hail from the Plains. Just outside the Capitol. Though I was born a Plainswoman, I never knew it. Perinith is my home."

"You carry the look of our women." Magnus stood and stretched. He'd been sitting too long watching the ridgeline. "Those green eyes. I was born and raised on the Plains, and lived there until the famine."

"Your family ... wife?" she asked, searching.

"No wife. Only a father and sisters. My mother died during the famine."

"I'm sorry." She rested a sympathetic hand on Magnus' arm. "I've heard stories of famine hardships, but Perinith insulated us. The sea provides what we need, as do the mines and the wealth of our people."

"Why Perinith?" asked Magnus, recalling geography lessons from his childhood, vague details about the far northern island known as Perinith. "A long way from the Plains."

"It is. A long, long way."

Veyra stepped to the edge of the treeline her gaze focused north. Perhaps towards Perinith. Towards home. For a time, she stood that way, pensive, silent. Magnus looked away, knowing her heartache.

"Did you know it freezes over?" She glanced back. He shook his head. "It's an ice-crusted wasteland nine months of the year. Breathtaking actually. Serene. Snow and ice carpeting every direction. You should see the light. The way it dances across the frozen barrens. Sunfalls are spectacular."

Magnus marveled at the thought. He'd never seen snow except on distant Tol peaks, wanted to ask what it felt like, but he waited, silent, as she continued.

"My parents claim a wandering peddler filled their minds with stories of Perinith. Snow drifts taller than a home's chimney, sleigh rides gliding across the tundra, giant white bears as numerous as the stars, the best spiced wine you'll ever try—they fell in love with it from a distance and knew they had to live there." She laughed wistfully. "No story is ever that simple. Truth is, my parents got mixed up in trouble back home and had no choice but to leave. And go far, far away."

She abruptly stopped in her telling. "I've taken up too much of your time, droning on about home, my parents ..."

"Not at all!" protested Magnus.

"It's okay," she laughed. "I know when men are just being polite." She rested a hand lightly on his arm. "Just wanted to say thank you. I owe you my life."

She smiled, those green eyes sparkling, and left him there, despite his continued protests. He regretted her leaving. She reminded him so much of home with those green Plainswoman eyes. The familiar ache settled in his gut.

Bochim returned with advance scouts, the regiment close behind. And so it was, eight days after first discovering Lumath, Magnus leaped back through the waterfall, surprising Col by his sudden appearance as if the Dorakian had forgotten all about the trail of markings he'd left behind.

"No. NO! You can't be here. It's not what we thought. Please just give me some time ..."

And then Aurelia burst onto the scene. She'd locked eyes with Magnus, the look of betrayal as raw as the guilt Magnus felt, and it broke his heart.

What have I done?

She struggled against Col as he tried to soothe her, eventually slumping in his arms, with only the occasional whimper. He dragged her clear of the rock-face opening as Ka soldiers streamed past, intruders in the garden wild, steel and leather carving through color and bloom.

The assault on Lumath had begun.

Chapter Nineteen
Lumath Shares Its Pain

Aurelia blinked in the harsh sunlight.

Where am I?

Gray Cloaks huddled nearby, while Ka soldiers kept a watchful eye.

The prisoners were a pitiful lot: old, gray-haired men and women, hard, pitted, emotionless faces, some sporting fresh bruises; and children, soft cheeks streaked with tears. Some slept fitfully, but most simply stared off into the distance, their skin and clothes marred with gray and black stains. Aurelia wondered why until she noticed her own clothes, her own hands and arms, realized she too was stained gray and black. She scrubbed at her arm, smearing a thin layer of ash.

She struggled to her feet, wobbling unsteadily, dizzy, before finding her balance. Once she felt confident she wouldn't fall, she took in her surroundings and immediately wished she hadn't.

Where once Lumath boasted a lush meadow with towering trees, now lay a smoldering wasteland, mounds of ash remnants of once giant trees. A clump or two of grass remained, testament to fire's random destruction. They waved in the breeze, foolishly so, as if daring the fire to try again, the only other survivor a lone tree, and though its trunk was streaked black, its leaves and branches gave shade to the soldiers sheltering beneath it.

Aurelia wept bitter tears.

She had known sorrow before. Never desecration.

The ash of Lumath bore silent witness.

She remembered Col restraining her as soldiers leapt through the waterfall. Remembered cries of terror and pleas for mercy echoing across Lumath.

Though Col consoled her, she was inconsolable. Where moments before she had wanted nothing more than his touch, now it disgusted her. He held her tight, but she fought back.

Col, what have you done?

Worn out, she stopped resisting, allowing time for tears. When Col relaxed his grip, she threw her weight against him, breaking free. He stumbled back and she lashed out with a punch. It connected with a loud crack, his nose spurting blood. He cried out. For good measure, she kneed him, hard, in the groin. With a whimper, he sank to the ground.

Aurelia ran.

Through the opening, into the garden wild, her heart aching at the sight of a crumpled Gray Cloak body.

Down the garden wilds path, into the meadow where chaos reigned. Soldiers herded men, women and children into makeshift rings. Smoke gathered thick above a fire feeding hungrily on the meadow. Anger blazed inside her, hotter than the fire. The smoke fed skyward into a gathering storm of roiling clouds and crackling lightning. Her fury found its target—a pair of soldiers laughing as they shoved an old man forward. The man's cloak hung in charred tatters on burnt skin an angry red.

Even now, thinking back, she remembered the soldiers' eyes. Empty. Remorseless.

With a bloodcurdling scream, she launched herself at the nearest one, sent him sprawling, a noise behind her the last thing she remembered before her world went black.

Bursting from the Gray Cloak prisoners, a child fell into Aurelia's arms. The same little girl who'd first led Aurelia down the meadow paths, a happy moment, so improbable now as she stared across the ruins of Lumath.

A soldier shouted, but the girl ignored him, sobbing, clinging to Aurelia, until the soldier pulled them apart and shoved the girl back into the crowd of prisoners.

Aurelia protested, a weak croak, her throat too dry for more. Another dizzy spell, throbbing head. She blinked, breathed deep, determined not to pass out. Her hair matted on the back of her head, she gingerly touched the spot. Sticky.

"The hilt of a sword got you there," said an elderly Gray Cloak woman, "last night ..." Tears sprang to the woman's eyes.

Aurelia looked away.

"Eken!" She noticed him then, lying nearby, filthy, as if he'd slept in a hearth's ash, his tunic stained a dark red.

He moaned, eyes fluttering open. "Aurelia?"

"I'm here, Eken. I'm here." They shared tears as she held him. Unknowing, uncaring, how much time passed until eventually the tears subsided. "Daphne?"

"I ... I don't know."

Aurelia didn't want to look, didn't want to know, but she peeled back his bloody tunic, anticipating the worst. There were bruises, black and blue, but no injury to account for the blood.

"I don't understand, all this blood -"

"Not mine. A Gray Cloak." He caught his breath, grunting. "The Ka beat me senseless when I tried to stop them."

Aurelia held her friend a little closer, to comfort herself or him she didn't know. She could think of nothing to say that would help.

"I ... I'm sorry. About yesterday," he said, "before the soldiers."

"Oh, Eken, I am too! I don't know what came over me."

An angry murmur as the crowd stirred. Soldiers dragged Daphne across the scorched earth, streaks of ash staining her cloak. Tossing her at the prisoners' feet, they walked away laughing.

The stone in Daphne's forehead was gone. Blood trickled from a jagged cut. Aurelia felt for a pulse and was relieved to find one, though faint. Her friend's skin was cold and clammy.

A violent and sudden surge in the prisoners' murmuring.

Col.

It was obvious the side he'd chosen. He strode towards them refreshed, clean, perhaps he'd even bathed that morning. No bruises, no stains of ash, no gaunt look to his eyes, and walking freely.

"Traitor!" cried a Gray Cloak. "You feasted at my table twice this past eight-day!"

A boy hurled a rock but missed. A woman spat in his face. The soldiers intervened, backhanding the woman, pushing the Gray Cloaks into a tighter circle.

Col wiped the spittle from his face.

"Aurelia, I -"

"Get away from me!" she hissed. "I want nothing to do with you."

"Listen to me, you foolish girl." He grabbed her and shook her hard. "I can have you both released into my care. But if you do anything stupid, threaten soldiers or choose her ..." his eyes flicked towards Daphne, "then I can't guarantee your fate. And I can't bear to think what your father would say if I return without you. So just shut up and let me take care of you."

The harsh words stung. She wondered what she'd seen in him the past several days and how she'd been so foolish as to fall in love.

How dare he talk like that to me!

She lunged, battling dizziness, but not caring. The crown of her head connected with the nose she'd broken earlier. A dull crack. Fresh blood spurting. A ragged cheer from the prisoners.

"You ungrateful -!" With one hand, he sought to stem the blood flow, the other, he raised to strike until another hand stayed his.

"That's enough."

Col turned to glare at Magnus. For a tense moment, neither gave way until Col lowered his hand. A bitter laugh, "You can have her, she's not worth it," before stalking off.

"I'm sorry," said Magnus, his voice cracking, "for all of this ... this horror."

Despite what he'd done, she felt sorry for him, for there was something more now. A new look in his eyes. *Shame.* He couldn't meet her eyes. And something more ...

"You feel it, don't you? Daphne called it Sensing. The land's magic. The way it breathes as if alive." She touched his cheek, tentative, searching his eyes. He finally dared look at her. "You sense the pain you've caused."

"I ..."

He exhaled, a deep shuddering breath. But his eyes, haunted, didn't break from hers. He held her gaze, covered her hand with his own, trembling, before finally tearing himself away. He didn't look back.

How strange, she thought, *that Lumath shares its pain with outsiders.*

Chapter Twenty
Hack at the Roots

Magnus couldn't run far enough away, or get there fast enough.

How can I be near her? With what I've done.

And she was right—he felt it. Lumath. Its pain.

At first, he thought his shame due to Aurelia's nearness. His betrayal of her. But it went beyond that. *Must be this Sensing*, as she called it. As the night wore on, the feeling only worsened.

The world was changing too fast. First Saan. Rumors of magic. Encountering the Binders and the reality of their powers. Now Lumath and its pain.

I must speak with Drael.

"Ah, Magnus!" The commander's greeting warm as Magnus entered his tent. "A spectacular night. Masterful work tracking them here. You shall be known as Breaker of Gray Cloaks!" He winked at Magnus, beaming a wide smile, an excited clap on the back. "Do you realize what we've accomplished here tonight? A crushing blow to their warmongering."

"I wish I could agree. There are few Binders here. Few with the stone. We've terrified a bunch of women and children."

The gleam in Drael's eye dulled before he eyed Magnus with a hearty laugh. "No need for false modesty, but fair enough, let others sing your praise. I'm submitting a promotion for you."

A promotion? For what I've done here? The thought soured Magnus' gut.

"I don't want it, and I should be nearly home by now. Remember?" Hands clenched, a deep breath, holding his anger in check. "What will become of Daphne and the Dorakians with her?"

"Bah, forget them." Drael waved dismissively. "They mean nothing."

"I can't. I made a vow."

"Curse your vows!" snapped Drael. "In war—empty promises. I questioned the Binder myself. Her companions may be unwitting accomplices, but she is guilty."

"What did she confess?"

"It's what she didn't say, more than what she said." Drael awarded his junior officer with a cold glare. "So I had her stone stripped. We'll take her to the Capitol for further interrogation."

"And when they're done?"

"Your insolence grows tiresome," growled Drael. "Be glad you led us here. I've a mind to strip you of your rank and have you flogged."

"Release them to my custody," begged Magnus, "I can accompany -"

"They'll hang her when done," said Drael, ignoring Magnus' offer, "Her friends too. You're dismissed. Go celebrate with your men."

"But I -"

Drael motioned angrily, and a pair of guards escorted Magnus out.

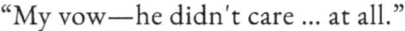

"My vow—he didn't care ... at all."

"The Binder got what she deserved." There was a distinct gleam in Kymn's eye, an ugly kind of fervor.

Magnus didn't care for it.

"How could you say that? After they rescued us?"

"It's time to pick a side." Kymn stretched a pleading hand towards his friend. "Our cause is righteous. Saan ... the valley ... what else must the Gray Cloaks do before you understand that?"

Magnus shoved away from his friend and started running.

"Wait, Magnus!"

He stumbled aimlessly through Lumath's ruins, passed soldiers celebrating, but he was in no mood to join them while the dead lay nearby silent and accusing.

Kymn's words rang in his ears—*it's time to pick a side.*

What about my vows? To the Ka. To Lavonshia. To Daphne, Aurelia, Eken and Col.

And what about home? His contract over, he could leave tonight. Leave it all behind.

The sounds of revelry faded. He glanced up to find his feet led him to the garden wilds. Flames had licked at the closest trees, only to sputter and die, leaving a line of blackened grass at the garden's edge. Plump fruits hung unblemished on tree and bush, though the bodies of fallen Gray Cloaks marred the otherwise pleasant scene.

To his surprise, Magnus felt a sense of belonging. *How can the garden welcome me?* His sense of guilt sat heavy, like a boulder resting square on his chest, threatening to crush him under its weight.

Around a bend in the garden's path, a cluster of pear trees offered shade to a cloaked figure, its back to Magnus. Though he couldn't see the face, he knew its form.

Magnus' fingers twitched at his sword, but something told him he didn't need it. Not here.

The shadowed man appeared solid, more flesh and bone than before, and he turned at the sound of Magnus' approach. A genuine smile brightened his face, and as it did, the last of the shadows fled. One could have mistaken him for Magnus' twin.

"Ah, I was hoping to find you here." The voice was decidedly human, unlike before, though lighter and more musical than Magnus' own. "I felt your nearness."

"Why are you here?" asked Magnus, relieved the man no longer terrified him, though whether he owed that to the garden's presence, or the man being flesh and blood, he wasn't sure.

"To answer the questions burning in your mind, of course. We have much to discuss. Come. Sit." He patted the bench beside him with a smile like a Tol lion.

Magnus considered bolting, without a backward glance. Away from the man, from this place, from his problems and his vows, even from Aurelia. But a moment's consideration was all it took to know he couldn't. He could never forgive himself if he did.

Eventually he sat, choosing the far end of the bench.

The predatory smile stretched wider.

"Who are you?" asked Magnus, "Why do you follow me?"

"You begin with those?" The man scoffed. "I've told you already—I am you. You are me. I'm here because we're connected."

"That's impossible." Magnus jumped to his feet, unwilling to hear such nonsense. "You can't be me."

"Fair enough. I suppose that's misleading, incomplete at best." At the man's concession, Magnus sat again. "I'm your shadow self; you can call me Sungam if you like."

"That's a clever one."

Sungam laughed then. Hearty and long, tears streaming, though it wasn't the sort of laugh that invited others to join in. He dried his tears on his cloak sleeve, a decidedly human gesture.

"My apologies. Never laughed before. That felt good." Sungam stood, and Magnus stood with him, their height identical. The once-shadow man stretched, his back, his shoulders, flexing his arms and cracking his neck side to side. "Much better."

"Are you human?" asked Magnus. "Does everyone have a shadow self?"

"Do I look human? Are you?" Sungam tried on another laugh, a harder bark of a laugh, shook his head, didn't seem to like that one. "And no, this is unique to us. Because you are the Day-Son. Don't you know sunlight casts a shadow?"

Magnus threw his arms up at Sungam's riddles. "Speak plainly!"

Sungam simply smiled and walked towards an apple tree.

There was something else different about him, and Magnus only noticed it as Sungam walked. When they'd last met, the man had glided; now, his feet touched earth.

"You're not like before. You're grounded, flesh and blood."

"You're observant. An admirable trait." Sungam studied an apple hanging low on a branch. "I do hope we can be friends. I ... have no friends."

"I can trust a friend, but are you one? Did you send the Shadow-Wolves?"

"No, not me," Sungam laughed again, a light and musical effort. He smiled, appeared to like that one. "Though I could guess who did. But that's beside the point."

He leaned in to pluck the apple, but as his fingers brushed its skin, a bright flame sparked. He jerked his hand back with a hissed *ouch,* sucking on burnt fingers, a petulant pout twisting his mouth. His gaze wandered about the garden. "Disgusting place, isn't it?"

"For you to say so makes me think we can't be friends. How could we when you're repulsed by a place I find so beautiful?"

Sungam shrugged. "If you truly knew what this garden was, you'd also find it repulsive. You're not yourself here, you know. What you feel, how you act, it's affected by this ... garden." He spat the word as if the word itself disgusted him.

Magnus' first impulse was to tell Sungam all the reasons he was wrong. But then the realization struck—Sungam spoke the truth. Magnus could sense it. *This place is affecting me.* Altering his thoughts, his opinions, so subtly he hadn't realized it until Sungam pointed it out. The question was could he trust it. Did it do so with evil intentions, or good?

"Would you?" Sungam pointed to the apple. "I do so desire one. But the garden resists me. You, though, are weak, and it takes advantage of you."

Magnus shrugged, too preoccupied with studying the apple to take offense. He'd never seen a more perfect fruit, its size robust, its sheen radiant, its deep red spotless. He'd yet to try any of Lumath's fruit and couldn't see the harm in doing so now and sharing with Sungam.

As his fingers closed around the apple, a whisper surged in his heart. A warning from the garden. Not of eating its fruit, but of plucking that apple in that moment. His grip tightened, so close to breaking it clean away. Tantalizing. Tasty. The warning grew stronger, like a fire's glow turned uncontrollable blaze. Magnus' hand and heart burned with the intensity of it.

"The garden speaks to you, doesn't it?" Sungam laid a hand on Magnus' shoulder. The touch—light, cool, comforting like that of a close friend—dispelled the warning's heat. He sighed as a wave of calm washed over, a feeling of relief that he would no longer have to choose, but could just listen to Sungam's voice. "Please. I need it. Pluck this apple for me, and I shall tell you all you wish to know. I travel as the wind; there is none to stop me. No knowledge is beyond me. I can tell you of ... your family. Your youngest sister ..." A sly look stole briefly across Sungam's face, but Magnus didn't catch it.

"My sister? What about her?" asked Magnus, his voice trembling. "Is she well?"

"The apple."

Sungam nodded again at the fruit.

Magnus' fingers tightened on the apple. Sungam radiated calm. Peace. Sungam could tell him of his family.

But Lumath warned me.

Magnus tore his gaze from the apple, from the shadow man, but nothing in the garden gave him answers. Now when he needed it, Lumath abandoned him. There was only Sungam's touch, calm, comforting, reassuring, but then it was gone. So too was Sungam, and the apple no longer spat fire, its skin now cool to the touch. When he released the apple, it bounced happily in place.

A polite cough. Magnus wasn't alone. He recognized Veyra, walking the garden path.

He blinked, a mental fog confusing his thoughts. *There was someone else just here. Wasn't there?* But he couldn't quite remember who; and the more he thought about it, the more he remembered being alone in the garden, until Veyra.

"Are you alone, Magnus? I thought I heard voices."

"I ..." Magnus peered through the trees, but there was no one else. "I um, just talking. Out loud. To myself."

Her head tilted while studying him, a quirky smile tugged at her lips, until she shrugged. "Join me for a walk?"

They meandered the garden path, Magnus content to walk in silence as he cleared his mind. The cool garden air refreshing.

Stealing a glance at Veyra, taken aback by how well she'd healed, though the scarring on her arm and leg would be permanent reminders, along with the scar on her jawline.

Veyra caught him staring. "See anything you like?" she asked with a wry smile.

He blushed. Looked away. "I didn't mean to offend."

She laughed, a playful nudge. When he didn't respond, she sobered quickly, remembering Lumath's ruin. "Wish I were anywhere but here."

He responded with a rueful laugh. "The company that bad?"

"The company's delightful. Circumstances less so." A slight pause, then, "Can you forgive yourself?"

If they'd been anywhere other than the garden, he might have protested such a question. But a sense of indignation didn't belong here. He looked away, unable to answer.

"I'm so sorry; there I go again." She winced, apologetic. "Always too blunt. It's not my place to ask."

"It's okay. I need that. I hoped for a pleasant distraction, but -"

"No one has ever accused me of being a pleasant distraction!"

"That's hard to believe. Surely in Perinith you were a pleasant distraction to many suitors."

"That's kind of you."

"So why join the army?"

"I ... well, I also ran into trouble back home," her green eyes flashed, "like my parents did in theirs."

He waited, patient, assuming she'd share if she cared to. They wandered off the path, found a bench fashioned from a log, artfully crafted with a motif of deer and bear, acorn and squash, an intricate carving, the Gray Cloak work stunning. *Is this the art of an evil people?* But he already knew the answer.

Veyra patted the seat beside her and he sat willingly, glad of the company, anything to distract from the guilt that weighed.

"I challenged our town council," said Veyra, picking up her story. "Called them frauds to their faces, accused them of cheating our people. Which they were. But let's just say that Perinithians don't forgive easily. A sympathetic townsman warned me the magistrate set a price on my head. I was no longer safe in Perinith and wouldn't be as long as I remained." She sighed, her tone melancholy. "So I left. Everything I've ever known."

Magnus nodded, understanding, missing home himself. *Though at least I'm welcome back.*

"That was two years ago, the famine in full swing. I couldn't believe how bad it was outside Perinith. When I couldn't find work, I enlisted in the Ka."

"Ever picture yourself a soldier?"

"Always been an adventurous girl," she said, though her tone implied doubt, "but the training was grueling, tough. Still, it surprised me how much I enjoyed it. I excelled even." She blushed, rushed to explain herself. "Not that I'm being prideful! It just ... fit me, somehow. Especially the bow."

"Why didn't you join the longbow troop?"

"Fate, perhaps." Her finger traced the carvings in the bench. "Or like these lines here, divergent paths we might have taken. I was considering transferring when our orders came. Took it as a sign and stayed with the regiment. We shipped out the next day, and now here I am ... and ..." she hesitated, surprisingly unsure of herself. From what Magnus gathered, that was a rare occurrence.

"It's alright, you're free to speak your mind. Here at least, in this garden, if nowhere else."

"This doesn't feel right. Being here," with a sweep of her hand she indicated Magnus, herself, their regiment, the garden wilds, "The Ka doesn't belong here."

Her eyes flicked, searching for unwanted listeners before gathering courage to continue. "Last night, my company flanked south through the meadow, stumbling upon a Gray Cloak family hiding in the tall grass. An older woman, bearing the stone, she bound air and grass and dirt, showering us in a cloud of debris. Caused little harm, though it blinded for a moment. In the distraction, they ran. We pursued. The woman tripped and fell. When I raised my sword to strike her down, she stretched a hand towards me, as if to ward the blow. The look in her eyes ..."

It was Veyra's story to tell, and Magnus understood the hesitation. A Ka's duty never easy. She searched Magnus' face, her eyes pleading for understanding. "I swung, but purposefully missed, striking the ground beside her instead. I couldn't do it. There was no malice in her eyes, no hatred. Only pity. As if she knew were I to strike her down it would undo me."

Magnus trembled at the confession, his eyes searching the garden as Veyra had moments before. Ka did not, could not, show mercy in battle, and for her to bear her soul now? A significant risk confessing treasonable actions to another Ka, let alone an officer.

He wanted to be angry. Angry at her for confessing, at their campaign against the Gray Cloaks, at the destruction of Lumath, at the famine that forced him into the Ka. But he couldn't summon it, his heart weighed by his own guilt.

"I knew I faced expulsion, or worse, from the Ka for my actions. But in the chaos, no one noticed. I'm not sure what I would have done next, but it didn't matter. Another finished what I couldn't. The last thing I remember is those eyes. Full of pity, but surprise too. And pain. I can't shake that image."

The clatter of soldiers interrupted them. The men bore axes and saws, their lively banter carrying as they spread through the garden, like a plague through an unsuspecting village, though not all joined in so easily. Some hesitated, eyeing the garden's beauty. An ax slipped from a soldier's hand, falling unused at his feet when he walked away. But another, unmoved, approached a tree and began to hack at the roots.

Chapter Twenty-One
It Was Magnus

Most days, Aurelia enjoyed the sun, the golden eye stirring awake from slumber, spreading warmth and cheer to all the world's inhabitants. But today it was cruel, indifferent, and far hotter than normal. It baked her and her fellow prisoners, as surely as her hearth oven back home baked a flatbread—baked them as they waited, miserable, for decisions over which they had no control and no say.

She gathered her friends close, cradling Daphne in her lap while Eken slept fitfully against her shoulder. When he did wake, he complained often and loudly.

"It's like I can't think straight," he said. "There's this pressure, this gritty buzzing in my head."

Though Aurelia checked twice, there was no visible head injury.

Daphne remained unconscious, her pulse weak. Despite her friends being close, Aurelia had never felt so alone. She missed home—her father, games of Ji with Koram, the tavern dances at night.

Why did you do this Col?

She cried herself to sleep only to wake to the barked commands of a soldier: "Hurry up, get a move on!" But when the huddled prisoners rose to their feet, he cursed, shoving Gray Cloaks to the ground. "Not you lot, just you three!" He jabbed a finger at them.

"Please, my friend here, she's badly injured -"

"I don't care if she's at death's door. Move!"

Their progress, carrying Daphne between them, was too slow for the soldier. He cursed and kicked Eken in the side while other soldiers jeered and threw rocks at Daphne's limp body. A cut opened above her eye, blood trickling down her face.

When Aurelia caught sight of the garden, relief flooded her. *It survived!* But only for a moment. Soldiers felled trees, laughing and singing as saws and axes bit deep.

It was too much, a final insult that broke what spirit remained.

Haven't they done enough?

She spotted Magnus with a female soldier, the one she'd helped save. They stood aside, seemingly calm and untouched, as the garden was destroyed.

Anger boiled, so hot she could have lashed out, the fire of it burning fast, until it too was gone, leaving her empty inside. A spear of lightning creased the sky as if to match her anger, but it was gone as quickly.

The soldier led them beyond the garden, to the grassy knoll where the waterfall thundered. She considered leaping into the chasm to end the mind-numbing emptiness. But she couldn't. Though she might not care for her own well-being, Eken and Daphne needed her.

The reason for the garden's desecration soon became clear: a bridge under way, first logs already laid and hammers ringing. Soon there would be a sturdy enough crossing to allow easy passage across the chasm, even for the wounded. If she'd cared for such things, she might have noticed that the wait was at least pleasant now, the air cooler with the sun hidden behind the towering rock face, while mist from the waterfall moistened their skin.

Whether it was out of kindness or simply to keep them alive, their guard shoved a flask into her hands. She shared with Eken and they drank deeply, coughing at the cold water. They attempted to force a little into Daphne's mouth, but spilled most of it for their efforts.

With the bridge complete, their guard escorted them across.

How strange, returning now through the waterfall, like this, a prisoner.

The Ka had cleared a trail through the thicket that was wide enough even for a wagon. Thorns just out of reach drooped unhappily, recalling their cheerful welcome to these same guests before, bemoaning their inability to say hello like the first time.

The regiment had established camp along the base of the hill, tents lined smartly in order, soldiers busy training, foraging the forest for food, and preparing an evening meal.

Aurelia's stomach growled as roasting meat overwhelmed her senses; a hint of pepper and rosemary tickled her nose; the pip-pop of sizzling grease striking flame delighted her ears.

The guard led them to a crude holding pen. In her present state, Aurelia almost wished it would collapse and crush them all.

"Keep your mouths shut and maybe we'll bring ya something to eat." The guard leered as he shoved her through a makeshift door, clasping a heavy metal lock into place. She found the extra effort amusing.

How far could we get, exhausted, hungry, with an unconscious Daphne?

"Take heart," said Eken, as though he read her mind. He forced an encouraging smile, though grimacing as he did, one hand clutching at his head. "They haven't killed us yet. There's always hope."

She smiled bravely in return, but the smile didn't reach her heart. She felt neither hopeful nor brave, only resigned to their fate.

"I'm glad you're here with me." She cupped his hand in hers. "I don't know what I'd do without you."

"If only we were back in Chelam." Closing his eyes, he shifted against stubborn protruding roots and rocks until he found a comfortable position. Moments later, his familiar snores pierced the air. Annoyed, the guard slunk away.

Light's glimmer winked out as night descended, like a last sliver of hope vanishing. The night brought with it a chill that seeped into her bones along with fits of uncontrollable shaking. She stank of smoke and ashes, sweat and blood. She'd have bartered her soul for a hot bath and a piece of that roasting meat.

Though the Ka celebrated late into the night, the camp eventually quieted, save for guards whispering, stray laughter, and the occasional soldier stumbling to the latrine.

When sleep came for Aurelia, it wasn't restful, tossing and turning as nightmares of blood and ash flooded her mind. Still, she preferred the troubled sleep over the waking doubts and fears.

Will I see Chelam again?

She hadn't expected such an ache for routine. Planting and harvesting, festival days, nights at the Plow & Lantern, games of Ji with Koram and her father. Surprised to find she could still laugh at the memory of her father's lack of strategy, no matter how many times he played.

Her thoughts turned to the Honored Ones she'd met in Chelam, to Ophel and her warning. What did that matter now? Their flight from the approaching army had been for nothing. It would have been as well to stay in Chelam.

Would Lumath have been spared?

They'd failed the prophecy, their band of four. In the black of night, it was easy to imagine darkness consuming everything.

Voices clawed at her. Muffled conversation, though in the dark it was hard to tell much. Likely a changing of the guard. But fresh guards, tired guards—*what does it matter?* She allowed the self-pity to wash over, too tired to wipe away hot tears.

"Aurelia!"

An urgent whisper. A figure approached, masked by darkness until it drew close.

It was Magnus.

Chapter Twenty-Two
Fatal Choices Bury Men

"We need to go, now!"

Magnus swallowed a knot of worry. Aurelia's stare was blank and blood matted her hair. She'd yet to answer him. He produced the key passed along by the guard and removed the lock. As he did, she finally spoke.

"Is this real?" She rested a hand on his chest. "Assure me this isn't a cruel joke."

He covered her hand with his own, before guiding it over his heart. "I made a vow, and I aim to keep it, pot drummer. This time I'm saving you."

When I call her pot drummer, does she know how often I've thought of her?

His heart flipped at the smile she offered, never mind it was weak, hesitant; and when a flood of warring emotions buffeted her face—anger, hope, joy, fear—Magnus' heart soared one moment and spiraled the next, until there it was: trust. When her face settled on it his heart settled too. He hadn't dared hope she could trust him.

Eken woke to the sight of Aurelia's hand on Magnus' chest. Cleared his throat. "Anyone care to explain?"

"Can you move?" asked Magnus, startled at Eken's stained-dark-red shirt, as if he'd plunged it in a vat of spiced wine.

"I'm okay, but Daphne needs help."

"Morco!" whispered Magnus into the darkness.

A bulky figure approached at a lumbering speed.

"Gonna give her an opportunity to surprise me." Morco winked at Aurelia, stepping into the cage and scooping Daphne into his arms.

Other figures emerged from the darkness. Tobias, Saul, Bochim, and Veyra, the last giving Aurelia an appraising look, though she included a friendly smile.

"I'm Veyra. Thank you. For what you -"

Veyra's thanks cut short as Tobias offered Aurelia her travel pack.

"Oh!" exclaimed Aurelia, with an instinctive hug in return. "You don't know what this means to me!"

She rifled through the pack's contents, relief plain as she withdrew a Ji set and hugged it to her chest.

"It was nothing." Tobias grinned sheepishly. "Helps when you're an officer's aide."

Magnus interrupted - "Time to go. Quietly. No more conversation until we're outside camp. If we're challenged, let me do the talking."

Despite his best efforts to lead them on a careful route, soldiers too often ambled close by; but focused on the ale in their flasks, they failed to notice the escapees. At the forest edge, campfires fading behind them, Magnus allowed a moment of cautious optimism until a man appeared, barring their path.

Kymn.

After the encounter with his friend outside Drael's tent, Magnus determined not to include him in their plans. Now, as Kymn spoke, it confirmed his doubts.

"Can't let you leave, not with her." The man nodded at Daphne's limp form slung across Morco's shoulder. Morco growled protectively.

"Don't do this, Kymn," pleaded Magnus. "They're not safe with the Ka. You know the vow I spoke. I won't let Drael deliver them to Capitol interrogators for a death sentence."

"What's happened to you, brother? We trained together. Battled together." Kymn paced, his face scrunched, perplexed. "This isn't the way. To defy the Ka? The King's orders? If you have a grievance, take it to the commander."

"I tried. He won't listen. And they've done nothing wrong. Nothing to deserve what awaits them at the Capitol."

"The Magnus I knew wouldn't sneak off in the night, aiding our enemies."

"These aren't our enemies. And perhaps I'm not that person anymore."

Kymn drew his sword. Magnus made no move toward his own, but then his fist shot forward, connecting with a sickening crunch. He followed with another, a low strike, hard in the gut. Kymn grunted, stumbling back.

Tobias leapt forward, aided Magnus in subduing their friend, stuffed his mouth with a bolt of cloth, while a strand of rope bound his hands. They pulled a fuming Kymn to his feet, face bruised from blows sustained in the scuffle, a cut on his cheek dripping blood. His eyes smoldered.

"What's the plan here?" asked Tobias, stealing a glance at Kymn, who waited sullenly for his fate to be decided.

End his life.

The familiar voice penetrated the recesses of Magnus' mind.

If you let him go, your friends will suffer.

He fought to shut out the whispers, but when his eyes closed Sungam's face appeared.

"Magnus, you okay?"

His eyes snapped open, to find his friends crowding close, their concern unmistakable.

"If we release him, he'll raise an alarm." Magnus hesitated, the whispers echoing still. "But I've no wish to harm him. He's only doing what he thinks right."

"Take him with us," said Bochim, "and he'll slow us down."

"He'll only betray us in the end, no matter what," said Saul, voicing darker thoughts Magnus hadn't wished to voice. "Better to be done with him now."

Is there no plan that doesn't include harming Kymn? Stalling for time, Magnus turned to Aurelia.

"How's Daphne?"

"Not good. Her stone's gone; she's barely breathing."

"Maybe I can help," said Eken. Up close, Magnus flinched at the sight of the haggard face, creased and weary, as though hardship had etched decades into it. Those lines hadn't been there before. "In Lumath I read a lot of books about history, science, magic and bindings, more books than I -"

"Eken, get to the point!"

"Right, okay, fine," he said, clearing his throat. "According to my reading, a Gray Cloak becomes an Honored One upon receiving a stone. But it's much more than just a stone; it's a channel for magic itself. For their bindings. And it has a name. They call the stones saphyr."

"How does this help Daphne?"

"A saphyr is grafted in a ritual that binds the Honored One to the land's magic," continued Eken, ignoring the interruption. "Removing it kills them. Immediately. It's like cutting out their heart and they can't live without it. At least, that's what I read. And if that's true, Daphne's hold on life is highly unusual."

"Did you read any more about the ritual?" asked Aurelia. "Maybe we could find a new stone, and somehow," she struggled for the right words, "re-attach one?"

"Not much on the ritual itself." He frowned, apologetic. "Seems it was an oral tradition they passed down. But they had a lot to say about the saphyr bond, speaking of the stone as if it were a living being itself. Attaching another one though? I don't know. Then again, Daphne still lives ..." He shrugged helplessly.

"We can't stay any longer," said Magnus. "We'll find a way to help Daphne. But right now, we need to figure out what to do with Kymn."

"We take him with us," piped up Veyra.

"Agreed," seconded Tobias.

Magnus nodded his assent, though Sungam's voice whispered within: *fatal choices bury men.*

Chapter Twenty-Three
Close to Her Heart

They fled the Ka's camp, destination unknown but eager to lose the trackers they knew Drael would send. No one spoke, worry gnawing like root mice burrowing into stored grain.

The ex-soldiers trembled over their futures and what it meant to abandon the Ka, knowing those they once called brothers would soon hunt them.

The Dorakians remained haunted by thoughts of captivity, and by the danger hanging over Daphne's life. Aurelia missed her friend's voice, her quick smile. Thoughts of friends reminded her of Col and the stinging words he last spoke.

You can have her, she's not worth it.

"Mind if I join you?"

She nodded, grateful to Magnus for interrupting dark thoughts. They wove through thick walls of barley stalks, in a field twice the size of her father's back home. Beyond the field lay swaths of farmland that bore a Dorakian look, though Aurelia didn't recognize their location. As best she could determine, they skirted northeastern Dorak. Chelam couldn't be far.

Home.

"Been thinking," said Magnus, "I didn't believe Daphne, that she sought to clear her people's name, but she spoke the truth, didn't she?"

"I haven't known her long," responded Aurelia, thumb and forefinger rubbing the pendant necklace around her throat, "but one thing I know, she's a truth-speaker. I've trusted few more than her."

"It's a rare thing to find people like that in our lives." Magnus ran a hand through his hair, guilt splayed across his face. "I ... I've been nothing like that to you. I betrayed you, and I despise myself for it."

"We've all done things we regret."

"Can you forgive me?"

Her eyes searched his, knowing she already trusted him. Forgiving him was the next logical step, but she scrunched her nose and twisted her mouth, before turning away to hide a smile, pretending to struggle with a response, sensing his anxiety building. And then, when she'd made him wait long enough, "I can, and I do."

"Thank you." His breath expelled in a sigh of relief so hard it knocked a barley stalk sideways. "Didn't realize how badly I needed that, and ... I was hoping we could be friends."

"I'd like that." Her heart skipped a beat. "Very much."

"And I want to help Daphne." Magnus paused, his jaw twisting, swallowing guilt before he could speak again. "It's my fault she's the way she is."

"No, it's not! Your commander did this." She grabbed his arm and they stopped so quick they nearly collided. A light breeze stirred, barley stalks waving merrily to the intruders. It reminded Aurelia of Lumath's meadow. Before the fire. But thoughts of barley and Lumath couldn't distract from the electricity sparking across Magnus' skin where her fingertips lay. Ash and dirt stained her fingernails, and she wondered idly if he noticed. "Father always said you can't undo the past, but you can live so the future needs no undoing."

"He sounds like someone worth listening to." Magnus took her hand and a step towards her. Barley stalks faded into the background. She drank in his scent, one of sweat, forest and field. Felt the calluses of his hand against her skin. Noticed a scar in the hairline above his left ear. *How'd it get there?* she wondered.

Magnus cleared his throat. "Um, was thinking, if we find Daphne's people ..." He pulled a map from his pack.

"Hey, let me see that!"

Magnus and Aurelia blushed as Eken shoved his way between them, the barley field coming back into focus, remembering they weren't alone.

"You reminded me," said Eken, oblivious to their embarrassment, "in Lumath I saw a map of Gray Cloak villages. Did you know Gray Cloaks are excellent cartographers?"

"Eken," sighed Magnus, "are you saying you can find them?"

"I can find a village. Whether there's a Gray Cloak there -"

"That's good enough for me. Lead the way then. And I think it's time."

"For what?"

Magnus drew a knife from his belt and strode towards Kymn. The man's eyes widened. With a swift cut, Magnus severed the ropes binding his wrists. Kymn flexed his hands as feeling returned and tore the gag from his mouth.

"Drael will use his wolfhounds," said Magnus. "He'll find us with or without your help."

"I'm free to go?"

"Take this for protection." Magnus tossed a dagger clear of the barley field. "Go. And I'm sorry, my friend."

"May we meet again in a better tomorrow." Kymn gave a final nod to Magnus, Tobias, and the others, before jogging across the field, scooping up the dagger as he went.

Magnus' eyes remained fixed on the shadows inside the treeline where he'd disappeared, long after he was gone. When Magnus turned away from the forest, Aurelia caught the slump of his shoulders and the resignation on his face, but he simply nodded to his companions, hefted his pack firmly across his shoulders, and walked deeper into the stalks of barley.

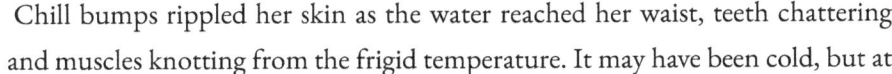

Chill bumps rippled her skin as the water reached her waist, teeth chattering and muscles knotting from the frigid temperature. It may have been cold, but at least Aurelia took comfort in finally knowing where they were, a day's journey from Chelam. She knew this because she'd spent many happy summer days with Eken there at Applemere Lake—so named for the orchards nearby—when they were young and the families needed a spot for the children to run and splash and play.

But it wasn't just lazy days with the Potterfelds she remembered so fondly. Every year, over a three-day span mid-summer, Chelam's citizens flocked to Applemere Lake for a festive party, unimaginatively called Lake Day Festival. Bonfires lit the night sky, and everyone, young and old, enjoyed sleeping out under the stars. It was one of her favorite times of the year. But those were hot summer afternoons when the water offered a refreshing escape from the day's heat. She'd never swum the lake in late harvest season. Only a fool would.

If only Magnus weren't a fool.

"This is perfect," Magnus had announced at the lake's edge. "With any luck it'll give the wolfhounds a cold trail and they won't pick it up on the other side."

Magnus shrugged his pack off his shoulders before stripping to his breeches.

"What are you ...?" asked Aurelia, shocked by his brazenness—never mind the chill in the air—before his intentions dawned on her. "Oh no. No, we don't. Swim across that? The cold will kill us."

Magnus shrugged an apology as he shoved his outer layers of clothing into his pack. The others followed suit, even Eken, minus his usual grin. Aurelia folded her arms with a smug *hmph* when Saul dipped a toe into the lake and gasped.

"C'mon, pot drummer!" The mischievous grin on Magnus' face irked Aurelia no end. "Though it's fine if you stay. You'll make a pleasant distraction for the wolfhounds."

He laughed, plunging in, his pack held high, but even he couldn't stifle a shocked gasp.

Aurelia expected he'd turn back. When he didn't, she applauded his determination—*or is it his stupidity?* Either way, she really hated him right then. Stamping a foot and throwing in a snort for good measure, she paced outside the water's reach as a blast of wind whipped across the lake, matching the intensity of her displeasure. *Great, that won't help matters!* Her tantrum accomplished little, as one by one everyone followed Magnus' lead.

"Got your pack," said Morco as he waded into the water, hoisting Daphne, his own pack and Aurelia's too, above his head.

Like a bag of stones, the water's chill slammed her chest. To breathe became a struggle, it was enough to suck shallow gulps of air as she waded in. When it got too deep for wading, she swam. She sought to distract herself from the cold, but her thoughts didn't help.

True to each other the four must remain ... The prophecy played like the steady rhythm she loved to dance to in the Plow & Lantern. Insistent. Repeating *... lest darkness consume all that is known.*

She wished she could forget that second half. If her wits had been about her at the Ka's camp, she'd have fought to take Col with them. He left Chelam by her side, and yet now she left him behind. But it wouldn't have mattered. Col chose his side.

Do what's right. Make your own choices. Leave others to theirs.

Her father's wisdom, right again. She had made her own choice, and Col his.

A strong swimmer, she closed the gap between her and Magnus. Still angry with him for forcing a swim in the frigid lake, she skimmed her hand across the water's surface. The spray hardly doused him, though the look on his face claimed otherwise. A moment later he was laughing at the wave of water he'd sent her way. She ducked under, swam deep into cold's deadly grip. She held her breath, gliding effortlessly underwater, knowing it was foolish in such temperatures. But Applemere Lake sang to her, remembering those summer days, reminding her of happier times, and for a moment she let go of her fears and felt free.

She popped above water, like she'd seen the otters do when they played, and found herself face to face with Magnus. His breath misted the surface, forming ice crystals that sparkled in the sunlight. Drops of water beaded his hair and along his jawline's bearded stubble. He tread water so close it unnerved her, the lake's chill forgotten.

"I um ... sorry about the splash." She wasn't, but couldn't think of anything else to say.

He looked as if he might have retorted, but instead noticed her chattering teeth and shallow breathing as the cold cramped her muscles. He reached out to steady her.

"If you two kids are finished playing," Bochim interrupted dryly as he swam by, "a Ka regiment will be at our heels soon."

Magnus stammered a protest. Aurelia dared not look Eken's way, anticipating the smirk plastered across his face. But when she thought of Daphne—what her friend might have said, were she awake, and no jagged tear where her stone once lay—the warmth slipped away all at once, leaving only the cold.

With the lake some distance behind, the sun continued its dogged climb above the mountains, its warmth welcome, drying clothes and brightening spirits.

Aurelia fell in alongside Morco.

"Any change?"

He shook his head. Grim. "Think she'll ever wake?"

"I want her to, with all my heart," she said, the thought of her friend not waking a knife between the ribs.

"I'm sorry." The hand on her shoulder surprisingly gentle for such a giant man. "I ... I'm ashamed to admit I witnessed the stone's removal."

A spark of hate ignited in her, like a fire seizing dried kindling. She tried to hold it, like she'd tried in the garden wilds, but it sputtered and died, unable to take root.

"Watching Drael cut out that stone," added Morco, "in a way, Daphne saved me. From who I might have become. But her scream will always haunt me. I knew then I could never be Ka again."

"Did she suffer long?" Aurelia didn't want to know, but had to ask.

"It was as horrible a death knell as I've ever heard. But it was over quick. One piercing shriek before she went limp."

Seeing her near tears, Morco pulled her into a rough but heartfelt embrace, even with Daphne draped across his opposite shoulder. His free hand patted her awkwardly while her sobs disappeared into his chest.

Aurelia recalled a boy in Chelam who had suffered a terrible fall and slipped into unconsciousness, never to wake again despite the healer's efforts. Though his body lingered, his spirit had fled. Many eight-days passed before the body finally surrendered. In her heart, she knew Daphne traveled the same path—she simply could not bear to admit it.

Dorakian farmland faded into the distant background, still Magnus urged them on. They spent the better part of the morning crossing a plain riddled with stones of varying size, all sun-bleached white, like the bones of a mythical creature where it had chosen its final resting spot. The once welcome sun beat mercilessly against their backs, long ago depriving their clothes of moisture and threatening to steal it from their bodies. Ahead, a stand of trees, a lone shelter in the field of bleached white stones, as if the mythical creature's heart had survived.

"This will do." Magnus was no longer a Ka officer, but he remained their undisputed leader. "Rest here tonight."

Aurelia knew she should help—scout for firewood, forage for edible plants or berries—but she couldn't. Instead she sat alone, her thoughts melancholy, until as true friends do, Eken came and settled back-to-back against her. The familiar touch was enough to steady, to draw her from grief's edge, and for once he was silent, knowing silence was better.

She couldn't count the number of times they'd sat like that, usually while Eken read a book and she daydreamed. It felt good to do so again, while the natural hum of conversation settled across camp. Bochim, Tobias and Morco left to hunt small game. Magnus and Saul built a fire and set up a spit in anticipation. Veyra worked on repetitions with her bow. Pull and release. Again. Pull and release. Again. Despite the obvious pain, her brow furrowed, concentrating, a slight grimace on her lips.

It was Aurelia who broke the silence when Eken rubbed at his head. "Still hurts?"

"Imagine your head in a vise-grip, like Runa uses in her forge, while your mind is clouded with ... with, well, what's the worst snowstorm Chelam's ever experienced? Think that and more. Snow so thick you can't see your way."

She tried to picture it but couldn't. A dusting? Sure. Every winter. But heavy snowfall was rare in Chelam. "Father claimed the worst snow recorded in Chelam, akin to blizzards on the Tol's peaks, happened when I was a baby."

"Isn't it always that way? Some time in the past they claim."

Aurelia snorted. *Sounds about right.*

"So yes, like that fabled snowstorm," continued Eken, "as if I can't find my way through it. Through my own mind."

"Too many books in Lumath?"

"Perhaps." His laugh rueful and regretful.

The hunters returned victorious with a pair of mountain squirrel in hand. The animals proved a nuisance to Dorakian farmers in harvest season, descending from the Tol like a horde, foraging fields and orchards for grain and nuts, preparing stockpiles of their own for winter. Tobias skinned, gutted and speared them through, securing them to the spit, the meat soon sizzling and popping over the fire. Hungry stomachs rumbled.

Aurelia perked up. She'd never been one to refuse a meal.

Loss has its season, dear little Aurie. Put those memories and those hurts where they belong—close to the heart, never forgotten, though we resume our planting and harvesting.

"What's that?" asked Eken.

A smile played on her lips—she hadn't realized she'd lent voice to her father's advice.

Abruptly she stood, her mind clear. "I think I'm hungry."

Her memories of Daphne were exactly where they needed to be, close to her heart, and it was time to eat.

Chapter Twenty-Four
The Colorful Scarf

Magnus studied Aurelia from across the fire. Though Daphne wasn't yet passed beyond the veil, it was apparent she wasn't coming back; and watching Aurelia struggle with that realization left a deep ache to reach out and try to comfort her. But barely removed from his betrayal, what right could he claim to that? Besides, she had Eken.

He sighed.

"You can talk to her, you know," said Tobias, seeming to recognize the sigh for what it was.

"It's all I want to do. I'm drawn to her, like ... well, like a moth to a flame."

"That doesn't end well for moths."

"I just forget about her then?"

"You described the two of you as moth and flame, not me. Honestly? She's kind yet fiery, obviously compassionate, and saved our lives. Your attraction to her makes sense ... and I've seen the way she looks at you. She's not looking at anyone else like that."

Magnus searched his friend's face. *Is he teasing me?*

"Aaah," he muttered, tossing a stick into the fire. Barely removed from treason he could hang for, on the run from the Ka, the girl's friend all but dead, and he was thinking about, what—love? *Who am I fooling?* And he barely knew her, which only made the idea all the more foolish. Besides, love was messy. His duty was clear: lead his companions to safety.

Dinner's aroma drew them to the fire.

"How is it?" Tobias nodded at Veyra's arm.

"Not good. The pain's fierce, and I've got no strength."

"Noticed you trying out your left arm for the pull."

"I aim far better with the right. Now ..." she shrugged, "I'll be lucky if I can hit a snow moose's flank." At his confused look, she laughed, "It's a Perinith thing. Snow moose are notoriously slow. Easy hunting and lots of meat."

"Doubt we'll be seeing any snow moose," said Tobias with a twitch of a smile.

"Just hoping to help if it comes to a fight. Right now I'm as likely to bury an arrow in one of you as in an enemy."

Eken cleared his throat. "What about me?"

"Yes, you'd be an easy target," said Veyra, "though not on purpose," she added with a toothy smile.

"No, I meant what about my helping in a fight? I don't know the first thing about it."

"Then your training begins tomorrow!" Morco's booming voice cut in.

"That's settled then," said Magnus, before addressing Aurelia. "And how about you?"

"Me?" she said, surprised, then a note of regret in her voice, "I, uh ... no, we had little need of sword or stave in Dorak."

"I can teach you."

His comment earned him a few snickers and an *I'm sure you'll be glad to*. He silenced them with a glare. "We'll need every able-bodied fighter if it comes to it," he said, his tone sharp, defiant.

Bochim sighed, stretched, patted a contented belly. "Wish there was more; that was delicious. No one could have conjured a better stew with what we had on hand. Well done, Tobias."

Eken cleared his throat again. "Um, that reminds me, speaking of conjured ... you see, sometimes a word or an object triggers a memory of what I read in Lumath -"

"Spit it out, Eken!"

"Right ... did anyone know that magic, bindings, used to be common throughout Lavonshia?"

Magnus tried to picture such a thing but couldn't. To think the power he'd witnessed Gray Cloaks wield, once commonplace? "Back home, our neighbor's herds birthed the healthiest and largest yearlings. There were whispers of magic."

Eken waved a dismissive hand. "We've all heard those sorts of rumors. A man's field yields more, a neighbor whose wine never runs dry, a village that's never lost a child to sickness."

"Coincidence," scoffed Saul.

"Exactly!" He wagged a finger at Saul. "Just coincidence, chance or fate, you could say. No, I'm talking about real magic. The kind the land itself possesses, that existed in creatures called midlings, and in people who could harness its power."

"So what happened?" asked Morco. "Where did it go? Why does no one speak of magic until Saan?"

"Does anyone know of the Red War?" Blank stares. A few heads shook. He nodded smugly. "I didn't think so. Read *History of the Kingdom Volume XIV*. It's where I learned how the Red War got magic banished from Lavonshia."

"Why was it called the Red War?" asked Bochim, ignoring Eken's know-it-all tone.

"It was a war of mages, Gray Cloaks who harnessed magic with their bindings. I remember the line that explained its name ... *as the Red War raged, the rivers ran red with the blood of our people.*"

Magnus had seen the devastation a handful of Gray Cloaks caused with such power. *What must it have been to endure a civil war of mages?* he wondered.

"The war was nearly four hundred years ago," continued Eken, "wreaking a devastation so tremendous that the King outlawed binding; even whispering of magic could lead to imprisonment. You see, Gray Cloaks didn't always live segregated lives; they were part of us back then, and woven into the fabric of our lives their conflict dragged all of Lavonshia into civil war. After the outlawing of bindings, I guess people gradually forgot. Hundreds of years later, and few

Lavonshians acknowledge magic's existence. At least not 'til Saan. But according to what I read, it's here, all around us." He waved expansively at the surrounding land.

"But I don't feel or see bindings around me," said Bochim, his tone doubtful, "and I've seen none of these *midlings* as you called them."

"Yes, that's a tough one," Eken pursed his lips while rubbing vigorously at his head. For a moment, as he spoke of magic, midlings, and the Red War, his eyes glowed fervently with the reflection of firelight, and the pained expression that had lined his face since Lumath disappeared. But it was only for a moment.

"Perhaps," said Bochim, answering his own question, "as time erased memories of bindings, even the land's magic fell into a kind of sleep. And these creatures, midlings, crawled off into hiding. Or maybe you read an exaggerated history."

"Maybe," Eken acknowledged, his eyes dull, a confused look settling his face.

"I felt magic!" piped up Aurelia. "In Lumath. Like nothing I've ever experienced."

"I think ... I think I did too." Magnus stared into the flames. "I didn't know it was magic then. But I felt something different in that place."

"I think you both hit on something!" exclaimed Eken, the gleam in his eye returning. "Magic is everywhere, but some places hoard it in far greater concentration. Lumath must be one of those. It explains everything. Why, and how, I'd spend my days absorbing more books than I could read in a lifetime, without a wink of sleep or a single meal. Why Daphne abandoned us, spending all her time with other Gray Cloaks, when that didn't seem like her. And Aurelia, it explains your falling in love with Col. Feelings you've never expressed before."

Magnus glanced up sharply.

Eken continued, "And even Col's changed attitude. From what Aurelia tells me, he was a kinder, gentler, person in Lumath. I think the magic affected us there, influencing our -"

"That's a terrifying thought," interrupted Saul. "Did Lumath play us like puppets on a string? Would we not have abandoned our Ka oaths and helped you escape?"

"Was none of it real?" asked Aurelia so quietly no one heard.

"I think it's not quite like that. Not like puppets at all. A book I read, *Of Magic And Its Properties*, by T.A. Shavil -"

Aurelia snorted. "Eken, we don't need to know every book and author name."

"- he explained magic in that it's gentler, more intuitive, influencing and awakening parts of us, parts we've buried or ignored. Take me as an example, I love consuming books -"

"That's an understatement," Aurelia muttered under her breath. Magnus chuckled.

"- to gain knowledge," continued Eken with a glare, "but Chelam stifles my desire. Our people aren't known for their love of books. No, Dorakians thrive on simple life structures. Planting. Harvesting. Family and festivals."

"Heard rumors of Dorakian festivals," rumbled Morco. "Always wanted to visit, never imagined I'd experience Dorak like this."

"My natural inclination stifled," continued Eken despite the interruptions, "I believe Lumath fed my insatiable desire. I couldn't leave the library because I needed it."

"What does that mean for Col then?" asked Aurelia. "Is there hope for him? He was so different in Lumath—until the Ka came. It makes no sense."

"You're right, that's confusing." Eken shrugged helplessly. "I wish I could say ..."

An idea popped into Magnus' head, though as soon as he voiced it, he wished he hadn't. "Maybe his love for Aurelia is less than what the Ka offers ... so, um, that, uh ..."

"That makes sense," Aurelia jumped in, saving Magnus his discomfort, while nodding slowly as if assembling the pieces, "at first, in Lumath, he existed only for me. Doting, kind, thoughtful, a deep listener, the man any woman would dream -"

"We get the idea," muttered Magnus.

"- but when the Ka came, he changed. Perhaps Lumath fixed his heart on what he cared most about. That was me. Until the Ka. Everyone knows they were his first love."

An uncomfortable silence settled around the campfire. Each lost in considering what Lumath had stirred inside their own hearts and minds, what influence its magic had wrought on their behavior.

"Still don't get the midlings," said Veyra, breaking the silence. "Where did they go? Why doesn't anyone ever see one?"

"I don't know, and it seems for all I learned in that library, it just leads to more questions."

"Midlings aside," said Magnus as he stood and stretched, "there's flesh and blood soldiers who, if not on our trail already, will be soon. I suggest we rest."

The following morning, Eken seemed far less certain about the location of Gray Cloak villages. When Magnus prodded him for specifics, his answers were vague, even contradictory, often mumbling as he stumbled over his words with a confused look clouding his eyes. But though it might prove a wild frit chase, Magnus had no better plan than Eken's.

Daphne's only hope lies at the hands of a Gray Cloak.

They had left Lumath far behind. Dorak and its villages even farther. From what he knew of the Ka maps he'd studied, they were deep into Gray Cloak territory. Eventually, a several days' walk eventually, they'd reach the Maldelea Sea if they were to head north. Or pushing in an easterly direction, they'd find themselves attempting to scale the Tol Mountains.

Time passed more slowly than watching wheat grow in the endless fields of the Plains. Not that Magnus ever wasted time watching wheat grow, but he felt sure it would feel like this. *Monotonous.* One foot in front of another, going somewhere but arriving nowhere, each forest and field a repetition of the last, while Daphne's condition worsened, her breathing grew more shallow, and her skin more pale.

Morco, who'd seen more death than most, whispered, "She's not long for this world, another day at most."

Drenched in such a melancholy mood, the companions stumbled upon an old man resting by their path. He didn't appear startled at such a strange mix of travelers—Dorakian villagers with armed soldiers and one who carried the body of a Gray Cloak. All bone-weary and smelling fiercely of sweat and dust. The man staggered to his feet and leaned heavily on a staff.

Magnus raised an arm in greeting.

"We seek help for our companion; she's badly injured." He hesitated, recognizing how foolish it was in the current political climate to speak of Gray Cloaks, but time wasn't on their side. "Do you know of Gray Cloak settlements nearby?"

The man appeared to ponder the question, scratching at his beard, and as he did, Magnus realized just how old the man had to be. Bits of fine white wispy hair sprinkled the back of an otherwise bald head, which contained more age spots than he'd ever seen on an individual. Thick white bushy eyebrows nearly obscured a pair of seemingly intelligent eyes peering out from underneath. The man was short in stature, quite stooped, bent nearly double, wearing a threadbare tunic and trousers, thin garments for the chill in the air, though what drew the eye was the clothing's oddity. In the Capitol, a melting pot of Lavonshia, Magnus witnessed an astonishing variety of clothing styles. But nothing ever like those the old man wore.

The tunic bore an unusual pattern of crisscrossing thread lines, as if the seamstress couldn't sew straight. The trousers though, these Magnus could never quite get the sense of. In one instant they appeared bound with moss and stone, at another sewn with squares of cloth, but then at the next, bits of glass and bead lined every stitching.

As a final accent to his unusual look, a scarf, jarringly and outlandishly colorful, draped his neck. The swirling colors rivaled the most brilliantly hued rainbow. It appeared especially soft, and Magnus had an itching desire to reach out and touch it.

The old man wore no shoes; long, yellowed toenails tucked beneath his toes. Though his hands were gnarled with age, he gripped his staff firmly enough. He spoke in a shrill whisper, so that one had to lean in to catch his words.

"Gray Cloaks, you say? Where? Point the way!"

For emphasis, he jabbed the air with his staff. Magnus ducked back to avoid a bruised rib. Somehow the old man remained standing, though he teetered unsteadily, wildly waving his staff before planting it on firm ground to lean heavily against it once more. The staff, despite its rather pronounced curves, seemed sturdy enough. At its top sat a polished sphere, the kind of cheap and shiny trinket one could buy off any peddler.

"No, that's who we're looking for," explained Aurelia kindly, "Gray Cloaks."

"Why didn't you say so! Of course I know where Gray Cloaks live. Come, follow me! Don't dawdle; keep up." Giving no pause for reply, the old man shuffled away at a surprising pace.

Aurelia hurried to catch up, dragging a confused and disoriented Eken along. *Don't follow, you can't trust him.*

The voice again. *Sungam.* Or his own fear wearing Sungam's voice? Magnus wished he could say, the voice echoing *I am you. You are me.*

"Cheer up, old friend," Tobias clapped Magnus on the shoulder. "Looks like Eken's lost his job. We've got a new nut to follow."

He laughed and hooked his thumb towards the old man and the colorful scarf flapping in the breeze.

Chapter Twenty-Five
Nothing

Aurelia had never witnessed such an odd little cottage, pieced together with bits of this and that, its patchwork construction remarkably similar to the old man's trousers.

It took the better part of an afternoon to reach the cottage, despite the old man's blistering pace. Intent on their destination, he never once looked over his shoulder. The path they followed led through a sparse forest of scattered trees, the ground bare save for a carpeting of hemlock needles. But it contained so many curving switchbacks, meandering like a side-winding snake chasing its own tail, that it was a marvel they didn't arrive back in the same spot they started from.

She kept a firm grasp on Eken's hand, all but certain that if she didn't, he wouldn't keep up. He shuffled along with his head sunk low, chin resting on his chest, muttering endlessly to himself.

"Why follow this path at all?" she whispered, half to herself, half to Eken, though she didn't expect a reply.

She jumped in fright when his head shot up, feverish eyes boring into her own, all while chanting, "Hobble, dobble, path and flight. Follow, hollow, till it's right."

But after such a strange outburst, he dropped his chin to his chest and resumed muttering. The moment came and went so quickly Aurelia wondered if she'd imagined it. She squeezed his hand, whether to assure him or assure herself she wasn't sure.

Aurelia could think of no rhyme or reason for the switchbacks; the way ran level, the forest so open it would have been an easy thing to veer off the path, walk straight ahead, and save a great deal of time and trouble. It was so entirely futile that before long she fell to grumbling and had decided to bypass the next curve and wait for the old man to catch up. But before she could, he cried out, "Stay on the path! Curves a-coming and curves a-going, but we stay on the path to reach our home."

As the curves kept a-curving, it wasn't long before she eyed another shortcut, but the old coot seemed to know her thoughts and always shouted his warning. She wasn't alone in her predicament. One by one each weary traveler decided to save a little time and energy, but inevitably each heard the old man's cry before acting on their impulse.

Honey.

Aurelia's fingers snapped, the noise a sharp echoing crack. It was like the honey she'd poured from the jar as a little girl, watching it ooze across the table, the sticky liquid following the furrows in the wood grain. She'd dipped a finger in its path, then another, diverting it, altering its course, sending it curving, delighting in its taste as she licked her finger clean, watching it ooze over the table's edge. With a delighted squeal, she'd broken every jar of honey in the house and played queen and commander to the honey's winding course. When her father discovered her and the sticky mess of fourteen broken jars, he was as angry as she'd ever seen, but she'd risk that kind of wrath again if a giant finger or two would descend from the sky and divert their path now.

Curve after curve, another sigh, another shouted warning, tension building as the sun inched ponderously slow. Questioning the old man why one must stay on the path proved fruitless, for he only repeated the same refrain: "Stay on the path. Curves a-coming and curves a-going, but we stay on the path to reach our home!"

When the first hint of twilight filtered through leaf and limb, mutiny hung thick with murmurs and questionings the old man ignored.

And then, they arrived. Without warning—a clearing, a cottage—and most bizarrely, for though one could easily view the path snaking off into the distance, none had caught a glimpse of the structure in advance. Gasps of surprise and relief echoed across the clearing.

The cottage was ... unique, to put it mildly. Where one might have expected its front porch columns to be made of stacked stone, a stack of boots instead. Where one might have expected leaden glass for a window, strings of metal beads. The siding, if one could call it such, consisted of a jumbled assortment, including the head of a hammer, bits of clothing, pots and pans, a woven basket or two, and even the crank-handle of a windmill. The whole mess appeared held together not by nails but by an oozing, glue-like substance that wept across its exterior, causing it to sway alarmingly in the breeze.

Aurelia eyed the cottage, wondering just how safe it might be.

"What are you waiting for?" The old man hopped onto the front porch, placed a hand on the front door—incongruously fashioned from one half of a giant clamshell—and regarded them with squinting eyes. "Don't stand there and gawk. You young people have lost all sense of politeness these days!"

With a muttered *tsk*, he disappeared inside.

"If he's lived this long, it must be safe!" proclaimed Tobias with a grin before following him through the clamshell door.

Aurelia caught Magnus' anxious peek towards the forest path and grabbed his hand before he could bolt.

"I sense something about this place," she said, her smile calming, "and the old man."

In fact, she felt it the moment the cottage appeared, a tugging feeling, similar to Lumath though not as strong. A fuzzy tingle, warm, the only way she could think to describe it, though that didn't do it justice. But she knew it was safe. They were safe. The cottage invited them in, as much as the old man had.

"I feel it too," said Eken, catching her off guard, his voice hoarse. It was the first intelligent thing he'd said all day. "It's safe. A good place." He smiled, reassuring, squeezing her hand, the dull haze in his eyes clearing, and she smiled back, glad to see the old Eken returning.

She ducked to avoid knocking herself senseless on the front-door casing. The clamshell was impossibly large but still small for a door. Morco managed to squeeze his frame through, though Daphne's limp form wasn't as fortunate when her head whacked alarmingly against the clamshell as it swung shut. Morco winced and petted her hair as if she needed calming.

"What doesn't kill you strengthens you," whispered Eken with a chuckle.

Aurelia gave him a look of daggers dipped in poison.

"What?" He shrugged. "A little dark humor goes a long way."

The cottage was surprisingly spacious inside, featuring a soaring ceiling and a spiral staircase that led to additional floors. Aurelia was tempted to step outside for another look at what she could have sworn was a small one-story cottage.

The first room to greet them was as large as her entire home in Chelam, not that Dorakian homes were especially large. Two doorways hinted at even more space the main level offered.

It hit her then. *Ah, a binding.* The only plausible explanation.

"Welcome to my humble abode!" the old man called over his shoulder as he disappeared through the closest of the two doorways. "Chockberry tea, anyone?"

A delicious odor wafted through that same doorway. It wasn't just the tea Aurelia smelled, but the scent of fresh-baked honey-bread lingering on the air. Her stomach rumbled; it had been a long walk on that path.

The old man re-appeared, carrying in his left hand a stack of mugs ten high, and in his right a pot of tea. The colorful scarf was missing, and he'd taken the time to step into a pair of house slippers.

"Take a seat, take a seat," he encouraged as he poured their tea, "no need to loaf around."

Sipping his tea, allowing its aroma to intoxicate, Eken puzzled over the invitation to sit. He didn't recall seeing furniture when they entered the home. But when the steam cleared from the spectacles perched on his nose, he was surprised to find—there, as if they'd always been—the exact number of chairs needed for everyone to claim a seat.

But what an odd assortment of furniture it was!

A room-centered coffee table had been fashioned from a giant horn. Eken gulped, awed yet curious about what sort of creature it might have come from. Each chair had an end table paired with it, and each end table had a distinct color painted over its metal, colors that reminded him of the vibrant scarf. The chairs themselves were bits and pieces of stick and stone strapped together with vines as thick as his arm. They looked uncomfortable, but when Eken lowered himself into the closest one, a contented sigh escaped his lips. He relished the feel of it, the way it cushioned every aching muscle just so, the chair softer than the premium resting cots Plow & Lantern offered weary travelers. Eken knew because he'd once snuck a rest while other guests demanded Proprietor Dunsill's attention.

His mind refreshed by the tea and his body by the chair, his gaze wandered, absorbing every interior oddity. The floor was grouted river rock, polished smooth as a marble floor; the walls constructed of intertwining vines, leaves and branches; while even larger branches, as large as tree trunks themselves, formed the ceiling, though worryingly unconnected to any supporting tree.

His throat tightened with rising panic and he wondered the whole lot didn't come crashing on his head while he sipped on his tea. But the old man continued pouring cups of tea with unconcerned ease, and as no one else seemed bothered by the questionable nature of the home's construction, Eken allowed himself to relax.

Besides the unexpected seating, the room was remarkably sparse; no artwork adorned the walls, save for one large wooden board hanging on the wall opposite the front door. Rows of black marks lined the board, and dangling below, a piece of charcoal, secured to a string.

"What do we call you?" asked Magnus after they'd taken a moment to settle in, sip on their chockberry tea, nibble on some honey-bread and gawk at the cottage oddities.

"Eh? Yes, yes, happy to have guests call on me," said the old man. "Not that many do."

"No, what do we call you? What's your name?"

"No reason to call me names. If you don't like my cottage or my furnishings, just say so." The old man glared.

Magnus sighed. Aurelia stifled a laugh and caught the old man's eye with a twinkle reserved just for her. The thought struck her—*he's having a laugh at our expense.*

"Do you live here alone?" She asked, curious, as she'd seen no signs of anyone else.

"Me? No, I'm never alone," he said, but didn't clarify, adding as an afterthought, "You can call me Tobwhit, pleased to make your acquaintance."

He asked their names and where they hailed from, leading to a few moments of idle chit-chat. Occasionally he nodded off to sleep, though he'd wake and not seem to miss a beat. He'd perk up at a random town name and ask if they knew so and so. The answer invariably being no.

When the pleasantries ended, old Tobwhit announced, "I'm much too tired for talk of Gray Cloaks. I'll need rest before embarking on that discussion!" He puttered about for a moment, cleaning up from the tea. "Your rooms are upstairs, third floor. Everything's arranged. And the pantry's through that door if you get hungry. Make yourselves at home."

With a contented sigh, he settled into his chair, sinking deep, folding into the chair's rows of rocks and sticks, so that he all but disappeared. A few wisps of white hair stuck out from the folds, passing for an animal curled up asleep. It was such an odd sight that Aurelia burst out laughing.

Magnus, impatience flaring, strode to Tobwhit's chair and waved his hand at what remained of the old man. When that had no effect, he grabbed a fistful of hair and gave it a yank. Tobwhit didn't stir.

"Leave him alone," said Tobias. "He welcomed us hospitably enough to his home. I believe he's done for now."

The guests dispersed, Aurelia found herself drawn upstairs, wondering how their host could have arranged their rooms when he'd never left the first floor.

She ascended the staircase determined to find out. On the second floor, Magnus studied a strange collection of objects cluttering a table. Tobwhit's scarf lay discarded on the table's edge.

That's odd, she thought, *how did his scarf get here?*

She hurried on, eager to see her room, taking the stairs two at a time until the staircase emptied onto a third-floor balcony. There it connected to a hallway running the length of the cottage, off of which Aurelia counted ten doors, enough for the guests and one for their host. As she walked the hall, she was only mildly surprised to discover an iron plate affixed to each door, and on each plate an engraved name. *Magnus Alwyn. Eken Potterfeld. Daphne Vale. Tobias Karrow.* And so on.

The doors weren't really doors at all but, like everything else in the home, were fashioned of something unusual. These were giant shields, like those she'd only heard of in stories, shields which hung from the bastion walls of the noble houses, displaying a family's coat-of-arms. She clapped in delight when she saw that these shield-doors also bore a coat-of-arms, each unique. She hurried on, looking for her own.

And there it was, beside the last door on the left.

Aurelia Talbot.

She traced the letter indentations, wondering at the exquisite craftsmanship. Beneath the name plaque a coat-of-arms centered in its design, hers featuring a dark storm cloud, so vivid she could smell the rain and feel the electric charge building in the storm. Her hand shook as she reached towards it. The rain smell thickened, tickling her nose. Was it more than just her imagination? She smelled damp earth, wet grass. The prickling sensation of an electric current coursed across her skin; the storm cloud pulsed with lightning; a breeze tugged at her hair.

Her fingertips brushed the storm cloud, and the sensations stopped. She blinked. Only a painting, though a moment ago so much more than that.

Hadn't it been?

Her heart raced, goose bumps prickling her skin.

Another feature of the design caught her eye—what looked remarkably like a Dorakian village. She could make out the towering Great Hall and the Tol Mountains an always present backdrop. In the village, four distinct human figures and, beside them, a stone severed by a jagged bolt of lightning.

Her curiosity piqued by the designs, she couldn't help but move from shield to shield, studying each with interest.

Saul Aldriomo. A blood-soaked knife embedded in a hand.

Morco De'ril. Two images. One of Morco himself, carrying a young woman with a stone on her forehead, the image so obvious it seemed to be of Morco and Daphne. The second image wasn't so much an image as it was a mass of dark swirling shadows engulfing Morco's likeness.

She didn't much care for that one. Even as she stared, the mass of shadows moved, twisting and writhing, a whisper lifting from them to fill her ears, an ugliness borne along by words that left the taste of curdled milk in her mouth.

Her hand drifted to the necklace around her neck. Its cool touch comforted. The whispers ceased. She shook her mind clear, wondering at the images. For the first time since meeting Tobwhit and arriving at his strange cottage, she felt unwelcome.

She glanced again at the image, but it lay still, simply a drawing of shadows.

Unable to help herself, she moved on to the next. *Eken Potterfeld*. A book centered heavily in the design, and she marveled at the words gracing its spine—*Of Magic and Its Properties*—the very book he'd referenced earlier!

She retraced her steps to the door past her own, the last on the hallway, the tenth door, a door she'd assumed led to a room for Tobwhit. But the plaque's name hit her full in the gut. It wasn't what she'd expected.

Col Blackwood.

He should have been here. She swallowed down bile, a sour taste in her mouth, felt the betrayal afresh, his words ringing in her ears—*you can have her, she's not worth it.*

Col's coat-of-arms bore a single image. A seated figure, head bowed under the yoke of a pair of scales. The left scale sagged lower than its twin, bearing a heavy weight—a soldier, astride a giant steed. Both rider and horse wore plated armor. In contrast, the right scale bore a lighter weight, for on it reclined a girl, wearing a simple blue dress.

She blinked and found she'd moved; her feet outside another door. The plate read *Daphne Vale*. For no reason she could explain, she pushed on the door and it swung open.

Inside lay Daphne on a settee.

How did she get here?

Aurelia could have sworn she'd been first up the staircase. She shut the door softly, more from habit than from fear of waking Daphne. *If only a slamming door could.*

The next door over, *Magnus Alwyn*.

Centered in its design: a woman cradling a baby, a blazing sun hovering over her shoulder. The woman created no shadow, though the baby did. Other drawings surrounded the central image, each featuring a woman. In one, she knelt before a blackened sun. In another, she held a bolt of lightning in her hand. Still another, the woman rested beneath a willow tree.

While she puzzled over the images, the door swung open. *Magnus.* His muscular frame filled the doorway.

"Pot drummer." He stood close.

Too close.

"I um ..." Aurelia twisted a lock of hair between her fingers. "How did you even get up here? No one else followed me up."

"You're confused; I was first up the stairs," said Magnus, shifting his weight to lean against the doorframe, before scratching at his head with a confused look himself, "But, no, there you were, holding Tobwhit's scarf, how did you -"

"No, uh-uh ..." Aurelia shook her head. "I saw you, there on the second floor, studying -"

She stopped mid-sentence. Was she sure? She'd been so eager to check out the rooms. *But I did see him on the second floor, right?*

"Studying ...?" prodded Magnus.

I must look a fool, she thought, mouth gaping wide enough to catch a moth, unable to think clearly or finish a sentence. The silence stretched between them, unbearable. She had to fill it with something. "How's your room? Comfortable? Delicious tea, am I right? And what a long day ... can you believe these shields and their designs!"

"Shields?" asked Magnus, but with a slight grin on his face listening to her ramble.

"The doors of course ..." Her gaze flicked to his door—plain unadorned wood. "I could have sworn ..."

She ran the hallway, door to door, confused, for they weren't shields any more, just plain oak doors. She returned sheepishly to Magnus, who'd watched her frantic search.

"You okay, pot drummer?"

"I think I need to lie down," and she meant it, the hall spinning.

Magnus took her by the arm and led her inside.

Unlike the furnishings downstairs, the offering here was resplendent: a marble washbasin to refresh oneself, a pitcher of tea and plate of crisps waiting on a nearby cart as if expecting company, and a broad settee couch with sloped ends for reclining as was fashionable in the Capitol. A smattering of pillows beckoned invitingly. At the opposite end of the room, an arched opening led to an alcove occupied by an ornate bed and fine silken sheets that looked nearly as inviting.

Aurelia sank gratefully into the settee while Magnus poured her a drink. In the washbasin he dunked a cloth square, wrung out the excess. She sipped the tea and nibbled on a crisp as he folded the cloth and laid it across her forehead. She reached to adjust the cloth and her fingertips brushed his. It was brief, just a moment, but the feeling electrified, like the storm cloud in her coat-of-arms.

She nearly told him then, all of it. Her experience with the coat-of-arms, the way he made her feel, his touch electrifying, but thought better of it. She turned away embarrassed as an awkward silence settled over the room, broken only by her hammering heart. He sat so close.

"Strange house ... isn't it." Magnus cleared his throat. "And a strange man."

"Yes," conceded Aurelia. "Though I'm fond of old Tobwhit."

She closed her eyes, to stop her head from spinning and because she found staring at Magnus' face, so close, unnerving.

"I should let you rest. I'll leave."

"No, don't," pleaded Aurelia, grabbing his arm. "Don't go! Stay. We can talk."

"About what?"

"Tell me ... your story. Tell me everything. Family, life back home, what you did before the Ka ... anything but the army. I don't want to hear about that."

"I was born in the sun's watch," began Magnus.

"What kind of start is that!" Her eyes flew open—*is he poking fun at me?*—but his face was serious.

"Are you going to let me tell my story, pot drummer, or would you like to?" he asked, swatting her with a settee pillow.

She threw up her hands, warded the blow, peeked between her fingers and found him studying her, a slight smile on his lips. She settled in, closed her eyes and prepared to listen, telling herself not to interrupt again.

"As I was saying, I was born in the sun's watch. Might seem a strange detail, but on the Plains, that never happens. Babies are always born at night, when it's dark. Been that way for centuries."

Aurelia appraised Magnus with a skeptical look. He shrugged, raised his hands palms up.

"I swear! It's true. No one knows why, but it's a fact of life in the Plains."

"If you're pregnant in the Plains," teased Aurelia, "but leave the Plains to give birth, will it still happen at night?"

"And that is why I never share this with anyone!" His eyes narrowed. "If you're not from the Plains, you don't get it."

Aurelia tried squashing her laughter, but it was a struggle to look at Magnus with a straight face. "So what you're trying to say is that you're special?"

His face darkened. "I -"

A knock at the door interrupted.

You are most certainly special, thought Aurelia.

"What's that?" he asked, turning back, his hand on the door latch. "I thought I heard you say something."

Aurelia's neck flushed red. *Did I say that out loud?*

"Nothing!" she squeaked.

Chapter Twenty-Six
The Spiral Staircase

Magnus studied Aurelia a moment longer. *Could have sworn she said I was special. Do I tell her I feel the same about her?* His heart hammered, threatening to rip from his chest, its beating so loud he wondered she didn't mention it.

"Magnus!" Another sharp rap at the door. "You in there?"

Disappointed, or perhaps relieved, Magnus opened the door.

"We have a problem," said Bochim before noticing Aurelia lying on the settee. "Oh, hi Aurelia, sorry, didn't see you there. You okay?"

"A little light-headed," answered Aurelia, but she swung her feet to the floor and sat up. "What's wrong?"

"You both need to see this."

Bochim led them down the spiral staircase to the second floor. Certain he'd never been on this floor, despite anything Aurelia said, Magnus whistled low and loud. Running the length of the second floor were three rows of six tables each, with the oddest assortment of objects cluttering the tables.

One table piled high with farming tools, some similar to those he used back home, others unfamiliar and strange. Another held an odd collection of weaponry, unlike anything he'd seen before. A large pottery wheel dominated the space on the next table, though the scraps of clay spilling onto the floor were twisted and warped beyond recognition. An angled chair waited expectantly beside the wheel, as if its occupant would return any moment, and Tobwhit's colorful scarf draped across the chair's back. At yet another table, stacks of books ceiling high, covering any and all topics one might care to read, and there sat Eken, eyes shining, obviously in a good mood, nose buried in an open book, though he made time for a quick hug with Aurelia and a nod to Magnus. On another table, glass containers of every shape and size littered its surface. Bubbling liquids swirled inside—midnight blacks, blood reds, pale greens, pumpkin oranges and sea-green blues—the colors as varied as the jars which held them.

"I know, I know," Bochim was saying. "It's all so strange, isn't it? But that's not why I brought you."

Bochim gestured to the far corner, where Magnus noticed the others—save Tobwhit—gathered at a window. As with most things in the cottage, it wasn't what one would expect. What served as a window was a set of oversized wooden spoons with deep gouges marking their surface, the lot of them bound by vines, while clear glass beads occupied the grooves between the spoons, creating a screen of sorts. The whole contraption rested on a hinge and so served as a covering for a small square opening. When shut, the window screen was remarkably airtight, but for the time being the screen had been thrust open, allowing the cottage guests to gather around, anxiously whispering among themselves, craning their necks to peer outside, though they quickly made space for the new arrivals. What Magnus saw beyond the window made his heart sink. His hand found Aurelia's and squeezed tight.

The Ka had discovered them.

Soldiers flooded the forest, some stalking across the carpeting of hemlock needles, others straying here or there on the path. Wolfhounds strained at their leashes, sniffing at the trail, baying in protest at their restraints.

I've failed. Let my friends down. The weight of it pressed like a millstone grinding his ribs.

"What do we do?" asked Aurelia. "Do we make a run for it?"

"I say we fight!" boomed Morco.

"Both are pointless," moaned a cynical Saul. "To run is a fool's dream. If the Ka don't catch us, the wolfhounds will. And we can't fight our way out, we're outnumbered."

"Saul's right," said Magnus. "I'll seek parley, negotiate terms, convince Drael this was all my doing."

Even as he voiced it, he knew how slim the chances. It was unlike Drael to show mercy, but he had to try, for the sake of his friends. *For Aurelia.*

"Nonsense," chided Tobias.

"We won't hide behind you," agreed Veyra. "We each chose this path, and I don't regret it. Whatever comes."

A chorus of *aye!'s* confirmed her response. Magnus nodded, grateful.

"Silly humans!" said a voice behind them. "Always looking, never seeing."

Startled, Magnus whirled toward the sound, but saw no one.

"Did you all -?" but it was apparent they had, for every eye scanned the room.

The voice bore a musical quality to it, perhaps not even human. A few days ago, he'd have thought he was losing his mind, but recent experiences had opened it to other possibilities.

"My point proven," said the voice, with an exaggerated sigh, "always looking but never seeing."

Magnus swore the voice came from the pottery wheel chair, but it sat empty. Someone had moved Tobwhit's scarf, it no longer draped across the chair's back, but lay on the seat, until one end of the scarf flicked and twisted, without human aid, swishing through the air like a tail.

"Did that just -?" asked Tobias.

"Yes, it did!" said Magnus, as the scarf expanded, puffing outward, or maybe his understanding did the expanding, his eyes finally seeing what his mind hadn't wanted to. Soon the scarf looked nothing like a scarf at all, and Magnus couldn't recall why he'd ever thought it one. Distinct features materialized. A head, an abdomen, legs and paws, or at least that was the best Magnus could understand of the colorful creature, its fur shimmering rainbow-like colors. Although it bore a slight resemblance to ...

"What was that animal in the Capitol? The pet that Drael's daughter carried around their estate?"

"Oh, you mean a cat," said Tobias.

"Yes, that's it! A cat." Though he'd heard of the exotic creatures that hailed from the Twelve Isles, Magnus had never seen one until the Capitol.

"I am most definitely not a cat. Whatever that is," disdain apparent in the furry shape's voice. As it spoke, it leapt from the table and sauntered towards Aurelia, furry legs vibrating furiously, propelling it forward. Its head contained the usual eyes, mouth, ears and nose of an animal, though they were oversized, even as the creature itself was rather large, at least twice the size of a cat. Two wickedly long claws poked from the end of each leg, clicking menacingly against the plank floor as it crossed the room. *I'd hate to be on the receiving end of those.* But there was nothing menacing about it as it butted its head against Aurelia, winding between her legs, speaking as it went, "Cat. Sounds plain. Boring. Don't like it."

Magnus held back a laugh. It most certainly wasn't the animal he'd first seen in the Capitol, though it could be that animal's distant magical cousin.

"What do we call you then?" asked Aurelia, tentative as she ran her hand across the creature's fur. Its throat rumbled, seeming to enjoy the attention, arching its body to meet her hand.

"I answer to NoNo," said the being.

"NoNo?" laughed Veyra. "What a strange name!"

"Not at all," he replied, a slight hiss to his voice. "I bear an older name, but my servant was the first to call me NoNo, and I rather like it. Has a delightful ring, wouldn't you say?"

The cat-like creature smiled, revealing a mouth full of razor-sharp fangs, begging anyone to disagree.

"Your servant?" wondered Magnus out-loud. They'd seen no one beyond Tobwhit.

"Yes, you met him earlier. The one asleep in his chair."

"He's your servant?" blurted Veyra.

"But of course. He feeds me, bathes me, brushes me, and when I allow it, pets me or plays with me."

NoNo meandered between each set of human legs, rubbing against them, or sniffing their feet. When he sniffed, his nostrils flared violently open. He jumped to the windowsill, stretching his two front legs on the wooden spoons, raking his claws down their length.

Now the deep gouges make sense, thought Magnus.

"What an interesting sight indeed," remarked NoNo, peering at the soldiers scurrying below. "Never have we had so many guests in our little corner of the world."

"They mean to do us harm."

"For what reason?"

"Until recently, some of us here were part of that army," replied Magnus, clearing his throat as he spoke, "But we, uh, we experienced a change of heart after they maimed our friend Daphne. Their commander ordered a stone cut from her forehead."

NoNo's eyes narrowed in tight slits. "Yes, I saw her. A nasty business indeed." Though his tone clipped tight, he stretched as languidly as if there wasn't a care in the world. He faced Aurelia, his big eyes close to hers as he sat on the windowsill. "Were you also part of their army?"

"No, definitely not." She laughed. "I'm a Dorakian. I live south of here, in the village of Chelam."

"Ah, a Dorakian! Never met one before, but I like what my servant tells me. Is it true, do you celebrate more than a hundred festivals each year?"

"We do. One hundred and eleven to be exact."

"Marvelous! Can I attend one with you? Please?" NoNo cocked his head sideways, striking the most pitiful of expressions.

"Yes, of course!" said Aurelia, and impulsively she leaned forward and rubbed her nose against NoNo's, who seemed to like the gesture. "I would love if you accompanied me home to Chelam."

"No one is going anywhere with all those soldiers out there," remarked Magnus dryly, "and we won't last long in here either."

"Nonsense, we have nothing to fear from them," the creature replied, waving a furry leg in a very human-like gesture of dismissal. "Like I said, you're looking, but you're not seeing."

NoNo bobbed his head toward the window, urging Magnus to look again. When he did, the soldiers were no closer to the cottage than before, though time had passed in their conversation.

"I don't understand."

"Thick as porridge, aren't you?" tsked NoNo matter-of-factly. "You recall your journey on the path?"

Magnus nodded.

"Without a guide forcing one to stay on the path, no one ever does. What crazy fool would? And the wolfhounds, smelling your scent directly to their right or left, are so confused they simply bound here and there, or worse yet, charge straight ahead, cutting across the path. You see, the only way to actually arrive at this cottage is to follow the path. Completely. Beginning to end, without exception."

"You mean we're safe?" asked Aurelia breathlessly.

"Yes." NoNo flicked his tail. "They are of no concern. They'll never find us."

NoNo's confidence proved contagious. Still, it was hard for Magnus to relax. Could the magic be so strong to keep Lavonshia's best-trained soldiers and wolfhounds at bay?

In a final act of mischief, NoNo turned his backside to the open window and discharged a nauseating haze. He leapt to the floor and sauntered across the room with a hint of feral amusement in his eyes, though they glittered dangerously. "If that doesn't send them scurrying from the forest, I don't know what will. Aurelia dear, close the window, would you?"

With that, NoNo descended the spiral staircase.

Chapter Twenty-Seven
They'll Be Mine Again

Back in Lumath, upon learning of the prisoners' escape, Drael promptly ordered the guard's execution. His anger seethed—at his soldiers, at the guards, at Magnus, even at himself if he was willing to be honest. *How did I not see it coming?* Magnus' fixation on his vows. That was the moment. Unusual for a Ka to hold that level of concern for a Binder and her companions.

Drael paced, ignoring the clerks who refused to meet his eye, fuming at this latest setback and the disastrous campaign into Gray Cloak territory. His heart yearned for the comforts of his Capitol estate, but the thought of meeting the King's displeasure turned Drael's gut sour. *Perhaps it's time.* The crusade for King and Kingdom no longer invigorating as they once were, and besides, his wife had urged his resignation for years. He sank into a chair, his old bones creaking. *Is this my end? Washed up, useless, a failure?* His wife was right, time to put his warring ways to rest, though he couldn't ignore the risk of returning to the King empty-handed.

A trembling guard interrupted his musings: Col, the Dorakian left behind, requested an audience.

Drael's gut relaxed just a bit, relishing the fear he elicited from Col once the man stood in his presence. *I may be old, but I still got it.* A large man at seven spans tall, the regiment commander was a formidable presence. Drael growled all the same, fear or no. "Don't have time for waste."

"Sir, allow me to accompany the wolfhounds, I -"

Drael considered ordering the boy whipped for his insolence. *To accompany skilled trackers?* The friends hadn't trusted him, neither did he.

But the guard escorting Col from the tent offered a quick bit of whispered advice: "See Tarn."

Tarn had little interest in helping Col.

"No."

"Please!" begged Col. "I can help bring them in."

"I said no. Go, before I impale you on the tip of a sword."

Dismissed, disheartened, Col wandered the Ka camp, dwelling on regret and the harsh words last spoken to Aurelia. *If only she'd listened, accepted my help. Stubborn girl.* Still, she hadn't deserved it, and if he'd been honest with himself, he would have admitted it. But Lumath wasn't his problem. His friends' actions forced his hand. Why couldn't they just cooperate with the Ka?

His wandering led him to the training ring, or the Pit, as the soldiers affectionately called it. Ostensibly for training, the Pit rarely served that purpose. More often than not, the Ka used it to settle a grudge, a practice known by officers but not officially sanctioned. In a Ka encampment, the Pit was little more than a scar of trampled earth, stakes hammered into a rough semblance of a circle, rope stretched taut between them. Room enough to fight, but nowhere to flee.

To prevent a mortal wound, combatants fit their swords with a set of blunting edges. The blunts added a slight weight, but few argued it limited the weapon's use, making it an effective solution for a grudge match. It wouldn't kill, but broken bones, concussions, and more serious injuries were common. Many a soldier's career ended abruptly following a grudge match.

Col wormed his way to the ropes and joined in the heckling of a round's loser. Or the round's winner if neither contestant fought well. After one such match, his taunts caught the winner's ear, who turned to rail against him.

"Think you can do better?"

"You wouldn't last a moment against me!" Col's mocking cry carried over the raucous crowd, earning him hearty cheers.

"Someone get this kid a sword!" The challenger strutted the field, prepared to teach the young upstart a lesson.

If he only knew, thought Col with a wicked grin.

As a young boy, Col had one wish—to join the Ka—a desire instilled at the tender age of six when a band of Travelers spent the summer in Chelam. Three times an eight-day their plays featured stories of glory won in battle. The vivid re-enactments filled his young mind with fantasies of becoming Ka. By summer's end, he announced to his father that one day he would be the Ka's supreme commander, second only to the King.

His father laughed.

But time did nothing to diminish Col's desire. As an unruly teenager, he picked fights with other village boys, even those many years his senior. Fed up with his son's reckless temper, Jusel Blackwood found a way to channel it: hiring a servant as a sparring partner.

A sparring partner at his beck and call only solidified Col's desire to be a master swordsman and join the Ka. He spent his days at practice, often late into the evening too, and by the age of fourteen was regularly beating the servant in their matches. Eager for a challenge, he demanded his parents secure the best the land offered.

For the Blackwoods, Chelam's wealthiest and most prestigious family, money was no object, though Jusel cringed at what it would cost to bring the best to Chelam. But sensing nothing less would satisfy his son, he paid the price. On Col's sixteenth hunter's moon, he presented to his son a master swordsman known as Cassian di'Loru.

The Blackwood's finance steward advised against such an acquisition, but more than being a doting father, Jusel was a shrewd businessman, recognizing an opportunity to both satisfy his son and turn a tidy profit. Cassian's skills with the sword were legendary and Jusel calculated that the man as a tournament headliner would help put Dorak on the map, in turn improving the Blackwood's other business ventures—including ownership of numerous inns and taverns. A revival of Dorakian tourism for the masses? Jusel could smell the coppery scent of the coin already.

That day, on his sixteenth hunter's moon, Col challenged the swordmaster to a match, and was promptly and soundly beaten. Despite the standard blunting edges, by the match's end Col's arm hung useless at his side and he trudged from the match with a noticeable limp. Jusel feared the embarrassment and the injury would discourage his son, fears grounded more in thoughts of lost earnings rather than concern for his son's wellbeing. But instead, when Col healed from his injuries, he plunged headlong into training, though he was more careful in bouts with Cassian, who for his part was pleased to have taught the arrogant boy a lesson.

Over the ensuing months, Col's skills steadily improved. Just before his seventeenth hunter's moon celebration, he won his first match against the swordmaster, and by the time he saw his eighteenth he was routinely beating Cassian one out of every three bouts.

Col was far from satisfied with these results, though his father reminded him that Cassian was the premier swordmaster in the Kingdom of Lavonshia, and Col's results against him exemplary. Few could claim to have bested Cassian. At only eighteen, his progress was remarkable.

But Col allowed pride to crush his spirit, convincing himself he'd reached the height of his skills, and while he was a polished swordsman, and could best most any man, or woman, in the kingdom, it meant nothing if Cassian held the upper-hand in their matches. Col hated losing.

He announced his retirement at the tender age of eighteen, dismissing Cassian on a day when the swordmaster had bested him narrowly in five straight rounds. Though Col would never lose his love for the Ka or the sword, Jusel lost any payoff on his investment. Cassian left promptly for the Capitol, fed up with the Blackwoods and their son, while a furious Jusel didn't speak with his son for a moon cycle.

But Col's mother, as perceptive women often do, recognized her son's decision had more to do with a certain girl in Chelam than anything else. He'd found a new passion: Aurelia.

With the same intense focus he'd applied to training, he wooed Aurelia. She became his obsession, and though she'd seen more hunter's moons and steadfastly denied his advances, he pursued her until that fateful day when the Honored Ones arrived in Chelam and urged her to flee.

The irony wasn't lost on Col. In pursuing Aurelia, he'd come full circle to his first love. She'd abandoned him, or so he reasoned, wounding him more deeply than he cared to admit, yet here lay an opportunity to showcase his skills and fulfill his dreams of glory. Not that he'd abandoned the dream of acquiring Aurelia as wife, but today he would prove his mettle and worth to the Ka. A little detour on the way to Aurelia, without pausing to consider whether it was Aurelia he missed, or simply the feeling of being chosen.

He ducked under the rope and stepped into the ring.

He ripped off his shirt, flexing honed muscles. He took care of his body, one of the early lessons Cassian taught him, and it showed. The onlookers hooted and crowed, enjoying the show as he enjoyed the attention, pumping a fist in the air, stirring up the crowd. When they placed a blunted sword in his hand, he checked its clasp, *snug but oddly tight* he thought briefly, before raising it to salute his adversary as Cassian had taught him. His challenger laughed, not knowing it would be his last of the day, the match over before the crowd's cheers hardly began, the soldier handily beaten without landing a single strike on Col. He lay bruised and broken in the Pit until friends assisted him off the field, accompanied by a round of hearty boos.

Adrenaline coursing, Col called for another challenger. He bested the second man, followed by a third, a woman who seemed as delighted to be in the same ring with him as to lose, before easily besting a fourth opponent as well. The crowd cheered lustily and he laughed with unbridled joy at the pleasure of the fight.

When he called for a fifth opponent, the crowd stilled, his challenge going unanswered. By now, they'd noted his skills, soldiers glancing uneasily at each other, no one eager to take a beating, until Tarn stepped into the ring.

Col studied his new opponent, recognizing the officer who'd dismissed him earlier. Though he'd dispensed with other opponents easily, he recognized this one would not be so easy.

Tarn was a massive brute of a soldier. Thick-chested, with a neck like an anvil, muscular arms twice the size of Col's, a mean scar angling across his cheek. It was obvious he'd seen his share of fighting, and by the way he held his sword and shifted his stance, Col sensed he was one to be wary of.

"Do you need a rest, boy, or shall we start?"

"I need no rest!" said Col. "A sip of water and I'll be ready."

The reply proved Tarn's suspicion. He'd been watching from the sidelines and the boy was good. Very good. But he'd noticed a weakness—Col was arrogant. Very arrogant. He tended to lunge off balance for a finishing blow, though none of his opponents had taken advantage. It was an error Tarn beat mercilessly from new recruits, and he planned to take advantage of the same cockiness he sensed in Col.

News of Tarn accepting the upstart's challenge spread like wildfire. The crowd swelled to record numbers, men and women jostling for the best view. A few of the old-timers stayed away, shaking their heads, wishing the boy luck. They'd witnessed enough of Tarn's brutal lessons.

Col raised his sword in salute as he'd done with every other challenger, but Tarn, holding to no such chivalrous rules, charged with a frightening bellow. His blows came fast and furious. Col backpedaled, desperate, parrying one strike and then another. His body ached from the force of the blows, and his arms shook, the grasp on his sword weakening. Sweat beaded despite the day's coolness. In a moment of clarity, he realized how foolish he'd been to enter a match against an opponent of Tarn's caliber without rest.

Driven to one knee, he cried out as Tarn chopped and thrust, striking blow after blow. Hate clouded the man's eyes.

I could die here, thought Col. *Beat senseless.*

The knowledge drove him. He shoved Tarn back, regained his feet, feinted left, tossing his sword to his right hand, a quick chopping stab at his opponent's knee. The man stumbled, crying out as pain lanced through his leg. The crowd gasped.

Gritting his teeth, Tarn stepped back. Recalculating. Realizing his mistake. The boy was more skilled than he'd shown; he'd been holding back.

Tarn charged again, screaming, cursing, bearing down on his opponent with superior size and weight.

Muscles straining, bodies bruised as blunted swords found their mark. The crowd, its noise, fading into the background; only the fight mattered. The need to win. To survive.

Bloodlust stirred in the crowd, a chant rising, cheers for the newcomer.

Col!

Col!

Col!

The fight slowed, each man catching his breath, sizing up his opponent, feinting right, left, striking, parrying. Waiting for an opening. For the right moment.

Tarn pursued a dogged assault on the younger man, though the strike below his knee had slowed him. Blood trickled from a cut above one eye.

The crowd sensed the tide turning in Col's favor.

But Col tired rapidly. Too many matches, too many blows, arms and legs trembling from the effort to keep Tarn at bay. His body screamed for rest. His thoughts dulled. *Just give in. Surrender.*

A hush settled as the crowd parted like a sea of wheat stalks before the scythe. Drael had arrived.

At the sight of his commander's snow-white head, Tarn renewed the attack, ferocious, hammering, chopping, thrusting. Though Tarn was a battle-tested veteran, Col held the advantage—youth, speed, natural ability, and swordmaster training. But as the match wore on, Tarn's experience and battle-forged stamina tipped the scales.

A charge by Tarn, pressing his weight against Col, who slipped, sword bucking hard against the ground, wrist snapping. He cried out, his sword clattered to the ground. But Col wasn't finished, able to handle the sword nearly as well with the right hand. With practiced ease, he scooped up the sword and jabbed sideways, hard and quick. Being blunted, it didn't pierce, but broke ribs. Tarn grunted, stumbled, rested his sword against the ground, struggled to breathe. He growled like a feral beast and wiped blood from his eye.

Sensing an advantage, Col lunged with a strike aimed at Tarn's throat. It wouldn't kill, but he'd never speak again.

It was the moment Tarn had waited for. An overzealous calculation. He side-stepped, the energy of the thrust carrying Col by as Tarn swung his blade in a downward arc. A sickening crunch. A blow to the back of the legs. Col's knee buckled. A cry of anguish as he crashed to the ground.

The match had turned in an instant.

Col struggled to stand, slipped, struggled to his feet again, legs threatening to buckle beneath him.

The crowd fickle, their chants changed.

Tarn!

Tarn!

Tarn!

"I yield!" cried Col.

It had been a bitter match, well fought, and though Tarn recognized a worthy opponent, he'd forgotten long ago what mercy looked like.

His eyes scanned the crowd, seeking one face.

He found it.

Drael nodded, all Tarn needed before his commander turned and walked away. The crowd noticed, some swore softly, a few veterans looked away.

"Sorry, boy," Tarn grimaced from broken ribs. "You fought well." He fiddled for a moment with the blunting clasp, blinking back sweat and blood. He slid the sword free; its blade glinted wickedly in the sun.

Col's fingers trembled as he struggled with the clasp on his own sword, struggling to free the blade so iron could meet iron. It wouldn't budge. Someone had soldered the clasp in place. He'd never had a chance; the fight rigged from the start. Tarn was not one to leave such things to chance.

Col limped backwards, desperate for time, scanned the crowd for help, for anyone with the sense to end the match without the loss of life. His life.

"I yield!" he cried again.

There was no help coming. The chants stilled. The watching mob silent, looking away. An eagle screeched as it wheeled overhead.

No blunting edges would save his life now.

Tarn's face lit in a malicious grin, the sweep of his sword a killing blow. But Col willed his wounded body to respond. He dropped to his knees, steeling himself against the pain and the desire to just give up. He lunged forward, seized Tarn in an embrace, one hand on the giant man's neck to pull him close, the other on Tarn's wrist, twisting, redirecting the sword's path.

It penetrated, slicing clean, deep into Tarn's side. Yet even while his lifeblood fled, the man yanked the sword free. A bellow of rage, death was close but not yet, fist plowing into Col's face, knocked him sprawling to the ground, sword raised in fury, one last act by the man named Tarn, a man history would soon forget.

Col twisted away, raising an arm to ward the blow that severed his right arm, just below the shoulder.

Tarn stumbled to the ground, chest heaving, clutching at his side where blood flowed between his fingers, eyes rolling back in his head as he died.

Col woke. Early evening. He lay on his back, wagon wheels creaking, jostling him forward. A bandaged shoulder throbbed angrily where his arm had once been.

"Water," he croaked.

A flask touched his lips, and he drank greedily before slipping back into unconsciousness, dreaming of the Ka and a girl named Aurelia.

He woke again, found himself in a tent, lying on a cot. Daylight streamed through an opening. His shoulder still ached, but not as it had. He was weak, very weak, but he was alive.

Lurching to his feet, he stumbled outside, where a noxious odor lingered.

"What happened?" he asked a nearby soldier.

"Isn't it obvious?" The soldier's face wrinkled in disgust, calling over his shoulder as he hurried by, "That's no natural smell. Binders."

Col hobbled through a camp in disarray, soldiers in various shades of pale, gathered near or heading for the healer's tent, liberally sharing buckets laden with puke, the sight and sound of their retching as bad as the smell. He was thankful to have been unconscious.

He found himself outside Drael's tent once more. Swallowed. Nervous. Fear clawed at his gut. *What will my punishment be for killing Tarn?* A guard admitted him inside, where a fire burned in a corner brazier, providing warmth and light to the interior. A few well-placed lanterns reached where the firelight didn't. The tent housed several field desks with men busy at work, furiously scribbling, while Drael stooped over the center desk, studying reports, muttering curses at problems and delays.

"Seems congratulations are in order." Drael spoke without turning, his tone unreadable.

"I'm sorry, I didn't know -"

"Tarn chose the fight," Drael waved a dismissive hand, "I've wasted little thought on it. You, though ... impressive. Despite your injuries, I ordered our healer take you under his charge. I had to know—where did a Dorakian learn to fight like that?"

"Cassian di'Loru. A master swordsman hired by my father to train me."

Drael stiffened though his expression remained neutral. Col didn't care for the gleam in his eye. The commander studied him for a moment, one hand rubbing at a weathered face, the other resting on the sword hilt strapped at his side.

"And where is this Cassian now?"

"Dismissed. Learned all I could from him."

"Cassian and I go way back. Fellow soldiers and all. If he contacts you, I'd like to know his whereabouts." When Col hesitated, Drael added, "I'd be indebted."

He liked the sound of that. Helping Drael could prove advantageous. He inclined his head. A nod of understanding.

"That's settled then." Drael turned his attention back to his desk. "In the meantime, we have deserters and a Binder to catch, and I could always use an accomplished swordsman in our campaign against the Gray Cloaks. Assuming you can still fight?"

Col's face broke into a wide grin, with a nod as he raised his remaining hand.

"Excellent. Now look at these." Drael motioned Col close. "Did we get it right?"

Approaching the desk, Col understood what the furious scribbling was all about. The desk was littered with images drawn in dark charcoal. The likeness of Aurelia stared back at him. A heading above the drawing in large block letters read,

1,000 DECRI AWARD FOR AIDING IN FUGITIVE'S ARREST, BY ORDER OF THE KING

The images weren't just of Aurelia, but of others too. Even as Col watched, a scribe finished another. A fair likeness of Magnus. A twinge of guilt pricked his heart. *My friends. On the run.* He swallowed a hard knot. Nodded. Though he didn't want to admit how spot-on Aurelia's likeness had been drawn.

"We'll plaster these in every town between here and the Capitol." Drael struck a determined fist into the desk. "They'll be mine again!"

Chapter Twenty-Eight
He Speaks of Himself

In the cottage, after NoNo sauntered to the stairs, Aurelia acted first, closing the window as instructed. She wrinkled her nose at a hint of NoNo's spray, her insides tightening in knots. Thankfully, the unusual window closed snugly, keeping the odor out. With the smell dissipating, she followed NoNo to the staircase. Her companions hadn't moved, seemingly still in shock from interacting with a talking creature. She laughed, glanced back, "What are you waiting for?"

Downstairs, NoNo was doing his best to wake Tobwhit, butting his head against the old man's chair accompanied by an ear-splitting wail.

"Worse than a cat's meow," whispered Tobias to no one in particular.

Aurelia didn't know what a cat or a meow was, but NoNo's efforts soon paid off. Tobwhit retracted himself from the folds of the chair, perking up considerably at the sight of the creature and their guests.

"Ah, I've seen you've met NoNo. I hope he didn't cause you any trouble; we don't get many visitors." Tobwhit's eyes stared into the distance. "Though now that I think of it, have we ever had guests, NoNo?"

The creature cocked his head as he considered the question, though he didn't answer, busy with a languid stretch, raking his claws across the chair.

"No! No! Stop it, bad animal." Tobwhit swatted at NoNo, who growled, jumping sideways before raising a fuzzy tail high and sauntering off towards the pantry.

"That creature will destroy this house," the old man muttered to himself. "Another four hundred years and we won't have anything left."

Remembering his guests, Tobwhit brightened considerably as he asked, "Have you rested? Enjoyed the collections on the second floor?"

Mention of the second floor reminded them about the soldiers outside, and they updated Tobwhit on the worrisome news. He raised a bushy white eyebrow upon hearing of NoNo's behavior, though he didn't comment. At the conclusion of their tale, simply offering a, "That's that then."

The remainder of the day passed pleasantly enough eating and resting, followed by more resting or more eating, depending on one's mood.

Tobwhit produced a set of Ji to the delight of Aurelia, who promptly challenged him to a game. For a moment her conscience pricked, thinking of Daphne at death's door lying in her room upstairs, but Tobwhit's smile reminded her of Koram back home and their matches of Ji, and she couldn't resist. When Tobwhit bested her easily in their first game, something Koram rarely did, she stretched, gathering her wits for a second game, and noticing her companions seemed rather at ease too. *Do we all forget Daphne so easily?* she wondered.

During the second game she swore a piece moved, unaided by human hand. She blinked. Maybe it had occupied that space all along.

"How do you keep winning?" she asked, suspicious after suffering a third humiliating defeat.

"My dear, when you've lived four hundred and sixty years, the game of Ji is a simple thing."

Reclining on a nearby couch, Magnus raised an eyebrow. "Say again?"

"Oh yes, you see, as complex a strategy as one can employ in Ji, it really comes down to -"

"No, not that! How is it possible you've lived four hundred and sixty hunter's moons? No one lives that long."

"Oh that. Sounds strange to my ears as well. But it's true. I keep track." Tobwhit nodded towards the board on the wall, the one featuring rows of black marks. "Each marks a hunter's moon. Four hundred years, or near enough, living in this cottage, and before that, sixty years elsewhere."

Magnus caught Aurelia's glance and rolled his eyes. She covered her mouth and looked away to keep from laughing before Magnus changed the subject. "What were you doing anyway, there by the road when we chanced upon you?"

"Waiting for you, of course. And that was no chance meeting."

"How's that?"

"Isn't it obvious? Fate sent you to me. I waited there every day for twenty hunter's moons, most time I've spent outdoors in years. Hmmm, maybe centuries. Though that's not the point. I knew you'd be coming; I just didn't know exactly when, so I waited. Four hundred and sixty years teaches one a little patience."

"But how did you know we'd be coming?" Aurelia pressed the point.

"To know might be a stretch, I'll give you that. A strong feeling, perhaps. But you have to listen."

"To what?"

"Why to the land of course. What a silly question!"

Once, back in Dorak, Aurelia would have dismissed him as a mad old coot, but her understanding of the world was changing swiftly. "Daphne spoke of Sensing. Is that what you mean?"

"Do youngsters nowadays not understand anything? Your parents didn't teach you to listen to the land? But yes, some call it Sensing."

"Never knew my mother, and my father taught me a great many wonderful things, but never listening to the land." She thought for a moment before adding, "You're referring to magic, to binding, aren't you?"

"Of course! Doesn't everyone know that?" asked Tobwhit in wonder.

"No, not at all," said Magnus. "No one talks about magic in Lavonshia." A thought struck him. "When did you last have contact with ... well, with anyone?"

"Hmmm," said Tobwhit, "hard to say exactly." He spent a moment counting on his fingers. "Could be ... no, not then ... of course NoNo doesn't count." He stopped, shrugged. "Four hundred years ago, give or take? After I fought in the Red War, I came here."

"The Red War!" A surprised chorus of questions as his guests gathered around, appraising Tobwhit in a new light.

"Yes, yes, to my shame. A horrible business that. I couldn't look my fellow creature in the eye after what I did. So I came here, and the longer I was here, the easier it became to never leave."

NoNo wandered in from the pantry, jumping into the old man's lap, settling in for a nap. Tobwhit petted him absentmindedly while he continued, "I think NoNo here saved me." The creature looked up from its nap and nodded its agreement. "If it hadn't been for him, I would have faded away. Not that death could have taken me; I'm not finished playing my part. And that has to do with you." He pointed a crooked finger at his guests.

"Let's come back to that," interrupted Eken, eyes gleaming, his hand patting the book in his pocket. "I want to hear more about the Red War."

"Very well, there's no harm in the telling. What would you like to know?"

"Why you?" asked Aurelia. "Eken told us it was between Gray Cloaks, between Honored Ones."

A troubled look crossed Tobwhit's face while a tear rolled down his cheek, charting a meandering path across his many wrinkles. Aurelia's heart broke, sensing even now, four hundred years later, how much pain he still bore.

When he finally answered, it was with a deep and shuddering sigh, "I fought because I was an Honored One."

Startled, Aurelia studied him with a puzzled look. "But where's your stone? I thought all Honored Ones bore the stone."

"They do, though with great difficulty one can remove, or even exchange, a stone."

Silence followed as his guests considered the implications. Aurelia leaned forward, nearly toppled from her chair as she dug anxious fingers into her seat. "Daphne? Can a stone bring her back? Do you have one we could use?"

"So many questions, and in such a hurry! You asked to hear of the Red War, rather rude to ask and not let me finish."

All that mattered to Aurelia was saving her friend, yet Tobwhit's reply stilled her. They were guests beneath his roof and the first souls he'd seen in four hundred hunter's moons.

"I'm sorry," she said, and meant it, "Go on."

Mollified, Tobwhit began, "The Red War. Aptly named. Too many lives lost, snuffed out before their time. And not just Honored Ones, mind you, countless others too. Humans. Midlings. Forever gone. But you were mistaken to assume the war occurred only between Honored Ones, or between Gray Cloaks as you call them. Perhaps at its core it began that way, but eventually it drew all into its conflict. You see, magic, the land's binding, called to us. To everyone. Demanding we choose a side. None could sit idly by."

He paused as his eyes wandered, glazed and distant, looking at no one and nothing in that room, while his guests waited patiently for him to continue.

"When the war ended, the very landscape of the world had been altered. Bindings wielded in ways never seen. It wasn't just humanity or the midlings that experienced loss. No, the land itself groaned. Did you know that the Tol Mountains didn't exist before the Red War? A result of a horrible binding used to devastating effect. You may find them breathtaking, majestic even, but the Tol Mountains are never to be trusted. They are a dark creation, a curse on the land that split the kingdom in two, a physical manifestation of Lavonshia's division, of the civil war that consumed us."

He couldn't have delivered more shocking news had he told them the sun didn't use to shine. Aurelia found it impossible to picture home without the Tol. They'd always loomed in the background, as constant an anchor as her father.

Tobwhit continued, "Those mountains killed more people and creatures then the rest of the war combined. When the ground opened and the Tol thrust upward to the sky, entire towns and villages vanished in an instant. Destroyed, gone. Unnumbered dead littered the valleys and plains. It was a horrific end to the war."

"No one had the heart to fight after that?"

"Yes, true to some extent, though the truth is never so simple. To kill the one who awakened to night, we performed an unspeakable binding, creating the Tol in its process. The horror of that act ended the war."

Aurelia stole a sharp glance at Tobwhit. *The one who awakened to night.* Not word-for-word the prophecy, yet close enough to stir a pulse of hope. Perhaps the prophecy's events had already occurred, and Gray Cloaks like Ophel clung to fairy tales long dead.

Tobwhit pressed on before she could ask.

"But at what cost I ask you? War is devastating, even when one vanquishes evil. So many dead, on both sides, and that one binding alone ... I shudder still thinking of it." Giant teardrops welled in Tobwhit's eyes. "I could no longer be an Honored One, so I forsook my people, clan Fi-jal, and came here to live out my days, overcome by shame for the part I played. But the land hasn't forgotten me. It's whispered to me throughout the years. I'm not finished. There's hope yet that I can redeem my past."

He must mean saving us from the soldiers, thought Aurelia, her gaze softening. He'd been nothing but kind, hardly the picture of someone responsible for the deaths of countless humans and midlings. Surely it couldn't have been all that bad. *Does his memory fail him?* True, Tobwhit was a little odd, but who wouldn't be after four hundred years without human contact? He seemed lighter now, as if confession had eased an old weight.

"I tire so quickly these days," he added abruptly. "I bid you good night."

Without another word, he withdrew into the chair, once again folding deep into it so that only tufts of white hair peeked out. NoNo leapt from his lap before the chair gathered him in its embrace too.

"But wait! Daphne -" cried Aurelia, trailing off when she saw it was no use. Tobwhit had chosen sleep, and she couldn't exactly blame him—Chelam's Elders were far sleepier than younger folks—she couldn't imagine how tired one must feel after experiencing four hundred and sixty hunter's moons.

"A game of Ji?" asked Eken.

Aurelia declined, apologetic, though glad to see his mind still sharp, the magic of Tobwhit's cottage doing him well; but her mind was too preoccupied, her heart too burdened for her covenant friend to focus on another game of Ji.

She checked the second-floor window, half-expecting to see soldiers still lurking, and felt a wave of relief at the sight of an empty forest; then to her room, delighted to find a nightgown waiting, an impossibly perfect fit. After refreshing herself at the washbasin, she slid, exhausted, into bed.

Some time later, she awoke, feeling more refreshed than she'd felt in days. *Even before harvest.*

She lingered in bed, delighted by its finery. The sheets were a luxurious silk fabric, finer than anything she'd ever seen at a Dorakian market. The pillow cradled her head just right, and the blanket was perfect. Not too warm or too cold, not too thin or too heavy, nor scratchy like her own back home.

A pair of windows framed the bed. She'd opened them before falling asleep, and a cool breeze stirred the air. Night had fallen while she slept, and moonlight spilled in through the windows. It was still dark, but she was no longer tired, so after a languid stretch she jumped out of bed.

There was a stillness to the cottage. She searched the first and second floors, looking for someone, anyone, but with no luck. *They must all be asleep.*

No sign of NoNo, or of Tobwhit either, whose chair sat empty.

She wandered idly among the second floor tables, examining the strange and delightful objects they held. But they couldn't keep her interest.

Truth be told, the person she'd like to see most was Magnus. To hear his voice and that story he'd begun, to simply be in his presence ...

There you go again, Aurelia! She exhaled hard, tried to banish thoughts of Magnus. If only she could speak to Daphne, about the desires weighing on her heart, or about nothing at all. The ache of missing her covenant friend pressed sharp and insistent.

Where's Tobwhit when you need him? She had so many questions, starting with, *what do you mean you can exchange a stone!*

She considered waking Eken, not that he could help with Daphne, but at least she could discuss her feelings for Magnus, until she remembered the last time she'd tried that approach. *Didn't turn out so well.* Though that wasn't fair. Lumath's magic had affected them both.

Perhaps I should go directly to Magnus. Tell him how I feel. How do I feel? she wondered. *I still barely know him!*

Lost in thought, she glanced up, startled to find herself at Daphne's door. The ghost of a smile played on her lips. *Seems these magical places have a mind of their own.*

A deep breath, a feeling that she wouldn't find her friend alone. She opened the door and stepped inside, her eyes adjusting to the dim light.

NoNo was curled at the bed's end, his head resting by Daphne's feet. Tobwhit sat bedside, a hand resting across Daphne's forehead, his eyes closed in concentration.

Or a prayer? Aurelia sensed she'd intruded on a moment she wasn't meant to witness.

Her feet scuffed the floor, and Tobwhit opened his eyes. His face bore the most pitiful expression, though at seeing Aurelia a smile brightened it.

"Come in, child, come in. It's okay, sit here beside me." He motioned to an empty chair, startling her. The chair hadn't been there a moment ago. "I rather expected you might come."

"You did? How would you - ?"

"One must listen. Magic fills this land, wishes to bind us to its purpose, but it takes effort and time to tune yourself to it. I've had many years to practice. The key is listening. Humans spend far too much time talking and not listening."

Aurelia had never considered herself a loud or talkative girl, but all the same, she'd much rather engage in a pleasant conversation with her father, with Eken, or with Koram over a game of Ji, then sit in silence.

"How do you know when the land talks to you?" she finally asked.

"It doesn't shout, or even speak in audible words, but whispers if you learn to listen." He turned back to Daphne, his face pensive. "But often it's only a feeling."

"Is there hope for her?" She took a seat by Tobwhit, her heart near breaking.

"While we yet live, there is always hope," said Tobwhit. "Hope not just for life, but for a life with purpose."

"But can you help her?"

His eyes closed once more, his response so delayed she wondered if he'd heard, but at last he spoke, words that pierced, sharp and cold like she imagined the three-span winter icicles that hung the Great Hall would feel were they to break away and plunge into her heart rather than the snow.

"It will take a terrible sacrifice. A life for a life."

Aurelia shuddered, goosebumps popping up across her skin, fear and resolve twisting together. Tobwhit said he'd been expecting her. Was this the reason? *Am I willing to lay down my life for Daphne? Or what if it's someone else who must?*

Would she be willing to lose Eken ... or Magnus, to save Daphne?

Tobwhit placed a gentle hand over hers. It was rough, weathered, wrinkled. But it was kindly, comforting.

NoNo stirred, a long stretch before lying on Tobwhit's lap, curling his tail protectively around his longtime friend.

"Calm your fears, Aurelia," said NoNo, his eyes brimming with pain. "He doesn't speak of you or your friends. Though I think you'd have the courage if needed." A long pause, then so softly Aurelia had to lean in—"He speaks of himself."

Chapter Twenty-Nine
He Wept

Morning light streamed through the windows, the bed's finery irritating after months of sleeping on regiment cots. Magnus stretched, muscles aching, a distinct feeling that he'd overslept, annoyed by the thought he should feel more rested than he did, but his dreams had troubled him.

Daphne was alive in one such dream, their joyful reunion short-lived when soldiers found and pursued them through the forest. Wolfhounds separated him from Daphne and Aurelia and trapped the two women at the edge of a cliff. When they hurled themselves to certain death, rather than face the wolfhound's mauling or the torturer's questions, he remembered sinking to his knees in horror and disbelief. Never had a dream been so vivid or so painful.

At the washbasin he splashed cold water on his face, rinsing away the night, rinsing away the dream, rinsing away the whispered doubts in his head. *Fatal choices bury men.*

Downstairs, he found Veyra and Saul fixing breakfast. His stomach rumbled.

"You sir have to wait," admonished Veyra, slapping his hand away, though with a playful grin and a wink she tossed him a sliver of salted herring from the frying pan.

He found Eken and Morco focused on a tightly contested game of Ji. Last night, he'd watched amused as Morco lost twenty-three games in a row to Eken before grumpily announcing he was done. A night of rest had apparently cleared his mind and improved his game. He was giving Eken all he could handle.

It wasn't, Magnus knew, that they didn't care that Daphne lay dying in her room upstairs, but a mind needs distraction from grieving. Searching for his own distraction, he chatted briefly with Tobias and Bochim, feigning interest in their conversation about the Red War, before excusing himself.

Where's Aurelia? he wondered. *Tobwhit and NoNo?*

He took the stairs to the second floor, but they weren't there. He wandered among the tables, idly perusing the strange objects littering the tables. But his thoughts on Aurelia, nothing held his attention.

At the window, he sucked in a sharp breath, and his heart sank. The Ka! No nearer than before, but they'd come back, stubborn as rot.

They hadn't yet found the cottage, though it looked only a matter of time, despite NoNo's claim. It shouldn't have surprised him; Drael was not an easily dissuaded man. Their scent led here, and even if momentarily deterred, Drael wouldn't give up. The path was an ingenious trick, but Magnus doubted it could keep them safe much longer.

I need to warn the others.

The floor pitched beneath his feet, a subtle lurch that told him the cottage was changing, unsteady, sick, as if its magic were failing. A muffled wail echoed and a warm buzzing sensation tickled his skin. He wasn't entirely sure he liked it, or trusted it, but knew it involved Aurelia. Only the third-floor rooms remained unexplored.

He bounded up the stairs two at a time.

There on the top floor balcony stood Aurelia, unharmed. Relief flooded, then disbelief. By her side, leaning on her for support, stood Daphne, alive but only somewhat alert, face pale, eyes groggy as if drugged. A stone sat centered on her forehead. Behind them, through an open door, poured a horrendous wailing.

"Daphne!" He rushed to her side, hugged her fiercely, surprising even himself at the strength of his emotion. "What happened? How ...? Who ...?"

"Tobwhit ..." said Aurelia, her voice unsteady. "I can explain later, but we have to go. Now."

"You're right—the soldiers, they're back."

"Wait, what? Really?" cried Aurelia.

The balcony lurched. Magnus staggered, catching himself against the railing. Daphne pitched forward but Aurelia grabbed her and steadied her. The house tilted dangerously sideways, Magnus stumbling into Daphne and Aurelia, knocking them over.

A shield door snapped from its hinges, whirling above their heads, splintering the balcony railing, and crashing to the floor below. Magnus rushed to the edge. Eken and Morco gaped up at him, their game of Ji flattened beneath the shield, though neither was hurt.

Cottage walls vibrated with tremors, vines and branches cracking and splitting apart. A limb the size of a horse fell from the ceiling, glanced off the stairway and slammed into the second floor, smashing a table, scattering its objects across the floor. The house creaked and groaned, sounding a death-knell.

He joined Aurelia in helping Daphne take the stairs, quick as they could, a treacherous descent, a constant guess which direction the staircase may tilt next as the house shook and rumbled. Chunks of ceiling and wall fell around them. Whether by luck or fate, they reached the bottom level unharmed.

"What's happening?" asked Tobias, as confused by seeing Daphne as he was by the cottage's breaking.

Another shield-door plunged over the railing, shattering into pieces as it struck the floor below, sending debris flying, a piece slamming into Bochim's side. He grunted, knocked to the ground, but Morco was quick to help him to his feet.

"We leave now, or we die!" shouted Magnus. *This place is coming down.*

The house groaned in protest as its foundation broke apart. Daylight streamed as a crack opened from floor to ceiling; it seemed the cottage yawned to swallow them whole.

At the front door, their packs sat in a neat row, as if someone during the night had known they'd be leaving.

"Where's Tobwhit?" asked Veyra. "And NoNo?"

There was no time to answer, only to run. They fled. The cottage groaned and folded inward, centuries of enchantment unraveling in a single roar. Through a billowing cloud of dust, NoNo leapt clear.

The binding that once protected house and path faded. The curving path groaned, a loud crick and a louder crack, the path protesting as an unseen force straightened it. An ear-splitting snap, its protests unable to stop the inevitable, Ka soldiers suddenly aware of a broad path that lay before them, with no curves and no switchbacks, and at the end of the path a jumbled pile of debris, while between them and the pile of debris stood a miserable lot of humans covered in dust.

For a moment, the element of surprise was theirs. But only for a moment. Soldiers shook off stupor, wolfhounds strained at leashes, baying with excitement until their handlers released them.

Magnus raised an arm in defense as a snarling beast leapt on him, strings of saliva spilling from its mouth. Its fangs pierced skin and sank deep. Feverish eyes of blood and death. The hound's weight slammed him to the ground.

A second wolfhound seized the hem of Veyra's cloak, dragging her screaming across the forest floor. She struggled to right herself as Saul and Bochim fought to free her.

Another leapt at Morco, claws raking his back. The man's booming cry filled the air before his meaty fists seized the hound's throat. He squeezed. The wolfhound's eyes rolled, lifeless, as he tossed the animal aside.

It was then the wolfhounds caught scent of the midling, and somewhere, deep inside, they recognized him as the source of their recent frustrations, when they'd been held at bay by a magical force they didn't understand, and been unable to locate their prey. Growls welling deep and guttural, they attacked.

NoNo stayed one step ahead, dodging nimbly when they slashed with claw or when they lunged with bared fang, while delivering his own deadly strikes. A wolfhound slunk away whimpering, its belly revealed a gaping mortal wound.

In the chaos, Magnus lost track of Aurelia and Daphne. Panic, like an iron fist, gripped his heart. He spotted them some distance off, running not towards him but away.

"Aurelia!" he cried.

The forest filled with Ka soldiers, spilling into the narrow stretch that separated him from the two women.

Aurelia turned, shouting, "Go, run! We'll find you!"

NoNo had made short order of the wolfhounds; they lay scattered—dead, dying, or limping away—while he sat calmly, licking a wound. A bright red gash ran the length of his body. He stilled, tongue lolling, solemn eyes fixed on Magnus.

"I can reach them," he said.

"Please," begged Magnus, "please."

With a nod, the midling leapt to the closest branch before scrambling up the tree. Soon he was bounding across the treetops, high above the Ka. A soldier cried an alarm at the sight of such a strange creature. NoNo roared, and the roar echoed. Branches and leaves trembled, the ground rumbled, a tree snapped at its base and crashed to the forest floor. Soldiers cowered in fear, while many fled. One, braver than most, mistook the midling for a mere animal despite the flash of its color and the size of its roar and loosed an arrow at NoNo, but the creature was too quick, darting aside as the arrow sailed harmlessly by.

"Turn back, you cowards! Get me that Binder!"

Drael sat astride his steed, the horse rearing, hooves striking soldiers who fled, while the rider's sword flashed, dealing death. The retreating tide stalled, men fearing Drael more than the unknown.

"We need to go," said Tobias, tugging at Magnus' arm as a band of Ka broke off towards them.

Magnus set a grueling pace. Though Aurelia and Daphne had drawn the larger contingent of soldiers, a sizeable group splintered off in their direction. Too many to fight. Their only hope lay in staying ahead of their pursuers.

A path wound more or less clear through the forest. There was nowhere to hide. The chase turned numbing, one foot in front of another, avoiding roots and branches, a stumble or fall deadly.

Magnus swore he heard the ragged breath of their pursuers, but a glance over his shoulder proved him wrong. The soldiers had fallen further behind, though a handful still shadowed them through the trees. But Veyra and Saul were faltering, not yet fully healed, unable to keep pace, and Morco—broad and heavy—was no runner. They needed time and Magnus meant to buy it.

Ahead, the trail wound through a boulder field, some larger than his Plains home, others forming towers of stacked rock rising forty and fifty span high.

"Bochim, Tobias, Eken—with me!"

As the trail curved through the boulders, for a moment they lost sight of their pursuers. The four darted into a gap between the boulders, while the others ran on.

With weapons drawn, they didn't have to wait long before the sound of pursuit reached them, jangling armor and heavy footsteps echoing through the rock formations. The first wave appeared. That they'd outpaced their companions only sealed their fate.

Magnus and Bochim fell upon them, dispatching a soldier each, while Tobias parried for a moment longer before dealing a blow to his assailant.

Eken leapt at a fourth, plunging his dagger into the soldier's chest. The man grunted, eyes wide, surprised, falling to his knees. A mortal blow. Eken stared, horrified by the blood pooling on the soldier's chest, his own knees weakening as he sank to the forest floor and vomited his morning meal.

With angry cries, a remaining two drew their weapons and engaged, while a third turned and fled. Outnumbered, the two soon joined their companions on the forest floor, empty eyes staring sightless into the tree canopy.

"Come, quickly—mourn their deaths with your life!" Magnus seized Eken by his collar and dragged him away.

Warned by the fleeing soldier, the Ka halted to confer, before scouring the boulder field in wary caution. By the time they realized no further ambushes awaited, their prey had slipped away.

The sun reached its zenith and began its inevitable descent to the distant horizon. With no sign of pursuit since the boulder field, Magnus called for a rest, while spreading a map across the forest floor.

"Here's the lake we swam," he pointed while Tobias looked on over his shoulder, "I'm guessing roughly here we first met Tobwhit, and somewhere in this area would be the cottage." He indicated another spot on the map. Tobias nodded his agreement. "And this strange drawing looks like towers of rock, doesn't it? Has to be where we ambushed those soldiers."

"If you're right about the cottage, look at what's due north of it." Tobias pointed at two curving lines running parallel, the words *Fereni Cliffs* and *Abinthar Gorge* appearing between the lines. "I'm guessing those rock towers we passed were south of the cottage; we didn't see any cliffs. So it stands to reason Aurelia and Daphne would have."

Magnus' heart sank.

The cliffs. My dream.

It wasn't possible. Was it? But he couldn't shake the icy dagger of fear penetrating his heart.

"NoNo's back!"

Veyra spotted him first, bounding through the treetops. Bright splashes of color danced across the forest floor as the sun reflected his fur, his smile grim as he neared.

"Yours was an easy trail to follow. A few still pursued you. I persuaded them otherwise." Fangs glinted dangerously.

"Never mind that," demanded Magnus. "Did you find Aurelia? Daphne?"

"I did, but -" NoNo hesitated.

"Tell me!"

"I'm sorry ... they're gone."

"I don't believe you. You're wrong." Magnus' eyes searched the way they'd come as if expecting to see Aurelia running through the trees.

"I couldn't reach them in time." NoNo hung his head in regret. "They climbed an embankment to a cliff's edge, the soldiers surrounded them ... I ... I'm sorry."

"No. It's not true," said Magnus, sharp and angry, as Eken sank to the floor in disbelief.

"I saw Aurelia take Daphne's hand ... no one could survive that fall. I know those cliffs."

"It can't be," whispered Magnus. Burying his face in his hands, he wept.

Chapter Thirty
Again, Her Green Eyes Sparkled

Ominously dark clouds descended from the eastern range of the Tol Mountains, first drops of rain heralding a coming storm. The strange band of travelers—seven humans and one colorful cat-like creature—didn't have to wait long. Moments later, the storm roared overhead, its force catching them by surprise with a heavy, dismal rain that mirrored their spirits. As thunder rumbled and lightning split the sky, they found refuge beneath a rocky overhang. It wasn't nearly enough. The storm whipped wind and rain into a fury, sending sheets of water sideways into their shelter.

Drenched through, they huddled close, studying Magnus' map. Tensions ran high, spurred by exhaustion and the death of dear friends, and by the fear the Ka might soon discover them. Only NoNo seemed removed from it all, sitting alone outside the shelter, rain pelting his fur.

Finally, the humans agreed on a path forward—no one offering a better answer—west to Hadil's Crossing and then, the Capitol. To the King as Daphne had wished, to see that the girls' sacrifice meant something. NoNo agreed to accompany them.

"I've lost my home." His ears, usually so perky, sagged limp against his head. "And my friend. Where else would I go? Fate binds me to you."

"It's decided then," said Magnus.

"A son of a Dorakian council member, six traitorous ex-Ka, and a magical midling," added Saul morosely. "How can such a strange company of travelers fail to sway the King's mind?"

The storm passed like a ghostly host retreating from the battlefield, turning to ravage southern lands. In its wake, a misty drizzle lingered. The sun remained in hiding.

They trudged westward, wet, cold, miserable, hearts heavy with sorrow. When tired legs could carry them no further, they made camp. No one attempted a fire, though it wouldn't matter if they had; there wasn't a dry piece of kindling to be found. Dinner masqueraded as a slice of stale bread and a handful of dried berries.

Tobias' breath frosted in the cool morning temperature, but at least the rain had stopped. The others slept, save Eken, whose rolled-up cot made Tobias wonder if the Dorakian had even tried. The morning dew, like frozen crystals on the grass, crunched underfoot.

He discovered Eken perched atop a boulder by a field, legs crossed beneath him, awaiting dawn. Perhaps he hoped its light would reveal Aurelia across the field and leaping from the boulder he would run and embrace his friend.

Tobias scrambled up beside him and they sat silent for a while, watching the world wake, rich golden sun softening the frozen dew, though its light revealed an empty field.

"Tell me about her," he said at last.

"She was ..." Eken paused, took a deep breath, "She was amazing. My best friend. Kind. Thoughtful. Willful and strong-headed too, not that she was difficult to get along with. It's just that she knew what she wanted ... well, usually."

Tobias' look made it clear he didn't understand.

"Well, men for one thing. She couldn't figure out Col. Whether she should marry him."

"Ah. Love's always a mystery."

"Until Lumath." Eken stretched his legs, allowing them to dangle over the boulder's edge. "She seemed so certain for once, and I got so angry with her."

"It was just one moment. You apologized afterwards, right?"

"In a way. But I think we were okay."

"Had you always been friends?"

"Always. Since the day we met. When I moved to Chelam, I was a pudgy kid. Loved pies, cakes, cookies, it didn't matter, I'd eat anything sweet in sight."

Tobias eyed Eken skeptically. The man was anything but pudgy now, hard to believe he'd ever been.

"What? It's true!" retorted Eken. "So there I was, an outsider in Chelam, in the Great Hall where every child under seven hunter's moons gathered for lessons. Elder Koram brought cakes, at least a dozen. I, uh … I snuck and ate the cakes. Every last one of them."

He glanced sheepishly at Tobias, who chuckled and nodded, encouraging him to continue.

"When Koram discovered the cakes gone, he demanded to know who'd eaten them. Every single kid there knew it was me. I'm sure I had guilt written all over my face; I could never hide anything. Besides, even if I hadn't done it, I was the new kid. They would blame me, and Elder Koram would pronounce the sentence. But Aurelia stepped in, said she ate the cakes. I don't know if they believed her, but being one of the oldest, they listened to her. In a single move, she brought me under her protection. She didn't have to do that."

"Was she always like that? Protecting people?"

"As long as I've known her, it's just who she is. Part of what made her so amazing."

Tobias rested a comforting hand on the Dorakian's shoulder, hoping to make the hurt a little more bearable. "You're blessed. To have known such a friend. Many never experience such a thing."

Eken nodded, mumbling his thanks.

A roaring fire cheered spirits and kept the cool evening air at bay.

It had been five sunfalls since fleeing Tobwhit's cottage and they had set up camp at the summit to Hadil's Crossing, in the shadows of the Tol's western range. Veyra returned triumphant from the hunt, a sloppy grin plastered across her face, recovering remarkably well from her injuries. In one hand she carried her bow, and in the other a pair of mountain rabbits. They wouldn't go far with seven hungry mouths to feed, but no one complained, remembering the stale bread and sour berries of recent dinners.

NoNo disappeared while they ate, returning some time later, licking his lips and reclining by the fire while grooming his fur. He declined to say what he'd eaten, but had apparently eaten his fill.

Magnus snuck away after dinner in search of fresh water.

"Mind if I join you?"

He glanced up from the map he studied as Veyra fell in step beside him, offering her an indifferent shrug. His heart wasn't in it, but he wouldn't send her away.

"Last we spoke," said Veyra, "you told me you had sisters. How many?"

"Six," he grunted.

"I have no sisters or brothers. Couldn't imagine so many! What was that like?"

"Messy," he said, reluctant at first, though warming to the conversation, "but lots of love and laughter. Seems the way a family should be."

"And if the Mrs. Magnus doesn't want a bunch of kids?"

"I guess we'll see." He glanced at her and noted the moonlight catching the early gray invading her short black hair. "I might can be convinced otherwise."

"Well I can tell you—having been an only child—I found it lonely. I'd love to have a large family. If you can't find another willing to bear you so many children, seek me out in Perinith." As soon as the words tumbled from her mouth, even she seemed surprised at herself. "I can't believe ... I am so -"

He waved off her apology. "It's refreshing the way you speak your mind. You've never held back with me, and I wouldn't expect you to start now. But give it some time, you may feel different when you get to know me."

"Actually, I like what I know and see."

Magnus cleared his throat nervously, uncertain about the sudden turn in the conversation. For a fleeting moment, he saw something he hadn't allowed in the days since Aurelia's death—a future where he could be happy. A loud house, too many children underfoot, Veyra arguing with him across a supper table somewhere in the Plains while that scar on her jawline pulsed red. An apology later. *Warmth. Laughter. Home.*

Then he remembered Aurelia, that she was gone, and his mood darkened.

Veyra noticed the change as it stole over him.

"There's many ways to mourn the loss of a friend. Some find solace in others. But enough of that, come! This stream won't find itself."

She ran ahead as Magnus hurried to catch up, hating himself a little for reaching toward comfort so soon after Aurelia was gone. Still, something in Veyra's green eyes felt stubbornly familiar—like the Plains after a long journey. Like boots and voices around an evening fire. *Like home.*

"See anything you like?" she asked mischievously, the same question she had in Lumath's garden.

"I um ..."

She filled her flask, lowered herself over the stream and drank greedily. He studied her out of the corner of his eye as he knelt to fill his own flask. When she caught him staring, again, her green eyes sparkled.

Chapter Thirty-One
Clasped Hands

Back in the cottage, before the Ka discovered them and the wolfhounds chased them, before Tobwhit's home collapsed, and before Magnus found them on the third-floor balcony, Aurelia dried her tears as NoNo had said to.

They sat in silence: Aurelia marveling that Tobwhit would sacrifice himself so calmly, NoNo fretting for his friend to summon the courage he feared was lacking, and Tobwhit waiting, patient, for his moment of redemption. He was not, as NoNo supposed, short on courage; only unwilling to rush what must come in the end.

Not having the patience-forging benefit of occupying a magical cottage for four hundred hunter's moons, Aurelia broke first.

"What can NoNo mean, Tobwhit?"

The old man squeezed her hand in a reassuring manner, but didn't answer.

"He can't mean you're leaving us, can he? But we ... I ... I've just gotten to know you! And this place, it's ... it's so wonderfully strange! I was thinking you'd explain all those marvelous gadgets on the second floor."

"I'd hoped to return to those." Tobwhit sighed, wistful, the regret in his eyes so haunting she glanced away. He squeezed her hand again, perhaps to reassure himself as much as he did her. "It's okay, child. I've had more time than most."

Tears welled as Aurelia looked fondly upon Daphne. "I wish for nothing more than my friend's return. But why a sacrifice?"

She was beginning to think adventures weren't such a grand thing. Since leaving Chelam, she'd encountered Shadow-Wolves, Ka soldiers who wished them ill, survived Lumath's destruction, seen her covenant friend brutalized nigh unto death, and now NoNo and Tobwhit spoke of sacrifice.

Tobwhit cupped her chin and lifted her gaze to meet his own. The regret was gone. His eyes shone. With hope and something more.

"My dear child, sacrifice is how we make the world right again. The greatest expression of love and the greatest antidote to self-love. And for some of us, we must sacrifice to right a wrong."

"What wrong? And what does this have to do with me or Daphne? You speak in riddles—I'm so confused!"

"Let me speak plainly then, and please, no interruptions. Though I'm patient, fate and time soon collide. Even now the soldiers return."

"They do? I must warn the others ... I -"

Tobwhit glanced crossly at her. "Didn't I say no interruptions?"

Sheepish, she hung her head, folded her hands in her lap, and waited.

He picked up where he'd left off. "I didn't share everything with your companions earlier. Certain things I wanted to discuss only with you."

She wanted to ask what those things could be, but closed her mouth at a look from Tobwhit.

"When I said before that I was an Honored One who fought in the Red War, you each assumed wrongly that I'm one no longer. Yes, appearances would make you think that's true. I don't wear their gray cloaks, or bear a saphyr stone in my forehead. But one cannot stop being an Honored One any more than one can stop breathing and still live." He paused as he picked up his staff, twisting it in hand, absentminded as he studied the attached polished sphere. "I may have forsaken Honored One ways and lived as a hermit in this cottage, but once the magic of binding connects you to the land, you can't live without it. Or more accurately, it's the saphyr you can't live without."

Quick and forceful for someone his age, he swung the staff with all his might against the bedpost. A jagged crack appeared in the once-smooth marble. Almost reverently, he laid the staff in his lap, closing his eyes, and hovering a hand over it. The marble glowed and bit by bit the crack splintered until a spiderweb of hairline cracks crisscrossed the sphere; and as those cracks spread bits and pieces of the marble fell to the floor, revealing that what Aurelia had assumed was a solid sphere was in fact only a shell, encasing an object within.

He held up the staff for her to see what remained. A stone, pulsing a deep dark, nearly black, metallic color.

"You see, child, I've never been far from my saphyr. Without it, I couldn't have lived, and never this long." He paused, drew a deep breath, "And now we come to the moment. It can wait no longer."

Aurelia stifled a cry. She'd been expecting this since NoNo had said as much, but it was still difficult to hear. Tobwhit patted her hand, a gentle smile upon his wrinkled face.

"Don't be sad, child. It's a good thing. An opportunity to atone."

"What will you do?"

"I'll transfer my saphyr to Daphne. In that process, I will die, and she will live. First though, an important detail you must know. Listen close, your very lives depend on it."

"I'm listening," she replied soberly.

"When my saphyr bond ends, it will cause the breaking of an old and powerful binding. One that sustained me and my home. These walls, these floors and ceilings, will crumble around you. I expect that in a short time this house will no longer be standing. As soon as I'm gone, you and your friends must leave without delay lest you perish here. The path outside, the one that hid my home, will become straight and plain, exposing you to the soldiers, who will pursue you." He paused, knowing the next part would be difficult for her to hear. "Listen now. You and Daphne must separate from your friends; you must go on alone. I cannot say why, and I know little beyond this. I can only say I foresaw it in a dream that must come true, else all will be lost. When you see the opportunity, leave your friends behind. The soldiers will chase you to a cliff edge, but don't be afraid; you must take a leap of faith. Off the cliff."

Confused, but eager to please, she nodded gamely at his instructions. "I'll try my best."

"No!" His voice turned cold, urgent as he grabbed her and shook her. "To only try will not do! You must do this, or my sacrifice means nothing. Promise me you will heed my words! Promise me."

"But how will I -"

"You will know it, for it will be obvious. The decision to keep your promise will be the hard part."

"I promise."

Relieved, Tobwhit closed his eyes and placed a hand on Daphne's forehead. "May the Great Binding speak to you as it speaks to all of us."

And then he began to hum, softly at first but increasing in volume and urgency, one hand still resting on her forehead, gripping his saphyr with the other. His hands trembled. NoNo arched his back and nestled his head against Tobwhit's chin. They needed no words; four hundred hunter's moons of friendship was enough.

At first, Aurelia sensed no change, but as the humming swelled, a tingling warmth filled the room. *A binding*. Ancient. Stirring as it was summoned. The stone's color shifted, a dull yellow glow consuming the metallic black, until a soft thrumming blue swallowed the yellow. Its pulse quickened, and the stone hummed a soft melody that mirrored Tobwhit's own.

Her heartbeat quickened as the melody roused a repressed memory. One she hadn't known existed until that moment. The memory was elusive, a fleeting image of a face, the focus hazy. A nose, an eye twinkling, mouth crinkled in a smile, jet black hair hanging over the woman's face, obscuring much of it. *Mother*. Instinctively she knew it was, and her heart burst with joy as in the memory her mother cradled her, bearing a smile of such warmth and love and light it put the sun and moon and stars to shame. The scent of lilac petal clung to the memory. A tune on her mother's lips—the same melody Tobwhit and the stone now hummed. Aurelia choked back a sob at such a precious gift, a memory she would cherish forever. It faded, but she sensed it hadn't left her, that she'd be able to recall it when desired.

Tobwhit's humming exploded in pitch and fervor, the stone keeping pace. The light engulfed the stone, expanded to fill the room, though not harshly, still a soft pulsing blue, bathing everyone and everything in its light. That warm tingling sensation intensified, tip-toeing across Aurelia's skin, seeping into her pores, filling her heart and mind with its presence. It pressed against her, from within and without, the pressure intense. But she welcomed it if this was how Daphne returned to her.

Closing her eyes, Aurelia allowed the melody and the light and the tingling pressure to wash over her. Felt the current of the binding as it crawled across her skin, tickling her eyes and nose and ears. Words accompanied the melody, so muted she hadn't at first heard them. They were not in a tongue she understood.

Abruptly, it ended. All of it, though the melody lingered for a moment, reluctant to be gone. When she opened her eyes, the pulsing light was gone, the chair beside her was empty, and NoNo paced the room, a pitiful wail in his throat.

Tobwhit...

Daphne sat up, bearing a gray saphyr stone in her forehead.

"Oh, Daphne!" cried Aurelia and flung herself on her friend, a fierce hug as giant sobs racked her body.

Daphne began to cry and laugh all at the same time. "I'm not sure why we're crying, my covenant friend, but it's good to see you too." She studied the room, confused. "Are we still in Lumath?"

Aurelia laughed, blinking away tears. "I have so much to tell you, but we must go; we're not safe here."

"Where exactly are we? This doesn't look like a Lower or an Upper."

"Can you walk?"

"Why couldn't I?" Attempting to stand, she buckled to the floor. "Why am I so weak?"

"Here, let me help you. NoNo, are you coming?"

"Who is -" began Daphne and stopped short, her mouth hanging open at the sight of the creature pacing the room, its fur shimmering in the light streaming through the windows. But NoNo ignored them as he continued to pace, his mournful wail echoing.

"NoNo!" yelled Aurelia while helping Daphne to her feet. "We're leaving—I promised Tobwhit."

This time she didn't wait for a response, the house shifting under her feet, knowing the binding was gone and knowing Tobwhit was right. The cottage wouldn't be standing long.

And as he'd predicted, the opportunity soon presented itself to leave their friends behind, but Aurelia hesitated. *What will they think when we abandon them?* Then she remembered her promise.

"Daphne, do you trust me?"

"With my life."

"There's no time to explain, but we have to go, just you and me. We must leave everyone else behind."

Daphne's face made it clear she didn't understand, but she nodded. They fled north, the Ka giving chase, separating them from the others.

Magnus shouted her name. Aurelia's heart skipped a beat at his voice, at how much she'd miss being near him.

"Go! Run! We'll find you!"

Heeding her own advice, she ran, Daphne in tow. The Ka chased them up an embankment, cornered them at the edge of a towering cliff. Against her friend's protest, Aurelia inched close and peered over. It was a long way down.

No one can survive that.

She hesitated, doubting her promise to a senile old man.

The soldiers' ranks parted for a man on horseback. To her shock, it was Col. His face looked years older, lined and haggard, an empty sleeve pinned where his right arm had once been while his remaining hand clung wearily to the reins. He slumped in the saddle, his usual air of arrogance gone.

She wanted to hate him, but couldn't muster it. Realized she only wanted to run to him and give him a hug, cry with him over his loss, forgive him for his betrayal. But he was with the Ka.

He reined in just shy of the two women. The horse snorted and pawed at the ground, eager to drive them over the cliff's edge even if its rider wasn't.

The always confident Col, so quick to speak, didn't, remorse in his eyes. *There's the Col from Lumath I might have married.* A commotion behind him drew her attention.

"Make way! Make way for the commander!"

Horse and rider thundered through the parted ranks and reared to a breathless halt beside Col.

"Binder!" shouted Drael, accustomed to being obeyed. "Come quietly, keep your powers in check, and I give my word I will not harm your friend."

"Please, take his offer ..." added Col, his eyes imploring.

Daphne turned to Aurelia and offered, "For you, I'll happily give myself up."

"Nonsense, you'll do nothing of the sort." Her eyes flashed as she snorted. "I don't trust a word he says." She took another step towards the cliff's edge and glanced over it again. Leaning close, she whispered, "This is going to sound crazy, but I promised an old man."

"You what?"

"I promised him I'd jump."

"How long have I been out?"

"Do you trust me?"

She spoke this loud enough for even the Ka to hear. Drael reached for his sword as Col extended a pleading hand toward the only woman he'd ever loved.

"The answer hasn't changed," said Daphne, "with my life."

The two clasped hands and leapt from the cliff.

Chapter Thirty-Two
they've found us

In the moment before her feet left solid ground, Daphne imagined only fools felt fearless leaping from a cliff. But surrender promised only Ka cruelty, if not now then later, in the bowels of a Capitol dungeon where it was rumored the King's men delighted in torture. *Could I keep my dignity and not betray my people? And then, at the end of all that nonsense, death?*

Leaping from a cliff seemed a better alternative, though the idea terrified her, for she was no fool. Besides, she trusted Aurelia, though she wondered what old man had swindled away her friend's brain.

There was no more time for thinking as her body plummeted. She screamed, but the sound choked off in her throat, the rush of air squeezing her in its embrace as she plunged to her death. She fought blackout. A canopy of trees suddenly and alarmingly close.

A violent gust of wind saved her from a certain impaling, though she knew immediately it was no ordinary breeze as a warm tingling sensation caressed her. Beside her a frit fluttered on the same gust and she could have sworn it smiled and waved, or perhaps it was merely its twitching fingers. The wind buoyed, slowed her descent just enough, before her body slammed into a patch of evergreen fir. Eyes squeezed shut as branches whipped past, lacerating face, arms and legs. Her gut slammed into a branch so thick it folded her body double across it, even as it knocked the air from her lungs. Head over heels she tumbled, knocked her head hard, and the world went dark.

A face flickered in and out of focus.

"Daphne. Wake up, Daphne."

She slept. Dreamt of home. Her mother. Her people. The shame of a decision made long ago.

She awoke again, tried sitting, a face she recognized. *Aurelia*.

"Careful, you took a nasty hit."

"You don't look too good yourself," remarked Daphne drily.

And she didn't. Aurelia cradled one arm delicate-like, a purplish bruise spreading across her right cheek, one eye black and blue and puffy, her shirt torn where a gash in her shoulder bled freely.

As Aurelia helped her stand, Daphne gave a frightened start. They weren't alone. Then a sigh of relief at noticing the cloaks they wore.

"You might know our rescuers," said Aurelia with a wry grin.

With a shout of joy, Daphne seized Ophel in a hug, the woman returning it with an awkward pat on the back.

"Hush, hush, child, remember who you are," Ophel admonished her. "You are not just a Gray Cloak."

The young man accompanying Ophel peeked out from under his hood. Daphne didn't know him well, though Liam had always been pleasant, if shy, but her nose wrinkled when she recognized the third, who spared only a frosty glare in her direction.

"You have Nezetta to thank for your rescue," added Ophel, "she and the wind have knit."

Aurelia studied the newcomers with curiosity. Ophel she'd met. The elderly woman appeared as focused and no-nonsense as before.

Liam was short and stocky, his hair braided in long beaded rows, a reddish birthmark gracing his cheek. The stone in his forehead the typical dull gray. He smiled amicably at Aurelia.

Nezetta was about her height and age. A mass of long, curly red hair cascaded, her lips pursed tightly together, a scarlet gloss applied, a recent fashion trend even some in Chelam followed, while a pair of high cheekbones accented the sharp angular features of her face. A pair of intelligent hazel-colored eyes stared back at Aurelia. She wore the gray cloak typical of her people, but a dark red sash around her waist was a startling nod to fashion that Aurelia hadn't seen in other Gray Cloak. The stone set in Nezetta's forehead was a blue, deeper than the shade of Applemere Lake.

When Nezetta spoke, Aurelia understood her friend's dislike for the woman. It wasn't what she said, though that was bad enough, but the frigid tone, the raised eyebrows, jutted chin, and dismissive attitude as she smoothed a wrinkle in her cloak.

"You must be a couple of very foolish girls to jump from that cliff. Be thankful my wind bond is well knit; anyone less skilled couldn't have gathered the wind as I did to cushion your fall. Perhaps the lashes you received will teach you a lesson."

"That's enough, Nezetta," Ophel reprimanded. "Surely they had good reason to take that leap," although Ophel's tone suggested she thought nothing of the sort.

"We aren't foolish!" Aurelia's fist tightened in a ball. "And I doubt you would have had the courage to jump." Thunder rumbled, and for a moment, Aurelia wished the heavens would open and drench Nezetta's fiery-red impertinent head.

The woman's eyes flashed, her mouth opened in retort, but surprisingly it was Daphne who intervened. "What my friend Aurelia meant to say, is that we had no choice but to jump, or face Ka torture."

Reining in her anger, Aurelia added, "I spoke hastily—we're indebted to you."

Hmph proved to be the extent of Nezetta's response, but she deferred to Ophel, who redirected the conversation. "Where are the others? Four left Chelam, now there are but two."

"The Ka came between us," said Daphne.

"Worse than that," blurted Aurelia, "Col betrayed us."

The older Gray Cloak frowned, her lips pressed together in disappointment. "I did not envision this. Tell me how."

The girls recounted a brief summary of rescuing the Ka, of fleeing to Belanor's Cave, of Lumath, Col's betrayal, and their subsequent escape from imprisonment, though Ophel interrupted before they could tell of Tobwhit and NoNo and the magical cottage.

"This Magnus, he was Ka and aided Col in his betrayal, yet he helped you escape?"

"Yes, and his friends too. They experienced a change of heart."

"On that point, we shall see. One must prove themselves before they can be trusted," admonished Ophel. "Come, we must go, lest the Ka have their far-seers. We are too exposed here."

"Where are we going?" asked Aurelia.

"To find your friends of course. And to speak with Magnus. He may prove useful as a Ka officer."

Aurelia clapped, delighted to learn the Gray Cloaks would accompany them, though she would have gladly traded Nezetta for another. On second thought, she knew little of their powers, perhaps Nezetta might come in handy again. She welcomed any protection from the Ka.

The valley floor spread steep and rocky below the cliffs, and the descent proved treacherous. Boulders blocked their way, evidence of past landslides, loose rocks and pebbles skidding under feet, threatening to turn an ankle or two.

Nezetta proved useful sooner than Aurelia expected, their path blocked by a yawning chasm and no apparent way across. Red curls bounced saucily as if anticipating their owner's use of power. Narrowed eyes concentrated as breathing stilled and hands swam a patterned flow. The first hint of a response, a slight breeze that ruffled Aurelia's hair. Then an urgent tug, until a moment later Aurelia found herself lifted bodily into the air. She let out a startled whoop, though the wind settled her safely on the opposite side of the chasm. Nezetta bore each in turn across until at the end she herself joined them.

"That's how you use a binding, Daphne," said Nezetta with a sniff and a toss of her curls. Daphne's eyes narrowed.

"Nezetta," counseled Ophel, "your binding was sufficient, you possess all the power one needs. But your hands. I couldn't hear them singing with the land. You rely too much on pure power."

"Yes, Elder-Mother."

Aurelia bit back a laugh when Daphne stuck her tongue out at Nezetta. Liam saw it too but he just winked and grinned.

The way became easier after the chasm, their route flattening. To the east rose the snow-capped Tol, their heights vanishing into the clouds, and to the west the cliffs towered stiff and unyielding. Her neck craned to study their soaring heights and Aurelia realized how fortunate they were to have survived. Had Tobwhit known a Gray Cloak would be there to save them?

The gorge itself was warm and humid, oppressively so. Aurelia thought it odd for the season until Ophel explained the warmth was due to the marshland that covered the southern end.

"It is muggy year-round."

The way no longer featured rock-strewn landscape as found at the base of the cliffs, instead transfigured by the encroaching marshland, wrapped in fingers of fog, dotted with clumps of grass and reed that hid treacherous pools of murky water. Despite the dangers, Ophel led them deftly, confidently, never once wavering in her steps. Shortly before sunfall, she called a halt for the day. For their sake, she explained, traveling the bog at night would be unwise, though she knew the way.

"Besides," she added, "the stream running here is the last clean source of water for some distance. We'll rest, fill our flasks for the journey ahead."

"Will it take long to be rid of this bog?" asked Aurelia, nose wrinkling at the black mud caked to her shoes.

"A full day and another morning," came Ophel's brief reply.

Their provisions on hand meager, Ophel ordered the others to forage for food while asking Aurelia to stay behind at camp, adding, "I have a matter to discuss with you."

An arched eyebrow betrayed Aurelia's surprise, but she simply nodded in agreement. Besides, she had questions that needed answers.

The older woman puttered around camp, clearing a space for a fire, gathering bits of debris and sticks for fuel, seemingly in no rush to talk, so Aurelia joined her and for a time they worked amicably side by side, saying little. The campsite Ophel had chosen was dry, but riddled with rocks of all shapes and sizes.

Sleep won't come easy, thought Aurelia.

But she needn't have worried. In a flurry of motion, Ophel bound the stones to her will, tugging them free of the earth, lifting them into the air before releasing them with a splash into a nearby murky pool. Her hands blurred, and the pockmarked earth vibrated, grains of dirt settling into depressions and lumpy mounds flattening, as if an invisible hand raked across them. When she finished, the ground was all but smooth.

Aurelia's jaw hung open at such a display of power. She meant to comment on it, but the words stuck in her throat. Ophel's hood, always secured so tight against her face, tighter even than most Gray Cloaks, had fallen loose at her shoulders, revealing a shaved head, a narrow gaunt face, a pinched nose and high cheekbones. Her stone a deep rich color, as Nezetta's, though Ophel's was a chocolaty brown.

She looked remarkably like Nezetta.

Aurelia's curiosity got the better of her. "Why do your stone and Nezetta's, bear such color? Most everyone's are gray, like Daphne's."

"To understand the stones, you must understand binding. What do you know of it?"

"Not much really. Just bits and pieces. I didn't understand its power until Tobwhit and his cottage."

She'd spoken his name rather absentmindedly, but Ophel seized her arm in a fierce grip. "What name did you utter?"

"Tobwhit?"

"And where is he now?" demanded Ophel, with a forceful shake, as if to make the answer tumble from her lips.

"He's gone," said Aurelia, wincing at the stranglehold on her arm. "Sacrificed himself for Daphne."

"Oh." With a resigned sigh, the older woman released her arm. "Tell me everything. Start at the beginning."

And so Aurelia did, from leaving Chelam to the fateful leap, leaving nothing out. When she finished, Ophel said, "And this creature, you said its name was NoNo."

It was a statement more than a question as Ophel gathered more kindling, before finally addressing Aurelia with a sharp tone, "I advise you now child, for your sake and for other reasons I won't explain, do not speak the name of Tobwhit again."

"Why not? Who is he to you?"

"He's a dangerous fool, and it would behoove you if none knew of your time with him."

Aurelia couldn't imagine Tobwhit dangerous or a fool. After all, he'd been right about everything so far, but she tucked the advice away for later consideration. She had rather liked Tobwhit.

"As for your earlier question, I shall tell you of stones and bindings. The Fiadha possess an innate magic within; and we descend from an ancient people, not originally of this country, some say not even of this world, but that is to be debated and not entirely the point. What matters is that binding, or magic as the unlearned say, calls to us from this land, and that call awakens what lies within."

"You're talking about Sensing."

"Yes. And no. Sensing is the ability to listen to the land, to feel its presence, the binding that rests within it. So, there is a binding that exists within us, and within the land. Separated, they can do little. But bonded, we manipulate the very elements of the world. Our stones are the conduit of these powers, the bindings we perform."

"If all Gray Cloaks possess this ability, why do only some receive a stone?"

"That is a simple enough answer—a limited supply of saphyr. Only a saphyr stone is the proper conduit for bindings; no ordinary rock will do. Only our best can become Honored Ones. Sadly, too few experience the joy and wonder of bonding with the land. For those who do not, it is a lifelong tragedy, akin to watching one's brother or sister live a fulfilled life, while handicapped in ways one cannot fully understand."

"That's awful. Can nothing be done?"

"Sadly, no. There are too few saphyr, for we have depleted once-rich deposits. As for the stone's color, a saphyr is gray. Initially. But when Awakened, what we call being knit, the saphyr's color changes. And we become Salel."

"Salel." Aurelia mimicked Ophel's pronunciation, but having never heard the word before, it rolled oddly off her tongue.

"It is not common amongst our people; only a handful of Honored Ones become Salel. I am one, as is Nezetta. She has sojourned in the Tol these past several months and completed her Awakening. For a Salel, the magic that infuses us is so rich it imbues the stone itself with color."

"Ah! Now I get it," said Aurelia, understanding dawning. "That's why you couldn't go with us from Chelam, and why you were with Nezetta below the cliffs, returning from the Tol. But why is her stone blue, and yours brown?"

"You ask many questions, child, though you are perceptive. Yes. I left to seek Nezetta. The Ka threaten our people, our land. We need those who can defend us, and Nezetta is by far the most powerful of her generation. Her Awakening offers hope in the approaching storm. She has only begun to tap into her powers as Salel, for in a time of great need, the land gives us one of our most powerful ever seen. As for the stone's color, it is the binding itself, the specific elements knit to it that determine the color. It is not of our choosing. But even those who will never be Salel, whose stones remain gray, have a natural inclination to certain elements over others."

"Most Honored Ones I've seen are female, why are there so few males?"

"It is uncertain," replied Ophel. "Some say men are too arrogant, too sure of themselves to listen to the land. Relatively few of our men possess the ability to Sense, whereas all our women do. Others say that long ago it was common for men to Sense and that they made for powerful Binders, but a war between male and female Fiadha resulted in women seizing power and curtailing the promotion of men to Honored One status. I am unaware of any histories confirming this war; it is only rumored legend. For whatever reason, be it our history, our customs or some innate difference between men and women, the number of women pursuing this path outnumbers that of men."

"I know you didn't ask me to stay behind just to answer my questions," conceded Aurelia, her curiosity satisfied for the moment.

"That is -"

The hunting party's return interrupted Ophel, while a beaming Liam held aloft a pair of foxes.

"There'll be plenty to eat tonight!"

Daphne's grin was more subdued, her dirt-stained hands cradling a clutch of wild potatoes. A fire soon cracked and popped as Liam prepared a stew of fox meat and potatoes. Aurelia's stomach rumbled as the aroma wafted across the campsite.

There was indeed plenty to go around. The tender meat and savory flavor of the stew proved a pleasant surprise to Aurelia. Content, with a full belly, she reclined by the fire. Though she still felt every bruise and cut sustained during her fall, she was grateful Ophel had cleared their campsite smooth.

She'd only just stretched out to rest when Daphne suggested, in a rather forced tone, they'd best clean their cuts at the nearby stream.

"Nezetta's hands bore nothing when you returned," Aurelia whispered as she joined her by the water's edge. "She refuse to help?"

"Oh, no, she helped." Daphne scanned their surroundings. "Let me warn you about Nezetta. Don't trust her. She'll stab you in the back with a smile on her face. She's a hateful woman. But today? Today I saw something that truly terrified me."

"While hunting?"

"When we left camp, of course Nezetta had to assume the lead. Her little red curls bounced saucily while she marched ahead of us."

"Is that what scared you?" teased Aurelia.

"Her attitude annoys me, but no, it's what happened with the foxes. Liam spotted them first, then Nezetta's hands weaved and lifted them into the air, squirming and kicking. Liam went to snap their necks, but Nezetta forced the air from their lungs, squeezed them so tight they suffocated. I looked at Nezetta, and what I saw ..." Daphne checked their surroundings again, hesitated before plunging ahead. "It was the look on her face, Aurelia."

She paused for so long in the telling, that Aurelia prompted, "What look?"

"It was -" Daphne appeared to struggle for the word to describe it. "Glee. Sheer joy at the killing, at the power she held over those foxes."

"Why shouldn't she be joyful to have caught us our dinner? I'm thankful for that stew." Aurelia patted her belly, standing from the stream and stretching. "Maybe I'm missing something—you did hit your head awfully hard earlier. Are you sure you're okay?"

Returning to camp, they whispered late into the night while the others slept, their first real chance to talk since Daphne awoke in the cottage. When Aurelia told her of Tobwhit's sacrifice, her fingertips brushed the saphyr, seemingly hesitant, reverent, as though it might still hold his heartbeat.

"It makes sense now. I feel ... different, ever since I woke up in that cottage. Still me of course -"

"But?"

"It's hard to explain. Like there's an echo that isn't quite myself. Fragments of memories at once familiar, yet unfamiliar. Does that make any sense?"

"Not really," admitted Aurelia.

"Imagine it's your thoughts, your voice, your words, but with an additional perspective there too, and it doesn't quite feel like your own. I never met Tobwhit, but ... it's like he's with me."

"Hmmm." Aurelia considered the strangeness of such a thought. "Have you ever known of a stone being transferred?"

"Never, though my time as Honored One has been short, and there's much they don't share with other Fiadha. Perhaps Ophel would know; we could ask her."

"We can't do that!" Aurelia rocked her head, eyes wide. "When I mentioned Tobwhit's name earlier, you should have seen her reaction. Told me I should never speak his name again. *A dangerous fool* she called him and that I wouldn't want others to know I'd associated with him. Who knows how it may change the way she looks at you if she knows that stone in your forehead is Tobwhit's."

"I'll trust you on that, but will always think kindly of him for what he did, dangerous fool or no. He gave me life again and brought me back to you. My covenant friend. But no, I won't ask Ophel."

Aurelia nodded in relief. "Do your bindings feel different?"

"What do you mean?"

"Well, you mentioned an echo in your mind. Has that affected your bindings, your power?"

"I ... um, I can't tell."

"You've never actually told me, or at least I didn't know to ask until Ophel explained how you bond with your stone—you know, what you're most attuned to."

"Well, uh ... I -"

"It's okay; you don't have to be so modest with me."

Aurelia wrapped her arms around Daphne, relieved to have such a friend. Had Nezetta been her introduction to Gray Cloaks, she would think much less highly of them. Where Nezetta was cold, distant, and haughty, Daphne was anything but. Her heart bursting with affection, Aurelia would have said more, but the words caught in her throat. Her lungs emptied as if a fist squeezed them shut. Her fingers clawed at her throat, she tried to breathe, but couldn't. The look on Daphne's face mirrored her own.

In the dark, a figure drew close, features sharpening into focus—*Nezetta!* The woman's hands turned, twisted, a binding sharp and cruel, so different from Ophel's gentle weave. An invisible weight pinned Aurelia and dragged her bodily across the ground, depositing her at Nezetta's feet. Aurelia's heart thundered and panic gripped as tight as the unseen pressure that forced air from her lungs. She tried to inhale but the world refused her.

This is how it ends then. Daphne was right. Nezetta can't be trusted.

Then she noticed two other figures crouched behind Nezetta.

Ophel. Liam.

What is going on?

Laying a finger to her lips, Nezetta leaned in close, whispered, "Hush. Quiet. We're not alone. The Ka. They've found us."

Chapter Thirty-Three
Weak and Losing Blood

"Search the marsh!" roared Drael.

The fire's ash still smoldered; the odor of a recent meal lingered. To be this close and once again find their prey slipping between his fingers ... his blood boiled at the thought.

Drael's instincts had been right, trusting Col's intuition, the man believing the Dorakian girl was no fool and no martyr. She must have had good reason to jump and reason to believe she would live.

But Drael had done more than trust Col, ordering his Far-Seers to search the valley floor for signs of life. Such strange little men with their slight frames and pale faces. The constant wringing of their hands, and whispering in those sniveling squeaky voices, staring unblinking from those pitch-black eyes. There wasn't much that spooked Drael, but Far-Seers were on that list. He believed in little beyond the physical world, a world he could touch, taste, and see; but Far-Seers caused men who held such beliefs to waver. Some claimed their abilities were the natural effect of a procedure performed at birth, but truthfully no one knew, save the Far-Seers, and they chose not to clarify. The Ka paid them well for their skills.

The three edged perilously close to the cliff, side-by-side, hands clasped like always when their eyes searched. Drael was certain a stiff breeze could blow them over the cliff's edge, but after a lengthy wait they returned with news. Movement below. Humans. With their view obscured by a thick canopy of trees, impossible to be completely certain, but they believed one bore a shaved head and another long black hair.

He didn't understand how they'd survived, but Drael assumed Gray Cloak magic was at work. When scouts reported a path down into the gorge, Drael led his Ka in pursuit. From the looks of the campsite, the two girls were no longer alone. Drael suspected Magnus and the deserters.

"It's them, isn't it?" The question voiced by Col, astride the steed secured for him by the quartermaster.

Drael nodded, distracted, studying the camp, the faint indentations where they'd eaten and slept, at least four, perhaps five individuals.

Then he noticed it, a scrape across the ground, leaving a faint trail—and there, another one—as if someone dragged two heavy objects across the ground. He signaled his men's attention and waved them forward.

Nezetta released her hold on Aurelia, but kept a finger to her lips. Shame pricked Aurelia's heart. *I doubted her, and she saves us again.* Whatever she felt personally towards the woman, she owed her a great debt.

They slogged deeper into the marsh. Mud clung, sucked at every footstep, hindered progress. Thick grass, razor sharp as blades, sliced at arms and hands but provided cover.

Aurelia couldn't help a surprised cry when her next step, instead of planting on a firm clump of grass, plunged her neck-deep into a filthy bog. Her cry stifled as a wind binding silenced her.

She managed a glare at Nezetta, couldn't help herself. *I didn't mean to cry out—anyone would have done the same!* Nezetta ignored the icy stare but released the binding so she could breathe again.

They waited, listening. Had Aurelia's cry alerted the Ka? For the moment it seemed not, though they could hear Ka in the distance. The occasional shout. The whinny of a horse. A jangle of armor.

Ophel skirted the pool of water as Aurelia swam across. Liam waited, his gaze intent on Ophel, noting the safe path she trod. With a grimace, Aurelia pulled herself up and out, on the far embankment. *Yuck.* Soggy reeds and chunks of dark filth clung to her hair and clothes.

A rustling noise. Aurelia screamed a warning. But too late. Liam's face contorted, anguished, a Ka sword piercing his back. The soldier yanked the sword free, and Liam slumped forward, his body sliding into the murky pool.

Chaos ensued. Nezetta whirled to face the threat, hands twisting, stuttering, violent movements, as she called on the wind to aid, hauling the soldier bodily into the air, slamming him to the ground with a sickening crunch. He didn't move again, but other Ka pushed their way through the reeds, some splashing into the bog, others finding safer passage around, swords raised as they charged the band of women. Three soldiers were upon Aurelia before she could react, the closest grabbing a fistful of hair to jerk back her head, baring her neck for his sword. With a jarring clang, another sword parried.

Col.

"Not her!" He spoke through gritted teeth. "She's my friend. She lives."

Using the moment to her advantage, Nezetta summoned the wind and hurled Daphne and Aurelia to safety, across another bog onto a far embankment.

"Seize them!" Drael appeared, directing his men toward Nezetta and Ophel. Ka flooded into the marsh, surrounding the two. The ground rumbled as Ophel joined the fray, hurling earth and rock at the approaching soldiers, knocking them unconscious, burying them alive in mud. But they kept coming, too many to stop. An unseen wind whipped into a frenzy, snatched soldiers by legs and arms, flung them across the marsh or drowned them in brackish waters. Still they came. Undeterred, determined, more terrified of Drael's fury than the women or their powers.

"Elder-Mother!" cried Nezetta, "together!"

Their hands twisted and wound in unison—Ophel's steady, refined; Nezetta's sharp, tearing—a mesmerizing pattern they instinctively knew. The soldiers fell back, awed and terrified as the ground beneath the women rumbled and a chunk of earth lifted from the marsh, carrying the women clear. Those unfortunate Ka who stood too close stumbled off balance and pitched forward into space where earth had once been. A flood of rock, mud and brackish water followed them down, entombing them forever in its embrace.

Drael didn't hesitate. He leapt across the yawning chasm, scrambled for a hold, clambering up behind Nezetta and Ophel. Absorbed in their binding, they failed to notice him.

Drael's blade pierced Ophel's side. The shock of it sent a ripple through the binding, slipping as she faltered. The platform crumbled. Drael stumbled sideways as once sure footing broke, his blade sliced at an angle, missing heart and lungs.

Ophel grunted, fell to one knee, groaned with effort to hold their platform together. With a shriek, Nezetta turned her fury on Drael. One hand held to her wind's binding, continuing the platform's flight, while the other gathered a fistful of wind. Released, the wind shot past Ophel with a shriek of fury all its own, slammed into Drael and flung him from the platform. He landed with a heavy splash in the marsh.

The wind blew their chunk of earth across the marsh. As the two Gray Cloaks tumbled from the crumbling platform, the girls rushed to their aid to find Ophel struggling to breathe, her cloak stained red. Supporting the older woman between them, they slogged through marsh and mud while the Ka regrouped behind. Ophel was weak and losing blood fast.

Chapter Thirty-Four
The Face Staring Back

The winding climb to Hadil's Crossing wasn't for the faint of heart, one more reason Dorak received so few visitors, the coming and going across the Tol an arduous journey. At Magnus' orders, they'd camped in sight of the crossing, but the steep ascent took all of the following morning.

Hadil's Crossing was nothing but hardened mud, a narrow wagon path squeezed between steep canyon walls. But oh, the view at its entrance! Everything Eken could have imagined.

He sucked in another lungful of thin air. It seemed the heavens themselves welcomed him; clouds floated by near enough to touch and the sun hung just out of reach. He stood eye level with snow-capped peaks where a herd of wild goats bounded across the steep inclines. There was something, too, about the air here, the way it cleared his mind and left him more refreshed than he'd been in days.

He wasn't the only one delighted; his companions drank in the sweeping vistas between gasps for air. Only NoNo seemed unaffected by the views or the thin air, leaping nimbly through the pass without a backward glance.

Eken followed Magnus and Veyra into the crossing, amused at their morning antics. He wasn't sure exactly what had changed, but something had, the night before, upon their return from gathering water. Oh, Magnus put on a brave front, appearing nonchalant, but Veyra's stares were enough to cause one to blush. *Bold like a Harvest Dance stare.* It was a pleasant distraction from recent struggles.

Since Lumath, except for their brief stay in Tobwhit's cottage, he felt less like himself and more like a stranger adrift in his own mind. At first he brushed the thought aside, but as it lingered, he fought to keep panic at bay.

What if I never recover? Will I still be me?

He often caught himself grimacing, rubbing at his head, or staring blankly into the distance. He attempted, in a muddled sort of way, to seek help. Tobias suggested he try willow bark for his headache. Morco recommended an afternoon of chopping wood: *nothing cures a restless mind like a little sweat and splinters.* Veyra offered to teach him the bow, take his mind off his troubles. Magnus urged rest. Eken reserved his highest hopes for NoNo—surely magical creatures offered sage advice—but his was the most banal of all. *Time will heal,* the creature said. But Eken sensed the truth was otherwise. Time would not heal. He'd lost a friend—two, if he were honest—and now he was losing himself.

"Come and join us, Eken!" Tobias' welcome genuine, as they strode through Hadil's Crossing.

"Will we reach the Capitol today?"

"No, before us lies the King's Forest."

"Oh," responded a disappointed Eken, who'd imagined the Capitol nestled tranquilly at the foot of the Tol. "So tomorrow then?"

A laugh as Tobias replied, "The forest is quite expansive; it'll take several days to make the Capitol. Don't worry, there's many a town along the way. Tonight—a proper bed and a hot meal!"

His ears perked at the pleasant sound of such things. *What wonders await me?* He dreamed of a comfortable bed in a lovely little inn, and a delicious meal prepared by its proprietors.

The bowl of cold gruel set before him at Numa's Inn sorely disappointed.

They'd arrived at the town of Hiedorn, settled where the slopes of the Tol met the King's Forest. To keep the townsfolk oblivious to his presence, NoNo leaped to Eken's shoulder and settled loosely around his neck, looking remarkably like a rather expensive and colorful fur.

A thick fog blanketed Hiedorn, a gift from a passing storm, meaning Eken's first glimpse of a town outside Dorak proved rather disappointing as he peered through the fog. Not that Hiedorn offered much to see had it lifted, its population small, with few visitors save those who endured Hadil's Crossing. This then was peak tourist season, while the crossing remained open: before their arrival Numa's Inn housed three guests.

As the King's Forest farthest outlying town, Hiedorn was a lawless place. Time had passed it by, of no real import or interest save to those who enjoyed anonymity from the law, or to those intending to access Hadil's Crossing. Its reputation well earned, Magnus warned Eken to stay close and not to wander off alone. Muggings were a common occurrence, even during broad daylight, but the townsfolk gave a wide berth to the group of armed soldiers, though some cast a curious eye at the man they protected. By the looks of the expensive fur he wore, they assumed him to be a wealthy lord with an armed escort. How exciting that such an important man visited their backwater town!

For the ex-Ka, it had been but a short moon cycle since their last stopover in Hiedorn. They returned now in very different circumstances. During that earlier visit, their commander requisitioned Numa's Inn for the officers' use, tossing a furious guest, the inn's sole occupant at the time. But Numa the innkeeper cared little, his eyes widening when a bag of decri coin landed with a heavy clunk on his counter. His three grown sons, laboring at the inn for a miserly rate set by their own father, happily cared for the officers, scrubbing laundry or fetching a drink of ale; the generous tips they earned in one night far exceeding their standard pay for a moon cycle.

Numa's eyes lit upon recognizing a returning Ka officer, and he smiled greedily, peering over the counter. But the smile faded after learning they were only seven, though they'd fill more rooms than his occupants the night before. He eyed the expensive fur around Eken's neck.

"Vere's the rest of yuns?" he grunted, a thick accent betraying Lavonshia wasn't his natural-born country.

"Just us, I'm afraid. Four rooms, please." Magnus slid a few decri across the counter.

Travel packs deposited in their rooms, the weary travelers descended on the inn's hall, famished. The gruel, as Eken soon learned, a major disappointment.

"Yuns miss dinner," the innkeeper's wife growled, brooking no complaints.

Then what is this? Eken wondered. He'd caught himself then, turning, ready to complain to Aurelia, before remembering and the words died unspoken.

While the recent arrivals ate, one son swept the floor, disturbing more dust than he gathered. The second son, smelling of raw meat and days-old dried sweat, refilled their drinks. Both Numa and his wife were broad-chested, big-boned and built sturdy. The sons had inherited every bit of that and more, hulking brutes short on brains but ready to brawl.

As he churned a spoon through the gruel, Tobias whispered, "Another night of squirrel preferable to this!" His companions stifled a laugh. The innkeeper's wife eyed them from her roost in the corner, where she'd taken up camp, needlework clicking furiously.

Assigned to a room with Morco, Eken retreated from the hall, glad for a few quiet moments alone as his chamber-mate had gone to seek provisions, though the thin, hard pillow did nothing to ease the pressure in his head as he settled under a threadbare sheet.

A heavy knock on the door startled him.

"Who is it?" He scrambled from bed, snatching up the knife he'd set close by, but someone was already fiddling with the lock.

The lock turned.

The door burst open.

He exhaled and dropped the knife from trembling fingers, relieved to see it was only Morco returned early, the relief short-lived as the man thrust a torn and damp parchment in his face. The charcoal on the page had run, ruining the words scrawled at its top, but the image on the document was clear enough.

The face staring back at him was his own.

Chapter Thirty-Five
Bound In Irons

"Leave me. You must save yourselves."

"It's too late for that, Elder-Mother," said Nezetta. "We stand our ground. Here. With you."

As the older woman's strength waned, Nezetta had assumed leadership of their tiny band, and the others fell in step, perhaps because she was Salel.

Soldiers burst through the clump of reeds where they hid, lifting cries of discovery even as Nezetta bound a shrieking wind to her will, silencing their cries. More soldiers followed, and she sent them flying or smothered them to the ground. Aurelia joined the fray with a shriek of her own, snatched a sword from a dying soldier's slack grip and flung herself upon another Ka. Her fury worked for a moment, surprising the man; but with no training or experience, she was soon subdued. Nezetta's focus split, the wind stuttered, and a club caught her temple. She crumpled to the ground, out cold. The howling wind stilled.

As Aurelia fought the soldier pinning her to the ground, she saw Daphne rocking back and forth, cradling Ophel in her lap, tears streaming down her face. *Oh covenant friend, why didn't you fight?* wondered Aurelia.

Perhaps with her binding, they might have stood a chance.

Daphne knew all too well why she didn't fight. Why she couldn't fight.

She was a fraud.

The result of a well-planned and elaborate cover-up.

It began when her father, Lothar Vale, secured a promotion to Fi-tor clan High Mage, the vote contentious, split eight to seven, but enough to secure his new position.

Lothar wasn't a powerful Binder, but he was shrewd, and his ambition knew no end. Within a year of the election, his maneuvering secured prominent positions throughout Gray Cloak society for other family members. By the time whispers of nepotism spread, it was too late. Lothar had solidified his power, his family's influence and status.

Daphne was born in Toma, her family's hometown, unaware of the stage set for her. From the moment she entered the world, the Vale family doted on her every whim and every move. If not for her mother, she would have been a very spoiled child. But Gyda Vale was a good woman and a better mother. She taught her daughter well and led by example. She taught her kindness, respect and compassion towards others. But most importantly, Daphne received from her mother what she failed to receive from anyone else in her family—love.

A perceptive child, she recognized the reality behind the attention her father and other family members lavished on her. It wasn't love. It was greed. Ambition. She was simply a pawn in her family's quest for power. In appointing family members to the positions of Ward, Guide, and Stone Keeper, Lothar Vale had circumvented a system of checks and balances intended to protect the sacred process one followed to become an Honored One.

That process begins with the Ward. While all Gray Cloak children possess an innate connection to the elements, the depth and power of their abilities varied. The position of Ward, than, was intended to weed out the weak, to recommend only the strongest for further training and the possibility of earning a stone. And so, as with any other Gray Cloak child, when Daphne witnessed her fourth hunter's moon, she was supervised by the newly appointed Ward. Gyda Vale. Her mother.

As Ward, Gyda observed in her daughter a distinct lack of magic. In private, to her husband, she admitted it was the least ability she'd ever seen in a child. The observation saddened her, for the heartfelt desire of any Gray Cloak parent is to see their child become an Honored One.

Lothar criticized his wife for not doing more to encourage their daughter's abilities. When Daphne showed no improvement, he withdrew emotionally. Even at a young age, Daphne sensed the souring of their relationship, though she didn't understand why. Gyda continued to love her daughter, as any good mother would.

But Lothar hadn't placed his family in positions of power for nothing. His vision of creating a family dynasty drove him to great lengths of manipulation, and he informed his wife she would recommend their daughter to the Guide.

Gyda had no choice but to comply, though she didn't agree, for she had long ago laid her will in her husband's hands, their arranged marriage a rocky one from the outset. He was abusive, physically and verbally, and by the time their daughter arrived on the scene, Lothar had long ago broken his wife's spirit.

For a year, Gyda watched as her daughter's inability, particularly compared to other children, became more and more apparent. But on Commendation Day, the day each year when the Ward recommends eight, and only eight, children to the clan's Guide from the current batch of four-years, Daphne's name was called.

Gyda's job as Ward was done.

It was now the Guide's role to lead the eight in further training. To aid them in understanding how to listen to the land.

And Lothar had also appointed the current Guide—Daphne's grandmother Asmi—who wholeheartedly embraced her son's scheme and knew that, when the time came, she would gladly choose her granddaughter for Ascension to Honored One.

There was little she could do to help her granddaughter though. The girl simply had no ability. True, she could Sense, feel magic in the land, or bindings as they occurred, but so could every female Gray Cloak. Daphne, however, had no innate binding abilities of her own, no real connection to the land. It did not call to her and seemingly never would. Nonetheless, Asmi Vale carved out time each day for a one-on-one session with her granddaughter, as expected for each of the eight. After all, appearances must be maintained.

They went through the motions, Daphne failing repeatedly to so much as create a whimper of a binding. There were brief moments that sparked fragile hopes—that time when the candle's flame flickered in her direction, but it was only a gust of air as Asmi entered the room; or when the wind seemed to howl in response to her efforts, but it was only an approaching storm; or when a pebble moved atop a pile of rocks, but it wasn't her, it was a bug scrambling to freedom, knocking the pebble aside.

Several years into the farce, without verbally acknowledging the decision, Asmi and Daphne stopped trying. Secluded away in the training hall, they read books, spoke of family or the latest juicy gossip. Any topic was fair game except binding and magic.

For those who survived the requisite time with the Guide, two hurdles remained.

First, the young man or woman must be Favored above their remaining peers at the Favoring, a ceremony on the first day of the third moon cycle each year, when all the clans gather. It was a solemn occasion, and an anxious one for parents whose child made it that far. For on that day, one child from each of the three clans would become an Honored One, the supply of saphyrs too limited to choose more, the Unfavored released back to society, never to become an Honored One.

It was a poor system. One that rewarded a few and punished most. A lucky few Unfavored assimilated well into society, aided by family that loved them or a kind soul that pitied them. But for most Unfavored, their failure was a life-defining moment they wore like a badge of shame. Shunned, avoided, passed over for meaningful employment, with little other training to fall back on, an Unfavored retreated into obscurity. Many left home, never to be heard from again.

For Daphne, the anxiety was less than for most. Because of her father, her Ascension was all but assured.

A part of her wished to shout her secret from the rooftops. To be done with the charade. But the life chosen for her was all she'd ever known—coming clean felt an impossibility. To do so would disgrace her family and ruin her mother, whom she dearly loved. She would be worse than Unfavored, she would be one who attempted to game the system. A lie. A cheat. She would be shunned and she would certainly never marry. Who would want her?

So she held her tongue and, as expected, in the year of her eighteenth hunter's moon, the Guide Favored her.

Lothar spared no expense for the party. Another Vale, an Honored One. As the evening drew to a close, the very inebriated father of a young man in attendance created quite the scene. The young man had shown spectacular promise in his bindings, but was no longer in the running now that Daphne had Ascended. The father's outburst an angry one, railing against the Vale family name, clamoring to any who cared to listen that Lothar had cheated his son, and that Daphne was a fake. Lothar's staff escorted the man from the party, and by an eight-day's end the man and his family had abandoned the clan, an unusual occurrence as Gray Cloak families rarely left their clans. Rumors swirled that Lothar might have had something to do with their disappearance.

With Daphne's Ascension, only one step remained: the Stone Keeper must transfer the stone to the newly appointed Honored One—a formality, by all accounts. No Ascended had ever been denied a stone or failed to bond with it.

On these points, Daphne was quite anxious, for why would a Stone Keeper hand her a saphyr? Surely they'd Sense she had no such power to bond with one. But the Stone Keeper was Daphne's uncle, Jeril, the final piece of Lothar's scheme, a position the most secretive of all in Gray Cloak society. So secretive in fact that outside of the Stone Keeper themselves, only a High Mage knew their identity, and only the two knew the sourcing of the saphyr stones. The clans jealously guarded this knowledge, passed down from High Mage to High

Mage, century after century. Daphne herself was unaware of Jeril's status as Stone Keeper, though she assumed it must be a family member for her father's scheme to work.

"How can I bond with it, Mother?" she had asked that day, the day of her Ascension, studying the stone. It was cold, flat, a dark gray color, identical on both sides, and for its size unusually heavy. A surreal moment to hold such a treasure in her hands.

She'd asked before, and knew what her mother would say, but she still doubted.

"You know the answer already. I'll do it for you."

"But will it ..." Daphne hesitated, never an easy thing to voice the lie, even to one complicit.

"Yes my daughter, it will still bond, and be as life and breath to you. So the ancients say, despite ..." Gyda hesitated too, before placing a gentle hand against her daughter's cheek. A daughter the family didn't deserve. Kind, humble, good and decent inside. Save for the lie. Her mother's lips moved in a silent prayer, as they had so many times before: that the lie wouldn't defile or define her daughter. "Are you ready?"

Daphne nodded, trembling. *What will it feel like?* she wondered. Her grip tightened on the stone.

"I'll need that," said her mother with a laugh, breaking the tension. Daphne laughed too and released her grip, allowing her mother to take the stone.

When her husband had set his scheme in motion, Gyda insisted on this one point. She, and she alone, would bind the stone to her daughter. She wanted no one else touching her daughter's mind and soul in that vulnerable moment.

If anyone had cared to take note, Gyda Vale took an unusual number of trips to Lumath and spent an unusual number of hours in its library, pouring over the renowned ancients' writings regarding Ascension. She discovered that, though rare, an individual could perform an Ascension binding for another. The reason for these rare exceptions remained shrouded in mystery, but Gyda reasoned that if it had been done once, it could be done again.

Don't mess this up—it still rang in her ears—the venomous words passing her husband's lips as he laid the stone in her palm. She had never despised him more. Thankfully, he hadn't stayed to watch.

The stone lifted as Gyda's focus intensified. Daphne watched, waited, and heard a gentle hum. Felt a tingling sensation crawl up her arms and down her legs. Her mother called to the land, to the stone, and to her daughter's mind and heart.

The stone spun. Slow at first, gradually faster. Its dark gray color lightened for a moment before it darkened again.

Beads of sweat formed on Gyda's forehead, wrinkles forming as she frowned in concentration.

Is it working? Daphne's anxiety spiked, threatening to overwhelm her. She nearly blacked out. *What if this all proves to be for nothing and I'm exposed?*

A high-pitched hum, from the stone. A blinding light. Pain, searing pain. Daphne fainted.

"Careful now, sit up slow."

Her mother hovered, concern etched on her face.

"Is it ...?"

"It is. How do you feel?"

"I ... I feel the same. I think." Truthfully, it was hard to tell. "I think I'm gonna be sick."

She remained in bed for three days, healing. Occasionally, in awe and wonder, her hand strayed to her forehead, trembling as she touched the stone. Her saphyr. It tickled where the stone grafted to her skin.

On the fourth day, Lothar paraded her before the clan, her gray cloak presented in a traditional Cloaking Ceremony, but all Daphne wanted was to hide away in bed or voice the thoughts in her head. *Please, I feel ill.* Away from the well wishes and the congratulations. *Don't, just don't. I'm a fraud.* From neighbors asking, How does it feel? *It doesn't feel like anything's changed at all.* Or wondering, Could you display a little Honored One magic for us? *No, sorry, I can't. I have no power to bind.*

Honored Ones from clan Fi-jal and clan Fi-dun attended the Cloaking Ceremony for clan Fi-tor's newly ascended member, and wondered at the lack of power they Sensed in the girl, though they kept the observation to themselves. It wasn't wise to confront Lothar or members of his family.

"It itches, does it not?"

Daphne had just slipped into her new cloak. It did, maddeningly so, and she didn't like it. She glanced up, surprised, recognizing the voice—a woman she'd met only once before, an Elder-Mother named Ophel from clan Fi-jal. A Salel.

"It will get better. I do not know if it is the skin getting used to the cloak, or the cloak getting used to you." The woman laughed, a stilted laughter like she didn't laugh often. "Walk with me. I wish to talk with our newest Honored One."

Out of respect for a Salel, the crowd parted, allowing Ophel and Daphne to pass. The two wandered, strolling by the town's river. For a woman wishing to talk, Ophel was surprisingly quiet.

The silence unnerving, Daphne spoke first.

"Will I ever get used to it?"

"I assume you mean the stone, not the cloak." A ghost of a smile played across Ophel's mouth. "I still remember that feeling, though it was many, many years ago. How odd it felt embedded in my flesh."

Daphne nodded in agreement.

"But then—oh, its warmth! The connection with it, to the land, and my power. Oh yes, you will get used to it. I am surprised you have not already."

The woman studied her, an expression on her face Daphne didn't quite care for.

"Oh no, yes ... that is, I meant to say yes. Most certainly. I feel those things." Truthfully, she felt nothing besides a cold, flat object against her skin, but what else could she say?

Ophel paused at the river's waterfall, what the locals called Hammod's Falls. When Daphne had learned why they called it Hammod's Falls, she never visited again. But today she was Ophel's guest and one couldn't refuse a Salel.

Ophel lifted a hand idly, distracted, her thoughts seemingly elsewhere. A pebble floated into the waterfall, danced under the sheet of water before plunging into the pool below.

"Your saphyr will become such a part of you it will be as air itself. As natural as breathing."

Daphne sighed, grateful her secret still safe, until the older woman's next words:

"There is something different about you. I can Sense it. You are not like other Honored Ones."

"I, um ..." Bile rose in her throat. Panic at the thought of being discovered.

"Do not worry, child." The Elder-Mother laughed. "It is okay to be different. It offers balance to our society. There are too many who hunger after power, but that is not your desire."

Relieved, Daphne calmed her beating heart. "No, you're right. It isn't."

"Though it is your father's." The statement spoken as one that was obvious, and with a note of disapproval. "A dangerous path, that."

Ophel turned from the waterfall to study the newest Ascended member of their order. She cupped Daphne's chin, lifting until their eyes met.

I hope she's satisfied with what she sees.

"Power is not everything," the Elder-Mother said at last. "Some who accomplish the most hold no power."

Daphne swallowed hard.

"Some will attempt to use you. Others attempt to break you. Do not allow them. Your power does not come from here." Ophel tapped the stone set in her forehead. "But from here." She placed a hand over Daphne's heart.

For the longest time they stood that way, the firm but gentle hand over her heart, calming her panicked heartbeat, the Elder-Mother granting her courage for trials to come. None, besides her mother, had ever seen her so clearly. Daphne fought the urge to weep.

In the days that followed, she ignored the whispers in her hometown of Toma, and there were many. People commented on the oddity of her Ascension. That she'd been sick for so long afterwards. Her unwillingness to display a little magic for the crowd, breaking from a time-honored tradition. What newly minted Honored One wouldn't care to show off a little, power coursing through their body, aided by a saphyr?

The whispers didn't last. Not with Lothar stamping them out. He'd worked too hard to establish his power and was not a man to countenance murmuring against him or his family. But in private and often in trivial ways, many in the clans disrespected Daphne. Chief among them, Nezetta. A member of a powerful family herself, she refused to be cowed by Lothar's threats and belittled Daphne every chance she could. It was a relief to the Vale family when she departed to pursue her Awakening, though they feared her growing power and influence should she return Salel.

When Ophel requested Daphne accompany her to Chelam, she set out with a mix of excitement and trepidation, thrilled to be out from under her father, though curious why the Elder-Mother would ask an Honored One with no power along?

She feared discovery of the fraud she was, sensing Ophel knew the truth yet hadn't outed her. Why? And could she trust her? Or did the woman scheme like her father? She tired of Gray Cloak schemes.

In truth, she was relieved someone else knew. For that reason alone, she trusted the Elder-Mother.

Her father and grandmother had coached her tirelessly over the years. *You must remain aloof. Distant. You can have no true friends in Gray Cloak society. You can trust no one with your secret, but as an Honored One you can wield influence. Political power. All that truly matters.*

But then the troubles. Saan. War looming. A mission to Chelam. She feared exposure should her missing powers be needed. Feared others' response, knowing it wouldn't be like Ophel's, who for reasons all her own kept Daphne's secret.

And then she met Aurelia, a covenant friend she treasured. Eken fast becoming a good friend as well, perhaps the others one day, the ex-Ka, though those relationships would take time. But none like Aurelia. And so most of all, the prospect terrified, that Aurelia would discover who she wasn't. Would learn that her new friend was a fraud, a liar, and that it would break their friendship. The secret gnawed like a creature's hunger never satisfied.

When Nezetta bound the wind against the Ka, and Aurelia leaped into the fray, Daphne sat weeping, cradling Ophel's head in her lap. She offered no resistance herself. Even Tobwhit's stone was no help to her, for it was merely the echo of another life.

Ophel's eyes fluttered weakly. "It is okay, child. I know. I know. It will all be okay."

She wept the harder as the older woman slipped into unconsciousness.

Drael pushed past his soldiers, a cruel smile parting his lips.

She looked up, tear-stained, imploring, "I'll go quietly, do whatever you ask. Please, just help her."

They bound the powerless girl in irons and led her away.

Chapter Thirty-Six
Stuck in Her Throat

Daphne found herself in Drael's tent, shackles removed, a meal spread before her. *No, more than just a meal—a banquet.* She counted five courses. Steaming food, the aroma rich and scented of exotic spices. Place settings for two, gleaming silver plate and cup and fork and spoon, with a luxuriantly soft naperon cloth to wipe her hands and dab her lips. Rarely had she seen such finery, a surprise in a commander's tent on a war campaign.

Earlier, Drael had ordered Ophel tended by the Ka's healer, her wounds stitched—she was resting now—while Aurelia and Nezetta were led away, gagged and bound, under guard. The guards had brought her here, to his tent, ordered her to wait, and wait she had, though the waiting got harder the longer she sat so close to the feast.

She swallowed a tight ball of fear, unable to keep her hands from trembling as Drael entered the tent and sat across from her.

"Please eat," he said, as attending servants poured the first course.

Mmmm. Cream and potato soup.

Before he could change his mind, she dipped her spoon in the creamy soup, slurped a mouthful, hiding her fear behind the sudden burst of flavor. "Mmmm! That's amazing. Delicious! Where ...? How ...?" She was at a loss for words at such exceptional flavor.

The commander's smile seemed genuine. "I spare no expense for what I eat. Even on the campaign trail, I bring my personal chef. He's from the Twelve Isles, you know."

Her eyes widened: the isles were mythical in their renown. An island nation, a protectorate of the Kingdom of Lavonshia, requiring a long and difficult voyage across the Maldelea Sea to reach—she'd heard near three moon cycles.

Drael relished the girl's reaction. He appreciated the gravitas it afforded him when others learned his chef was a Twelver. Unlike most, Drael had been to the Twelve Isles. Not all the rumors were true, as with most stories, but the islands did pride themselves on their culinary delights, as well they should.

He'd considered his approach with the Binder before ordering her brought to his tent, perhaps a gentler touch needed than his earlier heavy-handed removal of her stone, expecting the tantalizing aroma would soften her up.

He intended to lay it on thick.

The girl noisily slurped up every drop of soup. When finished, she stared wistfully at the empty bowl.

Drael laughed, a charming sound—he could turn it on when needed—you didn't remain a Ka commander on brawn alone. Wits and a little politicking were needed. "Don't worry. There's plenty of everything. Tell me about your life growing up. Were you privileged? Or destitute?"

"Definitely privileged." The Gray Cloak girl craned her neck towards the second course sitting just out of reach on the serving cart. "My father is a powerful man in our clan. Many of my family members hold positions of power or authority."

He noticed her eyeing the second course and sipped his own bowl of soup painfully slow. *Longing is such a persuasive emotion.* "You and I have much in common." He used his naperon to dab his lips. "I also grew up privileged. Could have chosen any life I wished."

Daphne cocked her head, considering Drael. Her family possessed all the power one could want, but that power hadn't trickled down to her. *How must it feel to be free to decide one's own fate?*

"Our similarity ends there then. I've had no say in my life's direction." She paused, before asking, "So why choose life in the Ka?"

It surprised her how easily the question came. The man terrified her at Lumath. Here though, he seemed at ease, as was she. She retained enough wits to realize the warmth of the tent, the pillows on which she reclined, and the tasty food were all affecting her. *What is he playing at?*

"I owe that to my father," answered Drael. "Needed to go as far from him as I could. Joining the Ka and seeing the world seemed the right place to start."

"Okay, you're right; we're not that different." She greedily accepted the next plate a servant handed to her.

"Smoked salmon," said the commander.

"I needed to escape my father as well," mumbled Daphne, savoring the tender, seasoned meat as it melted on her tongue.

"If we're not so different," Drael drove the point home, "then let us reach an amicable agreement. I wish for this war to end. There's no need for more Gray Cloaks to die."

"I agree!" She shoved another piece of salmon in her mouth, took a sip of spiced wine and sighed. *Exquisite.* "My people only wish to live in peace."

"There's Saan to consider."

"That wasn't us."

"It's the King you need to convince, not me." He shrugged helplessly as if he was on her side.

"Can you take us to him?"

"I can, but, and no offense meant, you don't have any power, do you?"

"I ..." Daphne turned away, hiding her blush. *How does he know?* she wondered.

"He'll want to speak with someone who has authority."

"Oh," she said, relieved he meant a different kind of power. "My father is our clan's High Mage. Would the King grant him safe passage?"

The third course arrived. Enormous platters laden with assorted fruit. Some she recognized; others, exotic and unknown, piqued her curiosity. She tried a piece of each. A smiling Drael watched.

"Here's my thought—I take you to the King. There you present your case, tell him of your father, and yes, I believe the King would issue a writ of safe passage for him and any traveling with him."

It was hard to argue with the man while enjoying his delicious food. His reasoning seemed sound. With a full stomach and a warm tent, her eyes fluttered.

"Agreed."

Her smile beamed across the table. He returned it, though if she hadn't been so sleepy she would have noticed its wolf-like appearance. A piece of fruit stuck in her throat until she forced it down.

Chapter Thirty-Seven
Never such a scene

Huddled inside Eken's room, they discussed strategy.

The vote was split—stay overnight and leave at first light before the town awoke, or go now.

Those favoring an overnight stay reasoned there'd been no attempt to seize Eken; besides, they were well armed, and well trained, a handful of backwater townsfolk posed little threat and those beds in the inn did look rather comfortable; while those arguing in favor of an immediate departure felt they were fortunate no one yet raised the alarm, and the sooner they were gone the better.

Magnus listened, weighing the arguments, but the words slid past without fully landing. *Overnight. Comfortable beds. Inn. Sooner gone the better.* He felt certain Aurelia would have had an opinion, Daphne too, but he shook his mind clear, refusing to dwell on such sad thoughts. The living needed him focused.

A fist pounding the door, "Open ze door yun fools! It's I, Numa ze innkeeper," and a moment later the man stood in their midst, returning Magnus' bag of coin.

"Yuns must leave. Townspeople gatzer to come and seize yuns companion by force. Yuns coin, less mine timez and troublez, and ze cost of yuns dinner. Be glad I vish no ill upon a guest of mine inn. Let no vun say zat vun staying at Numa's Inn could be taken 'gainst his vill."

"We're not afraid of a few villagers," said Bochim.

"Zen yun truly are fools! Perhaps yuns don't care zat a mercenary band come yesterday to Hiedorn to mine inn. Zey refused to pay mine price, so zey camped outside town. Ze people of Hiedorn aim to recruit zem and split ze reward. If yuns will not heed me, blood be on yuns own hands!"

Numa spat at their feet and stalked from the room.

"That settles it," said Magnus. "We go now."

"I noticed a backdoor while eating dinner," offered Veyra helpfully.

"If that gruel answers to being called dinner," muttered Eken.

"Bochim, Tobias, watch our back." Magnus laid out their plan. "Morco, Saul, at the front with me. Swords drawn. Veyra, be prepared to let your arrows fly. If an enemy seeks to engage us, let's hope a show of force discourages them. Eken, take this. Stay hidden in our midst."

He passed a hooded cloak to Eken, who pulled it over his head with a distasteful grimace, its wool coarse and itchy. NoNo wrapped himself once more round Eken's neck, though he protested the scratchy cloth with a pitiful mewing.

The backdoor proved a dead end.

"They've surrounded the inn!" Magnus startled the innkeeper and his wife as he slammed the door shut.

"Zer vill be no blood on mine fresh cleaned floors!" shouted the hysterical wife. "Yuns must leave! Go! Go!" Waving her apron, she shooed them towards the back door.

"We can't leave!" protested Veyra. "There's a murderous mob out there."

Numa growled and threw open the door to see for himself. An unruly mob had indeed gathered behind the inn, the gleam in their eyes betraying their intention, as did their odd assortment of weaponry—scythes, daggers, a staff or two, even an iron skillet. He recognized a few of the mercenaries sprinkled in the mob, lethal killers, with a look that said they knew how to handle themselves in a fight. They were better armed than the townsfolk.

The innkeeper slammed the door shut and barred it. He strode to the front door, throwing it open with such force it broke from its top hinge and wobbled at a haphazard angle. He grabbed a club from behind the counter on his way out while his wife and sons armed themselves in a similar fashion and followed him onto the inn's front porch. An even larger mob had gathered on the street out front.

"Yuns must leave!" yelled Numa, waving his club menacingly. Despite his thick accent, the mob understood his meaning. "Zer vill be no fighting. No harm to mine inn nor mine guests."

One would think the threat enough, but shouts of, *Bring out the wanted man!* and *We deserve the reward!* filled the air.

A dagger flew. No one could say later who'd thrown it, but it struck the innkeeper's ample gut. He grunted, pulled the dagger free, glared at the red tip and tossed it back at the crowd. As his gut was rather large, the dagger failed to do him real harm, but it succeeded in stirring the hornet's nest. With a bellowed rage, he waded into the crowd swinging his club.

Those closest went down, skulls crushed, knees shattered, limbs torn from sockets. Mercenaries and townsfolk alike fell before his fury. The crowd staggered. But as those in the rear surged forward, eager to earn a piece of the reward, their overwhelming numbers turned the tide. A mercenary plunged a sword into Numa's side, but he wasn't a man to go down easily, and seizing the mercenary with a meaty palm, he threw the man to the ground and crushed the life from him with a punishing blow.

Swinging, flailing, he waded deep into the mob. Spurred into action, his wife shrieked and hurled herself into the fray, the sons following her into action. Again the tide shifted, the mob retreating. Somehow, for a moment at least, it looked as if Numa and his family would win the day.

Inside the inn, the guests watched, stunned by the fight's brutality and how quickly it had escalated. But the innkeeper was slowing, as was his family. It was only a matter of time before they succumbed to repeated blows, and the inn's guests would be next.

"They're leaving!" shouted Veyra. Peering through a crack in the back door, she saw the mob leaving, surging toward the front, eager to join in claiming the reward.

A flaming brand shattered a front window. Fire leapt onto a laundry pile lying where Numa's wife had discarded it and began licking its way across the wooden plank floor. It spread quickly, hungry, devouring the dining hall's benches and tables.

It was time to go.

They cut through what little resistance remained behind the inn and vanished into the dark, the uproar in the street and the fire's glow masking their flight. Numa's Inn, the man's life work, was soon swallowed by flames; with dancing reds and oranges reflecting in his eyes, the innkeeper sank at last to his knees and breathed his last. His wife and sons fought valiantly, even after their patriarch's final breath, before succumbing to their own wounds.

Fire raged on all three levels of the inn, the street awash in blood, the dead and the dying in staggering numbers. Hiedorn had seen its share of violence, but never such a scene as that.

Chapter Thirty-Eight
If I Must

Skittish, the horse danced sideways across the narrow path, sensing the rider's anxiety and inexperience. Daphne's face blanched white as the animal careened towards a wall, picturing her leg, crushed and broken, pinned between the horse's heaving flank and the sheer rock face, but at the last moment it turned aside.

Disaster averted, she clung to the reins while scanning the crossing ahead.

"Are we close?"

"For the last time, yes," her escort grumbled. "They always move the wagons to the front for the crossing. It'll be there."

Not that her guard was disagreeable, though she feared the worst when Drael assigned her one. *For your protection,* he'd insisted. No, the aging soldier's eyes were kind, though the sword at his side suggested otherwise; and despite the unenviable task of guarding a Gray Cloak, he'd agreed to help when she asked.

"See. There it is," he smiled smugly, "as I told you it would be. Just ahead."

A lump caught in Daphne's throat. *Will she care to see me?* It would be the first time she'd faced her covenant friend since the marsh.

Ophel drifted in and out, mumbling incoherently. The healer who'd tended to her earlier claimed he'd done all he could, but the wound was too deep and an infection raged despite the herbs he applied. A foul odor wafted from the greenish-tinged pus soaking through the bandage. Aurelia didn't need her limited experience to interpret the look on the healer's face: Ophel wasn't long for this world.

A jarring jolt as the wagon cleared another of Hadil's Crossing's famous ruts, before Nezetta's white-knuckled grip on the bars relaxed. They appeared to be past the worst of it as the wagon rumbled clear of the crossing, rolling smooth now on the meandering descent from the Tol Mountains. Nezetta's lips thinned to a hard line as a rider approached, a Ka soldier shadowing close behind.

"Never have thought well of you, Daphne Vale. But this is a new low. Even for you."

"It's not what you think, Nezetta." Daphne struggled to steer the horse near the wagon. "I'm trying to help."

"You have a funny way of showing it."

The horse and its rider finally reached a mutual agreement. Or at least the horse gave up trying to unseat her. Snapping the reins tight, she dropped to a canter beside the wagon.

"I didn't know Drael would keep you locked up. I'm sorry."

"Heard your new friend treated you to a five-course meal," said Nezetta, her words frosted with ice.

"How ...?"

Nezetta shrugged, her usual haughty look settling across her face.

Aurelia had yet to look Daphne's way.

"Look, this is for you all." Daphne sighed. "Drael promised if I cooperated he'd provide a healer for Ophel, and that he wouldn't harm you."

"You think you can negotiate with a monster?" laughed Nezetta. With a sharp harrumph, she turned away and scooted to the opposite end of the wagon.

"Aurelia, please, at least tell me you understand."

"The healer failed." Her covenant friend's defeated gaze was heartbreaking. "She's not getting better."

"I'll go back to Drael. I'll -"

"Stop. Just stop. Whatever you're doing isn't helping. Just leave us alone."

Daphne tugged sharp on the reins, allowed the wagon to continue on without her.

Her escort nudged his horse alongside her.

"Never hide your tears from friends."

Daphne sniffled, rubbed fiercely at her eyes. "What's it matter to you?"

"Just a word of advice from an old soldier who's seen his share of heartache."

They halted at a town called Hiedorn, or at least that's the name Aurelia thought she understood. She strained to understand the local's speech, the accents this side of the Tol so strange.

The townsfolk approached the wagon cautiously, curious to see for themselves the butchers of Saan, as word spread that the Ka held captured Gray Cloaks. The laughable sight of three dejected and disheveled women proved disappointing, so they jeered and threw stones, rattled anything that made a noise across the wagon-cage bars, while the cruelest jabbed sharpened sticks. But when their taunts were ignored, they grew bored with the amusement and one by one drifted away.

It was early in the day for a stop, but Numa's Inn being a surprisingly decent and cheap stay for such a backwater town, Drael determined to board there for the night. Instead he found a smoldering pile of charred timber and ash where the inn once stood, fronted by a red-stained pebbled street. Only the inn's chimney stood fast, though it leaned at a perilous angle.

"What happened here?"

"Well, Your Generalness, a band of brigands." Hiedorn's mayor twisted his hat nervously in hand, refusing to meet Drael's eyes. "In the deads of night, while us good townsfolk lay asleep in our beds, they assaulted our gods-fearing innkeeper, murdered him and his family. Set the inn ablaze they did. We good townsfolk tried our best to save it. Honestly we did. But we was too late."

The commander's booming laugh startled the poor man and, like a skittish horse, he jumped back a step, ready to bolt. Drael knew no story set in Hiedorn was that straightforward or simple. And no Hiedorn mayor was ever that truthful.

"That's a good one, mayor." He wiped a tear from his eye, briefly considered appointing the mayor his personal jester.

"Your Generalness? It's true." Snatching a pamphlet from his tunic pocket, the mayor thrust it into Drael's hands. "Here, sees for yourself. Mans here was one of thems."

Drael's pulse quickened, recognizing the Dorakian staring back at him from the images he himself had authorized. He took a threatening step towards the mayor, grabbed the smaller man's collar, and hauled him bodily into the air.

"What night was this? And which direction did they go?"

"Uh ... night befores, Your Generalness," the man stammered, arms and feet flailing. "Wishes I could say which ways. Don't know. Honestly don't."

Drael dropped him unceremoniously to the ground. "For your time." He flicked a single decri at the groveling man's feet.

Emboldened by the sight of coin, the mayor dusted off his jacket and trousers. "If it please you, Your Generalness. Haves my town to consider. We lost a good inn, ones that attracted many guest. We be's nothing without it. Could the Kingdom spare further coin for our poor town?"

Drael's laugh barked at the man's boldness; considered ordering his execution, but he tired of the sniveling fool. Instead, settled on a glare and sent the mayor scurrying.

So they passed this way, mused Drael. He'd been right to send runners with those pamphlets. He cursed the Hiedorn fools unable to capture a ragtag band of men.

Where are you running? he wondered out loud, his knuckles rapping his desk, before pacing the tent, calculating. *To one of your homes?* Perhaps. *North to the coast, beyond to Perinith or even the Twelve Isles?* Maybe.

He ordered additional pamphlets drawn and distributed. To distant towns and villages. To the Capitol and beyond.

An occasional Hiedorn citizen still wandered by the wagon from time to time. Inevitably, they left after a brief stay. There was little fight left in the women and antagonizing them awarded little.

Aurelia sagged against the wagon bars, energy waning as she'd had nothing to eat or drink since the day before. She pleaded with a nearby guard, but he ignored her, so her thoughts wandered.

Where's Daphne?

She didn't care to admit it, but she missed her friend, though Daphne's consorting with the Ka troubled her.

She must have good reasons. Mustn't she?

Truthfully, she couldn't muster any anger at her covenant friend. What little energy remained she reserved for taking care of Ophel, the woman's delirious mutterings worsened, her lips cracked from lack of moisture, the wound at her side stank.

That Daphne and Drael made peace surprised her most. The man was a monster.

Would I have done any different? Made any better choice?

She herself had trusted and befriended a man who'd betrayed them, who'd led the Ka to Lumath.

Am I any better?

A man approached the wagon and spoke briefly with the guard.

Just another townsfolk coming to gawk.

The voice though, familiar.

"Aurelia."

"Oh Col!" Tears burst from her eyes. Unbidden. Unwanted. But they couldn't be helped. Too many memories, connections to home. Good to see a familiar face.

Col didn't flinch from her searching gaze. His eyes held regret. Guilt. Shame.

"Are they treating you okay?"

She gathered her thoughts, controlled her emotions, and realized she no longer hated him. How could she, when he'd saved her life?

"Aurelia, I ..." Hesitant, he reached for her; the opposite sleeve hung empty and limp. She couldn't help but stare, and he noticed. "It's okay. Rarely hurts anymore."

"How ...?"

"In a training exercise with the Ka, sparring. I won several bouts, until a man stepped into the ring, death in his eyes. He removed his blunts, and I ... I've never taken a life before ..."

"I'm sorry."

"Me too."

He drew a breath, gathering courage for what he would say next.

"It was wrong of me. To lead them to Lumath." His eyes betrayed the truth of his words. "I wanted to impress the Ka, waited my whole life to become one, and I think ... well, I think ..."

"It's okay, I understand." Aurelia smiled—a small one, not letting him all the way back in yet, though it was a start—before grasping the hand he offered.

"Thank you." He exhaled a sigh of relief. "I hurt you, badly, what I did and said ... I never wanted that."

Listening to the exchange from across the wagon, the mention of Lumath piqued Nezetta's interest.

"What happened at Lumath?"

Aurelia cleared her throat. Col averted his gaze as he dropped Aurelia's hand.

Nezetta scooted close, asked again, her tone demanding, "What happened at Lumath?" Her saphyr glowed, light pulsing.

Aurelia sensed it, recognized a binding, a prick against her mind, probing, demanding. She resisted.

Col didn't. Allowed the probe to force out truth.

"The Ka laid waste to Lumath and many Gray Cloak died."

"And you led them there?"

Again the stone glowed, its light expanding, pulsing.

This time, he fought the urge to answer, but the need to relieve his guilt was too much. "Yes."

Nezetta's eyes burned, feverish with malice, seizing Col's gaze, refusing to forgive him his burden. "Know that you shall die by my hand. This I swear. Justice for Fiadha and for a sacred haven."

Col drew a deep shuddering breath, a single tear rolling down his cheek as he tore his gaze away and left without a backward glance.

"He said he was sorry. Was that necessary?"

"You think an apology is enough?" Nezetta turned her glare on Aurelia. "His feeling sorry for it makes the death and killing okay? It won't be enough until he's dead." She leaned forward until her face was but a breath apart from Aurelia's. "And don't even think about getting in my way. If I must dispose of you to get at him I will."

Chapter Thirty-Nine
Headlong Into The Dark

Growing up in Luton, Saul knew the King's Forest well. Luton laid claim to being the largest town in the forest, which it was in both population and gross trade receipts. The prosperous town lay at the southern end of the forest, claiming the title *Gateway to the Highlands*. Though Saul and his companions' route to the Capitol wouldn't take them that far south, as the son of a prosperous merchant he'd often traveled the spiderweb of roads crisscrossing the King's Forest.

The youngest of five sons, he would never inherit the family business. But he was quick with numbers, and when times were good and the decri flowed, he accompanied the family on business engagements. When the family haggled over goods, his father relied on him for quick calculations during tense negotiations.

But prosperous times evaporated with the famine. Ashrot swept through stalk and bean and leaf until even the hardiest withered, so that all but the oldest son sought their fortunes elsewhere. But the King's Forest with its many roads and towns would remain forever etched on Saul's memory, and little had changed during his lifetime. Progress was slow in Lavonshia.

The others happily relied on his memory, for following the Hiedorn skirmish, he recommended less traveled routes that skirted large population centers. When dust rose on the road ahead, they melted into the forest, avoiding contact. When light flickered from a home or a campfire tucked in the woods, they bypassed those too.

But arriving at a crossroads, a hard decision awaited.

"Straight ahead lies the Capitol." Saul pointed west. A signpost bore a crude drawing of an arrow and the word *Capitall* charred into the wood.

Bookworm that he was, Eken snickered at the misspelling.

Saul ignored him.

"The problem being that route is heavily populated, with a number of towns and villages between here and the Capitol. It'll be impossible to avoid everyone."

"Surely the pamphlets haven't come this far west," said Bochim.

Saul shrugged before explaining their second option. "This route," he pointed at another sign bearing the words *Saan* and *Maldelea Sea* with another crude arrow, this one pointing north, "will take longer, on a roundabout path to the Capitol, but is much less populated. Though there are the rumors about what exists at Saan ..."

"Rumors?" asked NoNo.

"You haven't heard?"

The creature shook his head.

"Lost souls. Spirits that couldn't find peace after the vanishing. Some say any who enter Saan now, leave a raving lunatic."

"I like that idea," said NoNo. His ears perked. At Saul's questioning look he laughed, a squeaky, cat-like laugh. "Not the lunatic part. The lost souls. Always wanted to see a ghost."

Eken had only half-listened to the exchange, drifting onto the path that led north. A stirring tugged. He didn't know what it was or what it wanted, but it nudged his mind, urging him up the northern road. *How can I mention the feeling when I can't explain it?* But he knew with certainty the path he would take, whether he went alone or not.

"We go north."

It was the first decisive thing he spoke in days, and the others stared open mouthed. Recently, he'd kept his head buried in a book; if he spoke at all it was to mumble a complaint of the pressure in his head.

"North? After what I just told you?" asked Saul.

"I can't explain it. It's just what I have to do ... a feeling I have."

"Great idea! Let's listen to our feelings, that'll tell us the best way to reach the Capitol. I'm not saying we shouldn't go north, but we need a better reason than our feelings."

Eken shrugged, used to a little abuse, having learned to avoid the snide remarks. Col often treated him that way, as did others back home. Unless it involved book-learning, then they'd come to him for answers.

And there it was again. A whispered urging. *Come north*, it seemed to say. So strong a sense he thought its force might seize him bodily and carry him away, with or without his agreement. He wouldn't wait until that happened. Hefting his pack securely on his shoulder, he trudged up the northern path.

"You all coming?" he called, without looking back.

NoNo was quick to follow, excited to see the spirits.

Tobias laughed with a shrug and a cocked eyebrow for Saul, and hurried to catch up, as did the others.

Saul was last to go, standing alone at the crossroads, glancing between the two paths, before turning north with a sigh.

The rumors of what haunted Saan terrified him.

The regiment made good progress, or as good as a regiment can with wagons and prisoners in tow, an eight-day and a half having passed since recapturing the Binder and her friends. They camped now a day shy of the Capitol. Drael was pleased to see that, as ordered, reward pamphlets fluttered from every notice board and crooked signpost along their route.

He'd set his artists to work day and night. The Capitol alone needed hundreds if not thousands of the hand-drawn copies to post on its many streets, at its inns and market booths. He was determined every town in Lavonshia bear one if need be. And not just of Eken. No, the others too. Particularly that Magnus.

Drael's soul seethed with hate when he thought of that man. His top lieutenant. Betrayer of the Ka.

On the outskirts of camp lay a crossroads to continue west to the Capitol or north towards Saan, and beyond that, the coastline. Drael hunched over his desk, staring at maps he'd long ago memorized, every boundary line, every road and every village name.

Where are you, Magnus?

His fist pounded the table; clerks bent closer to their work, avoiding his gaze. A guard stepped inside the tent. "Commander, a report."

Drael motioned wearily. Likely another report of failure, as every previous scout had given. But the report, direct and to the point as he preferred, surprised him.

"We spotted them, commander. Late last night. North on the road to Saan."

"Excellent!" Drael exclaimed, clenching his fist in expected victory.

Is Saan their destination? Or beyond to the Maldelea Sea?

No matter. If Saan, they'd find little there. He'd been himself, seen little in the way of lost souls. But he was close now, his net closing around the deserters. Drael bared his teeth, a wolfish smile, and barked out orders to a nearby clerk.

Aurelia stirred groggily, her dream pleasant despite recent circumstances. She was home, at Chelam's square, on the brick pavers near the fountain, playing a game of Ji with Koram.

Aurelia.

A faint voice. Not Koram's and no other villagers were near.

"Pay attention, Aurelia." Koram tapped her gently on the shoulder, calling her attention back to the game. "Remember your defense. An offensive strike can throw your opponent off balance, but leaves your village vulnerable."

"Then how can I know when to strike?" she asked with a frustrated snort, perplexed as usual by the game's strategy. She loved Ji, and she'd spent countless hours at it. When she first learned the game, it seemed so simple, but the longer she played, the more she realized how tough its complex strategies were to master.

"Your village," Koram indicated her village piece, "best be outside the range of my warrior when you make your move." His warrior sat menacingly close.

Her thoughts wandered from the strategy to the details of the pieces. She loved the feel of the wood. The intricate carvings, the warrior's scowl, miniature sword and shield in hand. Elder Koram once told her his Ji set was more than a thousand years old. She loved the smell of the ancient wood. The rich color of the board.

Aurelia.

That voice again. She glanced away from the Ji board, perplexed, searching for it, the voice familiar.

Koram took her chin in hand, forceful but gentle, returning her focus to the game.

"What about my mage?" asked Aurelia, studying the pieces. "Can't she defend her home?"

The mage sat squarely between her village and the opposing warrior. But Aurelia sensed she was missing something.

"Ah. Therein lies the beauty of the game." Koram beamed, a wise, benevolent smile. "On the surface, yes, she can. But have you considered your treaties? Does one exist between King and mage? Or better yet, has enough time passed?" Koram indicated the bead counter on the side of the board. "If not, the mage has yet to learn her abilities. She will fail against the warrior. As in life, nothing is simple in Ji. The variables determine who lives and who dies."

Aurelia.

"What!?" she shouted, frustrated by the interruptions. She was so close to a breakthrough. Her mind struggled to recall Koram's words. Something about the mage, a treaty with the King, a way to protect the village ...? The details slipped as the High Elder's face faded.

"No, wait. Koram, please! How do I ... my village ...? Please, Koram!"

She startled awake, heart pounding, mouth dry, tried clinging to fading memories of the Ji board and Koram's instructions.

"Aurelia."

It was Ophel, voice weak but determined. She'd dragged herself to a seated position, resting against the iron bars of the wagon as it rolled and bounced along. Her face grimaced with every hard jolt. She coughed into her hand, speckling it with flecks of blood.

Taking a flask in hand a guard had gruffly thrust at her earlier, Aurelia scooted to the older woman's side and raised the tepid water to her mouth. She drank a little and sank back exhausted.

"There is something ..." Ophel coughed wearily, her breathing forced and shallow. "... I have wanted to tell you."

Aurelia leaned in close.

"I wish to tell you my name."

It wasn't what Aurelia expected. News from Chelam would be better. An update on her father. Perhaps a deeper revelation about the Storm Grazer Prophecy. Anything but this. *Her name? Is she losing it?*

"I am not losing my mind, child," scolded Ophel.

"How -?"

"No, I cannot read your mind. But you wear your thoughts plain enough on your face."

"I'm sorry, I didn't mean ..." Aurelia smiled, apologetic, unseen as Ophel closed her eyes and sank back against the bars.

"Ophel? Are you still awake?" Aurelia shook her and her eyes fluttered open.

"Of course I am awake, silly child. Now let me speak."

A coughing fit overcame her, and she held the back of her hand to her mouth. When she removed it, blood dripped. She muttered angrily at the sight, willed herself to sit up.

"Do you recall when we met? I told you then you may call me Ophel until you know my name."

Aurelia nodded. How could she forget such a strange statement?

"My soul-name is Ophel Tol Jalese Faolan."

The Honored One slumped against the wagon bars, exhausted by the strain of speaking. But the words didn't vanish as words do; they floated on the air, as if a weight bound them to the world. The power of Ophel's name, her soul-name as she called it, stirred Aurelia's mind, pricked her heart, and though she didn't understand its meaning, she knew it was significant.

Ophel Tol Jalese Faolan.

It was just a string of names, wasn't it? Though one caught her ear. Tol.

How odd to be named after a mountain range.

"There you go again, child," said Ophel, regarding Aurelia with a half-smirk tugging on her lips. "Wearing your thoughts on your face again. You wonder at Tol."

"How did you ...?"

"Lucky guess. Though I think any would wonder. It is an odd name, and one I have shared with few."

"Then why me? And why now?"

Ophel looked away, the first time Aurelia had ever known her hesitate. Deep lines spanned a face more haggard than a moment ago.

"Do you not know, child? I am dying."

"No, you're not! Don't say that."

"Tsk, child. Hush. No reason to deny the obvious. I feel my death approaching, though I give credit to the Ka healer—he tried. But all this blood ..."

Though Aurelia tried to reassure her, the words rang hollow. She couldn't deny the truth witnessed with her own eyes.

"I am exhausted, child. I shall say more later. Let me sleep for now."

Even before the words slipped from her lips, her eyes closed, and despite the rattling of the wagon, she was soon asleep. Aurelia stayed by her side, turning the name over and over again in her mind. *Ophel Tol Jalese Faolan.*

"I knew we shouldn't have listened to his feelings!" whispered Saul, fear palpable in his voice.

They had pressed northward, arriving at Saan near sunfall. It lay in total darkness, as if someone had thrown a cloak over the city and tucked the edges tight.

A series of three low walls encompassed the city, forming ever-widening bands around it. Outpost towers placed strategically along the walls provided encompassing views of the surrounding fields and afforded excellent positions for defense. No army could approach unnoticed. A sister city to the Capitol, Saan stood as a place of retreat should the Capitol fall.

Only two roads entered: from the west, directly connecting the Capitol, and from the south, the route they'd only just traveled. As for access, at each point where the road intersected an encircling wall stood a gate and a guardhouse. *This is no backwater outpost,* thought Eken. *Marauding Gray Cloaks against a poor defenseless city? Seems exaggerated.* It struck him as odd that anyone could have overrun Saan, considering the town's outer defenses lay undamaged, the ring of walls intact, as were the towers, the guardhouses and the gates.

Saul suggested they skirt the city altogether and seek the road exiting its western wall. From there, press on to the Capitol. There was no need to go through Saan. The plan being sound, all agreed, save NoNo and Eken, insisting their path lay through the city.

Eken suspected NoNo's interest lay in meeting spirits; his own far more desperate—the need for answers, for relief from his throbbing head that worsened with every step toward Saan. His scrambled thoughts twisted on themselves, memory unreliable, yet one conviction refused to fade: *my path lies through Saan.*

If put to a vote, the ex-Ka would easily win, but the Dorakian and the midling didn't offer that chance. They pushed on through the gates, past the guardhouses and the encircling walls.

The pressure against Eken's mind ratcheted to a new high entering the city. It hummed and vibrated, pinching his nerves, his pain spiking, moving to his chest, where he would have sworn a horse—pulling a cart loaded with melons from the Blackwood's fields back home—sat on it.

He gritted his teeth and planted one foot, then another, deeper into Saan.

Once a bustling city of commerce, the city lay eerily quiet. No people. No sign of movement. Not even a rat squeaked in a dark corner.

Here at last were signs of struggle. Shattered windows, battered doors, piles of rubble and burnt husks of once fine homes. Ash and silence. Goods and belongings scattered everywhere, evidence of citizens fleeing an attack. The clawing scent of fire and smoke lingered in the air. And here at last evidence pointing to Gray Cloaks, scrawled across buildings and homes.

A Free Nation For Gray Cloaks! read one, *Gray Cloak Before Lavonshian!* read another.

"Through there," Eken's voice echoed eerily in the silence. He pointed to a dark, cavernous opening, above which hung a sign: *Aqueduct.*

"Our flasks are full," said Saul. "Now can we please leave this gods-forsaken city? The western road's this way."

"Don't be so quick to dismiss him," rebuked NoNo. "I Sense something drawing him."

Eken had never been more certain of anything. He could sense it as the midling said, luring him in. It called, and he had no choice but to answer. He would go alone if he must. Like an unseen hand turning a dial, the pressure in his mind amplified, and snatching the book he carried in his pocket, he smacked it repeatedly to his forehead, shouting, "Stop it! Stop it! Stop it!"

His companions looked on, stunned, until he bolted for the aqueduct opening.

"Eken, wait!"

Ignoring their cries, he ran headlong into the dark.

Chapter Forty
The King's Presence

Mahan paced, restless as a caged frit, muttering under his breath. His companion, Ry, sat patiently at the room's table. A faint smile showed he found Mahan's antics amusing.

"She should be back by now."

"Patience," said Ry. "These things take time."

Mahan resumed pacing, knowing Ry was right, Eydis had to proceed cautiously. It wasn't every day you sought a guide to sneak you through palace grounds and assassinate a King. Were Eydis to ask the wrong person, it could mean their deaths.

If Mahan was honest with himself, his restlessness was more than just the wait. It was feeling suffocated there in the Capitol. The pressing crowds, the looming walls and buildings that blocked out the sun. *Oh how I miss Dorak! And Chelam!* Open fields and orchards, babbling streams, the familiar backdrop of the Tol. The comfort of his own home and bed, a quieter pace of life. The Capitol's hustle and bustle was no place for him.

His thoughts turned to Aurelia. He recalled that fateful day, when he'd returned home before attending the Harvest Festival and answered a knock at his door ...

"May I come in?" Ophel didn't wait for an answer, brushing past as she entered the home. She allowed her eyes to adjust, studied the one-room house. It was small, like she remembered. The ghost of decisions past still lingered. "It has not changed a bit in here, save for the extra bed in the corner."

Mahan studied the room, as if seeing it through Ophel's eyes for only the second time. "More's changed than that."

Ophel detected a note of bitterness in his voice, but made no comment. He had every right. She sighed. *Poor Mahan.* Saying he'd been through a lot would put it mildly.

"Why are you here, Ophel? It's been too long for friends, not long enough for enemies."

"The Ka are near and the time we feared has come. Aurelia must leave, but I have a plan." She turned to face him. "It involves you."

"Don't want to hear it." Mahan hefted a knife in his palm, studied it carefully. Picked an apple from a basket on the table. "Your plans have brought me nothing but grief and taken everything from me. I have no one left to sacrifice, and now you demand Aurelia?"

She winced at his words. Felt the weight of them, the guilt he imputed to her.

"There was no other way. And you knew this day would come."

"I won't win a war of words with you." His knife sliced through the apple and struck the table with a sharp *thwunk*. "Tell me the plan and let's be done with it."

"Two of our best Gray Cloaks. I want you to accompany them."

"Where?"

"To the Capitol. We must convince the King -"

"You want me to kill him?"

Ophel hesitated, considering the question before she answered. "If you must. Or make him see reason. His war against the Gray Cloak could drag Lavonshia into another civil war."

Mahan set the knife down slowly.

Can he kill again? wondered Ophel. It had been a long time since he had, and who wouldn't wish to die in peace and not on a sword's tip.

"For Aurelia," he said at last. "Not for you. Not for your people. For her, for a chance to live in peace."

"For Aurelia," agreed Ophel. She turned towards the door, opened it, stopped cold when Mahan said,

"And for Aisling."

"For Aisling." Ophel whispered quietly under breath and shut the door behind her ...

A sharp rap on the door returned Mahan to the present. Ry looked up, expectant, as Mahan slid the latch clear.

"Well?"

Eydis pushed her way past, removed the scarf secured at her forehead, revealing an embedded stone. She poured herself a drink.

Ry stayed seated, sipping from his own mug while he waited.

Mahan wondered how Gray Cloaks could be so infuriatingly calm and patient. Both the same as Ophel. Enough to drive a man crazy.

"It's done. As I said it would be," answered Eydis after tossing back the drink. Her hand trembled. "Tomorrow morning, early. He'll meet us at the gate."

She sat heavily. Shrugged off the black, green-trimmed cloak, glad to be rid of it for now. They'd agreed it wasn't wise to draw attention. Not after Saan. Once they'd crossed the Tol, both had exchanged their hooded gray cloaks for black, and donned scarves to cover their stones. Not a day passed since without their complaining about the inferior quality of the new cloak. It itched. It was too short. Or didn't fit well across the chest, or over the shoulders.

Mahan savored the thought of never seeing another Gray Cloak.

Eydis settled back in her seat, closing her eyes, but Mahan wasn't satisfied. "What's your contact's name? How does he plan to sneak us inside?"

"You worry too much." She waved away his questions. "Torsten and I go way back. He's not Gray Cloak, but he's a good man. He grew up in our clan."

"When did you last see him? Why did he leave your clan?"

"Is he always like this?" she asked, opening one eye to glance at Ry who shrugged noncommittally. Her question was rhetorical. Everyone knew Mahan asked a lot of questions. Eydis sighed, studied Mahan, sizing him up. "It's been some time. Eighteen hunter moons? Give or take. But he hasn't changed a bit. Same man I knew back then. I trust him implicitly. And if you must know, he was forced to leave."

"Why?"

"Must you question everything?"

"I'd like to know a little about the man I'm entrusting my life to."

"Fine. If you must know, he loved the daughter of our clan's High Mage; and she him. When her father learned of their love, he forbade the union and drove the family out."

"And what does he do now, here at the Capitol?"

"He's a mason, oversees repairs on the King's court and home. It's how he knows the passages and can get us inside. But he's no King's man. He's still friend to the Gray Cloak."

Mahan ran his fingers through his hair, continued to pace. He wished he could have met the man, gauged him. But Eydis insisted anyone accompanying her would spook her contact. *Makes sense.* He was raised a Gray Cloak after all; likely reserved, not quick to trust strangers.

Eydis waited as Mahan paced, knowing he'd reach the only conclusion remaining. The same conclusion her and Ry had.

Their resources in the city had dried up. Ry's contact a no-show. Spooked perhaps, hard to say. Mahan's contacts—of which he had a surprising number—refused the moment he mentioned accessing the King's home. Torsten was their last hope. Either they work through him, or return home a failure.

What Eydis failed to share was that she had once been close to Torsten. Very close. And that her heart had not entirely let him go. She was the High Mage's daughter in her story.

Why she hid the truth may have had something to do with Ophel's warning to her before they left Chelam: *"Mahan worries,"* the Salel had advised, *"too much. Tell him only what he needs to know."*

Eydis had also failed to share that Torsten's initial reception was cold. Oh he'd recognized her immediately, but the warmth she'd expected? Absent. The very warmth she still felt. Being in his presence rekindled love's flame, but it didn't seem he felt the same.

But he listened, and they talked. Long into the night and again the next day, thus her delayed return.

She, as much as Mahan, wanted to know she could trust the man she once, and still, loved. It'd been nearly twenty years after all. People change. But despite his initial coldness, the following day he'd been warm and inviting. Had even leaned in for a kiss, surprising her, delighting her to learn he wasn't married, never had been. *How could I?* he said, *when I've always loved you.*

He apologized for his earlier coldness, explaining that her sudden appearance had proven shocking. Eydis could have spent a moon cycle with him, their reunion so sweet, conversation so natural, catching up on everything missed in each other's lives, but she knew Mahan would be anxious.

So she finally shared with Torsten her reason for coming. That her people were being hunted to extinction. People Torsten once cared for, a community he'd once been a part of.

Torsten hadn't hesitated. Confessed his own hatred of the King and the proclamation against the Gray Cloaks. And yes, he could help. Could lead them directly to the King's bedchamber, through a series of seldom-used passages. Eydis knew then that fate had brought her and Torsten back together. Perhaps this time, forever. They kissed passionately, fiercely, before setting a time to meet early the following morning.

After Eydis said her goodbyes, Torsten had sat alone for some time, mind and heart in turmoil. The sun moved inexorably across the sky before a final wink, a final bow, as it dipped below the horizon, allowing moon and stars to take the stage. Still, he didn't move.

Seeing her brought memories bubbling to the surface. Beautiful, painful memories. Of a time when he'd loved a girl named Eydis. She'd been the best part of his life. Kind, sweet, amazing.

But he wasn't the same man he'd once been. Excommunication from Gray Cloak society had seen to that. Though he and Eydis had wept and begged her father, their pleas fell on deaf ears. Her refusal to flee with him, to elope, shattered any remaining hope.

His heart broken, it never mended properly, allowing a seed of bitterness to seize the throne. He became a hard man. Cold. Distant. The part of him Eydis had first seen.

He hated the Gray Cloaks, the shame of being sent away. Blamed them for his father's death, who'd taken to the bottle after their exile. Torsten's life spiraled out of control, taking to drink as his father had, only his skill with chisel and mortar saved him.

In the end, he did what he knew he would from the moment Eydis showed up unannounced on his doorstep asking for access into the palace. He went to the King.

As head mason, Torsten frequented his presence, speaking often and at length with him regarding repairs and new royal projects. The man had proven himself a capable leader, kind to his subjects, and he'd been no less to Torsten. The King's projects, coupled with military expansion, provided work, purpose, and pay, placing food on tables and saving countless lives during the famine.

Torsten lived comfortably on a head mason's wage. What had the Gray Cloaks ever done for him? And now this woman, who'd abandoned him, wanted his help?

As she divulged their plans, he hid the horror well—that she would ask him to betray his King. Still, it was a lie to say her presence had no effect. His passion in their kiss, at least that was real. It was for her sake, if nothing else, that he sat and stewed so long, but there was really no choice in the end. Not for Torsten, a King's man through and through.

Palace guards stepped aside without a challenge; he was a familiar sight on royal grounds. The King's personal bodyguard was a different matter. They searched him, as they searched any who requested an audience.

The hall echoed as Torsten approached the throne and bowed low. The hour was late. No one remained in attendance to the King, who sat alone on the throne.

"Rise, friend." The voice as always smooth like honey.

Torsten gazed into the eyes of the benevolent man he trusted. Knew that same familiar warmth, a slight tingling sensation. It was good to be in the King's presence.

Chapter Forty-One
The Last Divesting

The sun threatened to set on the day as it threatened to set on Daphne's decision to bare her soul.

How can I call myself her covenant friend if I'm not honest with her?

But as the sun coursed its western route across the sky, she found one excuse or another to delay the confession.

Her horse needed shoeing.

Or at least she convinced herself it did when she noticed the gelding favoring its right leg.

"You'll have to wait your turn," said the farrier once she'd found him. Sparks flew as he hammered a ribbon of steel into submission.

"How long will that be?"

"As long as it takes!" he snapped over the hiss of hot steel plunged into frigid water.

As long as it takes seemed longer than necessary, lengthened by patrons who came after her but left with finished work while she remained. She knew it was the saphyr. Few understood why Drael allowed her free roam, and few in the camp showed kindness upon seeing the stone, the old soldier by her side a rare exception.

But at last the farrier ran out of customers and excuses. The horse newly shod, Daphne's stomach rumbled. Confessing one's a fraud on an empty stomach would never do, and after a hearty meal surely one needs a nap.

When she woke, the sun hovered on the horizon. Still she dawdled, though unable to conjure further delays.

Unwilling to remain awake, even to witness a confession, the sun had set by the time Daphne approached the transport wagon. With a begrudging nod, her guard allowed a little space, hanging back in the shadows.

"Aurelia," she whispered in her friend's ear.

The occupants of the wagon slept fitfully. Daphne risked a glance Nezetta's way; wishing not to wake her. This confession was for Aurelia alone. Her friend mumbled and stirred.

"Aurelia, we need to talk."

One eye blinked open and Aurelia flinched at Daphne's face pressed so close against the bars. Nezetta shifted in her sleep.

"What do you want?" asked Aurelia grumpily, rubbing knuckles across her eyes.

"Keep your voice down. I don't wish to wake Nezetta. Or Ophel. But I need to tell you something."

"Why? I don't care anymore—why you're out there, why I'm in here, what your plan is. I'm done! I just want to go home."

"I'm so sorry," said Daphne, and she meant it. "How selfish of me—dwelling on my problems while you're the one locked up. Give me a chance to be a better friend."

"Are you? My friend?"

"I am. Always. I meant that vow when I took it." Daphne took a deep breath. "Which is why I tell you something now I've never shared with anyone. A secret I swore I would keep to my grave."

She burst into tears, overcome with the shame of who she wasn't. Though iron bars separated them, Aurelia took her hand and squeezed.

"Whatever it is, it's okay. I'll understand. You are my covenant friend after all."

Daphne ran a sleeve across her nose and blinked back tears. A small but grateful smile shone in dusk's dim light.

"I'm afraid I'll lose you when you know ..." She struggled to keep her voice a whisper; it hardly seemed appropriate given the weight of the moment. To finally unburden her soul. Screaming her feelings would have felt more satisfying. "I ... I -"

"Just spit it out already!"

"I'm a fraud! Powerless. I can't bind. My saphyr doesn't speak to me; I don't even know what it sounds like." The dam of silence finally broke and the truth spilled from Daphne's lips. "It's all been a lie. Every bit. From the beginning. My father, my mother, my grandmother and uncle. All part of it. We lied to ourselves, we lied to each other, we lied to our people. I stole a saphyr from someone else who deserved it more. Was never mine to have, but I took it. I'm a thief and a liar, a disgrace to the title of Honored One. Everything people think I am is smoke and mirrors. We defrauded everyone. Again and again and again. Oh, Aurelia, what am I supposed to do?"

"Is that it?" Aurelia laughed, a relieved *now I get it* sort of laugh.

Daphne stiffened, her shoulders squaring as her eyes flashed. "I confess my darkest secret, and you laugh?"

"I'm just happy you haven't sided with the Ka and turned against me."

"You thought ...?"

"When you didn't lift a finger at the marsh, and then after ... riding freely with the Ka. I assumed the worst. I thought our friendship was over. That you betrayed not only me, but your people too. It's such a relief to know you didn't."

"Oh."

"You don't need me passing judgment on you," Aurelia continued, more thoughtful now. "You've done that enough yourself. I get it, and you're probably right to be ashamed. No doubt you've hurt people by what you and your family have done. I'm just thankful you're still Daphne. You're still who you say you are, just a little lost."

"These stupid bars!" muttered Daphne. "I could give you the biggest hug." She pressed her forehead against the bars as Aurelia did the same. "Friends? Despite who I am and what I've done?"

"Not just friends," answered Aurelia. "Covenant friends."

At the opposite end of the wagon, Nezetta concentrated on controlling her breathing, keeping her eyes closed, and stifling a gloating smile.

She hadn't heard every word, but she'd heard enough, drifting back to a sleep filled with pleasant dreams of what was coming to Daphne Vale and her family. Saphyrs ripped from their scheming little heads. It had been far too long since the last Divesting.

Chapter Forty-Two
Hacked Their Way Clear

Why did you lead me here? Why insist I come—only to reach a dead end? Without answers, the questions did nothing to ease the constricting pressure on Eken's mind.

Before him lay an aqueduct, where water flowed to quench a city's thirst. At the present it lay undisturbed, for no soul remained to drink, save the current intruders.

"Why?" He punched the brick until his bloody and bruised hand objected.

He lifted his torch, casting its light upon the wall. But the light gave no answers. Just brick and mortar bearing silent witness to his pain.

What's happening to me?

He shuddered, unsure how much more he could take.

"Eken, what is it?" asked Magnus.

They had trailed him through the aqueduct, searched its dark and narrow passages, examined its rough-hewn brick and algae-stained troughs of water, the constant murmuring flow a soundtrack to their search, until arriving at the same dead end as Eken and perhaps the same conclusion.

I'm losing my mind.

He turned and faced Magnus, shook his head, eyes panicked. "I don't understand. I just knew I'd find answers in Saan. It led me here!" With a scream of frustration, Eken charged the wall, flailing against the brick.

"See," whispered Saul, "I told you we shouldn't have come."

Eken slumped to the floor, fished a book from his pocket and thumbed through it until he found a page he couldn't remember and ripped it out. Flipping past more pages, he found another, then another, tearing each one from their binding until he reached the book's end. He started over, numb, angry, lost, shredding page after page.

NoNo padded over, nuzzled his chest, wrapped his tail around Eken's shoulders. The creature's throat rumbled softly.

"Don't despair, young Eken."

"Why not? What's the point? I can't think clearly. It's like I remember everything I've read, but can't recall any of it. My mind's a jumble."

"Then stop thinking. Feel. Magic led you here for a reason. What is it? What do you Sense?"

As NoNo spoke, the pressure in Eken's mind eased, just enough, and a draft of tepid air teased his back where it rested against the wall.

"There shouldn't be a breeze here," he said, half to himself.

"What's that?" asked Magnus.

"The breeze. Makes no sense."

Eken pressed himself flat against the brick, arms spread, looking every bit like a spider set to scale the wall. To his companions, he seemed a crazed man, but he ignored them, his attention focused, his eyes closed.

NoNo's right—don't think, feel.

A hand on his shoulder.

"Eken. It's okay. Look, let's leave Saan, we'll get you to a healer, and ..."

"No!" He jerked away. "There's a reason I'm telling you! Here. Feel the breeze."

Magnus humored him, pressing himself against the wall as Eken had.

"Sorry." He shrugged, apologetic. "I don't feel anything."

"I tell you, there's something here," pleaded Eken, pacing feverishly. "I'm not crazy. I can feel my mind scraping against the edge of something I read in Lumath. It brought me here, but I can't put the pieces together."

He slid farther along the wall, splayed out, hands still searching until he reached the far end, where it butted against the perpendicular wall.

"Here! It's right here!" He pressed himself so tightly in the corner that it seemed sheer will alone would prove him right.

Willing to humor him one last time, Magnus leaned into the corner where the walls met. A damp breeze fluttered, on its current a twinge of an unpleasant odor and a strange sound, like a thousand claws scratching; and one could almost convince himself, as Eken had, that a thin crack revealed a passageway beyond.

"You see it too, don't you? A passage," Eken babbled excitedly. "I'm not crazy. This wall ... I don't think it used to be here."

As he spoke, he backed away several paces and studied the wall from a different perspective.

"See—the mortar—the color's different; it's not worn or faded. No chunks missing like the other walls."

Magnus stepped back to see what the man was carrying on about, his face registering surprise. "The Dorakian's right. This wall blocking our path is obviously newer."

"One way to find out," boomed Morco, his voice echoing in the tunnel.

The giant reared back, hoisted his warhammer, and swung straight at the wall where it landed with a resounding crack, spraying bits of brick and mortar. The others jumped back a few paces, to a safer spot. He swung again, the hammer demanding it be reckoned with. Brick splintered and broke apart, chunks fell from the wall, and what began as an indentation became a hole sizeable enough to squeeze through. Morco heaved a deep breath, leaned against his warhammer as he rested.

Visible through the hole, a passageway extended off into the distance, and through the opening wafted the damp breeze Eken first discovered. The odor was much stronger now. Foul and thick. Worse yet, they'd discovered the source of the scratching.

Rats.

They poured through the opening, an unending horde streaming past the humans. But eventually the river of rodents turned into a stream and the stream into a trickle. Magnus was first through, brushing a rat aside, holding his torch high, its light illuminating the truth hidden behind the wall.

Bodies piled high, to either side of the passage, with a narrow path between. The missing citizens of Saan. Lifeless eyes. Worse yet, cavities in the bodies where someone, or something, had removed their hearts. The stench was overwhelming. Rats scurried and darted everywhere.

Magnus pressed his tunic's hood to his face, covering his nose and mouth, while Veyra leaned against the wall, retching. Eken fell to his knees, gagging at the smell. NoNo's eyes narrowed into slits as an angry growl escaped his throat.

Fatal choices bury men. A voice whispered on the breeze.

"Magnus, did you say something?" It was Veyra, wiping her mouth clean, her glance puzzled.

He shook his head and stepped further into the tunnel, torchlight flickering across the gruesome scene.

"Where are you going?" asked Veyra.

"To see how far this goes. Someone must give account for what happened here."

"I'm coming with you then," she said, right on his heels.

Eken hobbled after them. The pressure in his head had eased considerably, its intensity gone, though his relief was tempered by the tunnel's horror.

"Compulsion led these people to their deaths," said NoNo. "I Sense its foul presence. An evil binding forbidden to Gray Cloaks. There's one who knew its pattern, but he died long ago."

The bodies continued for some distance, a silent witness to Saan's desecration, the number lessening until there were no more. The passage though continued on ahead, empty.

"I can't go back through that," croaked Veyra. Others muttered their agreement.

Magnus' torchlight revealed no end to the passage, but all tunnels must go, and end, somewhere.

"We'll keep on then, and rest ahead, away from the smell ... and the rats."

They marched in grim silence once the sound of scurrying rats faded, though the smell lingered far longer. Those who'd held back finally broke, silent tears wetting cheeks.

"How far can this go?" asked Veyra, voice echoing in the tunnel.

"Feels like we've walked far enough to reach the Maldelea Sea," muttered Saul, his tone caught between sarcasm and sincerity.

"Or the Capitol more likely," said Morco.

"That's it!" chimed in Eken.

"What's it?"

"What you said—I think you're on to something. Wager this does connect to the Capitol. I recall now a book in Lumath about the construction of Saan and the Capitol. Hailed as the two great cities of Lavonshia, connected by a series of tunnels."

"You're just now remembering that?" asked Saul, a hint of frustration in his voice.

"It's okay, Eken," assured Magnus, glaring at Saul in the dim light, "go on, tell us more."

"The tunnels gave the cities access to each other. In times of peace, serving as a passage for trade; in war, troop movement and supplies. But as centuries came and went, other towns and villages sprang up around the two great cities. And as peace persisted, trade followed routes through the King's Forest. As the tunnels became less frequently used they fell into such disrepair the King of that age sealed them for safety. Eventually to be forgotten. Or so the histories claim. This tunnel appears fine to me."

"So keep on down this tunnel and we'll end up in the Capitol?"

"I think so. And now that we know what truly happened here at Saan, we can tell the King."

"I'm not sure it'll help our cause." Magnus glanced back in the direction they'd come, considering what they'd seen. "NoNo says Gray Cloaks forbid this compulsion. But will the King believe it? A foul magic accomplished this, but who else besides Gray Cloaks uses such power?"

Another dead end, a wall Morco's warhammer made quick work of, then scrambling through, the passage sloped steeply, ending at a set of stairs. An iron gate barred their way, reinforced with lock and chain. The warhammer made quick work of those too. Beyond the gate lay an overgrown courtyard, obscured by weeds and twisting vines the size of a brute's forearm. The sound of a bustling city beyond the courtyard. A jumble of vines concealed an arched doorway. They hacked their way clear and stepped out onto a Capitol street.

Chapter Forty-Three
You've Earned It

"Aurelia. Nezetta."

Ophel's summons drifted, barely a whisper, but enough to draw them close.

"I wish ... with what time I have left ..." the Elder-Mother coughed, took a ragged breath. "Do you know the Storm Grazer prophecy? ... of what it speaks?"

The girls hesitated. Who truly knew what the prophecy meant? Aurelia had some ideas but didn't feel comfortable voicing them openly. But Ophel hadn't expected an answer.

"It tells of a great threat ... land—even ... darkness, rising. I can Sense it. Forces ... would ... ruin, destroy ..." Her voice cracked, fading in and out. "... the world under its dominion. That cannot ... must not, happen."

"What hope then is there?" asked Nezetta.

"The Storm Grazer ... must rise ... she ... tide of darkness."

Though her voice was weak, her eyes blazed fierce, searching Nezetta's face before her eyelids fluttered closed and a rattling cough shook her weakened frame.

Nezetta inched closer to her mentor, eager to hear more. "Tell me what I need to do."

Aurelia watched spellbound, hanging on every word.

The Elder-Mother sucked in another rattling breath, a coughing fit as she struggled to speak. "Help ... sit."

When Nezetta lifted her to a seated position, Ophel squeezed her hand and placed it over Aurelia's.

"My final wish ... to see ... Storm Grazer safe ... companion to aid her."

She coughed, blood spraying the wagon floorboard, before rallying again, words forced through clenched teeth. Her stone glowed, giving strength to overcome mortal weakness, her words no longer a whisper but a shout.

"I bind you to each other! By the authority of the first Salel of my generation. Who wounds one shall wound the other; where goes one the other shall follow; and what binds one shall bind the other. The land be my witness!"

Her saphyr pulsed, darkening to a deep chocolate hue. The now familiar sensation surged into Aurelia, a spreading warmth tingling through her veins, prickling needles on the skin. Not painful, but it was a tethering she could feel, an oath wrapping invisible cords around her heart, mind and soul, rooting deep inside. She didn't pull away, but neither did she yield blindly. Something in her had learned to count the cost. Nezetta did jerk away, her eyes and nostrils flaring, as if to her the binding were painful.

A last ragged breath and Ophel's body arched with a cry before sagging limp against the wagon railing. A smile lingered on her lips.

Aurelia waited for tears. When none came, she didn't force them.

Nezetta pressed her mentor's eyelids closed while she intoned a blessing, "May the Great Binding speak to you. Sleep well with our ancestors."

A band of Ka slipped quietly into Saan, the whisper of their feet against stone and brick stirring far less sound than clouds of ash, advancing into the aqueduct, discovering the hole created by Morco and the gruesome scene beyond it.

"Carry word to Drael." The captain informed a scout, averting his gaze from the horror. "This he must witness with his own eyes."

In the early morning hours, before the sun rose, the palace was at its quietest, though here and there staff stirred as palace grounds are never completely still.

Mahan waited, fist clenching, unclenching, eyes rimmed-red and heavy-lidded but refusing to close despite not sleeping a wink. Neither had Ry or Eydis.

As promised, Torsten met them at the palace's western gate. But instead of leading them through the gate, he led them away and down a narrow alley path to a door secreted behind thick ivy. Producing a key, he unlocked the door and hurried them in, paused at a crossing hall, glanced left and right before scurrying on to another door his keys unlocked.

"Where are the guards, the staff?" asked Mahan, finding the absence of anyone else unnerving.

"Shift change for the guards."

"How did -"

"Shush, Mahan, there's no time for this." Eydis' eyes blazed.

"Come. Quickly," urged Torsten, a finger to his lip, "and quiet now."

They entered a kitchen, occupied by a lone servant stoking a fire, too absorbed in her work to pay any attention to the intruders.

Exited to another door unlocked by Torsten's keys, and through a series of storage rooms they hurried. Here the inner bowels of the palace came to life—fine and fancy linens folded and stacked ten spans high; golden vessels of servingware for feasts and entertaining; silver-plated candles laid neatly in rows on shelves that soared above their heads; barrels of wine, ale and mead enough to drown Lavonshia in its deluge; jars and chests and casks of sundry other delights. But they weren't there to gawk at such splendor and Torsten urged them on.

A flight of stairs. A seemingly endless hallway. An alcove in the wall, with an ornate vase resting in the alcove. Torsten reached behind the vase, fingers searching, found the lever he knew was there and pulled. A door opposite the vase swung open without a sound.

Mahan's heart pounded, his ears attuned to every creak, every scuff, every pin-drop, Ry's labored breathing loud enough to rouse the palace staff, the royal guards and the King.

"We're close," said Torsten. "One more hall the chambermaids prefer. Keep quiet while I check."

He slipped through the door, closing it softly. Mahan, Ry and Eydis listened nervously to muffled voices, but it was impossible to make out the conversation. Footsteps retreated. A moment later, the door opened.

"Just another servant, she suspected nothing."

"But now you've been seen," said Eydis.

"Don't worry about me. I'll be okay."

"How long have you worked for the King, Torsten?" asked Mahan, innocently enough but digging.

"Fifteen years."

"A long time for no sense of loyalty."

"I ..." Torsten cleared his throat. "He's but a man, cruel and indifferent, and he threatens my friend and her people."

"Mahan!" hissed Eydis. "What's your point? We don't have time for this!"

"To put it bluntly, I don't trust him." Mahan crossed his arms.

"I do trust him, as I trust you." Eydis rounded on Mahan and thumped his chest for emphasis. "I've told you before, I know this man."

"No, you *did* know him," said Mahan, the worry in his voice rising in pitch, days of feeling trapped in the Capitol like a volcanic pressure in his chest, their passage into the palace too easy. "But now? To trust a man who rubs shoulders with the King so regularly and for so long?"

"A little late for this," said Ry.

"We can leave now. I shouldn't have agreed to this plan. It was a bad idea all along."

"My bloodline may not be Gray Cloak," Torsten butted in, "but I lived as one. I'd do anything to help."

"Eydis trusts him, and that's enough for me," said Ry. "Go if you wish, Mahan. But Eydis and I are finishing this."

Clenching his fists, Mahan glanced back at the vase, its convenient hidden lever, everything so easy for Torsten ...

"Think of Aurelia," said Eydis, "on the run from the Ka."

I'd do anything for her.

Mahan sighed, resigned himself to whatever fate might bring, nodded.

A quick glance down the hall, Torsten waved them across. "Quickly now!"

Safely through, down a narrow passage to a door bearing a distinctive pattern. The King's signet. Torsten motioned them close, perspiration beading on his forehead and upper lip.

"Best I know, he sleeps this watch of the morning. Bed's to the right."

Producing another key, Torsten inserted it into the lock, extinguished the lantern light, allowed a moment for their eyes to adjust and opened the door.

The bed was to the right as promised, though unease nibbled at his mind. *It's all been too easy.* Sliding his sword from its sheath, Mahan stole across the room. At the bedside, he paused, shadows obscuring his hesitation. But Ry was right—*a little late to rethink my choices.* Clutching the blade two-handed, he speared the reclining figure.

Something was wrong. The King hadn't made a sound. Mahan yanked away the cover, revealing a straw-stuffed form.

Light blazed as a dozen torches lit, sudden and blinding. The rush of feet, the jangle of armor, their eyes adjusted to the sight of royal guards pouring into the room. These were the Ka's best, hand-picked to protect the King.

Mahan's heart sank.

I failed her.

Eydis' and Ry's hands circled in patterned movement, the beginnings of a binding, until an unseen force pinned them against the wall. They squirmed and kicked, but it was useless.

A stunned Mahan assumed a defensive stance, but the guards outnumbered him. A man approached. His head bore a crown.

"You!" cried Mahan.

"Mahan, what a pleasure." The handsome face brightened with a sickly smile. "I was told Gray Cloaks sought to kill me. But you, I never expected to see again."

With a cry of rage, Mahan leapt at the King, sword raised. But a blur of movement and a crippling pain seared his hands. His fingers curled, bones snapping, wrists bent backward, and with a cry of anguish, he fell to his knees, sword clattering loose.

"I'm not what I once was." The King's look of pity at odds with the menace lacing his words. "You're nothing to me. A gnat. A fly. A nuisance to be crushed. It's a pity you came."

At a gesture, the royal guard secured the traitors while Torsten stood by the King's side.

"Torsten? How could you?" cried Eydis, as the guards hauled their prisoners away.

"You served me well." The King acknowledged his mason, crossing to a bedside table where he picked up a heavy bag of decri. He considered it for a moment before tossing it to Torsten. "Take some time away. You've earned it."

Chapter Forty-Four
After Sunfall

Aurelia's time in the Capitol hadn't gone as imagined.

In Belanor's Cave, when Daphne laid out the plan, she'd pictured a cheap inn near the palace, sharing a room with her covenant friend, with afternoons lost in the famous markets, and—eventually—an audience with the King.

Instead, the palace grounds had become the palace dungeons, and the shared room in a cheap old inn a nightmarish holding cell, packed with every manner of lowlife criminal and highborn citizen who'd run afoul of the law. An audience with the King? Not even close. She awaited her sentencing.

Will they send me to the gallows?

Aurelia fought to control the panic rising in her chest.

"Stop that! At once." Nezetta pressed a hand to her chest, face pinched. "Remember, I feel everything you feel now. That fool woman. What was she thinking?"

Aurelia swallowed hard, forcing down the bile in her throat.

"I can't help it." She scooted close to Nezetta while avoiding the leering gaze of another prisoner. "At least in the wagons there was fresh air, sunlight. Here …"

Her eyes strayed and wished they hadn't, meeting too many haunted expressions, too many vacant stares. Most there had already given up. The stench of the people was nauseating, while blotched stains of red, yellow and green covered the cell floor and walls. Bonded, she felt Nezetta's stomach roil, and it was all she could do to keep from retching.

"We'll hear word soon," Nezetta was saying, "Daphne, or even your friend Col. Someone will help us."

Though the Gray Cloak spoke with a note of confidence, the connection Aurelia shared exposed the hollow nature of her words.

"You don't actually believe that, do you?"

Nezetta bit her lip and shook her head, the arrogance drained.

Aurelia pitied the girl. She could taste every emotion, every flicker of doubt, understanding her now as she couldn't before. The arrogance was only a mask, a wall built to guard a fragile heart.

"Don't do that. I don't need your pity!" Nezetta withdrew to a far corner, though it did nothing to lessen their connection.

This is going to take some getting used to, thought Aurelia.

"My little Aurie? Is that you?"

"Father!"

And then Aurelia was hugging her father as fiercely as he hugged her while tears flowed freely.

"What are you doing here? How …?"

Aurelia studied her father. Dark bags highlighted his eyes. It looked as if he hadn't slept, or bathed, in days. His clothes were dirty, his hair and beard matted and greasy. And he smelled, confirming the lack of bathing, though she couldn't care less. His hands hung at awkward angles from his wrists, while jutting bones pressed ugly bruises into his skin.

"Oh, Father." Tenderly, she enfolded his hands in hers.

"Don't worry about me," he said, though he winced. "I've seen worse."

Aurelia snorted; she'd never seen him in such an awful state. Mahan led his daughter away from the crowd of prisoners, to an area relatively clean compared to the rest of the cell.

"Tell me everything." They spoke at the same time before sharing a quiet laugh.

"What are you doing here?" she asked. "I've never known you to leave Dorak."

"There's something different about you," he said, "but I'm not sure what."

"I've had some adventures."

"I'm glad to see you still have it." He nodded at the pendant necklace around her neck.

"Your story first," demanded Aurelia. "In Chelam, you said there was so much you wanted to tell me, but time was too short." She scanned the dungeon cell before fixing her eyes ruefully on her father. "I think you have all the time you need."

Mahan cleared his throat, nervous and unsure. "I don't know how to begin ..."

"Do as you've always told me. When the task is too big and too daunting—start. At the beginning's fine. One step at a time."

Mahan nodded and took a deep breath.

"Your mother was a Gray Cloak."

Aurelia's head spun. The prison cell lurched around her. *I'm ... a Gray Cloak?* The memory of her mother returned, that same sweet memory she'd gained at Tobwhit's breaking, but now the memory's focus sharp, her mother brushing aside jet-black hair, revealing an embedded stone. *My mother, a Gray Cloak!* Aurelia's heart leaped with wonder, re-evaluating her lineage and what it all meant. And then her mother spoke, adding to the sweetness of the memory as it evolved, and Aurelia could have bawled at the voice she never remembered hearing until now.

My daughter, oh my sweet daughter, the world-changer. I am sorry. For what I must do.

"Is that why the Gray Cloaks came for me? Did they know? That I am one of them?"

"Only Ophel. No other Gray Cloak knew your identity, we kept it secret."

"Why?"

"That's a longer story, though even I don't understand it all, perhaps for another -"

Aurelia's eyes flashed. "I've had enough secrets kept from me! Stop protecting me with lies."

He nodded, his eyes sad. "Okay then, well I should tell you, I wasn't truthful about your mother's name. It wasn't Thalara."

"Why would you keep all this from me?"

"To protect you." Mahan hung his head in shame. "Ophel demanded it, but I should never have listened. I should never have hidden it from you."

"My mother's name?" she asked, holding her breath, to hear it for the first time -

"Aisling."

"She didn't die in an accident, did she?"

"No," answered Mahan, quiet, remorseful. Another deep breath, plowing ahead, "She died for you. A sacrifice. Taking her own life so that you may one day live."

"I don't understand."

"Inside that pendant is a gift from your mother. Do you remember what I told you?"

Aurelia thought back to what seemed a lifetime ago, when he'd set the necklace in her hand, before Jusel Blackwood barged in to warn of Ka campfires.

"I think you said—*when all seems lost, use it*. Is now the time?"

"Only you'll know when it's right."

"What's in it?"

"An object of power."

Aurelia drew a sharp breath. Awe and nerves tangled in her chest as she glanced about, but none took notice save Nezetta, whose curious gaze met hers, tethered to the same pulse of wonder.

"My mother's stone. Isn't it," whispered Aurelia, more statement than question. She felt the truth of it.

Mahan nodded.

"I've never truly understood, why she had to take her own life. Why this stone coming to you was so important. Gray Cloaks have a way about them, and your mother was no different. We were madly, deeply in love. But there's nothing that infuriated me so much as the secrets she kept. Her and Ophel both."

Quite intentionally, Daphne and Col had avoided each other on their journey to the Capitol. Their reasons lay bound in the fact they'd never been close, as she and Aurelia were, and the shame they each carried for their deal making with the Ka, leaving them free—to an extent—while their friend lay bound in chains.

But upon their arrival in the Capitol, Drael ordered them to secure rooms at the same inn near the palace gates and posted a guard at the inn. On the second night of their stay, she encountered Col by chance outside their rooms.

"Your friend," he offered unexpectedly, "I'm sorry. I understand the Ka healer tried his best."

Daphne nodded her thanks, unsure what to make of him. Though he'd betrayed his friends, he'd also saved Aurelia's life.

"Ophel was a good woman; she didn't deserve to die."

"Perhaps that's true of all who die in war," mused Col, though he shrugged as if helpless. "I only want to serve the people, and my King."

"And if the King you serve is a threat to the people you serve?"

A troubled look crossed his face. "You're not a killer, I can see that. But that doesn't mean there aren't Gray Cloak who seek Lavonshia's ruin and the King's downfall."

There being little purpose in arguing, she bid him good night and retreated to her room.

The next morning found them again in close quarters, snatching breakfast from the kitchen pantry under the watchful eye of their guard. In silent consent, they sat across from each other, tearing hungrily into bread smeared liberally with fruit jelly.

"Any word from Drael?"

Daphne shook her head. Sighed. "Do you think he'll come through? It haunts me that while we wait, Aurelia and Nezetta rot in jail."

"I suppose if anyone can secure us an audience with the King, it would be Drael."

"Meanwhile, I'm going stir-crazy."

"Then come to market with me," whispered Col with a sideways glance at their guard. "Have you ever been to the Capitol?"

"I don't know, it doesn't feel right while -"

"How long should we sit here doing nothing? Look, one day won't hurt anything. The stories I've heard of the market! Don't you want to experience it?" He glanced again at the guard, at a rowdy game of dice nearby, and back to Daphne with a sly grin. "I've got an idea ..."

A few moments later and he'd convinced the guard to join him at dice where the players gladly made room for the newcomers' decri.

"A round on me!" shouted Col with a wave to the barmaid. A grin lit Daphne's face as she spied from across the room, realizing his plan. Five rounds later, he still sipped on his first tankard of ale, while the once grim-faced guard had merrily enjoyed every round.

Another losing roll of the dice and Col announced, "I think that's it for me fellows, I'm calling it a day," and, pushing off from the table, made as if heading to his room. A glance back at the guard, too engrossed in the dice to pay any attention, and Col slipped towards the exit with Daphne in tow.

Laughing until their sides ached, they tumbled from the inn. If Drael learned they'd slipped the leash, there'd be consequences, but it was hard to care for sunlight's warmth drenched the street and the market's hum beckoned. There was no need of directions—they followed the intoxicating smells. Pies, spiced buns and honey cakes, smoked sausage, rabbit skewers and mutton legs. The market was a sprawling affair and everything they wished it could be, with merchants hawking goods of every shape and style from stall and cart. There were expensive rugs from Perinith, Daphne marveled at the cost while Col whispered *a full year's wage in Dorak*; lamps, bowls and mugs crafted by the Plainsfolk; mountain lion furs from the Tol Mountains; weaponry forged in the famous smithies of the Highlanders; and food from every far-flung region of Lavonshia and beyond.

Col splurged on Twelve Isle delicacies Daphne had never heard of and together they delighted in the exotic flavors. She dreamed of wealth and status as she donned clothes befitting a high-born woman, howling with laughter as the merchant chased them from his shop upon learning they didn't have the decri for such finery.

Snippets of conversation joined a steady stream flowing from shops and stalls, blessedly normal conversation to Daphne's ear, free of the life and death ordeal of her own people.

"I'll take two of those, five of those there, and yes, that one too." An authoritative voice, fulfilling a shopping list.

"Please, Mother? You know if Taelith's wearing this at the ball, I must too." Whining, sniveling. Daphne could practically hear the impudent girl's foot stomp.

"Never seen so much plenty since before the famine." A hushed tone, awe-struck.

"We'll need a half dozen of those for the stew." Another meal to make, a tired voice.

"Bless the King, him being so wise, so kind and all. Without his openin' up his coffers, we'd never gotten through that famine." Daphne's ears perked, news of the King's benevolence encouraging.

"Is this right Uncle? The numbers seem off." A young boy, frustrated.

"Twenty-five decri," a merchant announced, startling Daphne. She stood by a stall selling dyed-blue dresses of silken cloth. She fingered the delicate material, dreaming of owning such finery while the calculating merchant studied her. "All the way from Perinith."

"From Perinith, you say?" Col eyed the cloth.

"Yes indeed. A deal. Normally I sell for forty," the merchant shrugged, nonchalant, "but, it's end of day. So a special price for you, for your lady friend."

"Mmm hmm," said Col. He smiled and winked at Daphne, studied the stall contents, rubbed the fabrics between his fingers, allowed the suspense to build.

"Here's what I think, dear merchant. If these were from Perinith, which they're not, then they're underpriced at forty decri, and you'd have sold out long ago. If, in fact, they're from elsewhere, say a local shop here in the Capitol, which I think more likely, then they're overpriced at twenty-five decri. Only a fool would pay that. And I'm no fool. I'll give you five."

"Ten?" The merchant smiled weakly.

An agreement struck, Col presented the dress to Daphne.

"For your audience with the King."

"Oh Col," she blushed at the gift, "it's too much. Besides, I intend to wear my cloak. The King should know who I am."

"Nonsense! That's a horrible idea. The King will know who you are. Wearing your people's attire simply throws it in his face. Surprise him. Be other than what he expects. Wear this."

Considering his advice, its wisdom surprised her, so she nodded and accepted the gift with a beaming smile.

As the sun set, he purchased a meat-pie to share for dinner, and they found a balcony with a view overlooking the Narthwich River as it bent its way around the Capitol. She was famished, exhausted, but happily so, after a day exploring the markets. *Meat pie never tasted so good.* Her belly full, she ran a sleeve across her mouth and leaned back to enjoy the sunfall over the river.

"I'm not sure I've ever had more fun," she admitted.

"You sound surprised."

"I am. Wasn't expecting Col the Negotiator or Col the Wise today."

"Not all Dorakians are simple farmers."

"Didn't imply you were, though there's nothing wrong with that."

"No, maybe not," he mused, "but I want more for myself. Father resented mother for keeping him tied to Chelam, and despite reaching the heights of success for a Dorakian, it never satisfied him. I think he wanted more for me too. Anytime outsiders found their way to Dorak, he made a point of inviting them to our home. I learned a lot from those outsiders."

"I'd say so. You got the best of the merchants today."

"If only all of life were so easy." The dwindling light dancing across the river's surface reflected in his eyes. "Do you think she'll love me again?"

"Did she love you before?"

"Hmm," a rueful laugh, he sighed, shook his head, "we were close, and I think we could have been happy. She accepted my hand, you know? But those stupid Gray Cloaks interrupted our dance and -"

"Hey!"

"Sorry," he added quickly, grin crooked. "Old habit."

"As for you and Aurelia, I'm not sure. But you could at least be friends. Sometimes that's enough."

"How about you?" he asked. "Anyone back home waiting on you?"

Home wasn't a pleasant thought for Daphne. There, she was a fraud, and couldn't allow anyone close.

I've never loved, or been loved, the way he speaks of.

She bit her lip, a slight shake of the head.

"Perhaps we'll both find love unexpectedly." Col stood, offering his hand. "Come, we should return. I'm told Capitol streets aren't safe after sunfall."

Chapter Forty-Five
Quite An Impression

"What's wrong with you?"

Nezetta's tone scalded, caustic as always, though a thread of concern wove across their bond. The thought touched Aurelia. *She might actually care.*

"I didn't know my mother; she died in an accident when I was little." Aurelia swallowed, nervous, unsure the girl would believe her, but with their bond, how could she hide anything? "I've just learned she was a Gray Cloak, who took her own life to preserve a gift I would one day need. To change the world, my father said."

She glanced at Nezetta, to know with her own eyes the girl's reaction. She hadn't needed to, bonded to the curiosity welling in her chest.

"This is what she left me." Aurelia lifted the pendant necklace from where it rested around her neck.

"A pendant?"

The jewelry was grotesquely large, a pale green with decorative markings. It appeared cheaply made, nothing much out of the ordinary, a trinket one could buy from any Lavonshian peddler.

"It's what's inside," clarified Aurelia.

Nezetta cupped the pendant in her hand, and as she did, her eyes lit with a wonder so strong Aurelia feared the strength of it would burst her own heart. But it wasn't wonder alone. Another emotion beat as strongly in Nezetta's chest.

Desire.

"A saphyr," breathed Nezetta.

"And not just any saphyr is it?" asked Aurelia.

She wasn't sure, it all being so new to her, but she sensed the stone, her mother's saphyr, was unique. She didn't need a verbal answer to realize she was right. Nezetta couldn't hide her desire for the stone's power. Her fingers closed tight around the pendant, but then Aurelia pulled away, and reluctance, longing, and loss spilled over their bond.

Nezetta cleared her throat. "Your father ...?"

"No, he's not. Never was. He's from a coastal village on the Maldelea Sea. Met my mother in the Capitol."

"You should give me that stone. Its power needs handling by someone who understands it, not by a silly girl like you."

"No." Aurelia's hand closed over the pendant. "My mother died for this."

"Listen to me—you want nothing to do with Fiadha power! That stone will curse you and all you love." Nezetta allowed the words to hang in the air for a moment. "Have you never wondered why you see so few Fiadha in the middle span years of their hunter's moons? Only young and old?"

Nezetta's guilt washed over their bond and seized Aurelia's heart, like fall plantings trapped in morning frost, squeezing mercilessly, threatening to crush her under its weight. She fought the horror of it until the feeling lessened. *What have our people done?*—the thought strange, *our people.*

"I'm not scared of magic, and I'm no stranger to Fiadha power. I've Sensed things before, you know, in Lumath. And there's my mind connection with Daphne -"

Nezetta glanced up sharply. "Your mind connection? That ability's been unheard of for generations! Not since ..." She studied Aurelia closely.

"Not since -?" prodded Aurelia.

"... the Red War."

The name of the war landed like a stone. *Not since the Red War.* Aurelia had no answers to the riddle: *Why now? Why me?*

"Is she in your mind now?" asked Nezetta.

Aurelia willed her mind to wander beyond the confines of their cell, pushing it outward. But there was only emptiness. No Daphne.

She shook her head.

"Work at it and your abilities will strengthen," assured Nezetta, tethered to Aurelia's frustration. "Though it will take effort, learning to listen -"

"To the land," finished Aurelia.

"How did you know?"

"A friend told me." Remembering Ophel's advice, she left out Tobwhit's name.

"What are you hiding from me? You know I feel it. Besides, you're one of us now. I can help guide you. Especially with Ophel gone."

"You were close?" asked Aurelia, gut-punched by the girl's sorrow.

Nezetta shrugged. "I respected her. A wonderful mentor, a tremendous loss for our people, though she speaks with the Great Binding now. There are so few powerful Honored Ones left."

"Why?"

"We give the stone to those who don't deserve it."

A dark flare of anger seared their link.

"Ouch, that hurt," said Aurelia, wondering who the anger was for.

"It's nothing." Nezetta brushed off her concern. "Perhaps there are so few strong because for too long we've remained disconnected. From the world, from each other. Isolation weakens us."

Aurelia sat for a moment, considering, grappling with the idea of this new people that would be her people. It reminded her of a question she'd wanted to ask since learning her mother's name. "I've only just learned my mother's name—Aisling. Have you heard of her?"

"Aisling is common among our people; I'd need more details. Did your father share more of her name?"

"Oh! I didn't even think to ask," Aurelia admitted with a small laugh. "Would it be as strange as Ophel's rather long name?"

"Ophel told you her soul-name?"

A bitter sting of jealousy shot across their bond.

"What's this obsession with names Gray Cloaks have? Such an odd thing."

"For Fiadha, a soul-name is your essence, your story. Past, present and future all rolled into one. To share it is to give away a piece of yourself. No one has ever told me their soul-name."

"Oh ... not even -?"

"No one. You'll find there's much we keep to ourselves."

"Great." Aurelia sighed. "Just what I needed. More secrets."

"When your father wakes, press him for details on the stone, and why your mother so foolishly took her life. Unbecoming of an Honored One." As the words left Nezetta's mouth, a hint of regret bled through their bond. Tears pooled in Aurelia's eyes. "I'm sorry. About your mother. What I said was ... unkind of me."

Aurelia knew the truth of the apology, so she smiled, nodded, accepted it. Nezetta returned the smile, the expression pained, as if she didn't try it on often, so unintentionally comical Aurelia nearly laughed. She marveled at their strengthening bond. *Who would have thought it possible when we first met?*

"My mother's stone—it's related isn't it," said Aurelia. "To the Storm Grazer prophecy."

Nezetta nodded. "Ophel's final wish was to see me safe, for a companion to aid me as Storm Grazer. Perhaps she knew of the stone you carry and bound us together because of it. I may need its power one day. And I won't let you fumble it into the shadows."

Aurelia cleared her throat. "She didn't actually name you as Storm Grazer, she -"

Nezetta's eyes blazed as a powerful wave of fury gut-punched Aurelia.

"Insolent girl! To think Ophel meant anyone but me. I'm the most powerful Honored One there's been in generations. You're a nobody!"

Aurelia snorted, indignation rising, but it was what Nezetta said next that really hurt.

"She may have bonded us, but you will never be more than a nobody! Never an Honored One! Your mother was a fool, and I can only imagine you will be too. So I will use you, take your stone from you if I must. To protect my people."

Nezetta stalked to a far corner of the cell, waves of cold hard anger pummeling Aurelia.

And to think, for a moment she imagined they could be friends.

When the summons finally came, Daphne wished it were anyone else keeping pace with the guard. He said little, setting a brisk pace, his heels clicking smartly against the stone floor, echoing through the palace halls. Her hands fidgeted, toying with her hair, smoothing her cloak, nerves frayed, head reeling with the excitement of meeting the King and everything riding on that moment. But when she set foot inside the court and those giant doors clanged shut, her stomach dropped.

There's a wrongness here.

The air tasted metallic, like a dream. Where she expected light, music, people of the court currying favor with the King, there was only darkness. Silence. The court appeared empty.

She couldn't be certain, as only the barest amount of light filtered through grimy windows set high into the walls and lanterns that hung at regular intervals remained unlit, the court's farthest end cloaked in shadows.

A timid step forward, towards indistinct shapes, their forms blurring into a nonsensical puzzle, a prickle of unease crawling on her skin.

"Hello?" she called.

No answer.

She edged forward and a closer inspection revealed floor-to-ceiling tapestries, once fine and glorious, now covered in filth and dust, hanging beside giant columns that bore the weight of the court. These too were similarly filthy, smeared with what she could not tell, while cobwebs of a size she'd never seen stretched between them. Unblinking eyes peered at her from the dark recesses of the cobwebs. *Shadows playing tricks on me.* She shuddered and scooted quickly past. Other shapes materialized in the dim light—chairs that once bore lords and ladies of the court, strewn haphazardly, overturned or shattered to pieces.

What happened here?

Her footsteps echoed hollow.

"Child, come here!"

A voice beckoned, the voice itself wrong somehow, like the place she found herself. She couldn't quite define the sense of wrongness, but it was ... off.

Every muscle ached to run, but for reasons she couldn't explain, the voice compelled obedience. Pressure, an unseen hand, punched the small of her back, shoving her forward. She stumbled and nearly fell, but when she glanced behind, there was nothing but shadows, curling through her hair, winding between her fingers. Thick and oppressive, they whispered her name. She struggled to breathe. Her feet disobeyed her heart as she took a step forward, and then another, deeper into the court.

A throne materialized into view, as tall as it was wide, stretching nearly the court's width, made of bronze, with winged statues, creatures cruel-beaked and sharp-clawed, adorning its back and sides.

Daphne willed herself to a stop, resisting the pressure that urged her forward. The shadows whined in frustration.

"I. Will. Not. Move." She spat the words through gritted teeth.

"I said come here!"

Shadows seized her, flung her bodily to the ground; they forced her to grovel, entwining ethereal-like fingers through her hair and with a sharp tug yanking her head upward to view the figure sitting the throne. A man. The voice deep, firm, masculine. A silver-plated mask covered his face, leaving only an exposed mouth and narrow slits through which a pair of calculating eyes regarded her. Even from her position on the floor, she could smell his breath, and it reeked of death and decay. Black liquid oozed from sore-crusted lips. He wore a tunic of red and gold, with the folds of a black robe concealing his legs. A pair of feet protruded from beneath the robe, and Daphne nearly vomited at the sight of pus-filled scabs and thick, curled toenails. He must have noticed her staring, for he slid his feet underneath the robe. The man himself was rather large, for the throne was a monstrous structure and his body threatened to overwhelm it.

"Where ... is ... the ... King?"

The man studied her before a slight motion of his hand released the pressure. She slumped forward, head sagging in relief.

"What is your name, child?" he asked, ignoring her question.

She considered ignoring him in return, but felt compelled to answer. "Daphne."

"Daphne," his tongue slithered across rotting teeth, as if tasting it, "why have you dared appear before me wearing ... that?"

A long bony finger jabbed at the gray cloak she wore.

"It's the common garb of my people."

"Do you not know I despise Gray Cloaks?" he hissed. "And yet you dare appear in my presence?"

He pursed his lips, fingers steepled at his chin, considering her. "There is something ... off, about you. I cannot put my finger on it." A fresh sore cracked open on his upper lip, blackish pus dripped into his mouth, while his tongue slid across the sore absentmindedly.

"Where is the King?" she demanded again. "I came for an audience with him."

The man's mouth curled in a snarl, and he shot to his feet despite his enormous size, voice thundering in the empty court. "I am the King!" And then quieter, in a whisper, sinking onto the throne as if his energy were spent: "And I will always be King."

She stared, horrified, at the deranged individual towering above her.

This is the King? We have no hope.

She disliked the way he studied her, as if she were an animal caged for his amusement. A wicked smile curled his face.

"I figured it out," he said, "the wrongness I sense in you."

Daphne's heart hammered. How far did his power extend?

Can he know my innermost secrets?

"You're a fraud," the King said with a mocking sneer. "A lie. And you know it."

Tears of shame fell unbidden from Daphne's eyes.

"You have no power!" He shouted gleefully with a deep throaty chuckle that became a full belly-splitting laugh. Blackened spittle flew, sprinkling her cloak. A dark stain spread where it landed.

The lanterns lining the wall blazed awake, casting their brilliance on the hall, suddenly packed with lords and ladies. They howled with laughter, joining the King in mockery.

"It isn't true!" cried Daphne, wishing she believed herself.

At her protest, the King and his courtiers laughed all the more. She gagged on bile as the lords' and ladies' heads spun full circle—once, twice—until they faced her with necks twisted all the way around. A lord leapt to grovel beside her, his leering face pressed against her own. His breath stank as the King's. Laughing madly, he seized her by the shoulders with such a violent shaking she thought her head might burst.

"No, it's not true! Please ... no ..."

She awoke from her nightmare.

"Wake up, Daphne. Wake up!" It was Col, giving her a good shake.

Her bedcover and sheets reeked of sweat.

"Oh Col! It was awful. The King saw right through me."

"Nonsense." He lifted her chin. Met her eyes. "It was a nightmare. When you see him, you'll impress him. Now try to sleep; it's still early."

The long-awaited summons had in fact arrived, but nightmares plagued Daphne's sleep. Col stayed with her until she fell back asleep. When she awoke, he was gone.

"How do I look?" asked Daphne as she descended the stairs.

A Ka officer seated at the inn's bar drew out a low whistle until an elbow jabbed him in the gut.

Daphne had never been one to spend much time on her appearance, but it wasn't every day you met the King, or needed to sway his opinion on a matter. A local hire had proved adept at applying a little color to her face, a darkener around her eyes, and a touch of rose petal pigment to her cheeks; while a seamstress altered the dress so it fit her to perfection, the rich blue complementing her eyes' natural shade.

Col met her at the stairs, taking her hand to descend the last step. As a gentleman would to any lady, he pressed his lips against her hand.

"You will make quite an impression on the King."

Chapter Forty-Six
Beyond a Visit with the King

Daphne couldn't stop fidgeting. The dress fit snug, and she preferred her tunic, trousers and cloak. Col seemed at ease in his Ka uniform, dressed smartly for the occasion.

The gate guard inspected their summons before returning it to Col and waving Daphne through.

"Just her, not you," the guard intoned. "Only her name on the summons."

"It's alright," she assured Col, quieting his protests. "I'll be okay."

Dejected, he stuffed the summons into his pocket and watched until the gate closed behind her. Ordered not to loiter near the palace, he wandered the streets in restless loops, always ending up back at the gate, but she'd yet to reappear.

During one such aimless wandering, he stopped short, neck craned beneath a looming structure with a harsh iron sign: *Capitol Dungeons*. The yard beyond boiled with motion, Ka soldiers shouting commands, urgency pulsing through every movement. Prisoners vanished behind shadowed gates, many would only return cold and flat beneath a coarse cloth veil.

He'd been taught many lessons by his father, chief among them: with confidence, one accomplishes a great number of things one couldn't otherwise. That and his uniform—a flash of the Ka seal at his belt—secured his entrance. He laughed at the ease of it, wishing he and Daphne had attempted access sooner, rather than pander to Drael's continued insistence they see the King first.

The dungeon was an unpleasant place, where muted cries hung thick in the air, assaulting the senses, accompanied by the pungent odor of too many unwashed bodies, but having come this far, he was determined to find Aurelia. *How delighted Daphne will be to learn I've visited her.* And the thought tweaked the corners of his lips in a smile.

That smile faded when the dungeon proved a maze. He blundered down its many stairways and corridors, past too many cells and too many dead ends, again and again. On his fourth pass down the same hallway, a guard eyed him, took a questioning step his direction, before Col plunged into a passage he'd missed earlier and darted down a flight of stairs descending deeper, scanning each cell he passed, shivering in the damp, frigid cold.

Another cell. A pitiful set of moans. Another criminal, curled on the stone floor. Col gave a start, whirled back to the cell.

"Mahan? It is you! What's happened?"

Mahan scooted weakly across the floor, eyes burning with fever, forehead beading sweat, broken hands extended before him. *In petition or to serve as evidence?* wondered Col. Impossible to tell if he was in his right mind or even recognized his visitor.

"Water," he croaked, "do you have water?"

"I'll get you some help. Hang in there, I'll be back."

Memorizing the cell number etched at its door, Col returned to the guard he'd passed earlier and demanded to speak with the prison commander. His tone brooked no argument. The guard led him to a bustling room, where his escort spoke briefly to a man seated behind a desk.

"I'm Lieutenant Mosi. You asked to see me?"

"Lieutenant. Col Blackwood, adjutant to Commander Drael, 2nd Regiment."

Col figured by the time the lieutenant checked his story, if he ever did, it might help save Mahan's life, perhaps secured that visit with Aurelia. A lie all around, though he used his real name. *Best stick as close to the truth as possible.*

The lieutenant's shoulders stiffened, his back straightening at the mention of Drael—a name ignored to one's peril—as his eyes drifted to the empty sleeve hanging at Col's side. Evidence of past heroics works wonders in the Ka.

"And how can I be of service to Drael's adjutant?" the lieutenant asked pleasantly enough.

"Commendations and greetings from Drael, Lieutenant." Col thought it always good to begin with a little flattery. "Just come from a prisoner here, one who holds some importance to Drael, and the man's delirious with fever. A healer must see to him at once."

After noting the cell number, the lieutenant asked, "Anything else?" his pen already scratching.

"Aurelia Talbot. Another prisoner. I need her cell number."

Puzzled, the lieutenant glanced up, replied, "Strange you would ask. Commander Drael signed her execution this morning. She's no longer in my custody."

Across the city, the lodging secured by Magnus and his companions had seen better days, but more importantly, it was off the beaten path. In its heyday, it had been a fabulously appointed inn that catered to wealthy patrons, but somewhere along the way of time's meandering drift, a swiftly expanding Capitol city had left the inn behind, tucked on a dead-end street, forgotten. Exactly what they needed, for upon arriving at the Capitol they discovered their faces plastered on reward pamphlets throughout the city.

While the others hunkered down, Saul—somehow escaping pamphlet notoriety—spent his days petitioning at the palace gate for an audience with the King; and NoNo—expressing his desire to explore the Capitol, *get the lay of the land* as he put it—left soon after. No one had seen him since.

Veyra found Magnus alone, in a corner of the inn's tavern. His fingers drummed the table as she joined him. "I feel so helpless, sitting here, doing nothing."

"You've gotten us this far," said Veyra, her eyes burning intense, searching his, "and you're an incredible leader. I'd follow you anywhere."

"Ah," Magnus looked away, uncomfortable, "nice of you to say, but -"

She seized his arm, a light touch but with sureness, pulling him towards her, "What I said before—if you couldn't find someone who'd have you, find me in Perinith. That wasn't a fleeting fancy. Everything about you draws me in, and I'll speak bluntly since it's what I do best. I believe I could be happy chasing the snow bear with you."

The comment was so odd it distracted Magnus from the gloom eating at his heart.

"I'm an idiot!" Veyra smacked her forehead, noticing his puzzled expression. "Can't imagine that made any sense to you. On Perinith, before considering marriage, a man and woman must hunt the snow bear together. If they succeed, a happy return to the village where their union is blessed. If they fail, well, there's no returning when they fail. But even the snow bear must eat."

Magnus shuffled his feet uncomfortably. *This conversation took a wrong turn.* She'd just proposed and expected him to survive a barbaric custom!

"You don't have to answer right away," Veyra hastened to add. "It's common for a man to hesitate; you men are never as ready to chase the snow bear. And ... I know I should have waited to speak my mind, perhaps after we'd seen the King. But I want you to know how I feel."

Her eyes sparked, locked on his, her lips parted slightly as if she dared hope for an answer. A *thwump* startled Magnus from the trance of her green-eyed stare as a breathless Saul tossed a bag on their table, hard enough to make their tankards jump.

"Had a thought," said Saul, seemingly oblivious to the moment he'd interrupted, "and hear me out. I'm not getting anywhere with an audience, so ..."

With a flourish he emptied the bag's contents. A jumble of cloaks, scarves and hats tumbled out, along with a large wedge of charcoal. "With these, you all can disguise yourself, charcoal to dirty your faces even. And if the guards refuse us entrance -"

Magnus snatched a scarf and hat faster than thought, eager for any excuse to escape Veyra's probing stare: "Then we'll find our own way in."

With Saul's disguises, they descended on the palace. Magnus, Tobias, Morco and Eken scouting its eastern exterior, while Saul, Bochim and Veyra chose its western. It was while studying the palace walls and contemplating a foolhardy plan that Magnus heard a familiar voice calling his name.

"Col?" Magnus whirled, surprised by the Dorakian's presence. "What are you doing here?"

"I'd ask the same, but there's a more pressing issue—Aurelia awaits execution."

"What game do you play?" Magnus' eyes narrowed. "She's already dead."

"No, she's alive! I accompanied her myself to the Capitol. I swear on my life she's alive. For the moment at least."

Words caught in Magnus' throat, his heart refusing to hope, but he couldn't deny Col's earnestness. The man believed what he said. *How's it possible after what NoNo witnessed?*

Eken leapt at Col, grabbed him by the throat and slammed him bodily against a garden trellis. "If you're lying, they'll be the last words you ever speak!"

The outburst attracted a guard's attention, who didn't care for the sight of a citizen's hands round a Ka's throat. Morco intervened, pulling the two apart.

"Eken, did you hear what he said?" asked Magnus. "Aurelia. She's alive!"

"I -" the Dorakian's response muffled beneath Magnus' embrace, before Morco engulfed them both in a joyful stranglehold.

Col adjusted his crumpled uniform and waved off the approaching guard with a shake of his head.

"Unbelievable," he muttered, "hugs for the man whose plan burned Lumath ... and I'm the villain."

"And Daphne?" asked Magnus, remembering the Gray Cloak.

"She's alive and well. In the palace as we speak."

"My friends," said Magnus, grinning at the irony, "it seems fate brought us here for a purpose beyond a visit with the King."

Chapter Forty-Seven
Horse and Rider

Daphne craned her neck at the giant double doors, intricately worked, plated in gold, featuring embossed scenes of life in the royal court, relieved they bore no resemblance to her dream.

Neither did the court.

Light filled the great hall, streaming through rows of windows and flickering from strategically placed hearths, the roaring fires providing both warmth and light. No filth or cobwebs were to be found.

And this court, a court utterly unlike her nightmare, echoed with life and laughter. Snippets of conversations floated across the hall. A trio of musicians played softly from a dais. Lords and ladies populated the court, lounging in chairs of various shapes and styles, some arranged close together, knees touching as they confided the latest royal intrigue.

Here or there, a lord or lady glanced curiously her way, while others stared more openly, witnessing the intrusion of another petitioner, a high-born lady. Col was right; the blue dress had been the right choice, while the extravagantly plumed headdress sat low enough to conceal her stone.

She cleared her throat and held her head high, forcing herself to walk calmly behind the guard, toward the large ivory throne at the opposite end of the hall. On the throne sat a man with a crown adorning his head.

The King.

By the throne stood or lounged his closest friends and allies, one eye on each other and the other on the man seated the throne. Theirs was a miserable existence. Trusting no one, always vying for position and influence with the King, though on the surface they appeared at ease. These were men and women who knew their place at court. At least for the time being.

Daphne swallowed against the knot forming in her throat, her stomach flipping as she fought the urge to vomit. She summoned courage, feigning confidence. The next few moments would determine the fate of her people.

The guard announced in a voice loud enough to carry the room, "Your Majesty, may I present Lady Daphne Vale."

He bowed low before stepping aside, leaving Daphne all alone.

The King inclined his head, the slightest nod, in greeting. He was an older man with graying hair and beard, although not far past his prime. Muscular and fit, it was apparent he did far more than spend his days seated.

She expected a harsh countenance, but his eyes and face were not unkind, and he appeared to hold a genuine interest for the people in court, including herself.

He descended from the throne, a move that surprised, having imagined he would pronounce judgment from above, and extended his right hand, palm down. The guard stiffened, shuffled forward, prepared for anything as the King approached his guest.

Daphne glanced at the hand he offered, unsure what to do. Her eyes caught a slight motion, a courtier signaling her. Grasping the meaning of his gesture, she leaned forward, took the King's hand and kissed it. The King smiled with a bemused expression.

"Lady Daphne. A pleasure to meet you." His voice rang clear, and in the wake of its echo, all music and conversation abruptly ended. "Drael claimed to send me a Gray Cloak, but I see before me a lady, one who could easily replace any woman here," adding with a wink and a whisper only Daphne heard, "Although no court lady bears a stone."

The ladies of the court licked their lips, eyeing their neighbors, seized on the delicious idea of a rival replaced, while shuffling nervously at the thought it might be themselves.

Taken aback by his greeting, Daphne tugged on the headdress. *Did he see the stone?* "You are too kind, Your Majesty, I ..."

"Please, no need for titles; call me Wymond," he exclaimed, for all to hear. A murmured ripple swept the court; none there had ever heard him offer such a thing. In a quiet voice, addressing only Daphne, "My wife always did, and you remind me of her. It's been a long time since anyone called me Wymond ... she passed some twenty years ago." A thin smile settled his lips.

Daphne didn't know what to make of it. He wasn't the man she'd expected, certainly not the King from her dreams. She sensed no malice or arrogance, and it emboldened her to speak freely.

"I'm sorry, Your Majesty ... Wymond, for your loss. I can't imagine losing someone so close."

"The ache never quite goes away," he mumbled, before gathering his robes, ascending the throne steps, and speaking loud enough for the words to carry, "But enough of the past. Let's speak of you. What brings you to our fair city, to my court? And are you a Gray Cloak as Drael suggested?"

At his question, heads turned as on a swivel, every lord and lady leaning forward in anxious anticipation of Daphne's answer. A Gray Cloak? In their midst?

"Your Majesty, Wymond, I ... I will not deny who or what I am. I am a Gray Cloak."

A shriek pierced the air, a court lady fainted, while more than one lord bolted from the room. The guard's hand strayed to his sword and made as if to seize Daphne, but the King raised his hand for silence and motioned for her to continue.

"But I bear you no ill will, and neither do my people. Rumors of our involvement in Saan are false," Daphne's voice gathered strength as she continued, "and if anyone says otherwise, I challenge them for proof. I beg you, King Wymond, please hear us out and learn for yourself that we stand not against you."

The crowd listened in rapt silence to her plea, the King watching impassively. Daphne swallowed, unable to read the man as he leaned back, his fingers steepled at his lips, resting his chin upon them, while he considered her and her plea.

He cocked his head as if to study her from a different angle before pronouncing, "I sense no deceit. Whether your report is true, you wholeheartedly believe the words you speak."

The King rose, imposing, regal, as the breathless crowd awaited his ruling. What would he do with this Gray Cloak who so boldly appeared in his presence?

In a voice once more carrying the hall, "Let it not be said that King Wymond the Wise and the Kind, First of His Name, Ruler of Lavonshia, Protector of The Twelve Isles, rules too harshly or too quickly. Let all know that he grants leniency and will hear the whole matter. Lady Daphne Vale, I grant you your desire. I will listen to the pleas of your people. Bring me your truth-speakers, your nobles and high councilmen. I shall determine for myself whether they speak truth or spread lies."

Unable to contain her excitement, Daphne clapped her hands in delight, a glimmer of hope blossoming in her heart. But the King wasn't finished. His eyes narrowed, his tone hardening, sharp and cruel.

"But know this. If you deceive me, if you fail to return as I order, I'll show no mercy. The whole of Lavonshian strength will visit terror upon the life of every Gray Cloak for which you care. This I swear, upon my crown and upon my sword." And seizing a sword propped against the steps, the King swiped it so violently across the throne's base that sparks flew across the room. The blade's steel rang sharp, though when the echo ended the silence was as deafening.

Sword in hand, Wymond the Wise and the Kind descended the throne steps.

"Hadil's Crossing closes soon at the Tol's first snow. I grant you an eight-day in which to return." As he spoke, he paused on each step, as if to emphasize his words, while his cold and calculating stare never left Daphne's eyes. "If you tarry, if you delay, I shall pronounce a death ransom upon all Gray Cloak and wipe them from the face of this world."

He snapped his fingers. A guard approached.

"Leave the Capitol immediately. My equerry shall saddle a horse for you in the courtyard."

The King turned his back on Daphne and proceeded up the throne steps.

"But, sire, my friends ..."

Wymond whirled to face her, snarling, "Do not try my patience, girl!" Spittle flew; he stood so close the stench of his breath roiled her stomach. "My decision is final. I care nothing for your pitiful distractions. For friends, or family, or your need to sit upon the pot, or stuff your mouth with food!" His hands and body trembled as he raged, neck muscles straining. "Even now the blood of Saan cries for vengeance. Do not try me! I may yet rescind my gracious offer." With a flick of his wrist, he signaled her dismissal before stumbling back to the throne, seemingly spent by his outburst.

An eight-day.

It was impossible. Or at least nearly, unless the wind itself carried her there and back.

Surely he can't mean it.

Daphne took a step toward the King, where he sat slumped, head resting in his hands.

"Sire -"

A hand seized her, yanked her away. She recognized the lord who'd gestured advice earlier.

"Stay another moment and you'll lose your head." His grim smile grotesque. "The horse will be fast. All the ones the King's equerry stables are. Perhaps you can make it."

He gestured toward the guard waiting by an open door.

"But an eight-day ..." stammered Daphne.

"I'll give you the benefit of the doubt," the man said, dragging her towards the exit, "and assume you don't know the King. It's unwise to protest his rulings—he's killed for less. Take comfort he didn't order you executed on the spot.

Next time, if there is a next time, don't let his welcoming nature fool you. Now go!"

He shoved her into the guard's chest, who dragged her bodily from the great hall, still protesting. A last glance back showed the King reclining the throne, eyes closed, an attendant massaging his temple.

In the courtyard, the equerry placed a stallion's reins in her hands. The beast stood seven spans tall, coat of black with a white-throated patch. It snorted, stamping a hoof while powerful muscles rippled its body.

"He's a lot to handle," said the groomsman as he hoisted Daphne into the saddle, "but give him his lead and tell him where to go. Somehow, he has a knack for it. Brilliant horse, this one."

She tried to recall the lessons learned during her recent time in the saddle.

Stay calm.

"Ha!" With a shout, the guard struck the horse's hindquarters. The stallion reared, nearly unseating Daphne, and bolted from the courtyard. Daphne's headdress tumbled from her head, exposing quite the sight: a magnificent black stallion, careening down Capitol streets, scattering patrons and merchants alike as it clattered across cobblestone, while its shaved-bald rider, bearing a stone in her forehead and wearing a royal blue dress that billowed in the wind, clung desperately to saddle and reins.

Horse and rider burst from the city gates, startling a colorful creature, vaguely resembling a cat, perched high atop a bailey wall.

Chapter Forty-Eight
Eating Away At His Heart

Nearly two centuries ago, the King of that age thought it uncouth to host public executions inside the Capitol, so he ordered the gallows removed and repurposed the courtyard where they'd once been held.

All executions now occurred beyond city walls, to the west across the Narthwich River. Officially, only family could attend, though guards cared little for the rules and curious onlookers frequented executions. The distance kept most away. When the spectacle had occurred inside the Capitol, it proved an easy diversion to attend; and the executions had assumed a fair-like atmosphere with merchants and hawkers selling souvenirs and food to the crowd.

But the new location required a half-day's travel and Capitol citizens found themselves too busy in their own pursuits for such a commitment. Attendance declined sharply.

Upon learning of Aurelia's fate, Magnus and company hurried from the Capitol, armed with only a general sense of the gallows' direction. Fortune shone, for on the Narthwich bridge, they encountered a well-dressed gentleman intending to observe that day's executions.

"Happy to show you the way. It's a little off the beaten path. But I'm a regular, attend them every eight-day if I can. Never know what dope you're kin to swinging on a rope."

His crooked grin revealed rotting teeth.

Fortune took an unfortunate turn as the man set a leisurely pace. No amount of encouragement persuaded him to lengthen his stride, for he assured them all executions occurred late afternoon, and seeing how it was still mid-morning they had time to spare. "It's a beautiful day! What's the rush?"

The day was rather dull, gray, the sun obscured by clouds, but his new companions held their peace and fell in step. The road meandered for a bit after crossing the Narthwich River bridge, before reaching an unmarked crossroads. Without a moment's hesitation, their guide continued down the left fork, passing through a wooded patch and arriving at a field where a small crowd gathered around a gallows.

To their dismay, a body already swung from a noose, while a guard escorted Aurelia, shoulders sagging, hands tied behind her, onto the platform.

Magnus rounded angrily on their guide. "You assured us it would be late afternoon!"

Their guide shrugged, flashed his crooked grin of rotting teeth and melted into the crowd.

"There's too many guards," bemoaned an anxious Eken.

"I have an idea," said Col and hurried towards the platform.

"If Col fails," said Magnus, "we go hard at them. Veyra, that knoll—now."

"Anything you ask of me," she replied, a hand on his arm, before scrambling up the knoll.

"Eken, you're with me. We come in from the side, while you four rush the Ka."

When Col neared the platform, guards barred the way.

"Official business," he snapped, the summons from the King in hand. "I am adjutant to Drael Rusk with orders from the King himself."

He'd seized on the idea as he approached the guards. *This better work.* The King's seal was clearly visible on the summons, though if he could help it he didn't intend to let anyone read the document.

The guards hesitated, not at his claim but at the seal.

"What's the meaning of this?" asked an approaching captain, absorbing the sight of a very flustered Col.

"A pardon for one of your prisoners." Col forced a note of steel into his voice. "That's her there at the noose."

"This is highly unusual. I've received no such -" the captain began before Col interrupted, flashing the summons. The captain couldn't help but notice the seal.

"You wish to incur the King's wrath?" asked Col. "You're a fool and an idiot. Personally, I don't care what happens to the woman; her blood is on your hands. As is your own."

He stuffed the summons into his pocket and turned away, fingers crossed. The captain didn't consider long, his face paling at the thought of displeasing the King.

"You! Hold there. I'll release her into your custody."

Concealing a smile, Col followed the captain to the gallows platform, to a hasty conferring between the captain and the executioner, none too happy at the prospect of losing a victim, though he reluctantly removed the noose from Aurelia's neck. The crowd booed as the executions came to a grinding halt.

Aurelia's knees buckled, and she stumbled forward, face pale as she touched her neck where the rope had cinched tight.

Ever playing the part, Col motioned disdainfully to Magnus and Eken. "You there! Help the woman down the stairs." Adding with a snide laugh to the captain, "I wouldn't touch such filth myself."

As he helped her down the stairs, Magnus leaned in to whisper, "I'm here, pot drummer. You're safe."

Aurelia blinked away grateful tears. "Please, in the pen ... Nezetta ..."

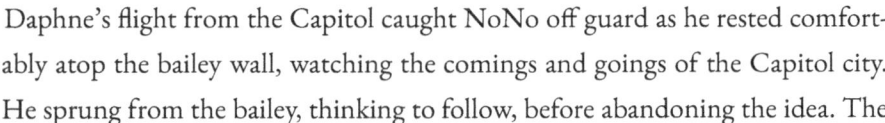

Daphne's flight from the Capitol caught NoNo off guard as he rested comfortably atop the bailey wall, watching the comings and goings of the Capitol city. He sprung from the bailey, thinking to follow, before abandoning the idea. The stallion was much too fast. But he was glad to see the girl still lived and Tobwhit's sacrifice wasn't for nothing.

Seeing her stirred a wave of guilt, reminding him of those he'd left behind. The guilt wasn't new; he'd experienced it plenty the last few days. It was just that he needed this—city chaos after centuries of cottage solitude—and he'd been content to wander, reveling in the marketplaces, the shops and warehouses too. He had particular fun there, giving chase to an endless supply of rats and mice. He caught his fair share, depositing each catch at the warehouse entrance for its owner to appreciate the following day. Eventually though he bored with the chase and continued exploring.

Just as he'd initially camouflaged himself to Aurelia and her friends, NoNo possessed the peculiar ability to blend in with his surroundings, invisible to any who glanced his way. With a whisk of his tail, he became a stray bolt of cloth tumbling along the street, or a mischief of mice scurrying across a room. To a casual observer, a momentary oddity, but one they inevitably dismissed with little thought, an ability that provided a delightful level of anonymity, and he enjoyed it to its full, exploring every Capitol nook and cranny. But eventually he tired of this too, and upon witnessing Daphne's desperate ride, reminded himself of greater issues at stake in the world than fulfilling his own curiosities.

It was no trouble slipping unnoticed onto palace grounds, sauntering the halls, occasionally distracted by an intriguing odor. He followed his flaring nostrils to the kitchen, where he sampled meats and pies placed kindly for him on the cooling rack.

Pausing inside the King's court to lick his talons clean, NoNo eavesdropped on the courtiers' conversations—useless gossip—though his ears perked at the mention of a Gray Cloak and her encounter with King Wymond. The popular opinion of the day? Her mission doomed from the start. Surely the King sabotaged it by giving her so little time to return.

NoNo frowned, not liking the sound of that.

The King was nowhere to be found. Not in court, nor his bedchamber. Try as he might, NoNo learned nothing of the King's whereabouts.

Where does a King go to disappear?

It was while investigating the King's bedchamber that NoNo Sensed it. The land. Stirring. A pulsing, angry groaning. Only once before had it felt such a way, and that memory still haunted him.

His Sensing told him the pain originated behind a bedchamber wall. His nostrils flared, sniffing the walls, and there it was, a seam, that ran a door's width.

There was no latch nor handle, only a binding woven into stone. Though the binding wasn't his it mattered little, for the wall was built of material from the land, and NoNo and the land were well acquainted. He closed his eyes, reached through the magic into clay and rock and soil. The wall resisted, but he was a midling and not one to give up easily. It yielded enough for him to slip through before snapping shut, missing his tail by a whisker. He hissed at the gall of it, before a wave of horror set his tail on edge and his body arching.

It wasn't the pitch black that horrified him; his eyes cut easily through the dark. No, it was the wrongness engulfing him, wave after pulsing wave. Something was dreadfully wrong, and he wished it wasn't his to discover.

The corridor sniffed of old mustiness, tickling his nostrils like the odor of Tobwhit's feet used to. Water beaded on the ceiling, falling with an echoing *plink* onto the stone-paved corridor, aged-slick with algae and mold. The passageway descended steeply, the temperature rising at an oppressive pace. As a midling he didn't sweat, but he still preferred the cooler breezes of winter and fall over sultry summer air.

The passage leveled, light spilling from an opening through which a timid NoNo stepped. The wrongness was thicker here, in a cavern seemingly larger than the palace itself, light illuminating its closer end while its far reaches remained swallowed in darkness. But what NoNo could see caused his fur to bristle.

A man astride a platform awash with the light of a dozen lanterns. The platform extended over a pit, from which proceeded the most awful wailing, while the man's hands traced lines of power and from the pit a wriggling mass struggled upward. Shadows swirled around the mass, solid, physical, and yet somehow very much ethereal. The mixture of shadow and mass wheeled and twisted, bobbing this way and that, dancing across the opening as if it struggled against the man's binding. But its struggle wasn't merely with the binding, for it soon became apparent the mass remained attached at the pit's bottom, shrieking and moaning and tugging against whatever held it in place. But at last it snapped free and settled near the man who'd summoned it.

Another pattern, a binding intricate and ancient, and the dark mass drifted to the platform's edge, to a vessel piled high with blackened, rotting hearts—and then one began beating. NoNo mistook it for nothing at first, merely a twitch, until the twitch became a spasm, the spasm a tremor, the tremor a steady heartbeat and the shadowed mass engulfed the heart.

The swirling darkness sighed, as if pleased, and spoke when it bowed, a decidedly human gesture.

"Master."

The man pointed wordlessly across the cavern, and the shadowed mass shrieked away. The man returned his attention to the pit and began anew. NoNo crept close, needing to see for himself, commanding his bristling fur to stay, for it would have fled his body if possible.

A thick black vein ran the length of the pit, an endless, unnatural streak, the blackest NoNo ever saw.

Unaware of the intruder, the man continued binding, plucking at the dark vein of land like one would pluck at a gooey substance. A sliver wrenched from the vein and once more the man bound the dark mass to a freshly beating heart.

It too spoke. Bowed. And disappeared across the cavern. The man returned to his work.

NoNo Sensed the man's binding was a twisted sort of Compulsion, and witnessing the horrific binding of shadow and heart, he realized where the blame for Saan rested.

Tucked away in Tobwhit's cottage, NoNo had all but forgotten evil's existence. He'd grown soft, forgotten evil's weight. Unprepared now, he was the wrong midling for the job. Surely he could leave this problem to another and slip away.

Overseas will work. Perinith. The Twelve Isles. Anywhere really.

Stepping back from the pit's edge, his paw dislodged a stone. It skittered across sloping ground, gathering momentum, dislodging other stones until a chaotic cascade tumbled into the pit. The man's concentration broke as the dark mass he'd summoned fled, and he whirled towards the sound, fury in his eyes. NoNo flicked his tail, blending with the terrain, becoming an innocent lump of rock.

This man though, was not so easily fooled as the average Capitol citizen, his eyes seizing on NoNo. For the second time in a matter of days, the man spoke an old friend's name. Not the name Tobwhit had taken to calling the midling, but an ancient one the midling hadn't heard in many years.

"Kynth-palla. This is a surprise, old friend." The man smiled, the fang-baring smile of a lion prepared to devour its prey. On his belt clip hung a crown. "And here I thought you'd faded into obscurity like the others. Why didn't your heart stop beating when the land stopped caring? My dreams of your death were pleasant."

"Morcant." A name that caused NoNo, or Kynth-palla as he was long ago known, to shudder. "You look remarkably well yourself for a dead man. Grasping after power not yours to take."

The King chuckled. "This pathetic symbol?" His hand strayed to the crown at his side. "It's nothing. A means to an end. True power? Is what I do here today."

"What foulness is this?" NoNo returned to the pit's edge, needing to understand what Morcant summoned.

"Can't you feel it?"

NoNo studied the dark streak, his Sensing groping for the truth. But just as he thought he might understand it —nothing. He growled, stomped a paw against the rock, the truth of it lost.

"Delights me to stump you, old friend. Like the riddles we use to enjoy, and my heart almost softens ... memories of a pleasant season. Of my wife -" Morcant choked on the words, turning away to study the pit, perhaps to hide tears. When he turned back to NoNo, his eyes had hardened to narrowed slits. "Why?"

NoNo hung his head. Ashamed. Not the first time he'd regretted his choices. Their choices.

"If I could change the decisions we made ..." Tears pooled at the corner of his large round eyes. "I am sorry. Truly."

"You're sorry?" Morcant's jaw clenched, fists balled so tight his knuckles cracked. "Is that all? Come now, Kynth-palla! Where's that sense of rightness you claimed when you turned against me? You, and Tobwhit. Ophel. Once my friends."

"I ... we did what we thought was right."

"Ha! That's rich coming from you." Morcant exhaled, releasing his balled-up fists, musing quietly almost to himself, "How many years ... close to four hundred? And it still wounds so deeply ..." His eyes fixed on NoNo, his voice gathering strength, "And are you *sorry*," he paused, allowed it to hang bitterly in the space between them, "for the tens of thousands you killed that day?" He laughed, as if the death of so many were a joke worth laughing at.

"We did what we must. To stop you."

"How easily you justify your actions. Consider then what your binding that day began! I call them my shadow midlings." And with a cry of delight, Morcant returned to his work, hands tracing a blurring pattern. Another tainted piece of earth lifted above the pit, and NoNo's Sensing revealed it to him.

He had done this. *They* had done this. For the tainted vein ran deep beneath the land, stretching beyond the Capitol and the King's Forest.

To its origin.

The Tol Mountains.

"You see it now, don't you, Kynth-palla!" Morcant cried, triumphant. "I may finish this grand work, but you began it!"

Another shadow midling born to life, bowing before shrieking away toward the dark end of the cavern. For an instant, the light chased its tail, and in that briefly lit corner NoNo realized the truth: the darkness wasn't light's absence, but an innumerable swarm of shadow midlings. His ribs threatened to crack as the horror of it threatened to burst his heart.

For the first time in his life, drops of perspiration beaded his fur. It wasn't the cavern's heat, but the shame of what they'd done. "Morcant, you must stop! Don't let what we began be your ruin! Be our world's ruin. You don't know what these foul creatures are capable of. Can you even control them?"

"Ah, my old friend. While you've wasted your life in obscurity, I've become more powerful than you could ever imagine. I haven't been idle these past four hundred years!"

The King seized hold of his tunic and ripped it in two, twirling as he did, pirouetting before an audience of one, a mad cackle reverberating off cavern walls. Saphyr stones covered his chest, arms, shoulders, and back, adorning his body like twinkling jewels, a colorful patchwork of blues, reds, greens, yellows, whites, blacks and every other imaginable color, a shockingly grotesque sight that sent NoNo stumbling backwards in an unconscious effort to get far away. And with it came two realizations.

He's a madman. Followed closely by the second, *I won't be leaving here alive.*

"Now it is I that am truly ... sorry," mocked Morcant, and with a slight flick of his wrist seized NoNo in an invisible grip, dangling him over the pit. "Enjoy your time with my new pets. They haven't fed in days."

Morcant released his hold on NoNo and signaled to his shadow midlings. As NoNo plummeted, the shadow creatures rushed into the pit after him, swarming his body, squeezing into his eyes and ears, through his mouth and nose, burrowing deep inside. The last thing he remembered was feeling their cold empty darkness eating away at his heart.

Chapter Forty-Nine
Pitiful Mews

"Nezetta?"

No one stirred. The prisoners had only eyes for the body swinging from the noose and ears for the crowd's swelling cheers.

"Nezetta?"

Tobias' whisper, louder this time, attracted their attention.

"Who ya lookin' for?" asked one, a rough character with a jagged scar across his shaved head.

"Can you get us out of here?" the only woman in the holding pen asked.

"You Nezetta?"

"Uh, yeah ... I am, yes." Her eyes darted, shifty.

"A mutual friend sent me," said Tobias.

"Her name ain't Nezetta," chortled the jagged-scarred man.

She leveled a stare of such poison the man scampered away. "Please, you've got to help me out here. I've done nothing wrong!"

The jagged-scarred man, perhaps hoping his assistance might secure their freedom, returned, having questioned the other prisoners. "There weren't none answered to Nezetta. But seems to me with that kind of name you's lookin' for a woman. They's leading one on stage now." He jerked a thumb towards the gallows, where guards led a woman wearing a gray cloak onto the stage, her hands shackled behind her.

Tobias offered a thankful nod. "There'll be a diversion soon. Make your escape then."

On stage, the executioner fit a noose around the woman's neck. When he cinched it tight, she whimpered, the crowd silent, awed by the sight of a Gray Cloak facing their end.

Tobias drew his sword, dragging it across the holding pen's bars. The clanging racket drew the attention he'd expected.

"Veyra!" he shouted, jabbing his sword toward the gallows.

Still positioned on the knoll, Veyra fit an arrow to her bow. With a sharp twang it leapt towards the stage where it nicked the rope, but the noose held.

With a cursing bellow, the executioner kicked the stool loose. Nezetta dropped. The noose cinched tight while her hands clawed, her body flailing and kicking.

Veyra notched a second arrow and let it fly. This time it sailed true, severing the rope in two. Nezetta crumpled to the stage. The Ka sprang into action, the captain issuing orders, guards converging.

Morco joined Tobias in a desperate fight at the holding pen, wind whistling as his warhammer attempted to keep the guards at bay. A guard's cudgel connected with Tobias' ribs. A sharp crack.

The crowd erupted. Guards shoved through with swords drawn, trampling spectators who fought back with fists and fury. The execution grounds turned into a riot.

Magnus charged the gallows, Bochim and Saul close behind. Steel rang against steel. Magnus leapt on stage. With an angry roar, the executioner hefted an axe, but a moment later fell with a puzzled expression, an arrow protruding from his back.

Magnus knelt by the woman's side to cut the noose free. An ugly red welt had taken its place.

"Are you Nezetta?"

"Yes, yes, I am," she croaked.

"Aurelia sent me. Come with us!"

The riot swallowed them whole, carrying them back to their companions before they fled.

Every jolt bruised another bone. Her body unused to riding so hard for so long. Daphne slid from the saddle and crumpled, exhausted, to the forest floor.

The horse was as swift as promised. She'd made good progress since leaving the Capitol, deep in the King's Forest by sunfall. *Perhaps the wind is at my back.* Her heart welcomed the sliver of hope taking lodge there.

She had no cloak or bag to use as pillow, and the dress would be precious little comfort against the frosty night air, but she didn't care. She was asleep the moment her head touched the forest floor.

Startled awake, she realized the sun had risen long ago and was far overhead. She berated herself for allowing so much time to pass, and worse, the horse was nowhere to be seen. *Must have failed to tie the reins. Hardly remember dismounting.*

Pain seared every muscle, but limping bravely through the forest, she searched for the stallion, didn't know his name, but took to calling, "Onyx! Onyx, here boy!" on account of his coat being so black. She prayed her voice would be enough.

She found him by a brook, guzzling greedily. His eyes—big, soulful—regarded her reproachfully.

"I know Onyx. I'm sorry."

He tossed his head with a fierce neigh, but allowed her hand on his nose. After consoling him, she collapsed by the brook and drank deeply.

Refreshed, she struggled to mount, until she found a log from which she could access the saddle. The stallion was eager to run, but she held back, her thighs and rear aching as they never had.

When the pain eventually dulled, she released her grip on the reins and gave the horse its freedom. The stallion snorted and reared, increasing its stride, the ground rushing by. Later that evening she once more slid wearily from the saddle. Foam gathered at the stallion's mouth, its coat slick with perspiration.

"You did well, Onyx." Her hand stroked his mane as she laid her head against his heaving flank. Finding a stream, she allowed the horse to drink before remembering to tie the reins to a branch.

Sleep was instant, as the night before, though this time it proved fitful. She woke repeatedly, muscles protesting their self-awareness. Before sunrise, she tired of fighting sleep and struggled bravely into the saddle. They made good time, passing Hiedorn at midday. But in the Tol's shadow, the stallion balked, jerking his head against the reins when Daphne tried to coax him up the slope toward Hadil's Crossing.

Their battle of wills wasted precious time she didn't have, but she refused to go on alone. *I'll need his speed on the other side.* The sun inched downward, but Daphne couldn't give up, her people's future at stake.

At sunfall, the stallion finally relented, allowing her to lead him up the slope. She camped at the yawning mouth of Hadil's Crossing, remembering the pockmarked path, unwilling to risk laming Onyx by venturing it in the dark.

The first glimmer of sunrise found her already mounted, waiting anxiously for light to penetrate the crossing's shadows.

Hope stirred afresh in her heart, to be close to Gray Cloak land so soon.

NoNo lost any sense of time, or of how far he'd run. When his body first struck the pit floor and the shadows began feasting on his heart, he'd been tempted to simply lie there and die. To allow the shadow midlings their feast. Fighting their emptiness, their darkness and their pain, seemed an impossibility.

But the land refused to let him die. It whispered to him until the whispers became a shout.

You must warn someone.

They need to know the truth.

Run.

Run.

Run!

He struggled to his feet and ran, his existence reduced to a series of simple truths—one paw in front of another, the same sickly dark vein threading an infinite spiderweb of foul tunnels. He wondered absentmindedly whether he merely circled beneath the Capitol. *Am I any farther from the pit than when I began?*

The tunnels were narrow, just large enough for a creature of his size. The shadow midlings with their ethereal bodies squeezed easily around him, engulfing him in a darkness even blacker than lack of light.

He wasn't sure which was worse, the wrongness he felt from the earth's sickly stain, or the loss he felt as the shadow midlings consumed his heart. They fed slowly, whispering and giggling as they hollowed him from within.

His mind turned numb, a blessed fog against the darkness, his ability to think diminished. Memories faded. There was a vague recollection of a cottage and an old man, but he could no longer remember the old man's name or where the cottage might be found.

Another face came frequently to mind. Ah. Morcant. His old friend. He remembered a ship, the stink of fish and salt spray, Morcant laughing beside him. He recalled clinging to the foremast as an island shimmered into view. A ceremony. Morcant receiving a stone and a feast afterward. Joy and celebration. The memories were pleasant.

Then the old man again, thick white bushy eyebrows, lips parted in a single phrase:

While we yet live, there is always hope.

The phrase repeated, drumming his mind. Insistent. Demanding. Often accompanied by the face of the old man, or that of a young woman, tall, with black hair and a kind face.

While we yet live, there is always hope.

She spoke the words too, though he sensed they weren't hers to begin with. But she liked the words, and he liked her as much as he did the old man. The words comforted him, though he couldn't shake the feeling of claws and fangs, real or imagined, digging deep into his midling essence, taking what wasn't theirs by right. The dark sorrow of the feasting creatures overwhelmed him, but the words playing in his mind infused him with courage.

While we yet live, there is always hope.

He resisted. A barely perceptible shift. A mental wall, a flimsy barrier against the encroaching shadow midlings. It worked, for a moment. He resisted again, straining, urging his mind to block out darkness, his heart to continue beating, his legs to carry on a little farther.

The shadow creatures giggled at his efforts. His resistance made the feast that much more pleasurable. The world's prey—a lamb here, a frit there, even a human Master wished to punish—had long since bored them. An occasional noble beast still excited, sensing its connection to a more ancient power, but even those succumbed too quickly. Certain of the shadow midlings had grumbled discontent, disappointed Master restrained their need to consume the world and everything in it. The pitiful humans and woodland creatures he brought would never satisfy. Oh, but now! He'd finally delivered. A magical creature much like themselves, another midling, but one without shadow or darkness in its heart. The feast was glorious.

"Leave me be! I choose hope!"

In desperation, NoNo called to the land, the shadow midlings screeching in delight at the burst of energy. He didn't call to the dark streak of earth, but to the untainted that lay beyond. His heart flared with courage when it responded, though its answer was weak, as if the rot had lain dormant too close, and for too long, corrupting even the clean.

But it was enough. Stalactites pierced the tunnel, nimble probing fingers. The land Sensed NoNo's presence, a friend, the one that called, and so the fingers missed him despite the narrow passage.

No, its target was something foul, beings not intended for this world.

The shadow midlings danced around the piercing fingers, for they were shadow more than anything else, and the land's efforts pitiful. They swirled and misted and danced, taunting the rock fingers.

"Is that the best you can do?" They hissed and laughed.

But like in a game of Ji, the earth learned. It struck quicker, deeper, probing for a weakness, and when one thin finger of rock finally pierced a heart carried deep inside a shadow, there arose such a racket of mournful screeching and wailing. The shadow midling died, and its brothers and sisters knew its death.

The triumph loosened NoNo's tongue, and he sang. An ancient song in a tongue only midlings knew. The shadows had a sense of it too, but perversions of midlings as they were, they would never grasp its essence. It only enraged them, for in the singing of it they understood themselves to be a wrong that shouldn't be. Their once gleeful laughter turned insane, a babbling of hate as they turned on themselves, feeding on their own hearts as much as they fed on NoNo's.

Infused with fresh hope, NoNo sang louder. The land responded, renewed its attack, aiming for the center of the swirling masses. Shadow midlings died as rock pierced heart. The land had discovered their weakness.

But there were too many, a countless horde of streaming, undulating shadows, and despairing, NoNo's song faltered. The shadow midlings pounced on his doubt, their whispers cruel.

"There is no hope."

"We are endless. We are everything and everywhere."

"You are alone."

"You are guilty."

"No one will save you. You cannot even save yourself."

The incessant beguiling clogged his mind and filled his heart with despair. No matter how many died, it didn't seem to matter. NoNo's song, once vibrant, faded to a whisper, no longer able to drive the shadows to madness. With renewed frenzy they fed on NoNo's dying heart. His pitiful mews echoed in the tunnel.

Chapter Fifty
A Rush of Wind

The wind swept over the Capitol, harvesting the market's chaotic din. It whipped through Grand Bazaar stalls, tasting the roasting scent of lamb and duck and pig, and plucking away the hawker's pitch. It wandered Merchant's Row, eavesdropping on whispered negotiations of merchant and buyer, caressing the hem of luxury fabrics and skimming the smooth-fired surface of Perinithian pottery. It whistled through the River Market, cooling as it crisscrossed the Narthwich River. It tore a screech from a gull's beak and rode the rippling gills of a fresh-caught trout before a fishmonger severed the head. Giddy with such fresh delights, the wind roared up the sheer bluffs on the Capitol's southern side, where a man stood at a courtyard wall.

Drael inhaled the wind's secrets, the ritual invigorating. His back straightened, shoulders stiffening, and for a moment he stood a little taller, imagining himself what he no longer was—a young man.

Behind him, the structures of his home thrust into the sky like Capitol guardians, keeping their centuries-long watch over the proud line of the Rusk family estate, anchored by his father, his grandfather, and their fathers and grandfathers before them. Brilliant pinks and oranges flared across the sky as the sunfall dipped beyond the horizon, and in the city below lantern lights winked on one by one as the night watchmen threaded through the streets.

Am I the lantern lights, awaking each night anew? Or am I the sunfall, never to rise again?

On that night, unlike most nights, the wind's delights couldn't save him from such dismal musings, troubled as he was by an earlier audience with the King. Not that the King had been angry. Far from it, he'd seemed distracted, a shrug and a dismissal despite Drael's campaign yielding so little. And now the Dorakian and Gray Cloak had escaped execution. Should the King rouse from his stupor, Drael feared the fury sure to descend on the Rusk family lineage.

Drael cared little for himself, content to leave the world when his time came. But he hadn't fought and scrapped and killed and tortured and outlasted to leave nothing for his wife—thirty hunter's moons his junior—and their precious daughter, coming soon of age. All his toil hung so fragile, a breath away from ruin. Subject to the whims of a capricious King.

But for once in his life, Drael's troubled thoughts extended beyond his own interests, at least a little. *Saan*. Drael had thought nothing could turn his stomach. He shivered, though not because he was cold, for he was well-bundled against the wind, and he sighed, his eyes twitching northward, towards the Maldelea Sea, and the Twelve Isles.

Aurelia held the leg of lamb over the fire, salivating as juices dripped and smoke curled around the meat, its aroma intoxicating. Her stomach growled. While a prisoner, she'd eaten little.

They'd encamped well outside the Capitol, to the north, past the curve of the Narthwich River. Fugitives, they knew the risks of being even this close, but couldn't leave without discovering word of Daphne, NoNo and Mahan.

At least here, the herds of grazing sheep outnumbered the human population, meaning the location held two chief advantages: sheep weren't known to betray for a handful of decri and they made an excellent source of food. Surely the shepherds wouldn't miss one or two.

A plateau served to overlook the Narthwich and the Capitol, offering cover in the thick woods carpeting it, and the high ground should the need arise to defend themselves.

Following their escape from the executioner, the reunion had been a happy one.

It's a strange thing, thought Aurelia, *all that's happened since Chelam.* New friendships kindled, old ones strained. Trust broken and trust restored. Or at least mended. A lasting trust would take time, fragile for now. Yet here they were, hugging and trading stories, though Veyra's strangely cool reception stung, and a grunted *careful* from Tobias and his broken ribs meant she'd need to hug a little gentler.

Nezetta grumbled most about lingering near the Capitol. With Ophel gone, she was eager to return home, to assume a place of prominence among her people, and Aurelia knew every twinge of impatience. It was a desire so strong that Nezetta left one night to do just that, only to return, gasping tearful breaths. If there'd been any doubt, Ophel's binding had seen to it they couldn't stray far from each other.

There shouldn't have been any doubt, for since their bonding they'd experienced the depths of that connection, and there was nothing off limits. Even hunger and sickness belonged to them now; when Nezetta fell ill, Aurelia doubled over with her.

When Eken learned of their bond, his face lit up. *That's why Gray Cloaks go in twos!* he'd said. *I read about it in Of Magic And Its Properties*—the others groaned in unison—*your bond is peculiar to Gray Cloaks, since the dawning of the first song.*

Despite Nezetta's earlier treatment of Aurelia, a fragile truce took root. Not exactly friends, but neither enemies. Perhaps they would never be close, let alone friends, but an understanding existed, and it was far easier to be civil and even kind when one experienced life through the lens of another.

Time dragged, slow and plodding as a plow through clay, Saul's reports of heightened security and frequent patrols discouraging, as were his failed attempts to learn of Mahan's fate. And still no sign of NoNo or Daphne.

So they waited, discussing rescue plans, though none seemed viable, each eventually discarded.

Aurelia chafed at the delay, consumed with worry for her father. Nezetta stewed with the same worry, a strange feeling when she'd never been that close with her own father. Storm clouds gathered on the horizon.

Saul wasn't as careful as he should have been.

But then, it wasn't really his fault. Rather, an odd chance of fate that Kymn would be on prison grounds the same day as he.

A string of bad luck led Kymn to seek work there that fateful day. Perhaps it was his own choices, but he didn't see it that way, so he blamed others, starting with his onetime friends, Magnus and Tobias. The three had been inseparable after joining the Ka. That they would abandon him so easily, choosing Dorakians and a Gray Cloak instead, planted quite a bitter seed. Magnus' interest in the Dorakian girl irked him. What did he see in her? She was a nobody, a troublemaker, at odds with the King and his policies. Whatever spell she cast, it had stripped Magnus of reason and duty.

After Lumath, Kymn struggled to fit in with the Ka. It wasn't as it once was, for now other Ka avoided him, viewing him as tainted. *Don't trust him*, they whispered, *he associated with the deserters*.

The bitter seed sprouted, rooting deep. His attitude spiraled, as did his attachment to the bottle. He drank to wake and drank to sleep.

Then came the fighting—quick to challenge any who crossed him. After a nasty right hook knocked an officer senseless, he'd been discharged by the Ka. Set adrift in the King's Forest, a kind family of peddlers offered a spot in their caravan. Their destination—the Capitol—to resupply before a scheduled stop in the Highlands, but he didn't care as long as it took him far away from Dorakians and Gray Cloaks. But upon reaching the Capitol, the peddlers politely disentangled themselves from their newest guest. They'd had enough of his melancholy demeanor and heavy drinking.

Alone in the Capitol, Kymn struggled to find work. The famine was in the past, but jobs were slow to return. With breath that reeked of spirits and a disheveled Ka uniform, no one would hire him. He slept on the streets, let his beard grow shaggy. His clothes stank as if he'd spent an afternoon rolling in a pigsty. Desperate, he went to the prison, hopeful they'd hire an ex-Ka. It was there he spotted Saul.

Kymn supposed there wasn't much reason to believe Saul had left Magnus' side, and *that* man carried a sizeable bounty on his head. Kymn dreamt of the decri and what he would do with it, starting with refilling the nearly empty bottle he nursed. So he followed Saul at a discreet distance, blending in with the crowd, just another down-and-out citizen, struggling to make ends meet.

He tailed him through meandering market streets, where Saul peeked in at shops and checked in at taverns and inns, apparently searching for someone. He never once checked for a tail. Kymn doubted Saul would recognize him anyway, what with his filthy appearance and shaggy beard.

At dusk, Saul exited the Capitol, and Kymn followed at a safe distance. They walked west and crossed the bridge over the Narthwich before turning north. There were fewer travelers heading north, and Kymn slipped farther behind, into lengthening shadows.

When Saul left the northern road to cut across a meadow, Kymn lost him in the gloom, but found his tracks in the dust. He tracked him across the meadow, to a path hugging a natural curve in the land as it wound between rocks and hills before beginning a steep ascent to a plateau. The moon slipped from behind clouds and shone a spotlight on Saul, who'd nearly reached the plateau. Light from a campfire twinkled, backlighting a figure emerging from the treeline.

The figure greeted Saul before the two disappeared into the thick of the woods. Kymn considered following for a closer look, but decided it wasn't worth the risk, confident he'd discovered the fugitives' campsite. He retraced his steps to the Capitol, whistling a merry tune, while mentally spending every decri that would soon be his.

A joyous whoop reverberated against cavern walls as the King's heart leaped, a joyful drum against his ribs. To know Kynth-palla's heart would give out soon! Though a shadow midling reported the creature put up a delightful fight, and the song was troublesome. The last thing the King needed was a meddlesome midling stirring the land, but the shadow assured him the song was but a whisper. Hope waned. The shadows gorged happily.

And earlier, an ex-Ka had arrived with news of the fugitives' camp. Weighing his options, Morcant remained seated on his throne long after dismissing his courtiers. At last, his mind made up, he retired to the bedchamber, with strict orders not to be disturbed. He needn't have reminded palace staff as he'd summarily executed the last man who'd dared defy his orders.

The bedchamber wasn't Morcant's final destination for the evening. With a flick of his wrist the hidden door slid open; bindings were a simple matter with such power at his disposal. He sensed it even now—the power—the stones thrumming against his skin, magic pulsing through every sinew and fiber of his body. A thought or a flick of a wrist was often enough. Only his shadow midlings, complicated and exhausting work, required the full use of his hands to create.

He considered using the Ka to silence the troublemakers, though recent events had caused his faith in them to wane. *Drael. A failure, washed-up. The man doesn't deserve his title or his estate.* But that was a matter for another day. These particular rebels seemed rather ingenious, and he needed assurances they would die. There could be no more hiccups with his plan's culmination so close.

He considered attending to the matter himself—he'd certainly have no trouble dispatching them. But then he remembered his shadow midlings and their pleas. Too many still crowded the cavern, jealous of their siblings' feast, for despite their ethereal nature, only so many hearts could squeeze into the tunnel after Kynth-palla. Perhaps this band of outlaws would satisfy them. At least for now, until he released them upon the Gray Cloaks. But before that, he would create more. He would take no chances against the Gray Cloaks and their powers.

With a flick of his wrist, he summoned the shadow midlings from across the cavern. They swarmed. Restless. Hungry.

"Master." They whispered his title as he stepped onto the platform. "Master."

"My children!"

He threw his arms wide, ecstasy surging as they embraced him, caressing him, their worship intoxicating. He marveled at their light touch as they grazed his skin, wove between his legs and around his fingers. His work as King had once been enough to thrill him. No longer. Only here in the cavern, surrounded by his creation, was he truly alive.

They sensed he planned a treat, shadow tails snapping as they nudged him playfully, begging for orders, demanding purpose.

"Fly, sweet shadows. You will find your prey on a plateau north of the Narthwich. Feed! Feed upon them!"

A rush of wind as shadows burst from the cavern into the night air.

Chapter Fifty-One
His Last Breath

Daphne allowed the stallion to pick its way across Hadil's Crossing. She wanted to hurry, needed to hurry, with three sunfalls passing since leaving the Capitol, but the light revealed her wisdom in taking care even now. The path was as treacherous and pockmarked as she remembered, and not one to rush. A misstep here would ruin everything. Besides, they'd soon be thundering across the narrow strip of Dorakian land that jutted from the south, before entering Gray Cloak territory.

A faint, quavering song, raw with agony, drifted through the gap. Daphne tugged the reins, but Onyx already pranced nervously, ears twitching at the unseen melody. She scanned the path ahead, but they were alone. The song was unfamiliar, yet oddly known, the words in another language; and though the voice was still fragile, the sound grew louder, as if the singer drew near.

With a gentle nudge, she led Onyx to a crossing wall and pressed her ear to the stone. She instantly regretted it. Instead of melody, a cacophony of such an awful chittering and chattering assaulted her ears. The strength drained from her limbs. Whatever foulness birthed the screeching carried death, and she wanted no part of it.

The wall exploded from the other side, blasting chunks of rock and dirt into the air. A ball of bloodied fur, engulfed by a cloud of shadows, burst through the rubble, causing the stallion to bolt and throwing Daphne from the saddle. The ground rushed at her, before the impact knocked her out cold.

When she woke, she knew it hadn't been long, but panic surged—she was blind—until she lifted a hand close and relief broke in a ragged sigh. *Thank the Great Binding.*

A flash of light pierced the dark, gone before it took hold. Another, just as brief. Her mind grasped the truth: she stood in the heart of a storm of shadows. Her eyes adjusted, and her stomach revolted at the sight of such a slithering mass. These were not normal shadows; their wicked whispers assaulted her mind, though they paid her no attention, focusing instead on the little ball of fur lying panting, bloodied, on the ground.

"Give up."

"You're nothing."

"Your life is pointless."

"You bring shame to midlings."

"The world shall rejoice when you die."

Daphne crawled through the dark, shadows whipping around her body, their tails and claws stinging, a thousand cuts on her face and hands. She reached for the ball of fur. Its sides heaved irregularly. It was the source of the song, and it still sang, but in a voice faint and fading fast. The ball of fur raised its head, and she recognized it, her heart breaking as she stifled a cry -

NoNo...

She'd only met him once, when she awoke disoriented in that cottage, but she would never forget her first sight of a midling.

There's so little left...

She swallowed back bile. He was more fur now than substance, the nibbling shadows tearing away flesh. His eyes glazed, heavy-lidded, his once beautiful fur matted by a dark thick oil, the excretions of shadow midlings. His breathing came in labored gasps. A hole, eaten away from the inside out, laid bare his heart, now abnormally small with chunks missing and slick with black oily streaks. He didn't appear to be long for this world, yet still he sang. A song of beauty and joy and light.

NoNo stirred, lifting his head with all the effort he could muster. His eyes focused on her in a moment of recognition. His smile, despite his agony, melted her heart. *A midling smiled at me. At me!*

"Daphne ..." his voice fading, "join my song ..."

"I don't know the words!"

"Just ... listen. Your power ... sing ..."

And with a loud cry of anguish, NoNo gathered his frail body beneath him and lifted his head and sang.

He sang for courage to end life well.

He sang for joy that arrives with dawn's first light, banishing night's terror.

He sang for Daphne and for himself.

And he sang for Morcant, a friend he'd once betrayed.

"Daphne ... help ..." NoNo's plea was urgent, his time for song at an end.

"But I can't!" she cried, tears flooding her face, great heaving sobs of helplessness. "All I am and all I've been is a lie—I can't sing. I have no power!"

NoNo dragged his body across the ground and collapsed into her lap. The shadows swarmed both human and midling, but still they ignored her, feasting on NoNo's power, ignoring the powerless human, rejoicing at the midling's end.

A final note rang clear and long, and when it ended, a deafening silence reigned. Even the shadows stopped their chittering and their feasting as if to acknowledge such a ferocious battle and the courage of a midling. NoNo's body sagged limp in Daphne's lap.

"I'm so sorry," Daphne bawled, sniffling through tears, "I'm so ... sorry I ... I couldn't ..."

A curious thing happened then. A marvel she'd never experienced. She Sensed a power tugging at her heart and mind, encouraging her to sing with it. She had never felt such power, but knew it was of the land. Its clarity and simple beauty stunned her. The pureness and rightness of it.

Her mother once told her *binding feels like singing with your hands while the land rises to join the melody.* So she sang, and her fingers twitched. It was more of a tuneless hum at first, faltering, weak, barely a thing worthy of taking note, but it was a start.

NoNo's ears perked as she hummed. He sang a faltering note. Then another.

Daphne hummed a little louder. Off tune. The sound of a singer finding their voice. She laughed at herself, for her tune didn't match NoNo's pure voice, however weak his might have been, and it didn't match the land's beautiful hymn. But it was her own, and perhaps it might improve, quickly even, with time and practice. The thought encouraged her, and she picked up the tune again. She stroked NoNo's matted fur as she sang, and he lent her his courage. Picking her way through the melody, she turned it over in her mind, seeking to understand it.

A shadow midling broke away from the pack, curious about the intruder. The voice was weak, and there was no power, just an echo of the land. The shadow giggled. Nothing would please like a second sumptuous feast, but it decided this one wasn't worth the effort, so it rejoined its brothers and sisters worming their way back inside NoNo.

Daphne continued to sing, while the land coaxed the song from her. She recognized a repeating refrain and fixed the spots in the tune where she'd been off-key. Her voice held firm, and the land responded, giving sudden clarity to the foreign words. She understood what NoNo sang, not just the melody of it now, as pure and sacred as that was, but the words that gave power to its melody. Words of hope and joy and love and triumph over evil, for every note blazed with hope, every chord swelled with joy, every word sang of love, the melody itself a weapon to unmake the darkness.

Her voice was nothing compared to the land's, for it contained such power, weak as it was, that it could drown her out if it wished. She sang anyway.

She didn't understand the swirling shadows, but she knew they hated NoNo, they hated the land and its singing, and soon they would hate her if she continued on. Fear gnawed upon her, and she faltered. A large pack of shadow midlings broke away from NoNo, intrigued by the fear's strength. They loved feasting on joy and love and hope, but fear was nearly as delicious.

"It's good, Daphne. A beautiful start."

Daphne looked to NoNo but he hadn't spoken. He lay still, his eyes closed, though his lips twitched as he sang brokenly.

"Never stop singing, Daphne. I hear your voice, others should too."

She peered through the shadows, but it was impossible to see any distance.

"Who's there?" she called.

No one answered, but she Sensed the answer. The land spoke. She clutched at the thought as one might clutch a precious jewel, awed by its splendor, for every Gray Cloak child knew the legend. As the stories went, the land once spoke audibly to their ancestors, thousands of centuries ago. In recent history, the land could barely muster a straining thought, and to know even that was a triumph. But to hear the land speak? Unthinkable.

Not caring about fears, or shadows, or who might overhear, Daphne burst into song. Delighted that the land spoke to her. Daphne Vale. A girl with no power.

As she sang, a part of her awakened, a part she never knew existed—an ancient and powerful magic dormant inside her. The ability to bind.

Her voice became the dominant one, drowning out NoNo's voice, then rising to match the land's. The shadows screeched, angry, fleeing from NoNo's body and clustering above the singing girl. Their denseness blocked all light from reaching the human and midling huddled there in Hadil's Crossing. But Daphne didn't need light. Power coursed through her, and setting NoNo's body gently aside, she succumbed to an inescapable need to rise to her feet as she sang. The shadows waited, studying, feeding on their own desire, anticipating the flower blossoming before them.

Eyes shining with rapturous joy, Daphne thrust her hands to the heavens, head thrown back in abandonment to the song. It filled her lungs, demanding to be freed, and she let go and danced, swirling through shadows, needing no light or sight, never once faltering, stepping sure-footed across potholes and trenches worn deep by heavily laden wagon wheels. The song became her own as NoNo's voice faltered. A song of forgiveness. All the pent-up anger towards her father, uncle and grandmother. The shame, regret, and lies. Even her mother, for yielding to the lie. She forgave all of them, even herself.

She sang as NoNo had. For the joy that arrives with dawn's first light, banishing night's terror. For her covenant friend, wherever she might be. She sang of NoNo's courage and for her own. She sang for her people and for the truth to come to light.

She even sang for the shadow creatures who violated NoNo's body. A song to heal their wrongness. They howled and whined, throwing themselves upon her. But the song protected her, repelled their attacks. Instead, they feasted on each other, whipped into a frenzy as the song grew in power and love and light.

Without knowing why or how, Daphne's hands swam on currents through the air, to dance a pattern she'd never known or tried. She'd failed every other attempt to perform a binding, but she didn't fail now, and with a final note the song broke in a glorious burst of light. Shadows fled. Those that didn't, dissolved into nothing, hearts falling lifeless to the ground.

Power drained from her, and Daphne collapsed.

Dragging himself an agonizing distance to where she lay, NoNo knew his heart was letting go. Only a few beats remained.

"Not yet!" he cried through gritted teeth.

He wished to thank the girl who'd saved him from a death consumed by shadows, a death that would cheat him of hope and light. He wished to thank her the only way he knew how, so his heart must hold until then.

His power, his gifts, would be hers.

With a final gasping heave, he flopped his head upon her chest and sang his life's song. The song told of his triumphs and joys, of friends and loss, of shame and guilt, of those he'd loved and of those who'd loved him. NoNo sang a final sweet and mournful note, the death note. He took his last breath, before his eyes closed in peace.

Chapter Fifty-Two
The Light Receded

The day little Nezetta witnessed her older sister bawling after being Unfavored, became the day Nezetta's heart chose status and power above all else. It was the day she decided those values were worth more than anyone, or anything, could ever offer. To her new way of thinking, people only disappointed.

Not that any trauma had broken her. She was neither abandoned nor abused as a child. Her father and mother loved her deeply. No, for her, it was a thousand insufferable stings—a friend's small lie, a mentor grading her work as less than perfect, family disappointments, and every breaking of trust no matter how small.

Her heart embraced a level of cynicism unusual at such a young age.

Cold, aloof, she blossomed into a young woman, her friends thinning like autumn leaves in a hard wind, until the branches stood bare. When she drove the last of them away, she built a fortress around her soul—stone walls encircled by a moat and locked behind a door with her heart hid deep inside. Buried where she thought light would never reach.

Until she fell in love.

She doubted his sincerity at first, but he proved his love in a thousand small moments, and she began to heal, the walls of her fortress crumbling stone by stone, each proof of love plugging a tiny hole in her cynical heart, and Nezetta dared allow love in. They made plans to marry, dreamt of their future, of building a life and family together.

He died on her twenty-third hunter's moon, from an illness the healer couldn't explain. Another disappointment. The healer of course, but also the man she'd once loved. That's how she referred to him now—the man—refusing to speak his name, holding him responsible for dying, for disappointing her and leaving her.

It was the last straw and her heart closed tighter than a shrewd merchant's fist. She abandoned all contact unless it served her purpose of becoming Salel, pouring herself into her studies, determined to know more of bindings than any other.

Achieving Salel proved cathartic, a hot searing iron closing up a wound. It stopped the bleeding. The problem lay in the bitterness that festered beneath the scab.

And then Ophel took the bizarre step of bonding her to Aurelia. And Aurelia was in love. Oh, the Dorakian girl hadn't admitted it yet, not even to herself apparently, but Nezetta knew it for what it was, and she loathed it. The quickening pulse, the flushing neck and pounding heart. The desire to be with him when apart. She waited expectantly for Aurelia to be disappointed. When it happened—for it would happen—she wouldn't think any less of the two. Perhaps, Nezetta reasoned, she could offer some level of comfort to the girl when he inevitably broke her heart.

It was on one such evening, as Aurelia's heart beat fervently for Magnus, that Nezetta stepped away from camp. She needed a little space. Not too far, of course. Separation from Aurelia was its own painful agony.

But she could stand for a little time away from people, at the forest's edge, looking out across the plateau. Alone. Like her time in the Tol. A happy memory.

Moonlight sparkled bright, reflecting off the Narthwich below. The air chilled her breath into frost. But it was what she saw, not the air, that chilled her inside.

A great swirling mass of shadows crossing the moon. Blotting out its light for just a moment before it winked back on. She sought to convince herself it was only wispy clouds floating by, or a flock of birds heading west for winter. But she knew that wasn't true.

What she'd seen was hideous, evil, a long trail of blackness that flowed from the distant Capitol, heading her way.

Fast.

As they neared the plateau, she could hear the chittering and screeching of the shadow creatures. She was Salel and their wrongness grated on her soul, Sensing the death they carried with them. And then they were upon her, darkening the woods with their shadows, grasping, clawing as they sought entrance inside her.

"I am the Storm Grazer; you will not defile me!"

Her hands moved in a familiar pattern, a technique she'd mastered during her pilgrimage in the Tol. A beam of light sliced through the trees, the moon's glow both illuminating and protecting her. Terrified by its power, the shadows recoiled, hesitating before realizing it was only moonlight and renewing their assault. They swarmed her, shrieking, popping and hissing as their forms touched the moonlight, but refusing to concede, searching for a vulnerability, certain they'd find one. Had it been sunlight, Nezetta might have shielded herself with a light strong enough to repel. Perhaps then it would have been enough. But the moonlight was too weak, and the shadows' relentless attacks took their toll. The light wavered and flickered.

A nightmare descended on the campsite, shadows enveloping all. Some fought desperately, swinging weapons and fists in a hopeless battle, while others lay kicking, shadows flowing through them. Saul lay motionless except for a leg still twitching. Eken curled into a ball, mouth open in a silent scream, one hand clawing at his head, while the other clutched a pair of crushed spectacles.

At Nezetta's cry, Morco had been the first to reach the edge of camp, and the first to fight back against the encroaching darkness, buying his companions precious time. Those first shadows met a surprisingly powerful will. With a bellowed rage befitting a man his size, Morco charged through camp, drawing the shadow midlings. Abandoning easier targets, they poured into him, breaking down his defenses, though his continued defiance surprised. But even as they brought death to every corner of his mind and heart, he raged against their disease.

His hands seized a heart hidden deep within its shadow and squeezed the life from it. But each moment of resistance only fueled their delight, and for a time, every shadow midling in the camp swirled in and out of Morco's body. When at last they finished, they fled his body, baffled that even at the end, with death so close, he resisted. He staggered forward, a hand outstretched, eyes clouded over, gazing upon a distant land only he could see, before crumpling to the ground.

Nezetta ran headlong into camp, defenses nearly spent. She spotted Aurelia, groping at tendrils of shadows dangling from her nose, her mouth, her eyes and ears as they fed. It appeared she grasped in vain; they laughed, mocking her as they slid by.

Nezetta had seen enough.

"Shadows!" The authority in her voice demanded obedience. "Hear me now. I am the Storm Grazer. You will learn to fear me!"

She reached for Aurelia, drawing shadow and power from her. Taken against their will, the shadow midlings screeched as their feast ended. Aurelia fell to her hands and knees, choking, gasping for air. Nezetta absorbed the power she took from Aurelia and felt the land's desire, to be rid of these shadows, a desire matched keenly by her own.

She turned her attention to the others—most lay twitching, at death's door. One by one, she drew out shadows wriggling and wailing, but Sensed no power to take.

When she came to Morco, she passed on by, for his body housed no shadows and no heartbeat.

Two others surprised her. First, Magnus. An unexpected power. She seized on it, greedily, drank it full until she might burst even as she wrenched out shadows. And then, Eken. He bore an old and ancient power, not as piercing as Magnus' or as full of vigor, but more capable of nuanced action. She delighted in both as the power surged inside, sparked down her legs and arms to her feet and hands. She imagined herself a firebomb set to explode.

The shadows rebuffed, they gathered, considering, preparing a last assault.

But having heard the prophecy since she was a child, Nezetta understood what it meant to be Storm Grazer and the rumors of what the Storm Grazer could do.

"Aurelia, you must come with me!"

It must be both together—Ophel's binding had seen to that. She couldn't go alone where she must go now. The distance would be too great, and the agony of separation too much. She needed full concentration for the task at hand, and she needed the stone hanging around Aurelia's neck.

Aurelia struggled to stand; her face pale, body weak and trembling. What the shadows hadn't taken, Nezetta had.

Nezetta, I need strength.

Through their bond, she Sensed strength and power returning. But she hadn't needed the bond to understand the urgency of Nezetta's command to join her. Their friends were dying, vulnerable to the shadows, and Aurelia would do anything to save them.

"Like this!" shouted Nezetta. Her hands blurred in movement, a pattern the land had never taught, but sometimes one must feel a binding rather than be taught it. There was no choice but to get it right for their lives depended on it. Nezetta's hands flowed and twisted seamlessly, perfectly.

"I see it too!" cried Aurelia, breathless at the image in her mind.

Aurelia, use the stone.

She had no time to wonder at the voice, though she Sensed it was the land. The necklace pendant floated at her chest and she seized it in hand, remembering her father's words—*when all seems lost, use this.*

But I don't know how! I'm just a girl from Dorak.

Hear the pattern and the song. The voice again. Not Nezetta's.

Her mind and heart reached out to the stone and as they did she felt Nezetta reaching too. Power flowing through their bond. Aurelia's fingers twitched, one hand slid across the other, her fingers lacing together in song and somehow, though not fully understanding, she worked the pattern as perfectly as Nezetta.

As their hands flowed and danced, the moonlight waxed in strength. It flooded the woods, the plateau, the fields, across the Narthwich and into the Capitol.

For a long moment it protected their friends, blindingly bright for moonlight as the bewildered shadows flew here and there with nowhere to go but knowing they couldn't stay. They sought refuge under rock, behind twig and leaf, beneath fallen logs, and in pockmarked earth at the plateau's edge. Anywhere to escape the light, though they sensed it wouldn't last.

But the work of Storm Grazer wasn't done. The flash of light merely a prelude, a moment's respite from the fight. Hands twisted, sang fast and sure, dancing intricate patterns of ancient design. A magic stored by the land since the dawning of the first song and imparted now to the Storm Grazer.

Thick, boiling gray clouds gathered, not puffy nor white, but neither black as the shadow midlings, for there was too much light in the storm. Nezetta looked up, her intent obvious, and at the same moment Aurelia realized what needed to be done and wondered at the Sensing of it.

Together they rose, into the air, straight up into the storm.

Winds whipped furiously, howling and shrieking, but the sound proved more delightful than terrifying. Funnels formed, tornadoes blustering and waterspouts drawing from the Narthwich.

Lightning ripped sideways, burst after burst, drawing power from an ancient well of magic, energy swelling, waiting to be sent. The lightning even coursed through the women, though they remained unharmed, for the Storm Grazer's power held the lightning in check.

Together, they sailed higher, above the clouds to where it was quiet.

"Calm your beating heart," said Nezetta, her face bathed in a smile, though her heart beat as wildly as Aurelia's in sheer awe of the storm.

"It feels like it could burst," shouted Aurelia into the quiet, her hearing slow to return, a smile plastered across her face too. It was impossible not to be intoxicated in the moment. *If Father could see me now*

The storm still gathered strength below, and they could feel the power nearing its zenith. Even the silence in which they drifted cracked from time to time, invaded by thunder and wind and lightning seeking release. As far as eye could see the storm gathered.

Does it cover the world? wondered Aurelia.

The women laughed, delighted, their bond as sharp and sweet as ever it would be. Enraptured by a moment they would always share.

"Are you with me, Aurelia?" asked Nezetta. Amplified by power, her voice carried easily above the storm.

"I am! I am with you!" shouted Aurelia in anticipation, with a longing to return and save her friends. *Magnus, Eken ... hold on. We're coming.*

"Then let us send these cursed shadows back to whatever foul pit they came from!"

As one, they extended arms and hands, fingers outstretched. Lightning crackled and spat, flowed over them and through them, straining the tips of their fingers, their eyes blazing with light. An immense power consumed them, ancient and mysterious.

They dove, free-falling through mist and cloud toward the earth, yet completely in control. They halted above the treetops as the storm raged.

Light ceased. Far across the stretches of the land, even to Perinith and the Twelve Isles. There was no corner of the world light touched, for the Storm Grazer consumed all light and a void so black filled the land that even the shadows recoiled in fear.

And then as one, Aurelia and Nezetta released the power they held.

Light blazed bright and fierce. Thunder rumbled unceasingly as lightning burned across the sky into Aurelia and Nezetta, bursting from their fingertips, their eyes and ears and mouths.

Shadows withered and died, hearts seared clean in half by lightning, never to beat again, for even the shadow midlings themselves ceased to exist as light erased them from time and memory.

The light receded, and moonlight, the dullest ever seen by human eyes, dared replace it.

Chapter Fifty-Three
Not Since the Red War

Daphne had believed NoNo couldn't die. What could kill such a creature? But seeing him lie so still, Daphne knew he was gone.

She had awoken dazed, disoriented. Not feeling quite herself.

How long have I been out?

It was late, sunfall, an unseen hand stretching night's blanket over the land.

NoNo's head rested in her lap, his face peaceful in death. He looked so small and frail, less than he'd been, and a gaping hole revealed the remnants of a heart that would never beat again. She tried to rouse him, refusing to believe he was gone. Her tears bled like sap from a tree's bark onto his matted fur, as her fists struck his lifeless body, begging him to come back.

But there was no coming back.

After a time, she stood, gathered his small form into her arms. *Why did I even sing?* It seemed such a bitter thing to be for nothing. Too little. Too late. A marvelous creature dead.

She cradled NoNo's body against her chest, stumbling down from Hadil's Crossing, wandering, lost, unsure of her next move, or what to do with his remains, but determined to honor him. She vaguely recalled something about a mission, but in light of NoNo's death it seemed rather insignificant.

When night fell, sleep came in fitful spurts. She still clutched the midling tight and dreamt of shadows and song and light.

Awoke more sure of herself. Remembered her mission, its urgency, and knew she had little time. But her body couldn't tell whether she'd slept a day, or two ... or more. *Where is Onyx?*

Hurrying across field and forest, she realized the world looked ... different, the colors more vibrant, a bird's trill pure and sweet. The land hummed with an energy she didn't remember existing before. *Or is it me?* She couldn't tell.

A Gray Cloak found her wandering the woods. She didn't know the man, but knew immediately he was a Gray Cloak. Not just by his stone or cloak, but by his aura of power. The Sensing of it heady, and for a moment the earth spun, tilted dangerously, she closed her eyes and when she opened them again, the world had stopped spinning.

"I'm Njal."

He glanced briefly at the stone lodged in her forehead, but had eyes only for the bundle she carried, laid a reverent hand on NoNo's body, recognized it for what it was, though he'd never seen a midling before.

"Could I?" he asked, his hands extended, pleading.

Daphne shook her head. "It's my duty, and mine alone."

"I'll take you to our encampment then," offered Njal, "perhaps Gyda will know how to honor a midling's passing."

"My mother?" exclaimed Daphne. "My mother's there?"

"Ah, so you're Daphne?" Njal studied her, glanced again at her stone, at the bundle she carried. "You're not what I expected, based on -" The words hung in the air, he cleared his throat, words tumbling, "Uh, right, um ... yes, your mother, Gyda, she's there, been searching the old writings."

"What do you mean?"

"To find answers, of course," said Njal. Daphne's puzzled look must have betrayed her confusion. "To the two mysteries? Three days past?" When she shrugged, he sighed. "Have you been shut away in a cave?"

"I, um, got knocked out," said Daphne. "Onyx threw me." Njal's turn to appear confused. Daphne rushed to explain, "My horse. Have you seen a black stallion?" Njal shook his head. Daphne's turn to sigh. "Tell me of these mysteries then, while you take me to my mother."

Njal's eyes burned with fervor as he recounted the first mystery, unfolding three days prior. An ancient song, in an unknown language, shattered the pre-dawn stillness. It resonated over forest and marsh, surging across mountains and into villages and homes, filling its hearers with wonder.

Daphne trembled at Njal's telling, but remained silent, unsure what to say. *Was this mine and NoNo's song?* Even if it were, what did she understand of it herself? And if it weren't, how prideful to assume the story was hers.

She trembled most for the number of days lost according to Njal's telling, her mind insisting the tale couldn't be theirs, but knowing in her heart it was, and if true, then she'd been unconscious far too long and had failed her people.

Tears threatened, but there were none left, they'd all been spent on NoNo.

As for the second event, resumed Njal, taking her silence as an encouragement to continue, it followed the mysterious song. On the same day but in the late evening. A breathtaking spectacle. A void of pure black, a darkness so absolute that many feared the light would never return. But it did, in a display of glory unlike anything seen, perhaps, since the founding of the world. It consumed the western sky before spreading north, east and south, accompanied by rumbling thunder and jagged lightning. The light blazed bright and glorious and died as quickly as it had appeared.

Daphne wondered at the hearing of the second story, though for reasons she couldn't explain, knew it involved her friends. She prayed they yet lived.

She found her mother buried in books and ancient manuscripts, poring over their pages. They hugged and cried and laughed, a relieved Gyda grateful to reconnect with her daughter and a relieved Daphne grateful to learn her father was away at a meeting of High Mages in another Gray Cloak camp.

"I failed, Mother," said Daphne, resting her head on the familiar shoulder, recounting the tale of her meeting with the King and her subsequent loss of time.

"Hush, hush, dear one," said Gyda. "What's done is done, and you did all you could. It was an impossible task; I'd say the King meant it that way. Now, let me get a good look at you."

Gyda held her daughter at arm's length, eyes squinting, nose wrinkled in concentration, studying her daughter and the metallic black stone in her forehead until her mouth parted in wonder. Daphne told her haltingly of NoNo's death at the shadows' hands, and of the song she'd sung with him.

"When did this happen?" Gyda fixed her daughter with a suspicious stare, an understanding dawning on her face.

Daphne gulped. "I don't know. Really, I don't. I was out, knocked out cold. Don't know how much time passed. I didn't think it was long." To pretend was easy. She wasn't ready to face the truth of the changes she felt.

Gyda didn't appear convinced, but she nodded—the way mothers do when letting a child tell a story. She glanced again at the creature in Daphne's arms. "A midling should be buried where the land sings most powerfully."

Lumath.

Despite its desecration by the Ka, the thought of its charred landscape somehow seemed fitting as NoNo's last resting place.

"Njal tells me you've been searching the old writings."

"I have, and I found something." Gyda dug through the pile of books, plucked one out and rifled through its pages. "A piece of the Storm Grazer prophecy. Ah, here it is: *When sung Hope's Dawning, when felt Void's Night and beheld Flame's Light, look to the horizon to witness the Storm Grazer Rising.* Now I don't know whether what we heard was Hope's Dawning or whether what we witnessed was Void's Night and Flame's Light, but could it be?"

The question hung unanswered in the air.

The following morning, Daphne departed early for Lumath. It would be a full day's journey, but she didn't walk alone. A crowd followed, so many that she marveled at its size. She assumed they came to witness the burial of a midling, and in part they did, but had she overheard their whispers she would have known they felt drawn to her. To the ancient power emanating from her.

Njal begged again for the honor of carrying the midling body, and this time she relented. He assumed the head of the solemn procession, joined by Daphne, with the swelling crowd close behind.

When Lumath's volcanic cone came into view, a cauldron of emotions bubbled inside Daphne. Precious memories of time spent in Lumath and terrifying ones too of the Ka's attack. They scaled the hill and entered the thicket, the sight of the bridge peculiar to Daphne, though Aurelia had told her of its existence.

She steeled herself, anticipating what was to come. Aurelia warned her that though the flames spared the garden, the Ka had desecrated its hallowed ground, felling trees to build their bridge. She expected stumps, and indeed there were. Too many to count. But her heart leaped at the sight of new blooms, most small and still fragile, sprouting from a stump here or there, in colors that sparkled, vibrant, unusual, surpassing anything the garden had ever offered.

As she walked the garden wilds path, her gaze shifted toward the babbling stream and she stifled a surprised cry at her reflection. The gray stone she'd received from Tobwhit was now a metallic, nearly-black color. Her face, too, appeared different. She couldn't say what exactly, grappling with the thought, but it was as if she'd aged just a little overnight.

At the garden's edge, a tall bloom, grown faster than any other, where an apple hung, strangely orange in color. She Sensed the garden's invitation to pluck and eat. She sank her teeth into it, the taste sweet, but not too. The flesh crisp, but not overly. In short, it was the most perfect bite of apple she'd ever had. She savored the juice, tempted to remain in the garden and wait for more fruit to bud.

But a question tickled her brain. One that only a firsthand look at Lumath's fields could answer, and for a fleeting moment, she allowed hope to flourish.

Can it be?

It was.

She wept. Tears of joy for Lumath and what it might again one day be. It wasn't that the scars of hate and evil had vanished—perhaps there would always be vestiges of those in Lumath, reminders of what unchecked evil can do—but here and there amidst the charred swath of land, fluttered patches of grasses and grains and stalks, while grasshoppers the size of her fist dangled from their ends, and the stalks bore a wondrous budding mix of pea pods, millet, chickpeas, fennel and sage, vetch and parsnips, ears of corn and amaranth grain. It was as if, in their hurry to grow, the fields had welcomed every possible seed borne in on boots and feathers.

Perhaps more spectacular was the sight of trees. Not massive yet as the ones that once dotted Lumath's field, in which her people built their Uppers, but still unusually large for less than a moon's cycle of growth.

But there was more than merely growth of flora. A gathering of workers, the contented hum and chatter of rebuilding, some discussing plans, while others added to a growing pile of stones, and still others applied mortar to stone in what appeared to be the first wall of a home.

Most shocking of all was the sight of those gathered that day.

Midlings.

Of all shapes and sizes.

And the midlings weren't alone. Daphne spotted a Dorakian, and a Gray Cloak. A Lavonshian with obvious Capitol garb. A woman with a full-length beard. And Daphne laughed, delighted. *A Perinithian woman, the stories are true!*

Her fists clenched when she spotted a Ka soldier trailing a midling. A warning shout formed in her throat until she realized the man carried no weapon. In place of a sword, he carried a trowel and a pail of mortar.

The workers paused, curious about the newest arrivals.

A pair of midlings, accompanied by a young man, approached. A stone in the young man's forehead made it apparent he was a Gray Cloak, but the cloak was gone, replaced by a simple tunic. Sweat glistened his forehead and his hands were stained dark from mortar. The two midlings with him could not have been more different. One was small in stature and resembled a rabbit. The other significantly taller, towering over the man and the shorter midling. This creature's face looked very much like a bear that had once invaded Daphne's village, though its body didn't carry the same bulky, bear-like size. Instead, it was lean and muscular with a fine covering of hair, a body more like a mountain lion than a bear.

Regardless of appearance, she Sensed both possessed extraordinary abilities. These were no ordinary creatures but were highly intelligent, and within them lived a wellspring of power.

Daphne had so many questions she wasn't sure where to begin. She began with the obvious.

"What's the meaning of all this?" she asked, the sweep of her hand indicating not just the rebuilding, but the strange mix of humans and midlings.

"We can't explain it really," said the young man. "Each of us, in his or her own way, drawn here. I arrived yesterday? No, that's not right. Two days ago sounds right. Or was it three?"

He didn't direct the question to her, but to the midlings with him, who seemed as confused by the timetable. The bear-lion stared perplexed at a paw, counting and recounting his great hooked claws, while the rabbit cocked its head to the side, ears twitching.

"Honestly, don't think it matters," resumed the young man, scratching his head, puzzled by the realization before his face brightened. "Time just doesn't mean much here. We're all chipping in to rebuild."

Daphne marveled at the thought of all manner of Lavonshians, together. *And with midlings.* Though how the Perinithians had reached Lumath in only a few days, from across the sea, confounded her.

"The name's Kentic," said the man.

"Ferca," offered the bear in a surprisingly smooth, honey-laced voice, placing a paw to her chest.

"And I'm Hilnon," the rabbit added in a deep gravely voice, bowing so low to the ground his giant ears flopped forward, the weight of them nearly toppling the rabbit over. If not for the creature's ancient presence deserving respect, Daphne might have laughed at the sight.

"Those gathered here," continued Kentic, "have appointed the three of us as the high council. To promote peace and resolve disputes. Though there've been none."

"Indeed, there haven't," Ferca picked up the story, waving her paw towards the workers, "Humans from across Lavonshia and beyond, and midlings who've lived in hiding for centuries—laboring side by side with joy in our common goal: to rebuild Lumath from the ashes of death."

The mention of death reminded Daphne of the burden they carried. She looked at the bundle in Njal's arms, her heart heavy again. Rebuilding Lumath wouldn't bring back NoNo.

"May I take him?" asked Ferca, though her tone implied it as a statement, not a question. Njal placed the body in Ferca's able paws. NoNo looked so small against the bear's chest.

The bear-like midling hoisted the body high above her head, then turned and walked solemnly towards the gathered workers. They moved aside, letting Ferca pass, her burden held aloft. So they would all see him. So they would all remember. Heads bowed in respect, and many knelt as she went by. Njal made as if to follow, but Daphne placed a restraining hand on his shoulder. This wasn't their moment.

A midling worker sang one mournful note. That was all. No one spoke or joined in the singing. The note hung on the air for some time until the wind carried it away. Perhaps elsewhere in the world, human or midling would stop and listen and know what it meant.

Ferca returned to Njal, to Daphne, the same way she'd gone. Her smile soft, her paws gentle, as she placed the body in Daphne's hands. She turned to face the gathered crowd, her words kind but firm carrying across the field: "Tears are proper today, but only today. When you think next of NoNo, dwell on his sacrifice and take courage. When you remember him, ask those who knew him best for his life's stories. For he lived a long life and a good one. We honor him here today."

Without needing to be asked, a worker began digging. No one spoke, not even to whisper, as Daphne laid his body in the grave. Her tears wet the soil prepared for him.

Not since the Red War had a midling died.

Chapter Fifty-Four
You Are

They buried Morco under a willow tree on the banks of the Narthwich.

Aurelia cried as they lowered his body into the ground, burying her face in Magnus' chest while he wrapped his arms around her. Col pretended not to notice.

Eken cried as bravely as Aurelia.

They all did, more or less.

Saul shared a story about Morco, involving a jumping game and a chair. The story fell flat for Nezetta and the Dorakians, but the ex-Ka found it funny.

Aurelia told of how she'd watched a giant of a man care for her friend, becoming Daphne's protector for a time.

A gentle mist accompanied their sorrow, carried on a warm breeze. A promise that spring would return after the coming winter.

Gray clouds, blessedly normal gray clouds, gathered in the distance, though Aurelia and Nezetta couldn't help but stare and wonder, a secret remembering of what they'd experienced together.

Through gritted teeth, favoring ribs still healing from the gallow's encounter, Tobias sang a Ka dirge only the ex-soldiers knew. The others didn't mind. It was a fitting tribute. A song of friendship and sacrifice. When he finished, there were no dry eyes gathered around the grave.

Aurelia took the frit carving Morco had given her those many days ago and tucked it between his lifeless fingers before they covered his body with dirt.

Fatal choices bury men. The whisper passed through the gathering unnoticed, settling only in Magnus' mind. His hands trembled as he placed a large rock at the head of the grave. Seizing the wind's power to use as a chisel, Nezetta etched words of remembrance deep into the rock:

Morco, a warrior, and champion among men.
Sacrificed his life for his friends.

"I'll come back."

"Promise?"

They sat by the edge of the Narthwich watching a pair of ducks battle the river's current. Despite the cool temperature, Aurelia had removed her shoes and dipped her toes into the water. *Isn't that cold?* Magnus had asked. *Absolutely yes,* her response—he sensed she wanted to laugh but couldn't find the voice to. Then she added, *but no colder than Applemere Lake you made us cross.*

The same mist from earlier still hung thick in the air, beading droplets of water on Aurelia's hair and skin. While she watched the ducks, Magnus watched her, committing that moment, her image, to memory. The tone of her skin, the worried look in her eyes, mouth left slightly open after she'd answered his question, the way a strand of hair she'd tucked earlier behind her ear had come loose.

"You know I'd rather stay with you, pot drummer." He took her hand in his. "But my family needs to know I'm okay. They'd have been expecting me more than twice an eight-day ago."

He left her there by the riverbank, a lonely silhouette framed by the mist. He was eager to be on his way, and just as eager to return.

"When ...?"

Magnus stood in the doorway, refusing to believe the news.

His arrival hadn't been met with the enthusiasm he expected. His sisters' welcome muted. Their reception bothered him until he learned the reason for it.

"Four days now. Hasn't said a word, hasn't eaten ... the healer says ... she ..."

Grief-stricken, Magnus' father buried his face in his hands. He sat by his daughter's bedside. A bedside he hadn't left in four days, where Magnus' youngest sister Ella lay, her skin pale and yellowing, eyes closed, breathing shallow.

"If I'd only been here," said Magnus, a tight knot forming in his throat, "I could have -"

"There's nothing you could have done." His father stood to face his only son and embraced him fiercely. Together, father and son, they wept.

Deep below the Capitol, Morcant stooped at the pit, shoulders hunched, head drooping. He kicked at a loose rock, listened for its sound when it broke upon the pit's bottom, though he didn't care. Not even when the dark stain called. It pulsed achingly, desiring his touch, his power, to shape it and remake it. As he had done now for the past many moon cycles. But today his heart wasn't in it.

He could Sense his children's death. Their slaughter.

He'd also Sensed the power that caused it.

First, a song. Morcant recognized in it something of Kynth-palla and he detested the song and everything it represented. When it finished, he knew his children's pain, Sensing their fear as they fled, Sensing that some had died because of the song, for he could no longer feel those who were gone.

But then, more ancient than the song, a troubling power. One he didn't know and didn't recognize. A blazing light that bathed the Capitol and beyond in a light brighter than the sun. And with its coming, the most horrid of death knells sounded by his children. In an instant, thousands dead. Not just their hearts but their shadows too. Gone forever. The power troubled him greatly.

"Master."

"My children!" Delighted, Morcant beckoned his shadow midlings near, these few who had survived Kynth-palla's song.

They needed little encouragement, swarming up through the pit and embracing him. He released a portion of his power, allowing them to feed off it. They were so weak and so needy.

"There, there," Morcant caressed and encouraged them. "All will be okay. You failed me, but I will remake you. Next time, you shall defeat the one who sings. And the one who brings a storm of light."

"He is dead already," the shadows whispered. "The Song-Bringer."

"We consumed him."

"But She has absorbed his song."

"The Flower."

"Yes, She is powerful."

"You failed us."

"We fear Her."

"You made us weak. Our beating hearts, our doom."

"You're to blame."

Morcant felt a stab of fear as the fingers of a shadow tugged at one of his stones. A second probed at another stone. He could Sense their anger and their thirst for power. Perhaps even at his expense.

The stones didn't dislodge, but the very thought of losing one was agony itself. For a moment he faltered, weeping at the thought and crippled by fear. But gathering courage, he called on his power. He would not show weakness.

"No, my children. I did not fail you. The stain did. It is not as resilient as we'd hoped."

The shadows considered the thought, pulsing, weaving around his body. Their presence still intoxicated, though he didn't care for their line of questioning.

"It is not I who failed you, but you -"

"No." As one, the shadows rebuked their maker.

"It is you."

"Always you."

"Not the stain."

"You made us."

"The stain is strong."

"You are arrogant."

"The stain is us."

"You failed us."

The shadows pounced, battering his chest, his arms and legs, everywhere the stones were bound. He cried out, backed away, slipped at the edge, and plummeted into the pit. The shadows surged after him, drowning out his cries as they engulfed him, entering his body, angry, feeding.

Morcant summoned his powers once more, feeding upon the shadows as they fed on him, laughter bubbling, bursting from his throat unsummoned, reverberating off pit walls, echoing across an empty cavern. But there was no one to hear or to witness the feeding.

Ella hadn't moved, not even a muscle twitch, despite his efforts to wake her. *I'm home,* he'd said. *Your brother's here.* He told her he loved her, and if she'd only wake, they could play her favorite games and sing her favorite songs. But she didn't answer, didn't move; she only lay still. Dying. Beyond help.

Magnus knew the yellow death would take her, knew because he'd seen these same signs before. With his mother. He witnessed anew how carefully his father sat by the bedside. As close as possible without touching, for healers claimed the sweat of yellow death transferred the disease.

When it was over, when she no longer breathed, they would come for her, as they had for his mother. They would come bound head to toe in clothes they would later burn, along with her body, her bedding, and anything she'd touched since falling ill.

When the waiting weighed too heavy, Magnus left his sister's bedside. In his old room, he stared at the four walls. A room smaller than he remembered. Time away had forever changed him, as had his experiences in the Ka. He was not the same young man he'd been when he left three hunter's moons ago.

Throwing his pack in the corner, he flopped down onto his old bed.

"Feels smaller, doesn't it?"

Magnus winced as he shot up in bed and slammed his head against the ceiling. He'd forgotten it sloped so low. The pain vanished at the sight of Sungam standing in the corner.

"You wouldn't know anything about it," said Magnus.

"Actually, I do. Because I'm you," replied Sungam. "I have your memories, to a point."

"I can't deal with this right now. My sister is dying, if not already dead."

"She still lives, though not for long." Sungam picked idly at a piece of loose mortar in the wall. "What would you give to keep her safe?"

"Anything," Magnus declared, leaping across the room with surprising speed and seizing Sungam's collar, demanding with cold unflinching eyes, "Is there a way?"

"For a price, yes." Gingerly, Sungam peeled back Magnus' fingers, brushed his tunic clean as if Magnus had made it filthy.

"Tell me. I'll pay anything."

"One day I'll ask a favor, one you mustn't deny me. In that moment, you'll repay your debt."

"What kind of favor?"

"I can't say; even I don't know yet what it will be. But in that moment you cannot refuse me, as compulsion will force your concession even if you are not willing. Then, and only then, will I release you from your debt. Do you agree to the terms?"

"But you can save her?"

"I can."

Magnus thought of his father waiting for his youngest to die. He thought of his sisters watching their sister die. He thought of Ella and the life she had yet to live. There was nothing else to consider.

"I agree."

Sungam drew a knife tucked hidden inside his boot and seized Magnus' hand before he could change his mind. He drew the knife across the palm, Magnus wincing as blood welled up through the cut. Sungam did the same to his own palm, though his blood ran thick, a red so dark it was nearly black.

Magnus drew back at the sight, but Sungam held his wrist firm and placed a bloodied palm against Magnus' own.

"It's done."

"That's all? I felt nothing."

Sungam shrugged. "It's not for me to say what you feel. But know that you will re-pay me. One day. Now go to your sister; the magic is already at work."

"Magnus! Your sister ... Magnus!" At the sound of his father's voice, Magnus ran from the room.

Eken found Aurelia sitting by the Narthwich, knees drawn up beneath her. She was as likely to be found here as anywhere these past few days, as if she thought being in the place she'd last seen Magnus might bring him back sooner.

Mist and rain had yet to relent since he'd gone. Today it fell in a steady drizzle, her hair and clothes drenched, but she didn't seem to care. Her eyes remained fixed to the west. Toward the Plains.

Eken sat beside her, fiddling with his ruined spectacles as he stared across the water. Farther upriver, Col fished for their dinner with a willow rod and line dangling from it.

It was the first quiet moment they'd had, and Eken found himself unsure what to say or how to comfort her. He needn't have worried; she spoke first.

"Do you think he's okay?" She asked. Eken hesitated, glad he did, as she clarified, "My father. Do you think he's okay?"

"I'm certain of it. Mahan's a tough nut. You know that."

"And Magnus? He said it was a day's journey. I thought he'd be back by now."

Eken scratched at the stubble on his chin and stared at his reflection in the Narthwich, the beard coming in thin.

"You worry too much," he said.

Am I any better? If forced to admit it, he grew the beard to hide from the shadows, in case they returned. Perhaps then they wouldn't recognize him, wouldn't remember how easily they'd infiltrated his mind and soul. It was a silly idea, but it kept him from the razor.

Aurelia sighed. "And the shadows? We beat them once, but what if they come back? And if we can't summon such power once more? I don't know if I can face them again. I've never felt evil like that. What were they?"

Eken thought for a moment, searching the knowledge jumbled in his brain. Images and memories of page after page, line after line of text, swam through his mind, but he couldn't recall anything he'd read on the subject. He shrugged, disappointed he couldn't help. *What's the point of reading all those books if they don't prove useful?*

"And I'm worried about Daphne," added Aurelia when he didn't answer. "Where did she go? What is she facing? Is she alone?"

"She's okay, I'm sure of it," although he wasn't.

"At least we had the Storm Grazer on our side." Aurelia sighed again, though this time it seemed a grateful sigh, rather than a worried one. "Without her, we'd be dead. Daphne first told me about the prophecy—I can't wait to tell her I've met the Storm Grazer!"

A memory fell into place inside Eken's brain. Details he'd read about the Storm Grazer. Lines of text on a page.

What was it?

He searched his mind for the book's title. Titles swam in and out of focus, books piled high, every space in his mind filled to overflowing.

If I could just ... He probed a corner of his thoughts, grabbed the title he was looking for. *Ah, there it is. The Storm Grazer Revealed: as told by Drustan the Wise, 328th Bookkeeper.*

He recalled it being a tiny book, tucked between the pages of a much larger, dusty old tome. A book unopened for many long centuries. He remembered the important details though. Drustan the Wise prophesying the Storm Grazer would be a girl. Born in a Dorakian village. Raised by a man she called father. A girl who never knew her mother. Until a day would come when events would force her to leave Dorak at great peril to herself and her friends.

He turned to stare at Aurelia, his mouth agape. His hand clutched excitedly at the worn book in his tunic pocket, a book thinner than before, missing many pages.

"What?" she asked.

"Aurelia, what did you feel when you went into the clouds? With Nezetta?"

"I um ..." Her eyes turned distant, unfocused. "It's hard to describe really. I was afraid, I think. Angry too, and ... I felt power. Immense, ancient power."

"From Nezetta ... or coming from you?"

"From Nezetta, of course!" She snapped, twirling a length of hair in her fingers. Thunder rumbled overhead. "I think. Or the stone. Oh, I don't know!" She squirmed, looked away. "It was all so much, and I was terrified of losing everyone I cared for. How can I explain what it's like to ascend above the clouds? To feel and see what I did."

She stopped, took a deep breath, stared at her lap, perhaps unwilling to admit the truth.

"Nezetta isn't the Storm Grazer," said Eken.

"What do you mean?" Aurelia glanced up, her eyes spoke her refusal still to accept the truth. "Of course she is!"

"No. You are."

Chapter Fifty-Five
Across the Narthwich Bridge

Morcant crawled through a jagged hole and fell headlong into Hadil's Crossing, grunting as a bone snapped and punctured his skin. It was a grunt of surprise, not of pain, for where blood should have poured, shadows leaked. He staggered to his feet, stared uncomprehending at an arm covered with an oil-thick black ooze. It clung to him like it would never leave. *Perhaps it won't.* His throat tightened, though it wasn't panic but shadows swimming his airways. His lungs screamed until he realized he didn't need air, that the shadows sustained him. He felt their presence inside and knew their need to consume, though his power held their consuming at bay.

He stumbled clear of the gap, skirted Hiedorn, trudged onward through the King's Forest. *My bedchamber. Rest. A bath.* Thoughts of home fueled him. Perhaps sanity would return and he'd awaken from this nightmare.

A pond shimmered, just ahead, though he wasn't thirsty. Or hungry. *How odd.* He trudged to its edge, his legs like watered-down mortar, every movement unnatural, stiff. Not because he was tired, for he wasn't. Rather it was as if the legs were new to him, like muscles he'd never stretched or used.

In the pond's mirror-like surface his eyes found a reflection he didn't recognize. His face reminded him of melted steel he'd once worked as a boy. Though where that slag had been fiery oranges and reds, his face was blackened by an oily sludge and swirling shadows. He could just make out a pair of eyes, bits of a nose and a mouth and ears, but only just. Shadows oozed from every orifice, but when he tried to brush them away he realized the shadows were a part of him. He scraped at the oily sludge but it only transferred to his hand, clinging stubbornly to his fingers. He stared again at the reflection in the pond, mesmerized by it.

Somewhere deep inside he knew he should be horrified, but he couldn't bring himself to feel any horror. *Or any emotion really.* He would have chuckled but couldn't. Only the need to consume existed. *What am I?*

Morcant pushed on, never tiring, walking through the night, reaching a crossroads where a signpost bore a crude drawing of an arrow and the word *Capitall* seared into it.

Feed us.

The shadows spoke and he trudged west, towards the spires and towers of the Capitol thrusting skyward—a beacon bright—high above the King's Forest, the Plains and the Narthwich River.

Aurelia Sensed Magnus drawing close, Sensed him before she could even see him. She knew Nezetta felt the excitement and wondered at its source, but didn't ask.

It was a windy day, abnormally so, and it whistled through her hair, black tresses billowing as Aurelia raced down the slope and across the Narthwich bridge.

Magnus.

Will he notice I'm different?

She certainly had. Slowly at first, and in little things. The way an electric current in a far-off storm tickled her skin. The way clouds gravitated towards her, so much so that she'd begun to miss the sun. The way raindrops tasted. She wouldn't admit it to a soul, but she could taste the storm and the clouds, knew where they came from and what they'd seen.

But it was more than that, more than storms and electric currents. The experiences since Chelam had forever changed her—she knew it, *felt* it, and wasn't sure she liked it. It was the way thunder rumbled when she snapped at a friend. She'd led a charmed life in Chelam and had little reason to snap before. Life then was pleasant, worries simpler. What fields to plant. Which crops to harvest. Whether to dance with Col at the Harvest Festival. But the worries were different now. Burying Morco had seen to that. She spent more of her days worrying how soon the shadows might return, whether she could protect her friends, and whether Daphne still lived.

Then Magnus was there, at the top of a rise, taking the slope at a brisk jog that broke into a flat-out run. She could Sense the smile on his face before she was close enough to see it. Who cared that sour-souled Nezetta lurked somewhere in the background?

"I missed you," he said.

She looked at him, really looked at him, and he seemed different too. She shrugged it off—her perception of the world and everything in it had changed—and returned his smile, took the hand he offered, an unassuming *I'm here. For you. To defend and care for you* kind of hand, so different from a hand offered at a Harvest Festival dance, and together they walked back across the Narthwich bridge.

Enjoyed the story?

The best way to support this book is by leaving a quick review on Amazon or Goodreads.

Even a sentence or two makes a huge difference and helps other readers discover the story.

Thank you for reading.

Visit my website *ericmunger.com* and sign up for my newsletter to receive exclusive bonus content, short stories, and updates on the forthcoming release of Book Two of The Lavonshia Chronicles:

Storm Grazer Forsaken.

Pre-orders available soon!

Acknowledgements

This book would not exist without the people who walked beside me through every storm and blank page. To Jessica—my wife, best friend, constant encourager, sounding board, travel companion, and the heart behind every mile of this journey—thank you for believing in me and my writing long before the Storm Grazer's world of Lavonshia had a name. To my family and friends who cheered me on and regularly asked for updates, thank you for your love and support! To my Beta Readers, you rock! Your discussing content with me, giving suggestions, and providing feedback proved immensely helpful. To my ARC readers, thank you for jumping on board and for your reviews of the book that encourage and support this author! And to the readers stepping into Lavonshia for the first time: thank you. I am thrilled to share the Storm Grazer world with you.

About the Author

Eric Munger is a fantasy author who writes stories of forgotten magic, shadowed prophecy, and reluctant heroes. He is the creator of The Lavonshia Chronicles, an epic fantasy series beginning with his debut novel *Storm Grazer Rising* and continuing with his upcoming second release, *Storm Grazer Forsaken*. When he isn't shaping new worlds, he and his wife often find themselves travelling, gathering inspiration from mountains, deserts, forests, and forgotten places along the way.

GLOSSARY

Abinthar Gorge

A valley bordered by the Ferini Cliffs and the Tol Mountains. It ends in an unpleasant marsh.

Applemere Lake

A large body of water in Dorak, fondly known as Applemere Lake for the numerous apple orchards surrounding it. Every year, during a three-day span mid-summer, all of Chelam turns out to Applemere Lake for the Lake Day Festival.

Ascension

The point at which a Gray Cloak receives a stone and becomes an Honored One.

Ashrot

A horrific spreading of a blight that ruins crops, rotting them through and making them inedible. Crops with ashrot take on an "ashy" look as they rot, thus the name. No one knows where ashrot comes from or why it starts. Most recently, it led to a two-year famine in Lavonshia.

Awakening

The process by which an Honored One becomes Salel. Few undertake it, few understand it. Shrouded in mystery, those who are awakened speak little of it. It is only known that they are Salel, and have Knit with the land.

Belanor's Cave

A large cave used by Gray Cloaks as a place of refuge and rest in their travels. With a narrow opening, it's easily defended. A stream inside provides an ideal water source.

Binder (Binding)

A binder uses the innate magical ability that lies within, and channeled through their saphyr stone, to perform a binding with elements of the land, thereby bending those elements to their will.

Breckei Valley

A primary route connecting Gray Cloak lands and Dorak.

Bresha

A red-tipped fern. Its fronds are harvested and used for healing purposes, to fight infection and aid in the healing of burns and wounds. Typically applied as a poultice.

Brightbeetle

An insect with a glowing abdomen pouch. Found throughout Lavonshia. Gathering a sufficient number in a lidded glass vessel allows those of little means to use them as a cheap source of light. Hunters and trackers also use them to leave glowing trail markers for others to follow.

Capitol

The political and cultural heart of Lavonshia, where the King and his palace reside. World famous for its three markets: the Grand Bazaar, Merchant's Row, and the River Market.

Chelam

One of the largest of all Dorakian villages. The home of Mahan and his daughter Aurelia, along with her friends Eken and Col.

Chockberries

A fruit with an elusive taste that's never quite ripe.

Clans

Gray Cloak society is divided into three clans—Fi-jal, Fi-tor, and Fi-dun—each with its own seat of power.

Cloaking Ceremony

A ceremony in which a newly ascended Gray Cloak, having bonded to their saphyr stone, is presented with the traditional gray cloak of an Honored One.

Covenant Friend

"I covenant to be your faithful friend, to be true as the night star. To give counsel where counsel is needed, to be silent where silence is needed. To utter only truth. This I covenant." – a declaration uttered by a Gray Cloak in choosing their very closest friend. Declaring an individual to be a covenant friend is considered a sacred honor within their community. The full implications of covenant friends are not well understood. Some say it can form a magical bond.

Decri

Lavonshia's monetary unit, the coins are comprised primarily of copper. The decri is used in the Plains, Tol Mountains, Highlands, the King's Forest and Capitol; whereas the eastern portion of the realm, such as in Dorakian villages and amongst Gray Cloak clans, primarily use a bartering system. The Twelve Isles, a protectorate of Lavonshia, also uses the decri. The island of Perinith, being an independent nation, has its own monetary system based on silver mined on Perinith. The exchange rate is typically twelve decri for one silver Perinithian coin.

Divesting

A rarely utilized punishment in Gray Cloak society, reserved for Honored Ones who abuse their powers and take advantage of other Honored Ones and Gray Cloaks. Divesting is a severe form of punishment as it severs the stone from its bearer, resulting in their death.

Dorak (Dorakians)

Rolling hill country east of the Capitol, known for orchards, farming, and frequent festivals. Dorakians are a hardy, welcoming people, who due to their proximity to Gray Cloaks (their northern neighbors) maintain friendly, though infrequent, relations with them.

Eight-Day

A manner of time-keeping in Lavonshia. A literal period of time that encompasses eight days.

Elders (High Elders)

Dorakian villages are governed by Elders, six of whom serve as High Elders. (High Elders can also be the male head of a Hearth Family household, though this is not a requirement.)

Elder Conclaves

Every other moon cycle, the Elders meet to discuss the mundane workings of a Dorakian village. The meetings are long and tedious, notes recorded in the Book Of Meetings, also known as The Records, giant tomes that each span a dozen hunter's moons worth of meetings.

Elder-Mother

A term of respect used by younger Honored Ones when speaking to an older mentor.

Eldihi

A mythical herd of stags, led by Belanor, a mighty beast with a many-pointed crown, thick golden fur, and the stamina of a dozen Eldihi stags. Belanor gave his life protecting his herd.

Far-Seers

Little is known of Far-Seers, where they come from, how they came about their ability to see distances no human eye can see. For the Ka, they play a pivotal role, providing intelligence in skirmishes and campaigns against the enemy. Some claim their abilities are natural effects of a procedure performed at birth, but only the Far-Seers know.

Favored (Unfavored) (Favoring Ceremony)

To be Favored is to be one of only a few Gray Cloak selected to become an Honored One. This occurs at the Favoring Ceremony. The Unfavored are released back to society, though typically shunned and outcast.

Fereni Cliffs

A dramatic bluff, towering above Abinthar Gorge. The cliffs lie on the southeastern end of Gray Cloak land.

Fiadha

The true name of the Gray Cloak people. Outsiders first gave the Gray Cloaks the moniker that most know them by, so named because of the Honored Ones in their midst who wear the gray cloak. Eventually the name stuck and even most Fiadha refer to themselves as Gray Cloaks.

Frit

Small, reckless creatures with tiny wings that provide limited buoyancy. Though they make their homes high in the treetops they spend much of their day foraging for food on the forest floor.

Gray Cloaks (Honored Ones)

A mysterious group of clans that live east of the Capitol, their territory lies nestled in between the Tol Mountain ranges. Northern neighbors to Dorakians. Rumored to have magical powers, known as binding. Honored Ones are Gray Cloaks who bear a mysterious stone in their foreheads, and as the name denotes this sect of Gray Cloaks are afforded an especially high place of honor among their people. They form the leadership of the clans and hold all positions of power in their governing bodies.

Great Binding

A popular belief held by the majority of Gray Cloaks that the world was initially formed by a powerful force that knit the world into its present state, along with all peoples, animals and plant life that would come from it.

Great Hall

The largest building in any Dorakian village, and the center of administrative activities and social life. A number of festivals are held here as are all Elder Conclaves.

Greeting Phrase (used by Honored Ones)

"You may call me (insert here Honored One's first name) until you know my name." – an unusual greeting the Honored Ones use. Its true meaning or significance is not understood by outsiders. *See: Soul-Name*

Hadil's Crossing

The only reliable pass through the Tol Mountains, a gap that connects the eastern and western provinces of the Kingdom of Lavonshia. Usable briefly each year after summer heat hardens spring mud, and before winter snows return.

Hammod's Falls

A trio of waterfalls situated outside the Gray Cloak town of Toma. Legend has it that in a time long past, a Gray Cloak named Hammod sacrificed his three children on this spot, once a dry desert plateau, in his unquenchable thirst for power. He was convinced the land would witness his sacrifice and grant him additional powers. For his wicked deed, he was banished from Gray Cloak society for all of time. It is rumored he still wanders the land, seeking a way to redeem himself. The townsfolk later discovered a trio of waterfalls where the three children's blood flowed.

Harvest Festival (Harvest Festival Dance)

One of the primary Dorakian festivals which celebrates the first fall harvest. The highlight of the celebration is three days of feasting that culminates in a dance, one that is particularly marked by young men courting young women for an opportunity to dance with them. A young woman who accepts a dance signals she is prepared and willing to accept her suitor's hand in marriage.

Harvest Master

Each Dorakian village appoints a Harvest Master, responsible for crop reports, and coordinating planting and harvesting details for all the village, ensuring there will always be plenty to eat.

Healers

The best of healers are known to be familiar not only with medicinal herbs and remedies to aid in the healing process, but also how to set broken bones or even perform surgeries with knife and hacksaw alike. Within the healers' community the debate continues over the efficacy of surgery, as a high percentage of patients die who go under the knife, usually from loss of blood or infection.

Hearth Families

Seven of the most influential families of a Dorakian village are chosen as Hearth Families. They shape village politics, festivals, and welfare.

Hiedorn

A lawless backwater town nestled against the slopes of the Tol Mountains, near Hadil's Crossing. Known as a refuge for criminals.

Highland (Highlanders)

The Highlands are situated south of the Capitol, at the southern end of the King's Forest. Highlanders are generally looked down upon by the rest of Lavonshia, considered to be a rustic and unlearned people.

Honored Ones

See Gray Cloaks.

Hunter's Moon

Approximately a one year cycle. Lavonshians mark the passage of their life in how many hunter's moons they've experienced. *See also: Moon Cycle, Eight-Day.*

Illyr

A village in Dorak, closest neighbor to Chelam, just a short half day's walk away. Its Great Hall recently burned to the ground.

Ji

A game played across the Kingdom. Typically played on a small square carpet with wooden pieces. A game of strategy.

Jilted Leaf

A plant which rarely grows wild, but is cultivated. When one inhales or ingests the leaves by smoking or steeping them in water, the result is relief from pain and an overwhelming sense of calm and peace. Some report experiencing an occasional hallucinatory effect.

Ka

The standing army of the land is affectionately known (or in some cases not affectionately known) simply as Ka, a simple abbreviation of King's Army. The King is the supreme ruler of the land and has final say in military decisions, though rarely does the King accompany the army in battle. The Ka is composed of peoples from all across the land. The size of the army was drastically increased by the recent famine.

King's Forest

A vast forest surrounding the Capitol, a natural buffer between it and the Tol Mountains, the Highlands, and the Maldelea Sea.

Knit

When an Honored One becomes Salel, their natural abilities are knit with the land, enhancing their powers.

Lake Day Festival

A popular summer celebration. Each Dorakian village flocks to the closest lake for three days of revelry, bonfires, and sleeping under the stars. For the villagers of Chelam, their Lake Day Festival takes place at Applemere Lake.

Lavonshia

A prosperous kingdom divided in two by the Tol Mountains, with most of its wealth centered in the Capitol and surrounding towns. Lavon is the common tongue and its people known as Lavonshian.

Lavonshian Blessing

A familiar phrase spoken at a time of parting, known by all Lavonshians: "May We Meet Again In A Better Tomorrow"

Liller's Creek

The main source of water for the village of Chelam. It runs behind the Great Hall.

Lumath

A hidden Gray Cloak settlement within a volcanic cone and home to their great library.

Luton

A prosperous town that lies at the southern end of the King's Forest. As such it lays claim to the title *Gateway to the Highlands*.

Maldelea Sea

An ocean on Lavonshia's northern border. Across the Maldelea Sea lay the Twelve Isles and Perinith.

Midling

A creature of magical ethereal qualities. They are not quite of this earth, but not quite of another realm either. Not all midlings were created equal, varying widely in looks, personalities, abilities and strengths. It is said that midlings were created by the first binders, who created them for companionship and as a help to perform the most intricate of bindings.

Moon Cycle

Lavonshians use moon cycles to mark the passage of time. One moon cycle is approximately thirty days in length.

Moon Festival

A Dorakian celebration of the moon and the guidance it provides at night. Always accompanied by extensive firebombs which explode in the sky to the delight of all in attendance.

Narthwich River

The Narthwich descends from the Tol Mountains, meanders through the King's Forest and north of Saan, until winding its way towards the Capitol. The Capitol was constructed overlooking the Narthwich River, which bends around it before continuing on across the Plains, and eventually emptying into numerous tributaries, rivers, ponds and lake through the Plains before drying up. Not a drop of it reaches the Serewild Dunes.

Oath of Defense

"My life is in your hands and should any raise a sword against you, I will defend your health and honor with my own." – a vow spoken, rarely, throughout Lavonshia. The phrase's etymology is of unknown origin. The oath is not sworn lightly as it binds the oath speaker to the recipient.

Pepper Tea

Pepper tea is made from the Pepper Plant (not to be confused with the seasoning spice). The yellow tipped leaves and brilliant white flowers are distinctive. The name of the plant has nothing to do with its look, but with the tea that is made from its flower. The tea has a spicy or peppery taste and is quite bitter. However the tea is a common cure for stomach ailments.

Perinith   (Perinithians)

The island of Perinith is an independent nation but a close ally to Lavonshia. Its inhabitants must survive extended harsh winter conditions as Perinith is far to the north across the Maldelea Sea. The island boasts great wealth and a ruling class of wealthy families, particularly those who control the numerous silver mines located on the island. Perinithian women are rumored to be especially hairy.

Plains (Plainsfolk)

A fertile land west of the Capitol. The region is known for its rich soil and is the primary food source for all Plainsfolk, the King's Forest, and the Capitol. Food from the Plains is also shipped to the Highlands and sold to Perinith. While there is some diversity amongst Plainsfolk after years of marriage with those of other cultures, there are certain characteristics that still dominate the people who descended from the original Plain's settlers. The most well known trait is the strikingly green-colored eyes of the Plainswomen.

Plow & Lantern

Chelam's only tavern—surprising due to the village size, one of the largest of all Dorakian villages. Some say its owners, the Blackwoods, have unfairly kept out other competing taverns. It is situated in the heart of town on the village square.

Red Oath

A time-worn oath memorized by every Lavonshian child, though none understand its meaning: "Though red is the night. We stand as one! Though mountains rise against us. We stand as one!"

Saan

A once prosperous and bustling city close in proximity to the Capitol. A city now of ash and silence.

Salel

Only a few Honored Ones ever become Salel. To become Salel is to achieve a full and complete bond between one's own innate powers of binding and the powers of binding that lie within the land. Salel are the most powerful and the most revered of all Honored Ones. To their people, it is obvious they have become Salel as their stone is no longer gray in color but takes on the color of the element to which they are most likely inclined.

Saphyr

The stone which Honored Ones wear on their forehead. Rumored to channel magical powers. All saphyr are gray until and unless its bearer has Knit with the land, at which point its color changes.

Sensing

The ability to feel magic.

Serewild Dunes

To the west, beyond the Plains, lies a vast expanse of desert. None have ever plumbed its reaches. It's rumored that should one reach the end of the desert expanse one will have reached the edge of the world.

Soul-Name

Gray Cloaks believe that one's name is more than just a first and last, but a true name, a soul-name as they call it, that speaks to one's very essence, to one's past, present and future and to one's life story. A soul-name is a closely guarded secret, shared with few, as Gray Cloaks believe by doing so you grant a piece of yourself, a piece of your power to the hearer.

Tiriman

Outlying Gray Cloak settlement, farthest west and therefore closest to Hadil's Crossing.

Tol Mountains

A massive mountain range dividing eastern and western Lavonshia. Hadil's Crossing is the only reliable route through.

Toma

A Gray Cloak town. Seat of the Fi-tor clan.

Travel Pack

A term for a commonly seen pack used throughout the Kingdom of Lavonshia. It is worn slung across the back and used to carry supplies when traveling on longer journeys. It is typically a rather large pack with side pockets and one large interior pouch covered by a flap and cinched shut with a drawstring.

Travelers

A term used to refer to a particular sect of nomads, famous for their charming beauty and handsomeness, and their stage plays which have entertained audiences across Lavonshia for countless centuries.

Twelve Isles (Twelvers)

The Twelve Isles, though an independent nation, is a protectorate of Lavonshia, and lies far to the east in the Maldelea Sea. While in reality the isles consist of several dozen small islands, most of those are merely a cluster of uninhabitable rocks jutting up from the ocean floor. Twelve islands hold the vast majority of the island nation's population as well as most of its livable habitat, thus its name. Those who hail from Twelve Isles are known as Twelvers. The islands are renown for their beauty, their wonders, and their culinary delights.

Wolfhounds

Ka-bred hunting beasts used to track fugitives.

Yellow Death

A most horrid way to die, with the sufferer succumbing to aches and sweats and fevers. One who contracts Yellow Death is considered highly contagious and cannot be touched, for the sweat of Yellow Death transfers the disease. Their bodies, clothes and anything they touched after falling ill are burnt.

CAST OF CHARACTERS

THE KA:

The King's Army, an elite military force, drawn primarily from the western provinces of Lavonshia.

Bochim Leving

An expert tracker. A trustworthy soldier and friend.

Drael Rusk

Commander of the regiment sent east to hunt down Gray Cloaks. Widely known for his temper. Most concerned with accomplishing the mission. A career soldier and a wealthy man with a large estate in the Capitol.

Kymn Blackmere

A close friend and ally of Magnus. A common foot soldier, not an officer or aide. Bears a strong sense of duty to king and country and to the oath he swore when he joined the Ka.

Magnus Alwyn

A commoner from the Plains west of the Capitol. Left home due to the famine and journeyed to the Capitol where he joined the Ka and became an officer.

Morco De'ril

A giant of a man, seven span tall. His graying hair betrays his age. Hails from the Tol Mountains.

Saul Aldriomo

Originally from Luton, in the King's Forest. A cynical, half-glass-empty sort of man.

Tarn Crowle

An experienced and hardened soldier. Willing to follow even the most heinous of Ka policies. Disliked and mistrusted by Magnus. The feeling is mutual.

Tobias Karrow

Best friend of Magnus, as well as his aide within the Ka. A man of integrity, he hails from the Highlands and from a family of Jilted Leaf farmers.

Veyra Fenwick

One of the relatively few female soldiers in the regiment. Hails from Perinith. An exceptional archer.

THE DORAKIANS:

A peace-loving people who delight in tending their fields and honoring their traditions through one hundred and eleven annual festivals.

Aurelia Talbot

Above average height for a Dorakian. Finds joy in the labor of the fields, attending the many Dorakian festivals, games of Ji, and dancing to the fiddle in the Plow & Lantern. Best friend is Eken Potterfeld.

Col Blackwood
The most eligible bachelor of Chelam. Son of a High Elder (Jusel Blackwood). Dreamt of finding glory with the Ka before becoming infatuated with Aurelia. An excellent swordsman, taught by a master swordsman named Cassian di'Loru.

Edme
Ringleader of a gossip circle in Chelam that Aurelia despises.

Eken Potterfeld
A good friend to all, hardly knows a stranger. Always cheerful and good natured. A bookworm. Has read every book in Chelam four times through.

Jusel Blackwood
Col's father. High elder of Chelam. A difficult and harsh man.

Koram
Kindly, older High Elder in Chelam. Aurelia's favorite elder, with whom she enjoys many a game of Ji.

Mahan Talbot
Aurelia's father. Famous for his many sayings. Often has fanciful musings about past adventures. A strong and fast harvester. Not a village elder, but for reasons Aurelia doesn't quite understand the people show him great respect and deference.

Old Lady Cridge
One hundred and three years old. Infamous for her too-thick sludge of a soup she makes every Harvest Festival, convinced it's a village favorite.

Proprietor Dunsill

Owner of The Plow & Lantern tavern and inn located in the village square of Chelam.

Runa

Blacksmith in Chelam. She has owned and operated the shop for nearly fifty hunter's moons.

Sari Potterfeld

Eken's second hearth-cousin.

THE GRAY CLOAKS:

A secluded, magically gifted people divided into clans:

Clan Fi-tor

Asmi Vale

Daphne's grandmother, the clan's Guide. Responsible for training those Gray Cloak children who have been recommended by the Ward, and ultimately selecting one child for Ascension to Honored One status.

Daphne Vale

A female Honored One. A little younger than Aurelia, also much shorter. Her face lights easily with a smile, she's kind, thoughtful and outgoing. Not as reserved as most Honored Ones are.

Gyda Vale

Daphne's mother, the clan's Ward, appointed by Lothar. Responsible for assessing Gray Cloak children and recommending eight each year to the Guide for further training.

Jeril Vale

Daphne's uncle, the clan's Stone Keeper, appointed by Lothar. Responsible for the clan's annual allocation of saphyr, for the stones' safekeeping, and for providing a saphyr stone to a newly Ascended.

Liam Shen

Accompanied Ophel in her journey to find Nezetta, who was in the Tol seeking her awakening to Salel.

Lothar Vale

Daphne's father and High Mage of the Fi-tor clan. Has solidified power around him with the appointment of family to prominent positions.

Clan Fi-jal

Eydis

Daughter of the High Mage of clan Fi-jal.

Kentic

A young Gray Cloak man who finds himself unexpectedly in Lumath.

Nezetta

Journeyed to the Tol Mountains to complete her awakening and become Salel. Intelligent. Strong willed. Haughty. Few friends. Bears a deep blue colored stone in her forehead.

Ophel Tol Sahana-Jalese Faolan

A very tall Gray Cloak. A Salel. Widely respected and looked up to in Gray Cloak society. Bears a dark brown stone in her forehead.

Ry

Accompanied Eydis on a mission to the Capitol.

THE MIDLINGS:

Magical, intelligent beings of mysterious origin.

Ferca

A bear-like creature of unknown age and origin. First appears in Lumath.

Hilnon

A rabbit-like creature of unknown age and origin. First appears in Lumath.

NoNo

A cat-like creature of unknown age and origin, hiding out in a strange cottage deep in the woods.

ADDITIONAL CHARACTERS:

Cassian di'Loru
A master swordsman, renowned in Lavonshia for his skills.

Peddler Ibben
A lone peddler. Wanders the world bearing the latest news and trinkets for sale.

Tobwhit
A mysterious man, lives as a hermit in a strange cottage deep in the woods.

Torsten
Head mason over royal projects in the Capitol.

Wymond (Morcant)
The King of Lavonshia.

www.ingramcontent.com/pod-product-compliance
Lightning Source LLC
LaVergne TN
LVHW040130080526
838202LV00042B/2863